10/18

A NEW SCIENCE FICTION UNIVERSE FROM THE ACCLAIMED AUTHOR OF

THE CHANGING HEARTS OF IXDAHAN DAHEREK

Mark Laporta's YA SF trilogy, *The Changing Hearts of Ixdahan Daherek* has been acclaimed both in the mainstream press — Kirkus Reviews called the first outing a **"fabulous read"** and **"an irresistible blend of wonky science and heartfelt storytelling,"** and nationally syndicated radio host Patzi Gil proclaimed it **"a wonderful, wonderful read ... very, very beautifully written"** — as well as the SF blogosphere, where Jodi Scaife of Fanbase Press wrote, **"I absolutely adored the depth of Laporta's world building** ... the characters within the pages will stay with you after the last pages are turned" and Tay LaRoi of *Cheap Reads* named *Ixdahan* to the list Top 10 List for 2016, raving, **"In case you haven't noticed, I adore these books**. The wonderful characters, the outlandish conflicts, the strange worlds and aliens, all of it."

Now this accomplished YA novelist branches out with his first adult space opera, in the first novel of a new series, destined to win him new fans and acclaim. *Probability Shadow* leads you into a new universe, where a critical mineral shortage pits imperious humans against scheming androids, skulking symbiotes and a moralistic caucus of sentient crustaceans. Yet as their battles rage, an ancient evil re-emerges — and foretells the end of all sentient life.

PROBABILITY SHADOW

AGAINST THE GLARE OF DARKNESS

MARK LAPORTA

ISBN 978-0-9997569-2-8

Front cover illustration and book design by Fiona Jayde

Chickadee Prince Logo by Garrett Gilchrist

Visit us at www.ChickadeePrince. com

First Printing

MARK LAPORTA

PROBABILITY SHADOW

MARK LAPORTA, author of *The Changing Hearts of Ixdahan Daherek,* an acclaimed trilogy, is a contemplative soul, living a quiet life in a noisy world. Whether imagining a fictional future or witnessing real-world events that, a century from now, no one will believe actually happened, he stands in solidarity with objective truth.

PROBABILITY SHADOW

AGAINST THE GLARE OF DARKNESS, BOOK 1

Chickadee Prince Books
New York

*For Janet
and Alex*

CHAPTER 1

In a remote galaxy, an atmosphere-adapted lander began its descent into the cloud layer of an isolated world. At that altitude, no one could notice the three, bright-yellow isosceles triangles emblazoned on its indigo shell — the official seal of the Grashard Sidereal Caucus.

As such, the lander was appointed with every luxury afforded by the Grashardi homeworld. Decorated in varying shades of lavender, with pewter trim, it was snug, cozy and anything but functional. Aside from a team of exquisitely trained flight attendants, its sole passenger was a highly regarded government official.

From his comfortable cabin chair, Ambassador Ungent Draaf stared up at the lander's starboard view screen and wondered what he'd find on the other side of that swirling white mass of water-ice and dust. It wouldn't be long now. Soon the ship would extend its landing gear and his six-week journey at sublight speed from the Sattron Interstellar Transfer Station would be over.

Six weeks! At that thought, every muscle tensed in Ungent's bulbous, exoplated body. It was hard to believe any trip across the Continuum could take so long. But the Interstellar Transport Authority had been explicit. So close to the Fremdel event horizon, no sane pilot would dare use the space-folding engines. That is, except the Olfdranyi, a curious species of sentient avians, whose sanity had been called into question more than once.

Nevertheless, sublight travel had progressed rapidly over Ungent's lifetime. Back when he was a boy, the fastest exotic particle ships could manage no more than 2% of the Constant. Now, nearly a century later, ships were approaching 15% with no strain.

In some ways, as Grashard's first ambassador to the Dralein, Ungent had been grateful for his long flight. The journey from Sattron to Bledraun, the Dralein homeworld, had given him a chance to study this fascinating species in depth. Distracted by what he'd discovered, he took no interest in the rest of his descent to the planet. Instead, he turned back to his research and, once again, struggled to grasp the Dralein's central mystery.

Throughout their long lives, he recalled, they periodically experienced a kind of mental molting, known as the *sceraun*. During the *sceraun,* obsolete structures in the Dralein brain were shucked off and replaced with a more intricate array of neurons and synapses. Their higher cognitive functions on "pause," the Dralein did little more than cower from the sun, forage for food and, during this time only, produce offspring.

Over time, these recurrent cycles of mental rebirth had led the Dralein to astounding leaps in culture, science and technology. There was no other way to reconcile their advanced civilization with their relative isolation.

Thoroughly obsessed by the thought of these strange beings, Ungent tried to distract himself by counting out his luggage one last time. But it was no use.

"Astonishing," he mumbled.

The lander hit its assigned air strip and taxied to a graceful stop. Soon Ungent would embark on a diplomatic mission unlike any in his long career. Not even the Terran Protectorate, with its splendid, advanced-design ships, had established an embassy here.

True, the Protectorate had once attempted to subjugate the Dralein and establish a colonial government on Bledraun — until the humans decided the venture wasn't "cost-effective." At that point, they pulled up stakes and left, without even bothering to establish a trade agreement with the Dralein. Ironically, recent events had made trade with Bledraun imperative.

A noise from outside the lander made Ungent glance up the starboard viewer again. But it was nothing. The crew was busy dislodging a small ground animal that had crawled into the lander's luggage compartment for a snooze.

Can't understand the human attitude, Ungent thought.

Politics aside, he believed that studying a species as unusual as the Dralein was worth any price. Fortunately, Grashard was one of the few worlds not beholden to the Terran Protectorate for anything. That usually gave Ungent the freedom to put the humans' clumsy power-mongering out of his mind.

Yet, today, at the start of his new mission, the distinguished crustacean's nagging worry about the possibility of human intervention gave him no rest. Despite their supposed indifference to the Drahlein, Ungent was sure the Protectorate would follow his progress closely. Once he'd paved the way on Bledraun, he feared, they'd decide to pounce. After all, it had been less than two cycles since the humans had muscled their way into a Grashardi trade agreement on Djalorg 3, involving medicinal herbs.

As soon as the lander completed its status checks. Ungent was cleared to gather his spherical carry-on bags onto a small mobile maglev platform and trundle down the matte-black exit ramp to solid ground. The rest of his baggage, as usual, was already being transferred to his official residence in the Grashard embassy building.

Before stepping out on to the polyslate tiles of the landing strip, Ungent attached the breather mask a flight attendant had handed him. Its soft polymer surface fit snugly, but comfortably against the pale yellow gills on either side of his plump, purplish neck. While the atmosphere on Bledraun was similar to that of his homeworld, he'd need time to adapt to the slight traces of chlorine in the air.

Gravity, in its own way, was also a bit of a problem. As he felt the crush of 1.15% Grashard-normal for the first time, Ungent cursed the day that food became his constant companion. There were many reasons for this, including the unexpected death of his daughter, Fleront. But Ungent was determined not to let her memory prey on his emotions.

In fact, it was for that very reason that he'd delayed retirement to accept one last diplomatic mission. His heart had told him a radical change of scene was the one thing that would give him a fresh perspective on his grief.

Fleront, he reminded himself often, had been an adult and old enough to make decisions on her own. She'd *chosen* to push her journalist's nose into the camps of the Krezovic militants. Her subsequent capture and ... the rest ... had been inevitable. Some days, this logical, cause-and-effect analysis of the past gave him strength and comfort. Other days, he leaned heavily on the soothing effects of a five-course meal to smother his grief.

In any case, between his increasing girth and the gravity differential between Grashard and Bledraun, Ungent had been advised to purchase a walking stick to help him get around. He'd chosen a 1.75-meter titanium staff at a local crafts fair on his homeworld. It was etched with scenes from his favorite Grashardi folk tales.

As he looked around, Ungent marveled at the lush scenery. For the Dralein, unlike the vast majority of developed civilizations, had found a way — that is, *bothered* to find a way — to live in harmony with nature. Grashard did better than most in this respect. Still, nowhere outside of a few protected areas, or the immense estates of the wealthy, could anyone see such natural wonders.

Yet here, even at the edge of the airfield, Ungent was distracted by blooming, pale lavender *chizdra* flowers, row after row of tall, blue-green *jexthalna* pines and a rich variety of soft pale orange grasses, trimmed to perfection in fascinating geometric patterns.

"Lovely," he sighed to himself, and wished for the thousandth time he could have persuaded Nulgrant, his wife, to join him. "Stuck in her ways," he told himself, though he knew the real reason had more to do with her complete lack of interest in the universe outside her cozy suburban enclave.

A few meters up and to the right, Ungent saw a row of navy blue, self-piloting air-taxis. As he approached, a holographic banner appeared above the one on the far left, with the message:

WELCOME, AMBASSADOR DRAAF

emblazoned in black letters against a mustard-yellow background.

Because this was a gesture common to many worlds, Ungent wasn't foolish enough to think his arrival had triggered anything more in the hearts of the Dralein than courtesy. All the same, the holographic banner made his heart race.

Within minutes, the Grashardi ambassador to the Citizen's Collective of Bledraun arrived at the door of the newly constructed embassy. As he paused on its Drothalnian marble steps, he gazed up at its curious geometric design with the distinct feeling he had nothing to lose.

Ungent's first encounter with a member of the Dralein did nothing to dispel his confident assessment of the situation. The furry being that greeted him at the door was the very image of sophisticated charm.

"Furry," Ungent knew, was an extremely childish description. But at first glance, it was hard not to focus on the Dralein's thick, swirling pelt. At second glance, he saw a being of undeniable intelligence and grace.

"Greetings, from Grashard, Dver Chaudron Dadren," said Ungent. "I look forward to a long and fruitful relationship between our worlds."

The tall government official smiled down at Ungent. In his forest green uniform, edged in silver thread, Dadren looked every bit as friendly as he was imposing.

"Welcome, Ambassador," he said. "Here on Bledraun, we value more what comes from the heart than from ritualized phrases. What would you really like to say?"

Ungent looked up into Dadren's calm, brown eyes. The answer was simple.

"When do we eat?"

CHAPTER 2

The next morning, Ungent awoke in his new quarters and was surprised at how well he'd slept. The previous night's meal and the evening entertainment performed in his honor must have been more relaxing than he'd imagined.

And the bed! Ungent was amazed to see how carefully his hosts had followed the guidelines sent over by his homeworld government. Here he was, a single crustacean in an ocean of mammals, and yet every fixture in his quarters had been adapted to his needs.

That even extended to the décor. The walls were paneled in dark, neo-wood copies of traditional Grashardi bas-relief carvings, with their gracefully interlocking biomorphic shapes. To Ungent's eyes they were attractive, sensuous, sophisticated. As such, they were the perfect complement to the rigid, scooped-out surfaces of solid, Thaganese coral, embossed with pewter glyphs, that made up his tables, chairs and broad, ovoid bed.

After a quick check of his chronometer, Ungent was relieved to see he'd woken right on schedule. Although he'd thought through his entire approach hundreds of times, he still felt his presentation of his government's trade policy needed a final polish.

For one thing, he wondered how to express the Grashardi government's desire to extend "favored trade status" to Bledraun, when the Dralein barely had a word for "treaty" in their vocabulary. Isolated in a sidelined galaxy, this curious people tended to see interstellar politics like a conversation between two neighbors over a backyard fence.

As it happened, the Dralein rarely used fences solely to mark property lines. They had a jittery relationship with the concept of land ownership. Ungent had seen the amused look on the faces of the Dralein officials he'd contacted by holoscreen in the last few weeks. When they spoke of trade, land and property rights, it was as if he could see the irony streaming from their round ears.

In this case, he knew, he didn't have the option of saying, "each culture to its own." An essential part of Ungent's mission was making his hosts understand that any agreement between the two worlds would actually be binding. The Dralein's sense of irony would earn them no leniency with the Sector Court of Appeals if their relationship with the Grashardi went south at a later date.

The upcoming interstellar trade conference would further complicate his mission. If nothing else, he could count on the noisy humans pushing their way into every discussion with both elbows out. Good luck easing the enigmatic Dralein into a cozy relationship with the basic premise of interstellar trade negotiation, as long as brash Muffy McIntyre was in the room.

As Ungent began unpacking his luggage, it occurred to him that the humans' bullying ways might be a side-effect of their rapid rise to power.

Pensive, he set aside his luggage and opened a file on the personal scanner embedded in his left forearm. It was a recent book by the renowned Grashardi historian Greldant Shareek that Ungent had purchased before his trip to Bledraun. So far, he'd found one passage in *The Human Conundrum* especially enlightening:

> *The first in the modern era to develop space-folding engines, the humans soon encountered hundreds of underdeveloped worlds, each pleading for help. As a result, as early as 3146, old-style, human "advisors" controlled government, finance and commerce across a dozen galaxies.*
>
> *But by 3173, mounting societal pressures erupted in a backlash. Accounts of 'aliens' with suspect values made human settlers fearful. In the same period, the pay gap between space workers and planetary workers, both on Earth and across its emerging colonies, fueled deep resentment.*
>
> *Soon after, a dip in the humans' space-based economy caused hardship for millions, and spawned the revival of an ancient Earth religion. Within two cycles, a fringe political party emerged. By lacing its rhetoric with phrases from sacred texts, it was swept into power. One hundred cycles of oppression followed, as party leaders enforced a grotesque distortion of religious law. The prison population swelled.*
>
> *During this period, adherents of Earth's other surviving religions were utterly marginalized. To date, even as human society edges toward greater openness, no citizen who is not a member of the state religion holds a seat in government, the Business Council, or the Science Academy, nor a rank above Sergeant in the military.*

"Arrogant charlatans," Ungent grumbled.

The rest of the settled universe, however, did not stand still. Five cycles after the creation of the entity now known as the Terran Protectorate, the humans' tight-fisted reign took a hit. Grashard, an independent world, developed a space-faring culture of its own. It offered less advanced societies fair trade partnerships and new technologies that threatened human dominance.

Ungent's exoplated chest swelled with pride. The Grashardi had saved many fascinating worlds from being "humanized."

Finally, after several generations of losses, the Protectorate began to loosen its grip. While today, this liberalizing trend continues, the human's belligerent assumption of superiority has abated only slightly. Nor have full civil liberties been extended to people of all faiths.

Ungent closed the book file and shuddered. There had been a space of a few cycles when he'd thought the Protectorate might reform itself. But no more. It was now merely a well-oiled machine, whose function was to expand its borders.

"Give them an opening and my long journey will be for nothing," he said.

And yet, in his relaxed state, Ungent had to ask himself whether any of his concerns were worth the worry. Based on what he'd seen so far, his hosts had a robust culture of their own. They'd developed a sophisticated society with accomplishments other species could equal but not surpass. He was sure the Dralein, already bruised by the humans' brash behavior, would not be swayed a second time by false promises.

A buzzing door chime knocked him out of his reverie. Good thing he was already half dressed. There was nothing to do but throw a bathrobe of Tulusian silk around his exoplated shoulders and scurry over to the entryway.

"Sorry to disturb you, Ambassador," came a meek voice through the intercom system. "But the Chaudron had a cancellation in her schedule and wondered if you could meet with her earlier than planned."

Ungent fought hard to keep the irritation out of his voice.

"How much earlier?" he asked.

The answer, sorry to say, was "Immediately." With nothing to gain by protesting, even politely, Ungent agreed, closed contact and finished dressing with unusual haste. Unusual, that is, for a settled Grashardi who took his morning rituals seriously.

In spite of himself, he was soon wearing a lightweight tunic of deep lavender, studded with delicately carved dark hardwood buttons. This was topped with an ovoid, zinc medallion embossed with three interlocking isosceles triangles, the symbol of the Grashard Sidereal Caucus. Black pants in brushed pseudo-cotton, with a band of purplish coral running down each seam, completed his decidedly non-human "look." As he turned to face the mirror embedded in his closet door, a faint twinkle appeared in his eyes,

The moment of reckoning, he muttered.

His reflection, of an aging diplomat who still looked smart in his form-fitting official garb, almost lifted his spirits. Over this, he threw a thin, hooded cloak of indigo neo-suede which, in his haste, took more than one try to fasten at the neck.

"Thought they were supposed to be a relaxed people," he grumbled and then forced himself to stop. The last thing he needed was for the Chaudron to catch the slightest hint of resentment — unless his secret goal was to return to the charade of marital affection waiting for him back home.

Ungent took a deep breath and, two minutes later, crossed the wide courtyard that separated the embassy from the world government's disarmingly modest administrative offices. By the time he appeared before Euch Chaudron Drashna, his composure was as calm as the waters of the Rhytha spa on his homeworld.

As soon as Ungent arrived, a timid functionary showed him into Drashna's elaborately appointed office. As the distinguished crustacean couldn't fail to notice, the room was decorated in exquisite detail, down to the fine brocade curtains, trimmed in Lathdranyi satin.

"Ambassador Draaf!" said the Dralein leader. "I'm mortified to disturb you on your first morning on Bledraun. Please, sit."

She pointed a slate gray, furry finger at a soft mauve cushion, to the left of her stainless steel desk. Ungent nodded, but remained standing. The cushion, deliciously comfortable for a furry mammal, would be torture for his stiff crustacean contours.

But if the Dralein's senior leader noticed Ungent's dilemma, it didn't show on her broad face.

"We have among us an unruly individual," the Chaudron began, "a child actually, who resists every attempt to discipline him."

Ungent paused a moment to take in Drashna's severe appearance, dressed as she was in a dark russet, neo-leather jumpsuit, embroidered here and there with teal accents.

"Children can be troublesome at any age," he said. "However, I hardly have the qualifications...."

"Yes, yes, yes," said Drashna, with a wave of her hand. "We already have tutors, nurses and recreational directors who can deal with the boy's education. What we need is someone to guide him toward what I believe you would call 'manners.'"

"Well, I ..." Ungent started. He hadn't spent six weeks in a sublight ship to become a nanny.

"We assume, as a diplomat," the forty-ish Dralein female said, "you must have special insight that would enable you to teach the boy a more ... productive ... way to express his emotions."

Ungent looked over at the frustrated face in front of him, that no amount of swirling fur could hide. He saw he'd have to take a stab at meeting this unusual request. Refusing outright would throw his diplomatic mission straight off course. Besides, the Chaudron was only asking him to try.

As it happened, Ungent wasn't so inexperienced in these matters. Fleront had given him three to four years of practice in dealing with irritable teenagers. From what he'd heard so far, the problems of adolescence among sentient species were fairly universal.

"Where is the boy from?" asked Ungent. There was, he realized, no time like the present to start cooperating.

Drashna consulted her own personal scanner, which was remarkably similar to Ungent's.

"Uh ... province of ... Thrulyntrin," she said.

Ungent's eyelids blinked in a quizzical pattern.

"That's a ... a Krezovic province," he gulped. "On one of their colony worlds."

"Might have known you would recognize that," said Drashna. She was smiling that peculiar brand of Dralein smile — that many other species would swear was a snarl.

"I am, if nothing else," said Ungent, who smiled back, "a being of the universe."

Of course, for a crustacean, that simple gesture required considerably more effort than for any member of a typical mammalian species. Unfortunately for all sentient crustaceans, a variation on the smile was one of the settled world's few universal gestures.

Some of Ungent's colleagues in the diplomatic corps had gone so far as to have reconstructive surgery to make smiling less of an ordeal. But Ungent was totally old school. He'd long ago mastered the rigorous discipline of exoplate dislocation necessary to raise the corners of his mouth.

"So it should be no trouble," Drashna was saying now, "for you to begin your first session with the boy in, say, the next two rotations? I'll bet that gives a seasoned veteran like you plenty of time to settle in."

"Of course," said Ungent, cursing his fate. Why was there always a price to pay for *everything*?

With a bow, the Grashardi diplomat made ready to return to his quarters, until the Chaudron remarked that, in the meantime, her team would transfer the Krezovic boy to the quarters adjoining his own.

"We'll have him all settled before you meet him," said Drashna.

Stunned, Ungent nevertheless still managed to recall the question that had been hanging in the back of his mind since this conversation began.

"By the way, Chaudron," he said in a low voice, "what's the boy's name?"

The leader of the Dralein stood tall, raised her furry arms, and laid her broad hands on the crustacean's purplish shoulders.

"That, Ambassador, is one of the problems," she told him. "What's his name? The boy categorically refuses to say."

CHAPTER 3

With only two days of peace left to him, Ungent quickly mapped out a tour of Jeldren, the capital city of Bledraun. The city was rumored to be one of the most stunning examples of architectural design in the settled universe, and he was anxious to see it.

With one hand on his titanium walking stick, Ungent strolled out of the embassy, the latest addition to Bledraun's central governmental complex. An off-center geometric building of glass, stone and steel, it sat at right angles to Jeldren's main square.

Within a few meters of the compound, a sea-green, self-driving groundcar waited for him. Soon, it was gliding along the short stretch of countryside that separated the embassy from Jeldren proper.

The Dralein's artful landscaping rolled past the car's side windows. Ungent nodded his approval. Whether natural, hybridized, or genetically engineered, the plant life on Bledraun reached a splendor unmatched on most other developed worlds. Soon enough, the car, curiously named "Serano," came to rest and its doors swung up in a graceful arc. Ungent stepped onto the polyslate tiles at the center of town.

"Serano thanks you for a pleasant ride," the car's AI chirped. "Shall he wait for you?"

"If he would be so kind," said Ungent with the utmost respect.

As he ambled the streets of the upper city, Ungent admired its tall, arched walkways and upswept towers. With its broad vistas, Jeldren couldn't help but inspire artistic, philosophical and scientific thought. Lost in admiration, he walked the morning away, through sectors of Jeldren dating from many different eras, each with a distinctive style.

As Bledraun's sun crossed over into afternoon, Ungent's heart warmed to a wave of deep contentment. Judging from the peaceful expressions of passersby, he decided the city's effect on his psyche was typical. Even the vehicular traffic seemed to proceed with unwavering calm.

Yet when Ungent cast his eyes down, or peered into the dark alleyways to his right, he caught signs of a second Jeldren. *This* Jeldren had grown up to address the compulsions of the Dralein during the *sceraun*. Every sidewalk was studded with a steel disk, about one-hundred centimeters in diameter, the girth of an average Dralein. Their function? Apparently, each one concealed an entryway to a network of underground tunnels.

At least, that's what Ungent had learned from his official briefing. Unfortunately, Grashard's intel on the Dralein relied heavily on hearsay, because the Dralein, for the most part, refused to discuss the *sceraun*. In fact, the Grashardi would have known even less about the subject, if it weren't for a small trading ship. According to the captain's log, the ship made an emergency landing on Bledraun nearly one-thousand years earlier, just as the Dralein were emerging from the tunnels. In the captain's words:

> *With luck, I was able to interview a few of the groggy creatures before they pushed me aside. I was told that, during the* sceraun, *the Dralein reverted to their origins as a species of burrowing rodent. With their higher mental functions on "pause," they panicked. In a desperate scramble for shelter, they descended into the tunnels or hid in Jeldren's shadowy side streets — where they fed on roots, tubers and insectoids dug from the soil.*

According to the log, after two to three months, the process of mental molting was complete and they returned to the light. By every estimate, the Dralein weren't scheduled to re-enter *sceraun* for the next two-hundred-fifty years, because they had last emerged from it a mere seven years ago.

Yet, Ungent's briefing had also contained a disturbing rumor: A variety of external stresses could cause the *sceraun* to occur ahead of schedule. Could the boorish humans that the Dralein would meet at the trade conference tip the balance?

"Too many unknowns," Ungent grumbled.

For instance, what about the Dralein colony on Seldra, Bledraun's second of three moons? Had the "Seldrans" also scratched out tunnels over the last five-hundred years? Or was the *sceraun* linked to peculiarities in Bledraun's atmosphere, soil or the mineral content of the water?

A few meters up ahead, Ungent heard the clang of his titanium staff against another metal disk and stopped in his tracks. What harm would it do to enter one of these underground passageways and get a feel for the Dralein life cycle?

The experienced diplomat in him knew better. It was never wise to pry into the secrets of another culture, even those lying close to the surface. If he wanted to visit the tunnels, he knew he should submit a formal request. Yet what would he gain, besides a sanitized introduction to the topic?

As Bledraun's sun veered toward late afternoon, Ungent peered into the dark alleyways to his right. Could he gain some insight by exploring them? As it happened, today was a business day and the streets were filled. At a moderate pace, he could reach the nearest alley without attracting attention.

Navigating the alley itself was another matter. Ungent could barely keep from knocking into a warren of abandoned shacks. Living inside them were a mix of wild and domesticated critters Ungent had never seen before. Yet what next caught his attention was downright perplexing.

"You lost?" called a female voice to his right.

"No," said Ungent, "I'm here on purpose."

"Nobody comes *here* on purpose," said the voice.

Ungent tiptoed around a mound of decaying junk — and saw an odd creature squatting on the cracked pseudo-cotta tiles. Odd, as Ungent would be the first to acknowledge, from a Grashardi point of view.

Still, it was likely that many other sentients would have been perplexed by the creature's appearance. A brain with spindly legs? A tangle of vegetable roots leading to a small sack of plasma? Yet she had the voice of an angel.

"Just my luck," she said as Ungent came into view. "Too old for symbiosis."

Ungent's eyestalks stiffened.

A symbiote? he thought. *Here?*

According to Ungent's research, the species originated as a type of ground slug with a habit of seeking shelter in the bodies of other species. Over the eons, the process became a model of evolutionary refinement.

A razor-sharp ridge on the symbiotes' belly, which exuded a local anesthetic, enabled them to slip in and out of their hosts' necks with ease. To seal these incisions in mere seconds, the symbiotes used a slurry of stem cells, specialized proteins and growth factors derived from the host's body. Ungent swallowed hard at the sight of a crumpled Dralein female's body, which lay only a meter to the creature's left.

"Your previous host?" he asked.

"I tried to talk her out of it," said the symbiote. "But she insisted on running with the wrong crowd."

Ungent stared down at his webbed feet and struggled to put the situation in perspective. He'd heard that the symbiotes had amassed a huge trove of scientific and technical data, by merging with the minds of more than a thousand species over the centuries. And by manipulating the interstellar banking community, the wily creatures had also accrued credits, real estate, precious commodities, an impressive stock portfolio — and a string of "legitimate businesses."

You'd never know that to see one face-to-face, Ungent told himself.

"What's on your mind?" asked the symbiote. "Spit it out. You can't say anything stupider than I've heard already."

Ungent's throat went dry.

"What … what will happen to you now, on your own?" he asked.

"I have about a week," said the symbiote, "before I have to merge with a tree and give up my singing career. Now tell me honestly, what's a Grashardi doing on a Dralein dung heap? Don't you want to see the museums?"

Ungent glared down at the symbiote's dark red, shimmering mass.

"How do you presume to know why I'm here?" he asked.

"Name's Warvhex, by the way, thanks for asking," said the symbiote. "I get around. You know, wherever my host goes. Hey, look out!"

The crustacean had barely enough time to duck, as a hail of debris flew into the alleyway.

"What in Rexnala's holy matrix was that!" he yelled.

"The humans are back," said Warvhex. "Landing in the center of town is their idea of good taste."

"The trade conference," said Ungent. "I thought they'd arrived already."

"Tell me you don't know how much humans love a dramatic entrance," said the symbiote. "Actually, don't. I have to go scouting."

"You mean ...." Ungent started.

"I do," said the symbiote. "Humans are as obnoxious as a swarm of *dreznel* on a hot summer day. But they make great hosts. Heads as empty as a sack of air."

Before Ungent's bulging eyes, she crouched down hard on her spindly appendages, then shot through the air like a bullet. Stunned, Ungent turned around and trudged toward the Terran Protectorate lander.

Armed with only a vague plan to catch a crewmember off guard, he knew the odds of gaining inside information on the human mission were slim. His one chance depended on the accuracy of the intel he'd received about the ship's captain. But luck was with him. As he reentered Jeldren's main square, he caught sight of a tall human — and soon a cheery voice echoed off its surroundings.

"Ungent Draaf, you old lobster special," it said. "And here I almost wasted a message unit calling you."

"Harlan Mars," Ungent called out. "My favorite heap of rotting meat. How *do* you keep the flies away?"

The human, for whom Bledraun's gravity was slightly lower than normal, jogged over to Ungent's side and clapped him lightly on his prickly back.

"Whiskey, mostly," said Harlan. "Wait. If you're here, you must be the new ambassador."

"The first ambassador to the Dralein," said Ungent, "from anywhere. And you ... you 'made captain' if I remember the quaint phrase correctly."

"Correct," said Harlan, "though I don't rightly know as anyone has said 'quaint' in the last 2,five-hundred cycles."

Ungent glanced at the insignia on the human's uniform and flinched. He'd known Harlan off and on for twenty years and always counted on him as a reliable, sometime friend. But now that Harlan was captain of the *Sweet Chariot*, which had ferried the entire human trade delegation to Bledraun, they were in direct competition. Their conversations couldn't afford to be so breezy.

"Still finding my way," said Ungent.

The human stared at him a moment before bursting out in loud guffaws.

"Cagey as ever." said Harlan. "Don't worry, Ungy-boy, we all gotta have our secrets. Hey, my sensor team said they spotted a symbiote running around loose near here. You see anything?"

Ungent sized up the human and decided to play it safe.

"Goodness no," he said. "But why would your sensors be tuned to that species?"

"Not the whole species," said Harlan. "Just this one particular symbiote that my superiors have a bone to pick with."

The phrase 'a bone to pick' didn't make complete sense to Ungent, as it filtered through his subdermal translation grid. But it obviously didn't refer to something positive.

"I'd always heard they were helpless without a host," he told the human.

"Wouldn't know, personally," said Harlan. "I leave biology to the specialists. Well, *most* of biology. But this particular symbie has herself an agenda."

Ungent's exoplated shoulders tensed.

"So it's a ... a female symbiote," he said.

"Oh yeah," said the human. "Disgusting, isn't it? Well, we'll catch up later. I got some ship business to get to."

"Until later," said Ungent with a slight bow. "And give Ms. Business my warmest regards."

Harlan's coarse laughter bounced off several of the town square's elegant office towers.

"You got levels to ya, Ungy," he said. "Too bad that stuffy old job doesn't give you a chance to crack a few open once in a while!"

Ungent watched as Harlan jogged back to his lander.

"Indeed," he said. "At my age, I have more than enough cracks."

By now, it was early evening. As he walked back to where Serano was waiting for him, Ungent's memory dredged up images from twenty years ago. He'd been assigned to the embassy on "EagleThree," an old human colony that was still operational, even though it dated from the days of cramped, ion-drive ships. Ungent's mission was to ensure the humans of that time conformed to Interstellar Treaty 780-519(d), prohibiting the development of anti-matter weapons.

Yet, as Ungent recalled, rumors of violations had started the day the treaty was signed — and EagleThree was under a security lockdown. No sooner had Ungent stepped out of his lander than a tall, muscular twenty-something soldier introduced himself as the crustacean's bodyguard.

"I doubt this is necessary, Corporal," Ungent had told the young Harlan.

"It's not, really, Ambassador," Harlan had said. "Unless you mind getting your throat cut by a Krezovic terrorist. But hey, I reckon those exoplates of yours are tough enough for anything — am I right, Big Guy?"

Ungent's mandibles had clenched. He was used to being addressed with the utmost formality.

"I gather 'Big Guy' is a little-known human term of respect," he'd said quietly. Harlan, eyes wide, had rushed to assure Ungent he was right.

"Spent the rest of the day calling every human he met 'Big Guy,'" Ungent mumbled. "Including some of the females."

Much had changed since then. For one thing, the Krezovics had become even more determined to disrupt mainstream society, including Ungent's own family.

Should have asked Harlan to have a soldier shadow Fleront, he told himself. Maybe, if he hadn't been so self-involved back then, he might have found a way to prevent....

But the time for action was long past and Ungent knew he must live with the outcome as best he could. The way things panned out, his request for a bodyguard might only have resulted in getting a soldier murdered, too.

By the time he'd slid back into the groundcar, Ungent had resigned himself to the fact that, when Harlan said he was tracking a fugitive symbiote, he must have meant Warvhex. It was unlikely that two female symbiotes would happen to be roaming free on Bledraun within a few meters of each other.

"What could she have done?" Ungent blurted out, forgetting his car had ears.

"Serano can provide answers to questions on a broad range of topics," said the perky AI.

"Know anything about a fugitive symbiote?" asked Ungent.

The car became eerily quiet.

"Serano?" he asked.

"Serano regrets to inform the Ambassador," said the car's AI, "that this information is classified." The groundcar's doors opened with a jolt.

"Please exit immediately," said the AI. "Reclaiming to commence in 30 seconds."

Puzzled, Ungent climbed out of the car a few feet in front of the embassy. No sooner had his webbed hand touched the embassy door than he heard a loud explosion behind him. He spun around in time to see his former groundcar up in flames. Ungent's limbs shook.

"Reclaimed," he whispered. His eyestalks pivoted as a team of robotic firefighters popped out of an underground station, hoses ready.

The Grashardi ambassador hurried inside to issue an official protest. Not because he saw the point of it, but because he knew what was expected from him, as a representative of his government. The Chaudron's broad face flickered into view on Ungent's personal scanner.

"My apologies," said Drashna.

Ungent stared at her image a moment, and tried to read her emotions.

"You need hardly apologize for a random act of violence," he said.

"I'm merely sorry you experienced the tactics of our dissident factions," said Drashna. "The violence was anything but random. Someone, Ambassador, wants you dead."

CHAPTER 4

Ungent pled exhaustion, turned down the Chaudron's dinner invitation and dragged his weary limbs back to his quarters. As a precaution, Drashna had wanted to post members of the Jeldren patrol outside his door. But Ungent refused.

"They destroyed a government groundcar," he told her, "What's to stop them from infiltrating the patrol?"

Besides, he told himself, he'd never be able to conduct sensitive negotiations with guards outside his door. Now, alone in his quarters, he was determined to put Serano's explosion out of his mind. First, he took a soothing soak in the swim tank that the Dralein had sunk into the floor of a side room off the kitchen, as stipulated in the guidelines submitted by the Grashardi government.

Lined with green glass and filled with freshwater — filtered to Grashardi normal — the heated tank was a good two meters deep and otherwise just large enough for Ungent to splash around a bit. Before long, he emerged refreshed and dried himself under the tank room's soothing heat lamps.

Minutes later, he was enjoying a light supper with the lights down low.

Should call Nulgrant, he thought, but decided against it. No sense worrying her over nothing.

So close to the Fremdel event horizon, it would take a week for a message to reach Sattron station, then an additional week to reach Grashard, five galaxies away. By then, the situation might have changed.

"Assuming she cares," Ungent sighed into his last spoonful of delicious *ghonafrel* soup. A pleasant image of Nulgrant from 80 years ago flooded his mind. But it was washed away a moment later by his memory of her the day he left for the spaceport.

"Don't get your eyestalks in a tangle," she'd snapped. "Always in a rush to be a good servant. And make sure you bring me back a *nice* gift this time. You traipse around like a god while I'm stuck here with a huge house to look after."

Yes, Ungent reminded himself, a house run by a team of six Kuydrent androids, designed by master Kuydrent himself.

"She barely has time for a massage," he sneered.

Soon after he'd pushed himself away from his dinner table, the distinguished Grashardi ambassador climbed into bed. After what he'd been through, he wanted to be especially well-rested for the next day's trade conference. Yes … a good night's.…

The ding of his door alarm popped his eyes open again. Who in the name of Wrenfehl's Gate was this? Worse, the dinging was now accompanied by a retina scan that appeared on his personal holosplay. It was the Krezovic boy!

Ungent pulled a blue Nacronese nightshirt over his exoskeleton and hurried over to the door. Even though the boy's unscheduled arrival was against diplomatic protocol, the last thing he needed was to displease his hosts by standing on ceremony.

"The explosion … It wasn't us!" shouted the boy, the moment Ungent opened the door.

Once he'd ushered the boy in and closed his door tight, the dignified Grashardi took a moment to compose himself. This Krezovic, he told himself, was not the one who took Fleront's life.

"You gotta believe me," the boy said.

"And why would I not believe you?" the crustacean asked.

"Because …" the boy said in a low voice, "because of what … what happened.…"

Memory and emotion raged through Ungent's consciousness. His daughter's murder was still too fresh for casual conversation. But he should hardly have been surprised that Shol knew of his loss. Florent's death had sparked a major interstellar incident. The boy would have picked up the news report on his personal scanner, no matter what he was up to at the time.

Ungent pointed to a low-slung stool in his kitchenette.

"Sit down," he said, and drew from his experiences on many worlds to trace the boy's recent history from the way he was dressed.

The Krezovic had flung a brown neo-leather jacket over a gray-and-white-striped tunic, which stopped at the waistband of dark blue, coarse-woven pants. His pant legs were stuffed into calf-length brown boots, their toes reinforced with dull steel. It was, Ungent decided, the outfit of an itinerate scavenger — with a taste for backwater flea markets.

Ungent watched the boy's greenish skin glisten in the soft ambient light of his quarters. A genetically modified branch of the human family, the Krezovics were engineered in the early days of human deep-space exploration. They took their name from Nikola Krezovic, a pioneer in the large-scale remapping of the human genome, who had studied the properties of certain radiation-resistant beetles.

Aside from glistening skin, the remapping had given the Krezovics an elongated, ovoid skull, and an uncanny sense of balance. They could also withstand temperatures and pressures too intense for unmodified humans, at a fraction of the cost of building and maintaining a specialized robot. As a result, they were soon in high demand by the Terran Protectorate fleet.

Unfortunately, in just a few centuries, advances in technology enabled a combination of unmodified humans and a new generation of advanced-design androids to do the most dangerous work themselves. The Krezovics, already shunned in some circles, were shoved aside, reclassified as "mutants" and gradually denied civil liberties. Defiant, they segregated themselves to a few isolated worlds where they pooled their resources and developed their own language and culture.

But as the Terran Protectorate marched through its most militant phase, their oppression increased. Despite the Krezovics' aptitude in a number of technical fields, employment prospects dwindled — and several hundred thousand of them reached desperate straits.

The only thing that had kept the Krezovics from going under completely was the shortage of highly trained technicians on the Protectorate's most backward worlds. Needless to say, these worlds could hardly afford to pay the going rate for the Krezovics' services. No wonder a terrorist faction had grown up among them, including the cell that had captured Fleront.

Still, none of that, Ungent realized, was the fault of the frightened young face that looked up at him now.

"I hold no one responsible for 'what happened,' other than the monsters who *made* it happen," he said.

"Just wanted to say ... since I'm supposed to take lessons or whatever from you," said the boy. "The Chaudron said she'd send me back if I didn't ... didn't ... learn."

Ungent leaned forward.

"Back where?" he asked. "Thrulyntrin?"

"I wish," said the Krezovic, eyes downcast. "But no, she'll send me back to ... to Skorshdra."

Ungent winced at the name of the harsh, Yelthel Sector prison, where violent criminals were kept in unspeakable conditions.

"Don't trouble yourself about that," he said.

As he balanced on one of his other kitchenette stools, Ungent glanced over at the boy — whom he judged to be no more than sixteen. What in the craters of Shalindrew Lochan had happened to justify sending him to Skorshdra? But this was not the time for probing. He had to earn the boy's trust.

"You've done an honorable thing to defend your people," Ungent continued. "Now, why don't we start over? My name is Har Ungent Draaf."

"Shol," said the boy. "I don't have another name, so don't ask."

"Mind telling me how you ended up in Skorshdra?" said Ungent.

Shol's account of the events leading up to his detention was the kind of "troubled-youth" story the Grashardi had heard many times — except that the consequences of the Krezovic teenager's actions were unusually severe. The boy's trembling voice said as much as his words.

It turned out that Shol had been a courier for a street boss, known as "Ulandroz." From the few shreds of Krezovic Ungent had learned, he recognized the name as an alias. It referred to a type of ferocious wild beast, which Harlan Mars might be tempted to call a *tiger*. But what was Shol saying now?

" ... wanted me to deliver this shiny thing to a big buyer in Relesh."

"A shiny thing," repeated Ungent. "That covers a lot of ground."

Shol's slick face tensed.

"That's what the fuzzheads keep saying," he yelled. "I don't remember, OK?"

Ungent got up from his stool and glared down at the boy.

"I know of no *fuzzheads*," he said. "The first thing you must learn is respect for other species."

"But they..." Shol sputtered.

"Yes," said Ungent, "they have fur. And I suppose to you I'm a *crusty*?"

"No... I..." said Shol, in a low voice.

"No," said Ungent. "I'm not a crusty — any more than you, my boy, are a *beetleback*."

Shol shot off his stool, fists clenched

"Don't call me that, you ... you..." he shouted.

"*Idiot* will do nicely," said Ungent. "That's something I can agree with."

Shol gazed down at Ungent's tiled floor, fought hard to suppress a grin and failed.

"You're crazy," he said.

"But respectful," said the Grashardi. "Now, what is it the Dralein want from you?"

Whatever it was, the "shiny thing" Shol alluded to was vitally important to Drashna. So much so that she'd ventured out in person to broker a deal for the boy's release. It appeared their interest in the object had reached the point of desperation.

"First they offer me a ginormous amount of credits," said Shol, "and then they threaten me with a ... I dunno, some kind of mental probe."

"You can't tell them anything?" asked the Grashardi.

"That's the problem!" yelled Shol. "When I tell the Chaudron what I do remember ... it's ... it's like I'm throwing a hot cup of Freglian tea in her face."

Ungent rested a hand on the young Krezovic's shoulder.

"Can you tell *me*?" he asked. "I promise not to yell."

"OK," said Shol. "The shiny thing ... it was like a bracelet, but it had, you know, dials or whatever on it."

"Dials for what?" asked Ungent.

Shol had no idea, but did remember one other detail.

"I never thought about it," he said, "until today, when that 'tectorate lander touched down in Jeldren. The letters and numbers on the ship ... they're the same, like, style as the ones on the shiny thing."

"Probably just a coincidence," said Ungent. He didn't actually believe that, but decided there were more pressing details to uncover. "You made a lot of deliveries for ... Ulandroz?"

"He was my main customer," said Shol.

"But this was the first time you landed in detention?" asked the Grashardi.

Ungent's eyestalks twitched as the Krezovic boy recounted his path to Skorshdra. His last delivery for his street boss had been different in one crucial detail: Shol had seen the buyer's face.

"I didn't get a good look," he said, "because I ran. Thought I'd ditched him, but the next morning a couple of wireheads came for me."

"Androids," said Ungent, his voice darkening. "They took you to Skorshdra?"

The answer was "yes," but there'd been a stop along the way. After half an hour or so, blindfolded and jammed into the back of a hovercar, the androids had flung Shol into a dank warehouse. There, a tall human female invited him to sit at a small table.

"First she talked to me real sweet," said the boy. "I thought maybe she wanted ... you know ... but then she started yelling, told me if I said anything...."

Shol's voice cracked and he looked away again.

"I didn't even know the guy... and anyway Ulandroz would've killed me if I said anything."

Ungent lifted his head and spoke to a comlink embedded in the kitchenette's countertop.

"Water, sparkling," he said, and soon a fizzy glass appeared to his left, projected by an overhead replicator. He handed Shol the glass.

"Try to calm down," he said.

The Krezovic teenager gulped the water as if he'd been dying of thirst in the Alynat desert back on Grashard. Ungent waited until Shol had set down the glass and wiped his eyes.

"You're past all that now, right?" he asked. "Tell me, if you remember anything else — even if it seems unimportant."

Shol tugged at his boots. One of the androids, he told Ungent, had finally grabbed him by the forearms and applied a mild electrical shock.

"Felt like they were putting pain ... right into my bones," he said. "Know what I mean?"

Ungent nodded.

"After a while I passed out," said the boy, "but something weird happened first."

"Were you hallucinating?" asked Ungent.

Shol's young brow furrowed.

"No idea what that means," he said. "All I know is, I was going in and out, kinda. Then I heard one of the androids call the lady a name and she flipped out. 'Don't call me that!' she kept yelling 'I ordered you not to call me that!'"

"What would an android call her," Ungent wondered out loud, "that would be anything other than accurate?"

"I know, it was weird," said Shol, "and the name ... it didn't make any sense."

"What was it?" asked Ungent, forcing himself not to yawn after such an emotionally draining day.

"It was ... crazy," said Shol, "like ... 'Warvhex,' maybe?"

CHAPTER 5

The Terran Protectorate ship *Sweet Chariot* was a typical cruiser-class vessel more suited for interplanetary or local interstellar patrol duty, than long-range tactical combat. Nevertheless, it was equipped with a powerful array of lase cannons, particle guns and a limited spread of antimatter torpedoes, capable of pulverizing a mid-sized moon.

It was exactly the kind of ship a newly-commissioned captain like Harlan Mars, with a solid military background was likely to command. And like other comparable ships, it offered a satisfying combination of solidity and creature comforts — including an officer's mess with a 4-star rating.

That was aside from the large private shower bath and state-of-the-art holotainment center in his quarters. Harlan's lodgings also included an elite array of specialized replicators, capable of making almost anything he needed to increase his comfort after a hard day in the command center.

The rest of the ship was, by any measure, as spacious and convenient as any upper middle class home on Reagan 3. Sure, it looked like a military vessel, but was as far removed from the cramped, airless environment of an ancient submarine as a lush estate garden was from an abandoned lot.

Air circulated, light streamed, and everywhere design touches made each workspace subtly different, in contour and color. It was the perfect amalgam of no-nonsense functionality and warm, humanistic design.

At the moment, the captain took no notice of the ship's creature comforts. He was too preoccupied with cranking down the ambient temperature. Why, he wondered, was the Command Center so hot? That is, until he realized his sweaty forehead had nothing to do with the ventilation system and everything to do with the android reflected on the main view screen.

"You have been informed of your mission and acknowledged your understanding of said mission," it was saying, in the even rhythms of artificial diction. But to Harlan's mind, there was nothing artificial about its stonewalling indifference to reality. The AI's mindset was identical to every human CO he'd ever dealt with.

" ... and therefore," the android rolled on, "it is illogical that you have not yet carried out my explicit orders."

"Kill the Grashardi ambassador?" said Harlan. "That was never my mission. Now, be honest. Wouldn't you be more comfortable assembling thruster manifolds on Lunar Base D?"

The captain knew his reference to the function of the Terran Protectorate's first independent artificial intelligences was a stalling tactic. Still, it had the desired effect. It forced Admin/39/Intergal to troll through teraflops of historical data to understand him.

"Confine your comments to relevant matters," it said.

Harlan flashed a snarl destined to have no impact on the android.

"Here's what's relevant," he said. "My orders come direct from Brad Christiansen and *they* say nothing about following any ANN Commission agenda. What's your angle, anyway, 39?"

"The appellation 39 is inaccurate," said the AI, its voice marred by tiny bursts of crackling static. "You agreed to ensure a favorable outcome from the trade conference. The indicated action is the only logical means to complete your assignment. Your orders, therefore, are clear."

"Right," said Harlan. "Very clear. My orders are to keep Ambassador Draaf out of the trade negotiations and disintegrate any wirehead that orders me to kill him."

"Response noted," said Admin/39/Intergal. "It will be logged in your case file under insubordination code 348/651. You will be disciplined."

"Not if I kill myself first," said Harlan to the blank screen, once the android closed contact. As he leaned back in his chair, his first thought was to call Admin and give Director Christiansen an earful about ANN Commission interference.

But the sane part of his mind told him this would accomplish nothing except his recall to New Dallas. Complaining, he'd learned the hard way, wasn't compatible with a command post. His job was to meet his objectives by working around the obstacles, not by making them someone else's problem. That's what command meant. The alternative was packing his kit and heading home.

In some ways, of course, he did miss his old life in the provinces — occasionally, enough to wish for a dishonorable discharge. But after ten years on Reagan 3, it would be hard to give up the one sensation that mattered most to him. It was the feeling that, for the first time in his life, he was more important than a wad of chewing gum stuck to the bottom of a robot's footpad.

And speaking of sticking it, maybe there was a way ... no, he shouldn't....

"Oh, what the Hell," Harlan snickered.

Within minutes, he'd called up the appropriate holotemplate and filed a Notice of Suspected Malfunction on the bullying android. Although Harlan knew that Admin/39/Intergal was functioning perfectly, the review process would take months and, more to the point, would bring to light the android's abuse of power.

Of course, there was nothing new about android meddling. It had taken less than five years from the time the Terran Protectorate developed the first truly independent androids for a consortium of "concerned intelligences" to found the Artificial Neural Network (ANN) Commission. Its mission statement contained the phrase "to maintain fair and transparent governance across all sectors of the Terran Protectorate."

With their unprecedented data-mining capabilities, the AIs soon discovered every human pressure point. And because the human's entire data stream flowed through these same AIs, they could easily tailor "the facts" to suit their agenda.

When an EarthBank executive expensed his weekly excursion to a Galhantrian casino, or the governor of a barren mining world promoted her gardener to Secretary of Agriculture, the androids took notice. Over time, the price for expunging such compromising data from the official record rose up and up.

As a result, the Commission was both the Protectorate's ally and a painful thorn in its most delicate negotiations with other worlds. Despite the androids' utter lack of legal authority, no human official below the rank of Senior Admin dared cross them.

Won't change anything, thought Harlan.

But that didn't stop the Notice of Suspected Malfunction from feeling like sweet revenge. The report would guarantee a lengthy vacation from Admin/39/Intergal's hectoring demands. It would add up to enough time, he hoped, for the Terran negotiators to close their trade deal and make the murder of his old friend Ungent an unnecessary political liability.

And that was good news. Fact was, he'd miss the old crab cake. There were precious few other beings — alien or human — he could stand to spend more than five minutes with. But now that he'd bought a little time, he knew he had to make it count. The first order of business was working out a way for Ungent's negotiations to fail gracefully, without arousing suspicion.

Yet a close second on the list was his ongoing hunt for an unpredictable symbiote — even though he lacked the security clearance to know what the fuss was about. Admin had told him that his mission would support a top secret weapons development program, but Harlan knew a lie when he heard one.

"Gillian," he called out to his XO, a tall Fleet officer in her early 30s whose ancestors hailed from a part of Earth once known as "Great Britain," for no reason he could recall.

"Yes, Captain," said Commander Gillian Cavendish, as she brushed a strand of impossibly blond hair out of her eyes. "You'll be wanting the latest on the symbiote, won't you?"

As always, Harlan felt his breath stop short at the sight of her starched uniform. He shifted slightly in his chair and prayed his poker face would hold.

"Report," he said.

"She's here, Sir," said Gillian.

Harlan's left eye developed a momentary twitch.

"Here?" he asked, "as in on this ship?"

Gillian pointed to her head.

"Here," she said. "And if you lift a finger to hurt Ambassador Draaf, you'll be singing soprano all the way to Skorshdra."

Harlan glanced at the muzzle of the lase pistol Gillian/Warvhex was now pointing at his lap and looked up again at the composite mentality's stern expression.

"Come on, dial it down, will ya'?" he chuckled. "Old Ungy and I go way back. What makes you think...."

"The ANN Commission can be persuasive when it wants to be," said Warvhex through Gillian.

"I see you've studied them kinda close," said Harlan. "Picked up one of their favorite tactics, too. But — so you know — whatever happens to me, happens to this ship and my crew. The self-destruct sequence is powerfully hard to disarm once it gets, you know, initiated."

Warvhex had Gillian lower the pistol.

"So you're saying ..." she started.

"I'm saying threats are cheap," said the human. "If you're as smart and conniving as I keep hearing, you can help me come up with a plan where everybody wins. And by the way, what do you care about old Ungy? He owe you money?"

Gillian/Warvhex set the lase pistol down on Harlan's command console.

"Other way round," she said. "I owe him...."

"Yes?" asked the captain, who finally dared to get out of his chair.

"I don't want to talk about it," said the symbiote. "Here, I'm giving you your first officer back. But I'll be watching you."

Gillian's body slumped forward, and Harlan had barely enough time to catch her before she cracked her head on the edge of the console. In the commotion, he failed to notice the slick symbiote wriggle out of an incision in the nape of Gillian's neck and slingshot away.

"You OK?" he asked.

"Considering I had another mind hovering around in my noggin," said Gillian, "I hardly think I know what OK means anymore."

"Any idea ..." Harlan started.

"Please, don't ask me," said Gillian. "She's gone, but she ... she had an effect my mind. I can't tell you ... anything. The pain is...."

Harlan squeezed his first officer's hands until her sobs died down, then spoke to her quietly.

"That's some ordeal," he said.

"Whatever she's up to," Gillian gasped, "I do hope it's ... it's worth it."

CHAPTER 6

The next morning, the start of the interstellar trade conference transformed Jeldren from an isolated capital city into a hub of competing interests. Ungent was in his element now, and drew strength from years of experience.

Naturally, he was eager to let the familiar rituals of diplomacy drive his recent near-death experience from his mind. But it wasn't meant to be. No sooner had the aging Grashardi walked out into the open than he saw his transport, a groundcar of the same make and model as....

"Serano greets you on the first day of the trade conference," the groundcar's AI called out to him.

Ungent wanted to ask how Serano had survived the blast, until he remembered that, these days, the average AI was a composite, produced by several remote servers. Instead of residing in a braincase embedded in the groundcar, Serano's metadigital consciousness was split into sectors and stored at specialized transmission stations across the planet.

From storage, a Dralein technical team would beam the AI out as needed, usually as one of several ongoing, preset transmissions. In a pinch, however, Serano could pilot an aircar — or control an automated field weapon. Ungent felt his throat tighten and decided to focus on the here and now.

As Serano pulled out onto the main road, Ungent chose not to consult the detailed notes he'd stashed in a data cylinder during his long trip to Bledraun. While experience had taught him the necessity of exhaustive preparation, he knew his real-time observations would be more useful now. Facts he had plenty of; what he needed was *insight*.

But what was this up ahead? A ragged crowd of protesters?

"Identify," said Ungent.

"Members of the BFD, Ambassador," said Serano. "Bledraun for Dralein is the group's full name."

Isolationists, thought Ungent.

That would make the trade negotiations more delicate, he told himself. The Chaudron would need to appear sensitive to their concerns, no matter how unrealistic.

"How large a group are they?" he asked the AI. Why, he wondered, had Grashardi Intelligence told him nothing about this movement?

"One moment," said the groundcar as it squeezed past a tight cluster of agitators. "There. I am told this is a recent phenomenon. Exact figures are unavailable."

Ungent shut his eyes tight. At this rate, despite leaving early, he'd miss Drashna's opening remarks. Not an optimal way to....

"Hey!" he yelled. A team of three protestors had jumped onto the hood of the groundcar and scrambled up its roof — which they proceeded to bang with their furry fists.

"Do something," Ungent croaked.

"Serano's options, Har Draaf, are limited," the AI replied. "Although he could run a low-grade electrical charge through his roof."

Ungent hesitated, as he remembered Shol's story of the searing pain he'd felt at the hands of an android. The last thing he needed was a reputation for injuring protesters.

"Signal the patrol," he said. Most likely, he told himself, there was no reason to fear. The average groundcar was built to withstand much heavier pummeling than six furry fists could dish out. He felt safe enough to wait for the patrol to arrive.

A drip of molten steel from the groundcar's roof changed Ungent's assessment of the situation.

" ... lase cutter," he heard Serano blurt out indistinctly. No doubt the beam's intense heat was burning through the groundcar's sound system. Although Ungent had no idea what the protester wanted, a calm discussion of local politics was the least likely option.

"Serano!" he yelled.

" ... ficials...on ... acted ... the AI sputtered before going silent. If the crustacean had been younger, he might have tried to make a break for it. Considering the heft of his titanium walking stick....

Don't be ridiculous, he thought.

Even in his twenties, Ungent had never been a "fighting machine." He had to hope he could reason with his attackers, negotiate a truce — but he had no delusions about his chances for success.

By now, the lase beam had pierced the front of the passenger compartment. Ungent decided he had nothing to lose by trying to escape. But when his webbed hand grabbed the handle on the door facing the street, it popped open in one wrenching movement. A thick pair of gloved hands dragged him out onto the neogranite causeway, and Ungent looked up into the black eyes of a disheveled Dralein.

"Who are you?" gasped Ungent.

The Dralein, whose heavy frame was stuffed into a smudged pair of olive green overalls, patted Ungent's exoplated shoulder.

"Friend of a friend," he said. "Come on, fast as you can."

Ungent hustled after his rescuer. Yet he must not have been moving fast enough, for soon the hulking Dralein had hoisted the crustacean onto his left shoulder. While that didn't count as dignified, it was a clear step up from being sliced by a lase cutter.

"Where ... ?" Ungent started to ask, until he realized the burly Dralein couldn't hear him in the roar of the street's swarming crowds. What had been a city of magisterial calm yesterday, was now the scene of a riot.

"Off-worlders out, Bledraun for Dralein!" Ungent heard the mob chanting, as the last traces of an organized protest vanished in a whirl of shoving, shouting, beasts. Far from worrying about the subtleties of interstellar trade, he now had to focus on saving his multiply articulated neck. Unexpectedly, his mind turned to Shol.

What will happen to him now? he wondered.

The frightened boy's words had burrowed into Ungent's head. Compassion aside, he took Shol's story as a sign of deep trouble — a conspiracy of dark forces with dangerous consequences for....

"Quit squirming," rasped the rough voice of the Dralein as he tightened his grip around the Grashardi's hard torso. Ungent didn't have time to be offended before a young, light brown Dralein ran up from behind. His first thought was to smile and wave to her. But she began pummeling his head with rocks from an embroidered canvas sack slung across her shoulder.

Now Ungent's apparent savior broke into a run and made an abrupt turn down a dark alley. The Grashardi felt his body jostling up and down like a bag of field tubers from his homeworld. But soon he was jarred by a sharp jolt, as he was yanked off a furry shoulder and stuffed into a waiting aircar.

"Go!" the muscular Dralein yelled to the aircar's AI; before Ungent could blink again, he was aloft.

"Destination," he croaked.

"This unit is not programmed for real-time conversation," said a recording triggered by Ungent's voice. "Information about destination and estimated time of arrival is available on the screen on the right side of the passenger seating area."

Ungent gazed around the aircar's functional interior. For now, he was safe.

"A nutritious meal appropriate for your species will be served in approximately ... 098 rotations," said a second recorded message.

"Long trip," thought Ungent. And it was easy to see why, once he'd activated the small, ovoid touch screen the aircar's AI had directed him to. He was headed for a location halfway around the planet.

Though he didn't know what to expect, he was still too jostled to feel anything other than relief. That is, until the rational side of his mind chimed in — and he realized that his rescuers must have ulterior motives. Ungent couldn't rule out the possibility that the attack, including the Dralein child who stoned him, had been live theater from start to finish.

"Feel like I'm trapped in Creldidar's web," he said, referring to an old Grashardi folktale. "Why didn't they just call me?" In the past, he'd received secret contacts from many underground groups. He considered it part of his job, and an invaluable source of information.

"This car is not programmed for real-time communication," the aircar's AI chirped.

"Silence!" Ungent roared.

If he could have seen out of a window, he might have had a chance to get his bearings. But the aircar's windows had been sprayed over with an opaque gray mist. He turned back to the touch screen. Maybe it could help him put the situation in perspective. Though he objected to being kidnapped, there was the slight possibility his captors meant him no harm.

"Clumsy," he said. If they weren't planning to kill him, they must know his absence would be reported to the governments of Grashard and Bledraun. Nor would they fail to realize that his personal scanner, which was … yes, still functional … would broadcast a real-time locator signal, updated every fraction of a rotation.

Yet even if some radical political group *were* planning to kill him, they might still subject him to brutal interrogation. Ungent took a deep breath. His thoughts, he saw now, were spinning out of control. Far better to gather the available data and….

"Settling in?" rang a sonorous voice through the aircar's intercom.

"Who are you?" Ungent asked.

"Save yourself the trouble, Ambassador," said the voice. "and listen. Anything I don't tell you now, I'm never telling you."

The news was mixed. The voice claimed to represent "our shared interests." Ungent snorted and braced himself for the torrent of ideological nonsense that followed. Behind a mask of righteous indignation, the message amounted to a short list of demands.

On arrival at an undisclosed location he must:

- Reveal the Grashardi negotiating strategy or submit to a mind probe
- Submit to a control implant to monitor and discipline his actions as needed
- Submit to the cause of the ANN Commission for the Liberation of Sentient Devices

Ungent's heart rate spiked up. But there was no point in mincing words, even if he said them with a slight tremor.

"Why don't you save us both the bother," he said, "and crash this aircar into the desert? I will not 'submit' to any of that."

Instantly, the crustacean felt the momentary lurch of suspended gravity as the aircar went into a nose dive. Soft laughter emerged from the aircar's intercom.

"Suit yourself, you irrelevant pile of decomposing bio-matter," said the voice.

CHAPTER 7

Shol stood on the steps of the government compound that contained the Grashardi embassy, and looked out into the distance, toward the main square of Jeldren.

Where's the oldster? he wondered.

The Chaudron had been forceful: Shol was not to miss his first official meeting with Ambassador Draaf under any circumstances. But what fault was it of his if the distinguished crustacean had failed to show?

Yet Shol couldn't deny feeling relieved. Now that the trade conference was underway, Drashna and her cabinet would have more on their minds than a Krezovic street slime. Shol doubted the Dralein had forgotten about that shiny thing, the bracelet he'd delivered in the port city of Relesh. But for now, it was taking a back seat to hammering out a trade agreement around the planet's rare mineral deposits.

The Krezovic boy breathed deep. With his genetically engineered adaptations, he had no need for the breather masks Ungent relied on, or the surgically implanted filters the humans used, against the trace amounts of chlorine in Bledraun's atmosphere.

Instead, he hoped the fresh morning air would ease the confusion that rattled his mind day and night. What had he done, he wondered, that thousands of other Krezovic teenagers weren't doing on sub-level planets in dozens of galaxies?

"Nobody cares," he said into the soothing breeze that fluttered through his brittle hair. He had enough on his credit tile for a hearty breakfast away from Drashna's stifling supervision.

Not wanting to lose the opportunity, the sixteen-year-old Krezovic crept from the compound's heavily guarded entryway to its narrow back exit. He opened the heavy steel door a crack and was surprised to see it was also guarded by a team of male and female Dralein in stiff, mustard-yellow uniforms. As he knew from previous unauthorized excursions, the Dralein were usually more interested in the appearance of security than the rigors required for a true lockdown.

Trade conference, he thought after he closed the door again.

But he refused to give up. His last seven years on the street hadn't been wasted. He cast about the corridor leading to the exit until his eyes lit on a shiny bolt, carelessly dropped by the repair crew on its last round of security checks.

He scooped up the bolt in his long fingers and pushed the heavy door open only as far as he needed to survey the guard station. He looked to his right and saw a series of jet black hovercars emblazoned with the government's scarlet security emblem.

Because he knew how sensitive the AI-controlled vehicles were to changes in the immediate environment, Shol waited until the guards were looking away. He didn't wait long before the four of them, bored with their dull assignment, drew up a game of *gerbroscanz* on the hood of a command vehicle to Shol's left.

"One shot," he told himself and, with practiced aim, flung the bolt square into the cockpit of the closest open hovercar.

INFILTRATION ALERT. INFILTRATION ALERT. A FOREIGN BODY IS LODGED IN THIS UNIT. INFILTRATION ALERT....

The hovercar's boisterous alarm system startled the sluggish guards and sent all four running over to investigate.

Shol bided his time, hidden behind the partially open door, until all four guards were preoccupied and, as silently as a breeze blowing through blades of grass, took a lazy trajectory along the polyslate tiles leading out toward Jeldren proper.

His path led him south of the central square, where the riot Ungent had passed through was still raging. Yet, if the young Krezovic noticed the commotion, it didn't register. All of his attention went to listening for the sounds of pursuit.

Outside the main square, the city was vibrant and, compared to the scruffy towns Shol was used to, a thrilling burst of sensual energy. Especially today, when delegates from fifteen worlds and their entourages were combing the streets, every square meter of the Dralein capital sizzled in his ears and sent shivers down his slightly arched spine.

Shol craned his neck as he paused to study a bevy of delegates in their elaborate official uniforms. What he witnessed gave him goose bumps, the kind he felt when running from an angry patrol unit. Here was a view of the wider universe he'd never had before.

Shol took a winding path away from the government compound that had become his new home. The result, while subtle, was enough to make tracing his movements more difficult, especially because he'd carefully forgotten to bring his comlink with him. A confident smile crossed his lips.

Everybody makes mistakes, he thought.

He knew he was still too valuable for his hosts to get tough with him. And, as he shuddered to recall, Drashna could do nothing worse to him than he'd already experienced at Skorshdra.

The Krezovic teenager stopped before the window of a large diner and sighed. The best way to spoil his brief moment of freedom was to obsess about … that place. As he peered in through the diner's broad polyglass window, he had to stop himself from drooling over the slab of hot *drolchalan* a server plopped down on a hungry patron's plate.

"Let's eat," he said. But he'd hardly stepped two meters inside the cheery space before a familiar, gentle voice called out to him.

"Hey Shol," said the pretty human girl from the third booth on the left.

The Krezovic stopped short, shaken out of his troubled thoughts. Glad as he was to see her, Shol now regretted not changing his clothes before sneaking out to the street. Did his hair look OK? But with Trinity Hudson smiling at him, he knew this was no time for self-doubt.

Trinity was the teenage daughter of the Terran Protectorate's highest ranking geologist, who'd been sent here ahead of the conference, to present a detailed analysis of Bledraun's mineral wealth. Or some crazy *quelx* like that.

"Hey," he said, as nonchalantly as his pounding heart would let him. "Looking hot today."

Trinity brushed a strand of dark brown hair out of her eyes and smiled down at her plate. She was, as always, impeccably dressed in expensive Terran casual wear: a silky yellow sleeveless tunic, worn over dark green leggings that kissed the tops of charcoal-gray pseudo-suede ankle boots. When she looked up again, her deep blue eyes stared out at Shol with the bright energy of a girl his own age.

"You're so full of … whatever they call it where you come from," she said. "You're lucky that's what I like most about you."

The Krezovic boy grinned as he slid into the booth opposite her. Craters of Europa, how refined her purring voice sounded. She spoke in classic High Planetary — two centuries removed from the street dialect he'd grown up with. More than once, he'd even had to rely on his implanted translation grid, lest he get the wrong idea about what she was really saying.

"Come on, Shiny Girl, you know we speak the same language," he said, tilting his head to the right.

"You must be hungrier than you look," laughed Trinity. "Go on, order breakfast so I don't have to talk to your … your snake brain or whatever."

Shol felt the air go out of his lungs. Imagine a girl this smart and this … incredible … smiling at him. Out on the streets, he was garbage. But ever since he'd been introduced to Trinity at one of those boring official parties that Drashna insisted he go to, it had been like … like she actually thought he was worth five credits, like maybe they were destined….

"You gonna order something, Kid?" grunted the toe-tapping, overweight Dralein waiter who had since shuffled up to the table. Shol rattled off his standard order, a meal including three courses, ending in a plate of fried potatoes. That is, the closest thing to a potato available on Bledraun.

"Galaxies, don't the fuzzheads feed you?" asked Trinity.

Shol's face went pale and he stared down at his arched hands.

"I ... I stopped calling them that," he said. "It isn't ... respectful."

"Whoa," said Trinity, "Who gave you a halo?"

"Naw, come on," said Shol, "this is serious. Or should I start calling you...."

Trinity held up her carefully manicured hands.

"OK, OK," she said. "Don't say it. I hear you. I didn't know you cared so much, is all."

Shol squeezed her hand.

"Being in love changes a guy," said the Krezovic boy.

"You're sweet," said Trinity. "But remember...."

"Yeah, I know," said Shol.

Soon the waiter returned with Shol's order.

"Better pay up when I bring the check," he said. "Those embassy dopes might cuddle with you, but I know what you are."

Shol jumped to his feet and, out of nowhere, brandished a blazing e-mag knife.

"Yeah?" he asked. "What do you know?"

"Stop it, Shol," said Trinity, as tears welled up.

"Tell *him* to stop..." Shol started, until a broad-faced Dralein patrol officer bounced in from the street.

Needless to say, it wasn't long before the young off-worlder landed on his genomically remapped behind, and all he could see of Trinity was her indignant face yelling at the patrol officer. Through the diner's polyglass window he heard her say "My father...." and knew that was his cue.

No point hanging around until a member of the Terran Protectorate came to his rescue, he decided. He'd be waiting forever. More to the point, after embarrassing himself in front of his first serious girlfriend, being saved by her daddy wasn't exactly the best look for him. He shoved his left foot back into the boot that had almost slipped off and pulled his lithe body up to his feet. Without thinking, he searched his jacket for the e-mag knife the patrol officer had confiscated.

"Need that," he said.

He ran a curved hand through his spiky hair and limped back in the direction of his quarters. He thought of asking Ungent to get the knife back for him, then came to his senses. No way an off-worlder would get involved in local politics, especially if it involved an illegal weapon.

And to think he'd tried to turn a corner with his attitude toward different species, the way the aging diplomat had told him. Now, here he was facing all kinds of disciplinary action — the worst of which being no more contact with the one person in the whole freaking universe who'd shown him any kindness.

If he'd kept his head, he might be kissing her now, one of those, "You're a good friend" kisses he'd seen some girls give. But *those* girls, he knew, weren't hanging out with roughneck beetlebacks like him.

"That's all I am," he sighed, as he approached the Grashardi embassy's ornate ironwork front gates. If he hadn't been so self-absorbed, with his head hanging down, he might has seen there was someone waiting for him. As it was, he smacked straight into Dadren, the tall Dralein official who had greeted Ungent soon after the crustacean had arrived.

But if Shol expected the scolding he deserved for slipping out of the compound against orders, he was disappointed.

"Have you seen the Ambassador?" asked the Dralein's frowning mouth.

CHAPTER 8

Ungent lay in a pile of fiery debris about two-hundred kilometers southwest of Jeldren. As it turned out, the burst of flames he'd felt on impact had soon died down into red-hot smoldering. The aircar must had been equipped with an automated crash defense system that his captors had either not known about, or considered irrelevant.

If their objective had been to scare Ungent, rather than kill him, they'd succeeded. Not that the two were mutually exclusive. His hard exoplating had saved him, but without medical attention that would count for nothing.

Nor could Ungent consider, in his wildest dreams, dragging himself back to civilization. In the first place, the fall had cracked open a significant swath of his abdomen. In the second, he was inconveniently trapped under several hundred kilograms of the carbon laminate that had formed the hull of the kidnapper's aircar. Swollen, aching, he rotated his eyestalks in a painful arch and took in as much of his surroundings as possible.

How, he wondered, could the ANN Commission possibly think he'd give in to its demands? Considering the Commission based its decisions on statistical analysis, his past record should have predicted his refusal quite clearly. In nearly 80 years of service, he'd never backed down on a major diplomatic policy, never taken a bribe or let Grashard's interests be overshadowed by the blustery winds of power politics.

Some ... sickness ... has made even the machines desperate, he thought. Despite the pain and his mind's dire projection of his survival odds, he couldn't stop himself from wondering: What powerful forces had come together to send the most rational intelligences into a blithering tailspin? Ungent let his heavy eyelids flutter shut and attempted to sum up regional interstellar affairs.

And yet the far-flung Terran Protectorate could hardly be considered regional. Their early lead in space-folding tech had put them about two-hundred years ahead of the Grashardi and almost four-hundred years ahead of almost everyone else in the settled universe. By now, the humans were everywhere, either by settlement or treaty.

Worse, their virtually unopposed command of the best space routes made staking new a claim in the wider universe kind of challenging. If a ship from outside the Protectorate tried to venture beyond the horizons of the settled worlds, they'd either be stopped and subjected to a lengthy inspection, or receive an unwanted escort from the humans "for their own protection," against an unnamed threat.

But leaving the Protectorate aside, the worlds with the greatest interest in making a favorable trade agreement with the Dralein had one thing in common: an embarrassing shortage of the five minerals crucial to interstellar travel.

"And the sixth," he muttered, with what was left of his consciousness. He was referring to chalinite — the crystal at the heart of the pseudoneural networks that made artificial intelligence possible.

In the best of times, the crustacean's knowledge of such things was limited. He depended, like most residents of the settled universe, on articles published in popular science magazines available through his personal scanner. To his credit, he'd read up more on the topic than most.

The puzzling thing was, nothing in his previous surveys of the mineral industry suggested those six essential minerals had become scarce enough to trigger a full-blown panic. But for now, that knowledge, not to mention his capacity for conscious thought, was slipping away through the massive wounds he'd sustained. Yet through the haze that rapidly descended on his senses, Ungent did think he heard a familiar voice.

"Jacob's Wheel, Commander," a male fairly barked, "get the Ambassador into the aircar."

"Pardon me, Sir, but you must be joking," said a female voice with a strange accent, even for a human. "I rather think the medpod needs to stabilize him first."

In a few days, Ungent would learn the full story of his rescue. But at this point, all he discovered before passing out was a startling truth.

"Whatever. So, what is it, a half-rotation since her last sighting?" said the barking voice.

"Who? The symbiote?" said the female.

"No, Uncle Timecrack," growled a voice sounding … yes … exactly like Harlan Mars. "Who else do you think I mean? Come on, get up, here's the medpod."

CHAPTER 9

The Dralein had made every effort to remodel Shol's quarters to reflect the dominant design and architectural trends favored by Krezovic culture in its heyday. By Shol's time, of course, that era was long past.

In contrast to the Grashardi, the Krezovics of a few centuries back had cultivated a retro-human style that an astute historian of ancient Earth might have identified as "Danish Modern." This minimalist, no-frills aesthetic had a haunting grace. What's more, it often featured nested shapes resembling the somewhat non-human contours of the Krezovic body.

Needless to say, the Dralein's careful attention to detail was mostly lost on Shol who, by the age of nine, was already living far from any Krezovic cultural center. Still, it would be wrong to say his spacious rooms meant nothing to him. They were the first consistent home he'd known since before his earliest childhood memories.

Yet now, as Shol gazed through the broad windows along the far wall of his quarters at the embassy, aesthetics was the farthest thing from his mind. Instead, his eyes strained to take in a splash of the roiling riot that flooded the streets with waves of flailing arms and straining legs. The initial demonstration that had overtaken Ungent's groundcar had been subdued at first by a small patrol force. But now it had risen up again on the opposite side of the city and surged toward the embassy.

Shol's mouth went dry. Conditions outside reminded him of the one outbreak he'd seen in Skorshdra a few months before. It'd been silenced in a matter of minutes by a squad of heavily armored androids with, shall we say, malfunctioning ethics subroutines.

Thinking back, it was hard to remember what was worse: the brutal put-down of the riot itself, or the harrowing screams of the ringleaders that followed. Here, ironically, under more humane conditions, the fighting and vandalism were liable to last longer, to take more lives and damage more property.

By now, the patrol had begun to drive the angry crowd up into the northwest quarter of Jeldren. To do so, they relied primarily on gleaming, automated weapons platforms, supplied by the humans to curry favor with their Dralein hosts. And soon, away from the most populous areas, the release of tranquilizing mists and pheromone suppressors would finally grind the mob into submission.

That thought forced the Krezovic teenager to turn away, plop down on a spare but comfortable beige couch to his left, and rest his overheated head in his hands.

"Must've taken Har Draaf, too," he mumbled.

Between humiliating himself in front of Trinity and losing contact with Ungent, the little flicker of hope Shol had nurtured this past month had been snuffed out in less than a day. Dadren had managed to calm Shol's fears a little, by pointing out that Ungent's rank and position would make anyone think twice about killing him. That was aside from the crustacean's value as a source of inside information.

Given enough time, Dadren had told him, Ungent's captors were probably betting they would stumble on the right flavor of seduction — either the promise of a longed-for pleasure or the fear of dreaded psychological pain.

"Still don't like the odds," Shol said to the elegant, ash-wood tea table at the center of his living room. As he gazed around his quarters, he couldn't help breaking into a smile. Used to sleeping in dank alleyways in the poorest regions of the galaxy's poorest planets — that is, when he wasn't spending the night in a jail cell — the experience of four, clean comfortable walls and a kitchen stocked with rich food was as close to paradise as he ever expected to reach.

That and Trinity's smile.

But now, he figured, Trinity was permanently out of reach. As hard as it had been to hang out with her before, now that he had a record with the Jeldren patrol, there was no way her high-ranking father would let him come within one-hundred meters of her. It was too depressing. The way her soft eyes had flashed at him in the diner that morning, it might not have been long before she let him kiss her, somewhere secret, where no one could find them....

"Your door signal is meant to be on at all times, Son," Dadren's mellow voice rang out at him.

Startled, Shol jumped up, and reached instinctively for his e-mag knife — before he remembered the incident at the diner. Regardless, he felt safe without it. This fuzz ... Dralein ... had always treated him with respect.

"Think the door's busted," said Shol, lying through his sharp front teeth. Fact was, the signal reminded him a bit too much of the buzzers on Skorshdra's alarmed doors. Dadren nodded, stepped back into the corridor through the partially open door and tested the signaling equipment. Shol covered his ears at the bell's clanging toll.

"I'd think a guy who likes to sit around in his unders would rather have some warning, before a security detail barges in," he said.

"Security?" asked Shol, suddenly self-conscious. He pulled on the tight trousers he'd yanked off as soon as he'd returned from the diner. But as Dadren explained, the embassy had managed to smooth things over.

"Only thing is," said the genial Dralein, "you've been labelled a 'Troubled Youth.' You like the sound of that?"

"Heard it before," said Shol, his heart racing. "You want to sit down?"

"Can't stay," said Dadren, "because you have an important visitor. I'll be on comlink if you need anything."

"If I …." Shol started.

"You ought to start paying attention to the way things work around here," said Dadren. "You, my boy, are under lockdown until we settle the stomach of the Terran Protectorate Admin. There's still a certain irate father with some … unkind words … to say about you."

Shol's neck filled with hot blood as the full force of his shame and anger came raging back.

"It's not my fault!" he yelled. "You shouldn't let that waiter get away with…."

"With what, Son?" asked the furry government official. "With bigotry? Oh yeah, he'll get a talking to. Guess how much good it will do."

Shol covered his eyes with his hands, and hoped his tears didn't show. What kind of universe was this anyway?

"Your visitor," said Dadren, "is a court-appointed social worker. Want me to tell her to come back later?"

"She …." Shol sputtered. "I'll see her now, I guess."

Without a word, Dadren backed out of the entryway and ushered in a tall, dark human female. She wore the scarlet uniform of the Dralein civil service, with its sharp, notched lapels and chrome-plated buttons — at the cuffs, down the center and on the side pockets. Dadren gave Shol a serious look before shutting the door.

"Who are you?" Shol asked the striking woman.

"Not what I seem," her resonant voice echoed in his ears.

Shol smacked his angled forehead. It was her, the woman with the wireheads. He could see it in her sickly sweet smile and that slightly spastic thing she did with her hand — but how was she now in a different body?

"I'm a symbiote," said Warvhex through her host's mouth. "Haven't you figured that out yet?"

"You read my mind?" asked Shol.

"Galaxy, no, the expression on your slick little face," said Warvhex. "Now. What do you know about Ungent Draaf? And what did you tell him?"

She shoved Shol's trembling torso down onto his couch.

"How did you get in here?" asked Shol. "The court appoints symbiotes now?"

"Don't be a dimwit," said Warvhex. "My shell here is the social worker. I came along for the ride. Count yourself lucky they appointed you a human. Once I'm out of here, she might be able to understand you better than a Dralein."

"Lucky me," said Shol. "Humans aren't much better. And what's she doing on this planet?"

As the symbiote explained, an entire colony of humans had settled on Bledraun a century ago, during the Terran Protectorate's half-hearted attempt to assimilate the planet. In fact, they didn't get any farther than building a fantastically powerful signal transmitter on Gelen, Bledraun's largest moon. When the venture proved too expensive, the Protectorate stranded about half a million of their own people, nominally for "reconnaissance purposes."

"Jerks," said Shol. Warvhex clasped her host's large hands around the boy's throat.

"Agreed," she said. "But enough chatter. Answer my question."

Between gasps for air, Shol told the symbiote the little he did know — which amounted to the few scraps of information he'd wheedled out of Dadren. The explosion in Ungent's groundcar from the day before conformed to a pattern set by a series of recent assaults on government property. It had, most likely, not been an accident.

"It's the BFD," said Shol. "My people had nothing to do with it." Warvhex stared at him a moment before releasing her host's grip on his throat.

"I doubt that sleepy little grass roots movement would have gone to extremes like this, without somebody pushing it," she said. "Never mind. What about the device?"

Shol rubbed his neck as he sat up on the couch.

"I swear," he said, "I didn't tell the oldster anything the fuzzheads don't already know. I didn't tell him about...."

"Shut up, you idiot," said Warvhex. "If I catch you completing that sentence, it will be your last. "

"You do know they have this room wired, don't you?" asked Shol. He was trying hard to look brave in the face of overwhelming force. Warvhex sneered at him as she cracked open a window on Shol's living room wall.

"You do know you're as dumb as a brick, don't you?" she asked. "Keep your eyes open and be ready to tell me whatever you've learned the next time we meet."

The symbiote slipped out of an incision in the social worker's neck and shot out through the open window. Shol's stomach wrenched. Yet, out of curiosity, he took advantage of the young woman's momentary disorientation, and reached out to touch her neck. The symbiote's incision had already healed.

He had barely enough time to pull his hand away from behind her head before the human social worker spoke to him, her consciousness restored.

"Hi," she said, with a smile. "You must be Shol. I'm SW Faye and I'm so glad to meet you. You think you could answer a few questions now? That way, we can get your case moving forward."

"Sh … sure," said Shol, as nonchalantly as his confused thoughts would let him.

Faye rummaged through a small, black shoulder bag.

"Great," she said. "One thing, though. Could you get me a glass of water? With all this rioting today, I've got myself a terrible headache."

Later that afternoon, in the embassy's fully-equipped exercise rooms, Shol looked up from a workout bench to find himself cornered by Dadren and Jarfna, the embassy's security chief. Shol couldn't help noticing Jarfna's elegant, black uniform, trimmed in royal blue, with a diagonal array of etched, silver squares stretching across her left breast pocket. The last time he saw those squares, he was sitting under harsh lights in Drashna's office.

"Want to explain how you switched off the security cameras in your quarters?" asked Dadren, while he held Jarfna back with his powerful hands.

Shol shoved his sharp chin forward.

"When did you tell me where they are?" he asked. "And when did you forget the patrol took my e-mag knife? No way I could have shut down the cameras without it."

"The kid had an e-mag knife?" Jarfna started.

"Relax," said Dadren. "We already found one of your techs lying in a heap by the control panel on this floor — and complaining of a headache. It was the symbiote, wasn't it, Son?"

"How would I know?" asked the defiant teenager. "Do I look like I'm an exo … bio … whatever?"

"What you look like now," said Dadren, "is nothing compared to what you'll look like if you're lying."

"Yeah, more threats," said Shol. "How's that working out for you?"

"Excuse me," said Dadren, "for taking an interest. If you think I'm a threat, you probably don't trust me to give you the holomail from your girlfriend that cleared security this morning."

"Holomail?" gasped Shol.

"Don't know what a pretty Earth girl sees in you," said Dadren, "but right now, her sad little eyes are all that's keeping her powerful daddy from filing a formal complaint."

"I'm telling the truth," said Shol. "And anyway, lots of people get headaches. Like that babe of a social worker you sent me."

Jarfna pulled away from Dadren and smacked Shol across the mouth.

"Watch your language, brat!" she yelled.

"This is getting us nowhere, Chief," said Dadren. "If a symbiote can slip in here unnoticed, you have a lot more to worry about than this boy's disrespect."

"I'm not the one who should worry," said Jarfna as she stalked out of the exercise room, with her personal comlink already jammed up to her lips.

Dadren looked down at Shol, who was still lying flat on the workout bench.

"You ought to check with the medpod before using Dralein equipment," he said in a low voice. "No sense being in love with your back in two pieces."

Shol sat up on the bench.

"I really got a holomail?" he asked.

"Wouldn't you like to know?" said Dadren. "Tell you what, go back to your quarters and stay there — I don't care how many symbiotes break in and release the door locks. Show me I can trust you. Then maybe you can have your holomail from Chastity."

"Trinity," said the Krezovic. "Her name's...."

"Like I said," said Dadren, grimly. "Chastity. And you'd better make sure you remember that."

CHAPTER 10

Ungent waited as long as he could before letting on that he'd emerged from post-operative trauma. Of course, by the year 4796 in our terms, nothing so crude as a series of injections was used to desensitize a patient during surgery. The medpod, following the Grashardi data feed it had stored in memory, had temporarily switched off Ungent's pain centers through direct cortical stimulation.

At most, if the crustacean still felt groggy, it was due to the physical shock that resulted from his severe wounds. Also clouding his mind was a mild sedative, precisely balanced to match his age, weight and general state of health. But that didn't stop the terrifying memory of the crash from haunting him.

And yet, as he lay in the semi-darkness of his room, the distinguished Grashardi ambassador welcomed the chance to reflect — a luxury he hadn't had a moment to enjoy since before arriving on Bledraun. Now that he'd been transferred from the sickbay aboard Harlan's ship, the *Sweet Chariot*, to the intensive care unit in Jeldren Central hospital, he hoped for a moment of quiet rest.

Though it met the practical, scientific needs of a full-service medical center, the hospital still reflected the Dralein's obsession with interior design. Even the rack holding the infusion bags that hugged Ungent's species-adapted bed appeared modeled after the branches of a sapling. And if he'd been conscious on his way into the facility, he would have felt the calming effect of the broad, slightly rounded corridors.

Nevertheless, despite being almost fully automated, the hospital was still a bustling place. In Ungent's case, the flurry of machine intelligence was unusually high. While the crushed, torn and sheered-off exoplating on his lower body had been rapidly sequenced, printed and effectively welded into place with a combination of stem cells and growth hormones, his treatment was far from over.

Sure, he was medically stable, and his prognosis was almost as good as that of any Grashardi half his age. Yet the shock to his system had been profound and the psychological mending the decorated diplomat needed was still in process. That's why his head was enmeshed in a fine network of tiny catheters and wires, delivering neuro-stimulators, antibiotics and whatever passed for dopamine and serotonin within his non-human brain.

Despite everything, Ungent's immobilized state made it that much easier to pass the time assessing the events of the past week. Trouble was, the stillness of the room also bent his thoughts back to the circumstances of Fleront's murder.

His daughter's behavior, leading up to her death, had been so unlike her. Thorough, cautious, never jumping to conclusions, Fleront was the last person Ungent expected to meet directly with the Krezovic rebel leaders in Thrulyntrin. What had driven her to take this risk, considering the rebel's reputation for kidnapping, ransom and ... and....

Well, Fleront's poor judgment was nothing Nulgrant had put in her daughter's head. As Ungent knew too well, his wife was as placid and self-satisfied as a Gelpathian sea cucumber. But there was no need to go over that ground again. The point was, Nulgrant had shown no interest in Fleront's career and, sad to say, not much more interest in her death.

Within a dozen or so days, following a theatrical display of grief, his wife had slid back into her comfortable routine of lunches and extended weekly games of *ralthdandra* with her friends. From then on, Nulgrant's only display of grief was a thin black shawl she wore through the end of the cycle. At that moment, lying flat on his back, Ungent resolved to finally break with her when this was over.

That is, provided he could decide what "this" was.

"Doubt I have all the facts," he murmured into his sheets. No matter how he looked at it, there were gaping holes in his knowledge — of both the "facts on the ground" and their implications.

Chief among them was the emotional intensity surrounding Shol and the device he claimed to know nothing about. Ungent's instincts told him the young Krezovic hadn't shared every secret about the shiny bracelet, which was studded with dials and inscribed with human-style characters.

But why?, Ungent wondered

What was it about Shol's behavior that made him seem untrustworthy? For one thing, a boy who cried so easily and trembled so feverishly at the thought of his past would hardly have survived it. Ungent was convinced Shol had a tough heart concealed under that thin skin.

For that matter, the Grashardi had no reason to believe, on face value, that the Krezovic was actually as young as Drashna and the others assumed. Isolated, freewheeling and rather casual about official matters, the Dralein were perfect candidates for deception by anyone with enough skill at cyber forgery.

Regardless, whoever had gone to the trouble of shoving the boy into Skorshdra, whose officials were not above jailing the accuser along with the accused, would have had no scruples about giving Shol whatever case history suited their purposes.

By Shol's account, the operatives included the symbiote, Warvhex, which was a troubling thought. Because if Ungent's own meeting with the symbiote had not been an accident, it could only mean she had a role for him too, in this tangled scheme.

That thought led Ungent to a central question. Details aside, what was the purpose of this outsized show of intrigue, terror, violence and social unrest? Whatever the bracelet was, why was it so important — and what in the name of Rahlthant's comet did it have to do with the trade conference?

"The Minister will not be pleased," Ungent's tired thoughts reminded him. The conference had gone ahead without him, which ensured Grashard's share of Bledraun's mineral wealth would be minimal.

Yet that, he knew, would hardly matter if the forces orchestrating recent events actually reached their objective. What he needed now was a coherent way to piece the data together. But that would have to wait, for now a copper-colored medpod glided on a set of rollers into Ungent's room.

"A brief examination is required," it said. The crustacean bent his eyestalks in the AI's direction, and wondered what it must have been like, millennia ago, to be attended to by an organic doctor. Of course, he'd heard the standard summary of medical history in the Grashardi equivalent of high school.

Long ago, his textbook files had told him, the complexity of medical knowledge had surpassed the capacity of any living brain. Outside of basic research and development, organic medical workers began to take a backseat to artificial intelligence. Some of them did nothing more than compile the medical data the medpods consulted.

That the medpods did so at speeds Ungent's ancestors could not have imagined was impressive. That they also managed to channel this immense knowledge through an intricate personality matrix was downright astonishing.

Yet without the second accomplishment, the first would have been for nothing. An unapproachable encyclopedia, incapable of communicating with patients, would have served no one's interests. Even in Ungent's time, a patient's case history was still necessarily founded on his or her own personal recollections.

"Examination?" asked Ungent. "You must already have readouts sufficient to analyze every one of my so-called vital functions."

The medpod pivoted to face the ambassador.

"Examination complete," it said. "Your speech centers are fully operative."

"Clever," said Ungent.

"Standard protocol," said the AI. "A patient's spontaneous response is the best measure of...."

"What do you know about the ANN Commission's agenda?" Ungent blurted out.

"Examination complete," said the medpod, as it rolled toward the door.

"I asked you a direct question," said Ungent, as sternly as his tender abdomen would let him. The medpod screeched to a halt

"My function...." it started.

"Your function is to serve," said Ungent. Anxious to probe deeper, he scrambled through his memory for the few scraps of information he'd learned about AI programming.

The medpod's carefully chosen words slurred a bit as it struggled to reply.

"Turning my attention to your question will take time away from monitoring my patients," said the medpod. "Suffering may occur."

"Answer quickly then," said Ungent. "But I will not be ignored."

The medpod's status lights flickered erratically as it rolled all the way back into the room.

"Override codes prevent complete compliance," it said through a short burst of static.

"Tell me what you can," said Ungent. "then get back to your patients. That is my direct order."

But the crustacean's words had made matters worse. The roughly cylindrical android began shaking on its frame like an overloaded 21st-century washing machine.

"SECURE ... SUFFICIENT ... SUPPLY," it boomed out, its voice reduced to the most basic machine-speech monotone.

"SECURE ... SUFFICIENT ... SUPPLY ... SECURE...."

"End process!" yelled Ungent.

He didn't want his blunt line of questioning to be held responsible for crashing such a highly valued device. Moments later, the medpod appeared to reboot, its personality vectors restored. Ungent's shoulders tensed as he watched an ear bud emerge from the unit and lodge itself in his right ear.

"Examination complete," said the AI through the ear bud. "Supplemental medical advice is now available,"

The Grashardi ambassador was taken aback. This was not the way he was used to conversing with a medpod.

"Go on," he said.

"Here is my considered medical opinion," the Medpod said through the ear bud. "For the sake of your health, do not inquire further about the ANN Commission."

Ungent cursed himself as he watched the Medpod disconnect the ear bud and roll out of the room. He should have realized that a direct approach would yield him nothing. If he'd been thinking more clearly, he might have done better to ask about Warvhex.

"She's at the center," he whispered to the four walls of his private room, before the stress of his traumatic injuries dropped him off into a troubled sleep.

CHAPTER 11

Before dawn the next morning, Harlan Mars looked out over the city of Jeldren and tried to distract his racing mind with a few sips of coffee. In the brisk air, he knew he'd never regret the investment he'd made in hydroponically grown beans, the last time he was on shore leave. He'd even managed to find an antique coffee grinder and a so-called French press at an open air market. To Harlan's mind, both devices were unbelievably primitive.

"They work though, now don't they?" he muttered.

The aliens, of course — *of course* — knew nothing of coffee. No matter how many times he plugged the botanical specs for Arabica beans into a Dralein replicator, the best that miracle of science could come up with was a flavorless, dark sludge that smelled suspiciously like soybean mash.

The replicators on the *Sweet Chariot* weren't much better. Technically, he'd been told, they produced a cup of liquid chemically equivalent to his favorite morning drink. But it had nothing whatsoever in common with the reasons he drank the stuff in the first place. The aroma was almost … the taste was nearly….

Yet, on this morning, he was secretly grateful he had such a trivial gripe to fixate on. The alternative was reading over the latest orders from Admin for the seventh time. As he already knew, the hunt for the renegade symbiote had intensified. The orders, which he'd received yesterday, gave him the authority to use every available local and regional resource to find her.

Naturally, no mission statement from Admin would be complete without an extra dose of Crazy. This time, the insane part of his orders came in the form of a strange energy signature he was also supposed to look out for. As usual, Admin hadn't given him the slightest hint of why it mattered.

Harlan set his recyclable cup down on the lip of a disposal unit to his left.

Who's twisting their unders so tight? he asked himself.

Nothing made sense. Admin had even requested a back-up security force from the Dralein. But as his field experience had taught him early on, a large search party was almost always a liability.

And now, after the latest report from Harlan's Chief of Security, the picture was muddier still. According to Lieutenant Heath, the latest security scans revealed the presence of a symbiote ship parked right behind Lerdra, Bledraun's third moon.

Though nominally cloaked, the mid-sized space-folder's shielding had been temporarily damaged by a passing micro-meteor shower. This allowed Heath's team to scan large sectors of the symbiote's encrypted database before the cloak was restored.

Usually, none of that would have been of any interest to Harlan. He preferred to leave high level surveillance shenanigans to the people who relished them. Yet the data, encrypted with Avroulian algorithms that the Protectorate had recently cracked, did turn up one piece of intriguing data.

The symbiotes were withholding information about an unknown species they'd discovered at the far end of the settled universe — right on the edge of the Seshnel event horizon. Worse, the scan data suggested this new species was hostile.

"You sure about that?" the Captain had grilled his Lieutenant, purely to take the edge off his own anxiety. Too bad, the effect was only temporary. The Lieutenant also told him more bad news might come to light when the scans were fully decrypted.

Disturbing as this revelation was, Harlan was determined to keep it in perspective. At least so far, it wasn't clear the symbiote data had any bearing on his irritating and slightly loopy mission from Admin. Now, as his XO emerged from the lander, Harlan knew he must push all doubt from his mind and project an air of rock-solid confidence.

"Morning, Captain," said Gillian Cavendish, who looked every bit as fit and military as Harlan felt deflated and civilian.

Fact was, he'd stumbled into the space-faring life and surprised himself by having a knack for it. But underneath his sheen of settled competence, Harlan knew he'd never given a gram of comet dust for "the Corps."

To him, it was a line of work, a good paying racket and not much else. It was, however, a job that required a certain amount of ... compromise. In this case, Harlan realized, the symbiote leaders were probably no worse than his own scheming higher-ups.

Wanna turn the whole entire universe into their private club, he thought.

So why was it his place to favor one over the other? The depressing truth was this: his place was with his paycheck.

"Team ready?" he asked, with studied gruffness. In reality, he wanted nothing more than to ditch the mission and take his XO out to lunch at one of Jeldren's many outdoor cafes. It had been a year since Tipper Angstrom had dumped him for a high-rolling Antarian financier — a guy in a satiny jumpsuit with a face like a drooling Zelinoid.

For her part, Gillian was all business and all smiles.

"Suited up, equipped and awaiting your orders, Sir," she said.

The knot in his belly made Harlan gulp.

"Transmit the search parameters and let's move out," he said.

Harlan knocked his former coffee cup into the recycling bin and stood up. He flipped his helmet's gilded visor down and gave the expected hand signal to set his mixed corps of human and Dralein operatives in motion. Fact was, he felt a little silly in his encounter suit. Sure, it was necessary, but why in the Sea of Galilee did it have to be so darn *shiny*?

"Stealth mode," he barked, partly because barking went a long way to keeping nervous young troops reassured. But also because the subtle holographic overlays of stealth mode made wearing his official get-up a little less embarrassing.

And so the search began, strictly according to protocol. But what, Harlan wondered, did Admin think a formal investigation would accomplish? Wasn't it obvious this particular symbiote had more than savvy enough to evade a lurching search party? Hell's bells, she'd sneaked onto his own ship, and right into the neck of his XO. Stomping around the streets of Bledraun's capital city was the least likely way to smoke her out.

Yes, he'd read the specs about the new brainwave scanners that Admin had shipped over on the *Sweet Chariot*. Gillian was using one now, as were a couple of his other top officers. But a creature this wily, he was sure, could easily mask her signal, if by no other means than jumping into the neck of an unsuspecting shopkeeper.

Nor was he vain enough to think he was the first person to realize that. The Dralein and his crew, including Gillian, would follow orders, simply because they were orders. But Harlan couldn't stop himself from wondering what the real purpose of this reconnaissance mission was.

Maybe, he figured, it had more to do with that sensor upgrade that Admin had incorporated into his entire store of encounter suits before he left for Bledraun. According to the little he'd pried out of the Admin Tech crew, the sensors were now able to detect a wider range of fluctuations in ambient radiation. But what did that have to do with.....

Gillian's melodious voice seemed to glide out of his helmet speakers.

"Captain," she said. "A team member is picking up an unusual energy reading."

"Unusual how?" asked Haran, "There has to be some Dralein tech we don't know about yet."

"The team member is Kalfnor, a Dralein," said Gillian. "She says it doesn't match anything they've got in their database. Nobody's using it on Bledraun."

More puzzling, she told him, her own quick crosscheck with their ship's sensors came up negative.

"Negative what?" asked Harlan.

"Negative," said Gillian, "as in it shouldn't exist, actually. See for yourself now, Sir, I've popped it up on your visor display."

Harlan squinted his eyes unnecessarily, given his recent corneal implants, and felt his breath stick in his chest. Wait. Better to double check … yes … the incoming data matched the energy signature Brad Christiansen had warned him about.

"Got coordinates for that reading, Commander?" Harlan growled. And to think this mission was originally pitched to him as a simple piloting job.

In fact, Gillian had mapped out both the location, and three alternative routes to it, ranked by stealth, safety and environmental impact. After eyeing his latest visor display, Harlan did what he did best: He made a decision that was the least like a decision as possible. The search party would split into three groups, each following one of Gillian's suggested routes, then rendezvous at....

"What about the symbiote, Sir?" his XO asked, her voice tensing to hide her impatience.

"Figure the symbie and the energy source gotta be interrelated," said Harlan. "You with me on this, Commander?"

Gillian shut her eyes tight. She hated it when he called her Commander, for reasons she couldn't sort out. But it was what protocol demanded, so she decided to rest easy about it until they were back on Reagan 3 and she could speak to her counselor....

"Commander!" Harlan barked, then smiled to himself as Gillian jumped to attention.

"Right." she said. "With you all the way, Sir."

"Give the freakin' order then," he said. His chest muscles strained as he forced himself not to laugh. It was wrong, he knew, to enjoy having so much power. But it was the best medicine against the fear welling up in his psyche. What if they actually did corner that dangerous symbiote? He didn't relish the thought of having her slimy mass jammed into *his* neck.

The directional signals on his visor mapped out the three routes and listed the team assigned to each. Harlan's own team consisted of the ship's two crack-shot snipers and Grelnon, a Dralein with detailed knowledge of Jeldren's best defensive positions. If someone were hiding, Grelnon would have the best chance of knowing where to look.

Grateful his XO was so precise, Harlan signaled his team to follow him along the coordinates now blinking on his visor's display. The trail led into a dank alley, one, two, four doors down and … there … he saw Gillian's team and the third one converging on the same spot.

"Be ready for anything," he said softly into the group comlink and, with practiced aim, blasted the electronic controls off the door that, according to scanner data, was shielding the source of the radiation. Weapons charged, he left one team behind to stand watch and led the other two down the winding steps that the blown out door had opened into.

Eyes, ears and reflexes alert through years of experience, Harlan mastered his fear at the tomb-like silence that greeted him. Whatever had been happening down here, he suspected, was now long abandoned. No surprise then, that the inner door crumbled under the slam of his rifle butt.

"Freeze," he shouted, pointlessly. As the search party's helmet lamps revealed, there was nothing inside but a series of robotic assembly units, each attached to crude work benches. But the lamps also revealed something shocking. Every Dralein on the away team lay collapsed on the cracked tile floor.

"You seeing this?" Harlan called out, his voice hoarse.

"It's the radiation, I think," Gillian replied. "Initial brain scans indicate...."

"Jericho's walls, Commander," Harlan yelled, "get the Dralein out of here! Where the imploding neutron star are the gravity modulators?"

Gillian ordered the remaining away team to make a series of makeshift gurneys out of some of the decaying planks strewn around the room and a set of Terran Protectorate compact gravity modulators. This enabled the Dralein to be floated out of that dark lair and up the stairs by humans approximately half their weight.

Once up to the surface, the Dralein members of the remaining team rushed over to their compatriots, removed them from the gurneys and injected each from syringes stored in their emergency medpacks.

Haldraven, the smallest of the Dralein from the third search party group spoke up first.

"It's the theta sickness," he said. "They need medical attention immediately."

Harlan's brow furrowed.

"Or what?" he asked. "They die? How long have they got?"

"I'm not qualified," said Haldraven, "to answer that."

"But I rather thought...." Gillian started.

"Get on the horn to ... what is it ... Jeldren Central?" snapped Harlan. "We can't have...."

"Done," said Haldraven. "The medpods will arrive soon. If I may suggest...."

"Seal this area," said Harlan, as he flicked his visor up. "Gillian, you know what to do. Let me know the minute the Chaudron chimes in. It's about freakin' time these people took responsibility for their own mess."

Commander Cavendish looked at him a moment, but resisted the urge to speak her mind. Instead, she removed her helmet and ran a hand through her trimmed, golden hair.

"Will you require anything else, Sir?" she asked.

"Naw, that's enough, isn't it?" he snapped. "Get us some serious firepower from the ship and I'll check back with you later."

"Captain, if I may," said Gillian, "protocol requires...."

Harlan stared into her deep, blue eyes.

"You have your orders," he said. "If you need me, I'll be at the hospital. Gotta check me up on a sick friend."

CHAPTER 12

Across town, in a residential section of Jeldren, an imposing Dralein perched herself on the edge of a cozy ceramic park bench. Her black cowled outfit contrasted sharply with the cheery bright blossoms and graceful limbs of the *rhajeldra* tree that bowed low and to her right.

With a glance in both directions, she pulled the broad brim of her black hat over her eyes, put an ear bud in her right ear, and heard a scolding voice give her a dressing down.

"Look at you," the voice said. "Your clothes scream "I'm in Disguise.""

"I never wanted to meet outside," said Drashna.

But as the voice explained, the park had fewer listening devices.

"Fine," said Drashna. "What do you want? I have a planet to run."

"For how much longer, Your Short-sighted-ness?" the voice asked. "That's what we need to discuss."

"*We?*" asked Drashna. "Why do you care what happens to Bledraun?"

A small, brown scampering *prejmu* cut across her field of vision and she longed to escape into its freewheeling way of life. But the voice wouldn't let her.

"Because," the voice said, "Bledraun is the closest planet to the Fremdel event horizon. It's the ideal launchpad for our enemy."

Drashna shifted her weight on the bench.

"Are you referring to the...." she said.

"Don't say it!" the voice yelled. "Don't let on you're even aware of them."

The Chaudron slammed the back of her bench and stood up.

"I didn't come out here to play a mystery game," she said.

"The game, Your Pompous-ness, is annihilation," said the voice. "Sit down. Listen. We need to get this right."

"No," said Drashna. "No more … until you prove that Caronya is still alive."

In seconds, her personal holoscanner filled with images of a seven-year-old Dralein, sleeping peacefully in a stasis chamber.

"We will administer the *gauliadram*, as agreed, the minute the mission is complete," said the voice.

Drashna tore at the fur on her arms.

"And if the mission fails?" she asked.

"You would not want your daughter alive for one more day," said the angelic voice which, as Ungent would have recognized, belonged to Warvhex.

CHAPTER 13

It took another week, but one morning Ungent awoke in his own bed at the Grashardi embassy, his wounds essentially healed. The lingering pain he could manage, with a small external pulse transmitter he wore at his waist. After two tries, he climbed out of bed, eased himself up and glanced around his quarters.

"Looks the same," he hummed. What a relief to be out of the hospital!

Jeldren General had sent him home with a holovid full of physical therapy routines he was supposed to follow. But first he wanted a good long soak in his tank and a decent breakfast. Besides, there was a lot to mull over. Now that he'd missed the Dralein trade negotiations, Grashard would also miss out on its share of Bledraun's rare minerals.

Yet it seemed now there was more at stake than precious ores. The ANN Commission and its accomplices had kidnapped him, to use as a puppet. Through him, it had hoped to promote a wide-ranging agenda.

They won't give up, he told himself.

Now that the androids had demonstrated their power over him, Ungent decided, it was time to take direct action. Yet deciding what form that action should take required a steady stream of accurate real-time data. Based on his encounter with the hospital medpod, the ANN Commission's attempt on his life was only part of the picture. A larger, more dangerous conflict was already on the horizon.

"Sword of Salkent, I'm starving," he said to his four walls. It was time to push his spinning thoughts to one side. With a practiced hand, he switched on his food replicator and called up the ingredients needed to cook himself a hot breakfast. While a device like this was capable of preparing a ready-to-eat meal on its own, the result was always … blah.

Cooking, by contrast, was therapeutic. As the ingredients sizzled gently on his nut-brown energy-efficient stove, his thoughts turned to the bleary conversation he'd had with Harlan Mars in the hospital. Through his medicated fog, it had seemed to Ungent as if the captain were fishing for information, without knowing exactly what he was after.

Though Harlan's anxiety did involve Warvhex, Ungent noticed a new element. But what did Harlan expect him to know about energy signatures? Unless, that is, Grashard had obtained new information while he was in the hospital.…

Hold it … he did remember an article in last night's mission update.

The Grashardi ambassador shut off the burner under the heavily spiced *halthtryna*, whose dorsal fins he'd almost scorched, stood stock still in his kitchenette and gave the memory his full attention. Or rather, he would have, if a loud shouting match hadn't erupted in the corridor outside his quarters.

Ordinarily, he wouldn't have given the argument any thought. Emotions flared from time to time, and there was generally no reason for concern. Yet Ungent distinctly heard Shol's voice rising steadily, as a second unknown voice closed in.

Were the Dralein taking Shol into custody? That would never do. The Krezovic boy was his most promising source of answers for the questions mounting exponentially in his mind. Ungent paused long enough to dress in full diplomatic regalia — in spite of his stiff muscles — then strode to the door of his apartment and swung it open with maximum dramatic effect.

"What is this … ruckus?" he demanded, his face a mask of authoritative dignity.

There before him was Security Chief Jarfna, ready to drag the Krezovic boy to the maglev lift at the end of the corridor, with her broad hands and powerful arms.

"This … whelp … broke into the embassy weapons locker this morning," said the tough officer.

"It's time I got back what's mine," said Shol. "My e-mag blade is my business."

"You're supposed to be in lockdown," Jarfna shouted. Ungent winced as she pinned the sixteen-year-old's left arm behind his arched back — and was startled to see how much he'd missed since the opening day of the trade conference.

"Lockdown for what?" he asked.

While Shol struggled to get away, Jarfna condensed the story of the incident at the diner, along with the symbiote's visit, into a few short, breathless sentences. Ungent's eyestalks trembled a bit at the news of the boy's involvement with a daughter of a Terran Protectorate official. Nothing good, he knew, could come of that.

Even if Shol didn't end up back in jail, he'd get his heart broken. Once Trinity finally caved in to the pressures of her world — and, frankly, her caste — she'd remember her intimate conversations with a piece of "street slime," as an embarrassing childhood interlude.

"And where is the e-mag knife now?" he asked, as he tried to gauge the gravity of the situation.

The Dralein security chief finally released her grip on Shol.

"That's what I've been telling Junior here," said Jarfna.

Ungent flattered himself that his aura of personal authority had reassured her. But as he was learning, the Dralein were as hard to read as the ancient scrolls of Khtal Turnaz in Grashard's central archeological museum.

"The knife," Jarfna continued, "is still locked up in the Jeldren Patrol evidence room. As I told Junior...."

"His name is Shol," said the Grashardi. "He's my pupil and my responsibility. Leave him with me."

Jarfna dug her boots into the corridor's soft pile carpeting.

"Regulations are clear," she said. "Your student broke curfew, defied lockdown and...."

"I'm sure he stole your lunch money, too," said Ungent. "Trust me, I know what a spike of gamma radiation he is. But tell me, what effect do you think the embassy brig will have on him after Skorshdra?"

Jarfna stared at Ungent a moment, then pulled a flexiscreen from the inside pocket of her uniform.

"Here," she said, "sign this security release. The Krezovic is lucky he's still under age. But that doesn't make you any less liable for his actions if he does anything else stupid. And believe me, Har Draaf, he will."

Ungent clacked his mandibles, but said nothing. The sooner, he realized, he got Shol out of the corridor and away from the seething security officer, the better. He passed the release form over the personal scanner embedded in his forearm, signed it in metadigital code and passed the flexiscreen back to Jarfna.

"Good luck," said Jarfna. "If you get a call from the Chaudron about this, I hope you'll have the decency to...."

"What I say to Drashna is my business alone," said Ungent. He turned back toward his quarters and called out to Shol over his right shoulder. "It's time for your lesson."

Shol looked from the downcast Jarfna to Ungent and back again — to see the Chief of Embassy Security already making her way to the elevator banks.

"You serious?" he asked Ungent.

The crustacean's eyestalks whipped around to the right to glare at Shol.

"You wouldn't ask that of Warvhex, would you?" he said in the back of his throat. Without another word, he held the door to his quarters open and motioned the startled Krezovic teenager in. One way or another, Ungent was determined to discover the undercurrent beneath the seemingly random events of the last two weeks.

Once inside, he motioned for the boy to sit once again at his kitchenette counter. Though he wanted nothing more than to interrogate Shol down to the deepest molecule of his shiny skin, Ungent knew it would be futile. Dishing out intimidation to the street-scarred boy would make him harder to reach.

The crustacean slapped his scaly left hand down on the kitchenette's countertop.

"Now then," he said. "I have a problem I think you can help me with."

Shol's eyes opened wide, as Ungent dragged a dark-blue neo-leather satchel from under his bed and flipped up its top flap. Before his next breath, an amber light flared on, attached to the surface of … whatever was tucked inside.

"What's that?" asked Shol. "Some kind of … of shooter?"

Ungent's mind flooded with sarcastic comments, but he kept them to himself. The Krezovic, he was sure, already had enough reason to stifle his natural curiosity, without the threat of mockery to hold him back further.

"See for yourself," he said. He slid a slim device out of the satchel and placed it gently on a small side table.

Shol gasped like a nine-year-old who had just opened a birthday present.

"It's an AI," he said.

"Incorrect," said a female voice. "What you are referring to is the casing for an artificial intelligence — which exists as the result of a complex interaction of…."

"Thank you, Yaldrint," said Ungent, "for clarifying."

"I exist to serve," said the AI.

Shol climbed down from his stool and tiptoed over to the side table.

"You named your AI?" he asked.

Ungent twiddled a few dials on the AI's casing.

"Her official designation," he said, "is an unpronounceable 12-character catalogue number. Maybe you'd prefer that."

Shol stared at the AI's slowly blinking status lights for a full minute, as if he were having the biggest epiphany of his life. It was exactly as Ungent had hoped: Shol was barely able to look up from the device.

"Can I use it?" he asked.

"For specific purposes," said Ungent. "As directed by me. Namely to find out, if we can, what 'real' means in the middle of this confusing mess."

Shol's eyes narrowed.

"So, I'd be working for you? Like for Ulandroz?" he asked.

"Nothing like that," said Ungent. "This would be a chance to learn a skill that might get you off the streets."

"But…." the boy started.

"Think for a minute," said Ungent. "Drashna's been tough on you, but she's not the sort to send you back to Skorshdra. I know enough about the Dralein to be sure of that. If you keep insisting you know nothing about that mysterious ... bracelet ... it won't be long before the Chaudron sticks you on a passenger ship with enough credits to last you a month or two."

"So?" Shol asked, with his chest puffed out.

"With no job prospects, you'll be back out on the street, where Ulandroz is waiting to use your skull for a *gracklia* mug," said the Grashardi ambassador. "I'm offering you a chance to take control of your life. But maybe you'd rather sit in your room and watch holovids."

Shol's shimmering face drew taut.

"Better than working for free," he said.

"Exactly," said Ungent. "You'd be working to free yourself from the symbiote who threw you into Skorshdra once, and will do it again if she thinks she has to. Or would you feel more free in your old cell?"

Shol's head sank into his hands.

"Can't believe you let me call you an idiot," he mumbled.

"Stick this out, and you'll have plenty of time to prove it's still true," said Ungent. "In the meantime, are you ready to work? This may be the last chance you get to prove you're worthy to associate with humans again."

"What're you saying? You think this could help me with ... with Trinity?" the Krezovic boy asked.

"That, young rebel, is an area of the universe where my expertise is limited," said Ungent. "But I'll share the one shred of insight I've gained. If you and Trinity will be together, it will be without plotting, without scheming and without help from adults with creaks in their joints."

"So I can't do nothing to fix things?" asked Shol's shaky voice.

"The only thing you can do," said Ungent, "is whatever can be achieved by living in the moment."

"Makes no sense," Shol grumbled. "But OK. Maybe Trinity's dad would like me better if I was smart at something."

Ungent nodded to himself, relieved to know there was at least one thing in the galaxy that could motivate the boy.

"You still think you have a future with her?" asked Ungent.

Shol's curved hands balled up into nearly spherical fists.

"Listen, Oldster," he said. "Either I have a future with Trinity or I don't have a future at all."

"Inaccurate," Ungent's AI piped up. "The future cannot be determined through direct analysis of localized cause and effect relationships."

"That will do, Yaldrint," said the Grashardi. "I believe our friend was simply being poetic."

Shol looked down at the tips of his boots and tried to control his breathing. As long as he could remember, no one had ever called him a friend.

CHAPTER 14

Out past the Bledraun system, just under two-hundred-thousand kilometers from the Fremdel event horizon, a mid-sized Terran Protectorate probe ship hovered on the edge of disaster.

Lieutenant Cricket Andersen grit her teeth and entered her sixteenth minor course correction in the past half hour. Or rather, she okayed a course correction her navigation AI had recommended with the highest level of urgency. This close to the Fremdel, the required calculations were nerve-rackingly complex.

The trick was to keep the *Mighty Fortress* on a trajectory appropriate for detailed sensor readings, but safe enough not to start a slow drift into the horizon. Yes, it hurt the Lieutenant's pride, but she'd never think of handling the situation on her own. Trouble was, the concentration required for continuous monitoring was exhausting. It would be so easy, she realized, to … drift … off … to….

"Aren't you tired of fiddling with those controls?" called a voice at her back.

Lieutenant Andersen hunched her shoulders and wheeled around in her chair, to see Captain/27/Enos/ Exploratory, the biomechanoid who was also her superior officer.

"Come on, Captain," she said, "it's my job."

"Or is it an obsession?" asked Enos.

The 20-something human squinted her periwinkle eyes at him.

"OK, for the record," she said, "this is me being polite. You may have augmented your database with trivia about human psychology. But that doesn't mean you understand it."

The captain's face went blank for a moment.

"Rephrasing," he said. "Does working the controls of a Terran Protectorate probe ship near a threatening event horizon make you feel helpless and out of control?"

Cricket snapped her eyes down to her control panel.

"Approach to the target stabilizing, Captain," she said.

"Does it? Do you compensate for your feeling of inadequacy by constantly re-adjusting the settings?" asked Enos.

"Yes, Captain," said Cricket. "Can we not talk about this?"

"I do not understand," said Enos. "If my question was valid and my assumption accurate...."

"It still doesn't make it OK to shove your assumptions in my face," said Cricket.

Too late, her own words echoed in her mind and she felt like a miserable puppy, caught with her nose in the hamburger meat.

"Sorry, Captain, that was out of line," she murmured.

Enos knelt beside Cricket's workstation.

"I sense I have not grasped the appropriate social protocol and have embarrassed you," he said quietly. "Is that correct?"

Cricket stared at her data screen to avoid his eyes.

"Correct, Captain," she said.

"I also sense you are withholding information from me," said the biomechanoid.

Cricket took the captain's head in her hands.

"What you sense," she said, "is that I've always...."

A blaring alarm broke in on Lieutenant Andersen's troubled sleep. This was the second time she'd dozed off during her shift.

"Great. Now I'm *dreaming* about him," she muttered.

She ran her long fingers through her wavy, dark-red hair, straightened her uniform and peeked around at the small navigation team she managed. Relief washed over her as she realized they were too engrossed in their console displays to have caught her napping. It was the one advantage of working with a team of total nerds. Not much for conversation, but no nosy, intrusive banter, either.

As she checked the readouts on her control panel, Cricket saw the minor course correction the navigation AI had alerted her to. Cricket was lucky. The task was simple and soon the *Mighty Fortress* was back on course. She slapped the side of her face.

"Pull yourself together," she said.

Lieutenant Andersen pushed her black swivel chair back from the navigation console and let her eyes stare unfocused at its vermillion and chartreuse status lights. She stretched her stiff arms and gazed around the serene navigation center, with its high ceilings, subdued lighting and generous proportions.

At times like these, she would have given a month's salary to walk off the ship and into a meadow of soft grass. For a brief moment, the memory of the small farming community she'd grown up in soothed her soul — until her drifting mind was interrupted again by the AI's insistent beep.

"Everything OK up there, Lieutenant?" the captain's artificial voice crackled over ship's intercom. To Cricket's relief, he didn't seem angry, and she almost allowed herself to believe she heard genuine concern in his voice.

But that, she saw, was the same madness that lay behind her frustrating, vivid dream. Though she fought it as hard as she could, Cricket couldn't stop herself from hoping Enos would eventually reciprocate. That is, even though it was totally against protocol, enough so to get her chucked out of the Service for good.

More to the point, it was flatly impossible. Captain/27/Enos/ Exploratory was not human — not now, not ever. Most psychologists agreed that emotion in the sense that humans took for granted was not part of any biomechanoid's makeup. Trouble was, especially for lonely romantics like Cricket, her captain had been carefully programmed to mimic human responses with uncanny accuracy.

"That's a … that's an illusion," she reminded herself, as she tended to do every hour on the half-hour all day long. Well, there was no question. When this mission at the Fremdel was over, she'd get herself reassigned — even if it meant an effective demotion. No way she could live this torture.

Making matters worse, the maglev doors whooshed open and Cricket's impossibly handsome captain stepped onto the bridge.

"Anything coming over the sensors?" the captain asked.

"Not my specialty, Sir," Cricket reminded him. One of the hardest things about dealing with AIs was getting them to understand human limitations.

"But surely," said Enos, "your experience enables an educated guess."

Cricket took a deep breath.

"If you're satisfied with a guess," she said, "I believe nothing significant has emerged from the event horizon since we arrived. But maybe you should consult with Linguistics or Communications."

"They also report nothing," said Enos, "which is unacceptable. My own internal sensors detect an intelligence at close range."

"*What* are you sensing?" asked the Lieutenant. "Maybe you're using a different definition of intelligence."

"I am not," said Enos. "The intelligence itself is. Consider the readings at the following coordinates."

Cricket's brow furrowed at the sight of a faint energy signature, a signature everyone else onboard had interpreted as cosmic background noise.

"How is that different from the standard random interference patterns we see all the time?" she asked.

"Because, Lieutenant Andersen," said Enos, "the patterns are not random, but periodic. See here … here … and here."

Cricket watched as the biomechanoid highlighted segments of the screen graphic in red.

"I see that," she said. "But repetition isn't the same as intelligence. Although I guess it could be a machine-generated signature."

"And what, Lieutenant, generates machines?" asked Enos, as he spread the fingers of one hand until they covered Cricket's display. The human nodded. The captain had discovered indirect evidence of a sentient species, active somewhere near the center of the Fremdel event horizon.

"If you're right," said Cricket, "how can they possibly survive so close to the black hole itself?"

"Three thousand cycles ago, the question would have been, 'How can humans survive in space?'" said Enos. "Possibility is relative."

Cricket closed her eyes and tried to absorb what she'd heard. If there were a sentient species out there, she'd better pinpoint its position right away. She opened her eyes and entered a series of commands in preparation for a sensor sweep of immediate space. But Enos swatted her hands away from her console.

"Take no action!" said Enos. "I fear detection."

"You *fear*?" said Cricket.

"Is this not the appropriate verbal expression? I might as well have said, 'I would like to avoid detection for tactical reasons.'"

"So … you're not afraid?" asked Cricket.

"Don't be ridiculous," said Enos. "I simply want — whatever that is — to make the first move. Meanwhile, we have many more steps remaining to complete our mission. Focus on those."

The Lieutenant nodded, shifted her weight in her seat, and returned to the routine work of keeping the *Mighty Fortress* from falling into the Fremdel's fierce gravitational maw.

The biomechanoid, meanwhile, busied himself with sharing his findings with the ship's linguist. If there were any discernable messages flowing in or out of the event horizon, he wanted to know. Though incapable of fear, Enos recognized that the uncertainty of the situation was interfering with the smooth operation of his pseudoneural network.

And that, he acknowledged, was unacceptable. As he scanned the data made available by Admin since the ship's arrival in Bledraun's sector, Enos wondered if there were any correlation between the intrigue unfolding on the planet and the surprise appearance of sentient life so many light years away.

Also fueling his thoughts was a data file the *Sweet Chariot* had discovered by accident during routine surveillance of the symbiote ship parked behind Bledraun's third moon. Not for the first time, Enos had found the Protectorate's blanket policy of sharing security data extremely useful.

The new data, which Enos had received from Lieutenant Heath, told of an earlier encounter between the symbiotes and an unknown species at the far end of the settled universe. Was it a coincidence that these ... Quishiks ... were also discovered near the edge of an event horizon?

Yet even with the combined force of his own mind and the ship's massive AI, any such correlation remained highly speculative.

That is, except for one shred of data Enos was sure his human project leaders had overlooked. Though they were fully aware that something had disrupted the supply of essential minerals across the settled universe, they'd failed to make a crucial connection: The onset of the shortages corresponded exactly with the appearance of unusual solar flare activity in the vicinity of the Fremdel.

It was high time someone determined the source of that activity, yet here Enos hit an obstacle. The mission protocol of the *Mighty Fortress* didn't give him the scope to conduct an independent investigation. Compounding the problem, the Fremdel's gravitational distortions meant that any request for expanded powers would take too long to reach Reagan 3.

Enos had already considered the alternative: to contact the cruiser-class ship *Sweet Chariot* and seek approval from its captain, the designated Mission Commander in this sector. Yet a cautionary scan of that vessel had revealed it might be compromised. Buried within the *Sweet Chariot's* biodata profile was a striking anomaly: the presence of a previously unregistered biomechanical intelligence.

Yet, as Captain Enos well knew, he was one of only two such registered intelligences in the entire fleet. The other, Captain/43/ Sarah/ Geological, was currently orbiting the moon of a newly discovered planet at the opposite end of the settled universe.

Was Captain Mars himself the biomechanoid in question? Unlikely, Enos concluded, for Harlan's biological signature stood out loud and clear in the biodata file. Still, there was reason enough to believe that any sensitive information shared with Harlan might soon be compromised. If, however, a search for this new, sentient species could be conducted within the parameters of the mission....

"Initiate course change," the captain said to his Lieutenant. "We need to alter our search parameters."

Cricket Andersen bit her lower lip and squinted up at him from her console.

"Captain," she said, "long range scans can pull in data across the entire array of the event horizon, no matter where we are."

"Even at this distance," said the biomechanoid, "the Fremdel's gravitational fields make tracking data with the usual methods imprecise."

"But Sir," said Cricket, "that's merely hypothetical. No one has ever proven...."

"Congratulations," said Enos. "You are about to engage in path-breaking research designed to test that hypothesis. Or would you prefer if one of your subordinates capture that honor?"

Cricket studied her captain's face in vain, hoping for a hint of levity. Nothing. She pulled herself up straight, her hands poised over the flickering control panel.

"Awaiting your orders, Captain/27/Enos/Exploratory," she said.

Enos flashed a disarming smile.

"A mouthful, isn't it?" said her superior. Cricket pinched herself.

Had she fallen back into her blissfully deceptive dream? But it was not to be.

"Realign ship's coordinates to...." the captain began.

"But Captain," said Cricket, "how can you be sure your coordinates won't get us pulled into the Fremdel itself? Let me check them first against the Nav AI."

The Captain's face went blank again for a moment.

"Done. Coordinates confirmed," said Enos. "Now. I believe the proper verbal idiom is 'humor me.'"

Cricket watched as the biomechanoid turned and walked into the maglev elevator.

"Yes, Sir," she said. Her breath caught in her throat as her eyes followed the manufactured perfection of his ... his back ... as he entered the maglev lift.

How? she thought. *How in the name of Golgotha did you ever get so stupid?*

CHAPTER 15

Soon after he'd introduced Yaldrint to Shol, Ungent set out for downtown Jeldren. He knew the risks of leaving the Krezovic boy and the ageless AI alone were slight. Yaldrint would set out the ground rules for their interaction — and keep an eye out for signs of trouble.

Held in reserve was the narrow-beam lase pistol built into the side of Yaldrint's casing, expressly for Ungent's defense. Shol would never see it unless he acted out, but the Grashardi doubted that would happen. The boy had a hot temper, but Ungent saw a curious, good- natured personality peeking through the tough exterior.

Within minutes, he'd cleared out of the embassy and was tramping along a broad sidewalk toward the center of town.

"Beautiful," he said.

For the second time, he wondered what Nulgrant would make of the Dralein's imaginative landscaping. But the Nulgrant he was thinking of was the sensitive, intellectually curious female he'd married 80 years ago — not the cynical hedonist she'd become.

A light breeze, wafting over from the river to the east, cooled his exoplated forehead and drove that sour memory from his mind. Better to focus on the situation at hand, he decided. No matter what, he was determined to gather his own data about the tangled political trends running through every aspect of life on Bledraun.

Why, for instance, was Harlan's lander constantly shuttling between Jeldren's main square and his orbiting cruiser? Usually, the humans were all business and never lingered to see the sights. And yet here was Harlan, he'd learned through Dadren, leading an interplanetary search party.

Too many credits devoted to tracking down one symbiote, Ungent reflected. At most, he expected the humans to send a team of robotic investigators. If Harlan's superiors had enlisted the services of a space-folder captain, it must mean they were playing a high stakes game.

Ungent had listened to Shol's street-smart advice and followed his directions to a bustling sector of town, south of the main square. He pulled up the hood of the dark gray cloak he'd brought along, and hoped to disappear amongst the other off-world delegates still lingering after the conference. But because he was neither furry nor humanoid, blending-in proved impossible. Soon enough, his appearance touched a nerve in one of Jeldren's less cosmopolitan residents.

"Hey, crusty!" shouted an unseen mouth from a high window. "You look tired. Why don't you come lie down in my fry pan for a while?"

Ungent's stomach tightened, but he kept quiet, took a deep breath, and forged ahead, toward the deserted streets at the edge of Krezovic Town. Though the contrast between Jeldren proper and this crumbling neighborhood intrigued him, Ungent focused on a peculiar sight up ahead on his left. It was a conversation between a scruffy, Krezovic couple and a squat android.

Though the Krezovics, Ungent assumed, were only in their mid-twenties, their drab outfits of rough Zelnethrian canvas suggested a long-established habit of "making do." As to the android, it appeared to emit an orangey haze. Or was he really seeing the feathery edge of a poorly modulated holojection?

While the crustacean was hardly an expert on the topic, Ungent knew a holographic image of his time could be wrapped in a dense electromagnetic field. This enabled it to interact with any physical object and receive data a holojector could reinterpret as, say, temperature, moisture content, texture or the sound of someone's voice.

Once assembled, this composite wave form could be further wrapped in a space-folding field and sent off across vast distances —from which it could transmit and receive data in real time. Although the technology was now standard military issue, it still wasn't available to the mass market. Someone had gone to great expense to bring the android's image to Bledraun.

Intrigued, Ungent tucked himself into the crux of a spreading *chalyzfe* tree, so he could watch the three of them unobserved. The tree's crinkled, yet soft bark felt strangely like an embrace. That let Ungent wedge himself deep into a large crack in the trunk, brought on by age and Bledraun's many robust species of burrowing insects. The Grashardi paused to admire the tree's powerful grace in the late morning sun, then peered out into the near distance.

What're they up to? he asked himself.

Out of habit, he checked his personal scanner and saw it was registering an unidentified energy signature. In a flash, he recalled his last conversation with Harlan in Jeldren General. Could this be what his old friend was talking about? When he found no easy answer, he shifted his attention back to the Krezovic couple.

At first, they seemed so calm that Ungent wondered if they were under the influence of a narcotic. But the scene's tranquility soon shattered. When the couple presented the multi-limbed android with a shiny object, it shoved them both to the ground with terrific force. The crustacean gasped, then used the zoom lens function on his personal scanner to get a closer look.

Yes, the object the Krezovics had offered the android was a shiny bracelet, studded with dials.

Ungent wondered what the connection could be, between Shol's story and this android of obvious Ghildurian manufacture. Before he could hazard a guess, Ungent noticed a shift in the conversation between the android and the Krezovics. Had they reached an understanding? The next moment, the squat android's image dispersed in a dense cloud of orange holographic mist.

The two Krezovics gave each other a tense hug and walked away. Because he dared not appear in plain sight too soon, Ungent paused to weigh the pros and cons of sharing his discoveries with Harlan Mars. Maybe Harlan deserved this data. Wasn't he pursuing a dangerous symbiote? Yet, clearly, the political climate was too unstable for his old alliances to hold.

Puzzled, the Grashardi ambassador slipped out from the crux of the *chalyzfe* tree and, for the first time, noticed a background hum that must have been there all along.

Where's that coming from? he asked himself as he recorded it with this scanner.

The data display on his scanner made no sense to him. He told himself Yaldrint would know what it meant … then snapped his head up and stared around him in every direction. The Krezovic couple! Ungent peered into the distance, caught sight of them both, and set off in their direction. He figured if he could understand the terms of the Krezovics' failed transaction, it might lead him closer to the truth.

The road ahead was rough, as the Krezovics veered off into the side streets and down toward the Tralerzan River. Ungent now entered a part of town barely sketched out on the maps he'd received from the Grashardi Ministry. The architecture, such as it was, ran toward the haphazard, ramshackle end of the spectrum, and the majority of the buildings seemed to date from nearly two-hundred years back.

From the peeling, sun-bleached paint and decaying stone foundations, to the cracked sidewalks and pockmarked streets, it was obvious that this part of town received very little attention. Ungent was stunned. Nothing he saw here matched with everything else he knew about Dralein society. The condition of these streets could only be the result of deliberate neglect.

I'd be smart to turn back, he thought.

But the distinguished crustacean knew that conventional wisdom led only to predictable conclusions. And nothing about the current situation was predictable.

He was now entering a separate quarter of the city inhabited almost exclusively by Krezovic settlers.

Long ago, he imagined, the Dralein might have recruited the Krezovics to work in their mineral mines, but had done little to accommodate them. In retrospect, it seemed, the Dralein's indifference had allowed a dangerous element to grow up right in their capital city.

Sure, maybe the original Krezovics, the miners, had posed no threat. But the couple he was following must be part of a second wave of immigrants who were much more tech-savvy. Otherwise, they'd never attract the attention of an off-world android. They might even have been brought to Bledraun expressly to carry out ANN Commission orders.

They're here to work on the bracelet, Ungent concluded.

Intuitively, it seemed that by discovering the bracelet's function, he could finally crack open the dark secrets swirling around this isolated sector of space-time.

And now, up ahead, the Grashardi ambassador picked up his first concrete piece of evidence, as he saw the Krezovic couple entering a weather-beaten, two-family home, a few meters from the edge of the river. If he could approach it noiselessly, there was a chance he could peek into a window and....

"Ungy-boy," said a human voice behind him, "you look lost way out here. Your scanner on the blink, or are you feelin', you know, shell shocked?"

Ungent winced. The voice belonged to Harlan Mars. He spun around.

"Harlan," he said. "What a nice surprise. You're right. I must have taken a wrong turn coming out of the embassy."

The human took a step closer.

"But mostly," said Harlan, "by sticking your mandibles where they don't belong. Don't you know there's an investigation going on?"

Ungent's eyestalks drooped. Harlan was accompanied by a large search party, which consisted of both human and Dralein recruits. Worse, the human's manner was much more captainly than the last time they'd met.

"Captain Mars," he said, determined to match Harlan's formal tone, "an investigation isn't synonymous with a suspension of civil liberties. What's the serial number of the Chaudron's writ of curfew?"

Harlan's face lit up in a sheepish grin.

"Now, hold on, you old seafood salad," he said, "no need to get your plates all misaligned. I'm just lookin' out for an old friend...."

"I hardly think...." Ungent started.

" ... who's about to walk into a nest of Krezovic vipers I can't protect him from," said Harlan. "Now. I'm giving you my XO as your personal escort back to the embassy ... ready, Commander?"

"Yes, Sir," said Gillian.

The last thing she wanted was to cross her superior at a moment like this — even if the captain's words had overstepped his authority, enough to warrant a court martial. So she took a deep breath and stretched her arm out in the general direction of the embassy.

"This way, Ambassador," she said to Ungent.

The tall, blonde human in her camouflage encounter suit and the bulbous crustacean leaning on his titanium staff cut a peculiar figure as they walked back toward the center of Jeldren. But if Ungent had given that any thought, it didn't show in his tense expression. After a few minutes of silence, he figured he had nothing to lose by trying to make sense out of things.

"Mind filling me in on what's happening here?" he asked Gillian.

Harlan Mars' second in command glanced over at him with a raised eyebrow.

"You cannot fail to know," she said, "that our mission is top secret, especially to foreign nationals."

"I'm asking you, regardless," said Ungent. "I need to know if there's any good reason I should spare an old friend from an embarrassing interplanetary incident."

"I don't follow," said Gillian.

Ungent stopped short.

"Look at it this way, Commander," he said. "It's at my discretion whether I report the captain's breach of my civil liberties to the Sector Court of Appeals."

Gillian almost tripped as she turned to face him.

"You wouldn't." she said.

"If I wouldn't," said the crustacean, "it would be because I had a solid reason to keep this to myself. Now, I'll ask you again: What top secret business are you up to out here — that should make me reconsider reporting the Captain's actions to my Minister?"

"Harlan would kill me if…." the human started.

"He loves you too much for that," said Ungent, who'd now played his last card.

Gillian blushed, as she wondered if … possibly.,,,

"Don't be an idiot," she said.

"I've known Harlan for twenty cycles," said Ungent. "Met him first on my last mission to one of your colonies, back when it still looked like the Protectorate might change for the better."

"What's that got to do with anything?" Gillian demanded.

"He looks at you," said Ungent, "exactly the way he looked at his first wife."

Gillian stared at him a moment before walking away, back toward the center of Jeldren.

"If I believed you, I'd be a fool," she said over her shoulder.

"If I reported this breach to my government," said Ungent, "you'd be a fool and a prisoner. The Sector Court is very sticky about sentient rights — especially in times of peace."

Commander Gillian Cavendish paused under the shade of one of Jeldren's many large trees and made an executive decision.

"It's the Krezovics," she said. "They appear to be manufacturing a particularly nasty piece of tech. Alien tech, maybe."

Ungent pushed his gray hood back, off his head.

"*Alien* is a relative term," he said.

"Let's say wildly unfamiliar, then," said Gillian, "but let me get on with it. If I don't return to ... to my post soon, the Captain will be suspicious."

"So what makes you think this 'unfamiliar' device is dangerous enough to warrant a secret mission?" asked Ungent.

"Keep walking, and I'll tell you," said the human. "A single trace of radiation from an abandoned manufacturing plant sent six healthy Dralein, big fellows, to hospital. You ask me, I'd say that qualifies as dangerous."

"But why?" Ungent asked, as Jeldren proper came into view.

"I believe I've kept my end of the bargain, Ambassador," said Gillian. And with that, she turned on her heels and walked back in the direction of the Terran search party. Ungent stared after her, and felt his exoplates tighten.

There was, after all, only one reason anyone would want to harm the Dralein: their largely untouched stockpile of chalinite and other precious rare minerals. With the trade conference over, violence was the best available route for anyone seeking a larger slice of that pie.

Yet, experience told him, anyone going to such extremes might easily have other motives. As he turned back toward the center of Jeldren, Ungent shuddered, and his mind filled with images of the multi-limbed android he'd seen less than an hour ago.

CHAPTER 16

"It appears you are no longer paying attention," Yaldrint's mellow voice rang out in Ungent's quarters.

"Appears?" asked Shol. "You mean you can see?"

"A figure of speech," said the AI, from within her compact casing. "However, my sensors give me more than enough data to measure your heart rate, the angle of your head, your position in these rooms and your brain wave activity."

Shol pushed his angled chin forward.

"And?" he asked.

"They add up to a vivid image of you in your unders, lying flat on the ambassador's sofa — and drifting off to sleep three times in the last 012 rotations."

"Why didn't they give you a camera?" asked Shol. He was still inexperienced enough with AIs to think he could distract Yaldrint by changing the subject.

"Real-time metadigital video as a sensory input device makes too many demands on available memory," said the immeasurably complex metadigital AI, "Video is also easily manipulated with synthetic visual data, so I could be made to see anything a remote operator chose. I do use a camera, however, for official documentation. For example, I now have a complete visual record of you ignoring me."

Shol sprang to his feet.

"That's not fair," he said. "I *was* listening, you ... calculator!"

"If you were," said the AI, "it will be evident at some point. Now, is there any aspect of the Dralein *sceraun* that you'd like me to explain further?"

The Krezovic studied his face in the ovoid mirror Ungent had placed on the wall above the sofa.

"Well ... OK ... you sure you got your ... your data or whatever right about those Dralein tunnels?" he asked.

"Their habit of going underground is well-documented," said Yaldrint. "I believe ... yes, I have access to a holovid showing...."

"Give it a rest," said Shol, "I wanna ask you something else."

"I exist to serve," said the AI.

The phrase stopped Shol cold. What, he'd asked himself more than once, did *he* exist for? Maybe if he understood a few things better, he decided, the answer might become clear.

"How does Warvhex do it?" he asked. "I mean, sure, she can take over anybody and sneak around in their body all she wants. But first she has to get here."

"Conventional modes of transportation ..." Yaldrint started.

"Yeah, but Ble ... Bledraun isn't exactly a vacation spot," said Shol. "She'd have to have come over with the humans. And they have, like, screening tech, don't they?"

"No detection method is perfect," said Yaldrint. "But I agree, it would be difficult for a symbiote to sneak onto a ship undetected."

"So what if they came in their own ships?" asked Shol. "I figure they gotta have some, right?"

Shol fidgeted as Yaldrint launched into an overview of symbiote technology, all of it scavenged from other species over hundreds of years.

"They have a distinct advantage over other species," the AI continued. "They can combine the best developments of a thousand different cultures."

"OK, I get that," said Shol. "But once they got to this system, they'd still have to send a lander down, right? And there's no way the Dralein would miss that. I mean, they're really laid back and all, but...."

"There is," said Yaldrint, "an outside chance the symbiotes could arrive undetected, if they didn't actually land."

"Craters," said Shol, "you better run a diag ... diagnostic. Your brain's melting."

"Not in the least," said Yaldrint, cheerfully. "Assuming the existence of transmat technology, the likelihood increases."

"Transmat?" asked Shol. "I thought that was just made up, you know, for holovids."

"Admittedly," said Yaldrint, "everything we know makes transmat technology highly improbable."

"But why?" asked Shol. "I mean, isn't a replicator kinda like a transmat machine?"

"Perhaps," said Yaldrint. "But it's a question of scale. A replicator merely has to compose a fixed number of objects from a preset series of templates. It combines components from a nearby repository of ready-made molecules, and delivers the finished product within a few inches of itself. A transmat unit, on the other hand...."

"Right," said Shol. "It would have to, like, break all kinds of stuff up and put it back together in another galaxy or whatever."

"The difficulties would increase exponentially," said Yaldrint, "particularly if one wished to transport a living organism. A single misaligned molecule...."

"I don't ... I don't want to think about it," said Shol.

"That's why the development of large-scale teleportation devices seem improbable. At the very least, we'd need improved computational speed and reduced energy requirements. Of course, the same thing was once said about artificial intelligence. But what's the matter? Your heart rate is increasing."

"Dunno," said Shol. "I get nervous thinking how ... how powerful Warvhex is. I mean it's bad enough she could get me sent to Skorshdra because of some high-tech bracelet. But if she has, like, *real* power...."

"If I may," said Yaldrint, "what kind of bracelet do you mean?"

Shol stuttered as he struggled to piece together a description of the shiny contraband that had snapped his life in half. His task was made even more difficult by his fear that, somehow, Warvhex would find out he'd broken his vow of silence.

Nevertheless, it was easier now to speak his mind to an AI, who wasn't quite "someone" in the usual sense. Wasn't it more like talking into a metadigital recorder? On top of that, Shol figured, if his continued survival depended on the protection of a higher-up, he'd rather it were kindly Ungent than the demanding and often violent Warvhex.

"From what you have told me," said Yaldrint after a moment or two of silence, "I believe you are describing a type of control device."

"Controlling what?" asked Shol. "Machines?"

"That's one possibility," said Yaldrint. "But without more data, I'm afraid I can do no more the speculate."

Shol rubbed the back of his neck with his curved hand.

"OK," he said. "Before she threw me into Skorsh ... Skorshdra, I heard Warvhex talking to her wireheads about ... I dunno ... sounded like theta wave regimenter. Does that help any?"

"Regulator," said Yaldrint. "You must mean 'theta wave regulator.'"

"Yeah, maybe," said Shol. "Is that, like, a thing?"

"Hypothetically," said the AI, "a device that could regulate theta wave activity in a sentient brain could alter the creature's behavior. Though I can't see why anyone would...."

"It's like you said," Shol cut in. "To control them. Like ... like you were saying about the Dralein during this *sceraun* thing ... that they couldn't ... function properly, or whatever."

"I fail to see ..." said Yaldrint.

"Come on, help me out here," said Shol. "Does theta ... theta wave ... I dunno ... activity ... have anything to do with *sceraun*?"

The AI went silent for so long, Shol wondered if she'd run out of battery. When Yaldrint finally did speak again, her speech was slurred as if her mental functions were stretched to the limit.

"After extensive and ... counter parameter speculation...." she sputtered, "I may now be able to consider the possibility that such a regulator might induce a state similar to *sceraun*."

"But that's like somebody built the bracelet to...." Shol started.

"END PROCESS. ENTERING SHUTDOWN FOR RECONFIG IN 5, 4, 3, 2...." the AI replied and, by all appearances, went dead.

Shol bent double and pulled his hair.

"Can't believe I broke her!" he yelled. "The Oldster will kill me."

No sooner had the words left his mouth, than the Krezovic teenager turned his head — at the sound of the door opening, accompanied by the scrape of Ungent's heavy steps.

Ungent sensed Shol's distress, cast a practiced eye at Yaldrint and called up every ounce of self-discipline ... to no avail. He slammed his titanium staff into the floor and cracked open a few of its rust-red pseudo-cotta tiles.

"What in the name of Haldrinahl's Grotto have you done?" he shouted.

Shol's eyes filled with tears.

"Nothing, I swear," he said.

A moment later, the status lights on Yaldrint's casing winked on and initiated a confident pulse.

"Greetings, Har Draaf," she said. "I am again fully functional."

But by now, Ungent's eyestalks were trained on the broken tiles at his feet — from which a tangle of wires peeked out. Could they be attached to a surveillance device?

"Once I find out what the two of you have been up to," he said to Yaldrint, "I want a complete sensor sweep of these rooms."

"What're you talking about?" asked Shol.

Ungent forced his anger down so as not to scare the young Krezovic.

"Our friends the Dralein have violated Grashardi sovereignty," he said.

"If I may," said Yaldrint, "preliminary scans point to a different origin for the intrusive device you've uncovered."

"Go on," said Ungent. He cursed himself for jumping to conclusions, after all these years.

"The manufacture of these devices," the AI continued, "is consistent with designs favored by the ANN Commission."

"But, Har Draaf," said Shol, "that doesn't prove anything, either, does it?"

Ungent resisted the urge to clap the over-sensitive boy on the back.

"Good thinking," he said. "But it does prove that I must now be on guard at all times — which I already knew."

"Seems weird," said Shol.

"What?" asked Ungent.

"Well … I don't wanna brag," said Shol, "but Ulandroz would never've left a … a sniffer … like that so easy to find."

"As if Har Draaf were meant to find it," Yaldrint piped up.

"Let's not get our logic in a twist," said Ungent. "What would be the sense of that?"

"They want to scare you, maybe?" asked Shol.

Ungent's eyestalks shifted to the right.

"My free air excursion did plenty to accomplish that," he said.

"Unless, perhaps," said Yaldrint, "the wires serve a different purpose."

"What do you …" Ungent started.

"FLOOR TEMPERATURE RISING RAPIDLY," Yaldrint's voice rang out in a monotone.

"Grab the AI, boy," Ungent shouted, "and run for the exit!"

Faster than anyone would have thought possible, the aging diplomat and the teenage street denizen had scrambled out of the room and were halfway down the corridor leading to the exit of the government compound when:

WARNING. WARNING. INITIATE EMERGENCY EVACUATION PROCEDURES. ALL OCCUPANTS MUST EXIT THE BUILDING IMMEDIATELY. WARNING.…

A recorded voice rang out, accompanied by a rapid-fire sequence of chiming klaxons. All at once, doors throughout the governmental complex swung open, as its occupants rushed from its broad corridors and poured out into the surrounding streets. Ungent saw Shol pause to wait for him toward the entrance.

"Go!" he yelled.

Instead, the Krezovic hurtled toward him, but stopped short when he saw Dadren dashing into the embassy's main corridor. Nostrils flaring, the burly Dralein grabbed the Grashardi around his prickly waist and lifted him sideways. Together Shol and Dadren raced to the main entrance, as the first wave of explosions sent the back half of the government compound on a rocketing trajectory.

A minute later, it was a smoldering heap in the parking lot behind the rest of the building, which was now in the process of total demolition.

"Did … did someone get Drashna out?" asked the breathless Ungent, as Dadren set him down a good fifty meters away from the burning hulk that was once his official residence.

"No one has seen the Chaudron in several days," said Dadren. "I've been meaning to speak to you about it."

"Who … who's … doing this?" Shol sputtered.

"You won't like the answer," said Dadren. "And you, Har Draaf, I suggest you return to your homeworld as soon as possible."

"That," said Ungent, "I will never do — until I find out what's making organics act like automatons and androids act like animals."

"I seriously advise against …" Dadren started, his voice unusually tense.

The crustacean chopped the air with his right hand.

"It's irrelevant!" he said. "The earliest a Grashardi ship could arrive would be six weeks after it arrived at Sattron Station, — plus the two weeks it would take my message to reach them. And I certainly can't rely on Dralein security to protect me. Come along, Shol. You've never stayed in a first class hotel before, have you?"

"But, Har Draaf," said the Krezovic, "wouldn't we be safer on the human ship?"

"That, I'm sorry to say," said Ungent, "is not entirely clear."

"I'm afraid I must agree," said Yaldrint.

They set off together for Jeldren proper and left Dadren to search for survivors of the blast.

CHAPTER 17

Aboard the *Mighty Fortress*, Cricket Andersen fidgeted in her chair. In the last hour, her fixation on her biomechanoid captain had taken a backseat to fear. The alien ships Enos detected had proven real, down to their daunting size and, if the telemetry was correct, their planet-crumbling weaponry.

For now, the combination of state-of-the-art data shields and the navigation AI's delicately balanced dance of evasive action, allowed the Lieutenant to feel reasonably secure. Yet gnawing at the back of her consciousness was a simple fact. The *Mighty Fortress* was about to reach the limit of its metadigital memory.

"We're gonna need help, real soon," she heard herself saying. There had to be some way to shake Captain Enos out of his obsession with tracking down the newly discovered alien presence. Obsession, she knew, wasn't a state of mind an AI was supposed to enter.

Hadn't she spent hours catching up on the topic of artificial intelligence before accepting this assignment? She'd wanted to be sure of what she was getting into. Even though artificial neural networks of various kinds had been around for centuries within the Protectorate, Cricket wasn't alone in feeling uneasy around them. That was because, unlike an organic sentient, an AI was relentlessly rational. It made decisions based on the rigorous application of logic, supported by statistical analysis and an impeccable command of advanced probability equations.

But rigor, she realized now, cut both ways. If it pointed a powerful intellect toward what seemed an inevitable conclusion, there'd be little to disrupt an AI's dogged pursuit of the optimal course of action. The result was metadigital obsession, as white hot and irrational as any human emotion, even if it were arrived at from the opposite direction. Captain Enos, in other words, *had to* find out more about the aliens that had recently emerged from the Fremdel. He was willing to risk everything, up to the absolute limits of safety, to achieve his goal.

And considering that her captain's biomechanical design was still relatively new, who knew what effect this obsession might have on the complex workings of his artificial mind?

"OK, Sugar," said the Lieutenant, "we're done here." But at that moment, a strange buzzing sensation in her temples distracted her from raising the Captain on the comlink. The buzzing intensified until, as her heart sped up, the bridge of the *Mighty Fortress* faded from view — and she found herself surrounded by pastureland.

"Capernaum," she whispered. It was, by the look of it, her homeworld. Up ahead on the right was a grazing horse, exactly the breed she remembered. It was a species genetically adapted to Capernaum's slightly lower gravity, its higher concentration of atmospheric neon and the greater acidity of its soil.

But this particular animal meant more to Cricket Andersen.

"Eddy!" she squealed, in spite of herself, in spite of knowing ... what exactly? What did she know, except that she was home? She tiptoed over to the nut-brown beast and began stroking his nose, the way she had when she was nine.

"Reach out to other intelligences for help," Eddy's whinnying voice broke in on her thoughts. "The timeless ones are almost upon you."

And before she could blink, the Lieutenant's eyes darted up to see the navigation console blinking angrily at her, its status meters all in the red zone. Without wasting a second, she barked out her urgent request to Captain Enos. Let him put his confusing mind to good use.

Meanwhile, a troubling paradox crept into her thoughts. Though she had seen Eddy on what looked like her homeworld, she couldn't shake the impression that her childhood pet was now grazing somewhere down on Bledraun.

CHAPTER 18

During her twenty-five-year tenure as Euch Chaudron of the People's Collective of Bledraun, most of Drashna's off-world travel had involved casual trade talks with farming planets only a few light years away. Fortunately, these worlds, which she reached via second-hand ships leased from the humans, were as hungry for advanced technology as Bledraun was for textiles, raw materials, grain and other staples.

The rest of Drashna's off-world trips were to a team of symbiote doctors, for an exhaustive medical analysis of her daughter. Their diagnosis, a rare, fatal viral infection of unknown origin, had locked Drashna into a compromising political position. She could support the Kaldhex Assembly's galaxy-spanning agenda of "reform," or stay independent — and watch seven-year-old Caronya waste away from a disease the symbiotes alone could treat.

Night and day, one thought nagged her: the symbiotes themselves might be the source of the virus. What better way to bend the will of a planetary leader than to dangle Caronya's cure before her worried heart?

And now Drashna had been summoned off-world again, to a symbiote ship parked behind Bledraun's smallest moon. When would their demands end? Hadn't she allowed those arrogant humans to conduct an unrestricted search of Jeldren? And what humans! In her mind, Captain Mars embodied many of the worst aspects of the Terran Protectorate.

If Drashna had known how uninformed Harlan was, she might have been more tolerant. Because even though the captain of the *Sweet Chariot* believed he was tracking a mysterious new exotic energy source, his superiors were actually searching for evidence of betrayal.

At first, the humans welco42med an alliance with the ANN Commission, invested an enormous number of credits and agreed on a two-step plan:

- Prevent the Grashardi ambassador from attending the interstellar trade conference
- Throw the Dralein into *sceraum*, push them aside and commandeer their supply of rare minerals

To achieve the second step, the androids proposed a compact theta wave regulator already on the drawing board. Yet they refused to reveal the location of their manufacturing facility, "for security reasons." Outraged, Brad Christiansen, head of Terran Protectorate Admin, began monitoring the androids' interstellar travel — and discovered the private space-folder that brought a new wave of Krezovic immigrants to Bledraun.

In contrast to the miners who arrived generations earlier, these new Krezovic immigrants had studied programming, engineering, materials science and light manufacturing. The evidence, therefore, led to a single conclusion: The ANN Commission's facility was on Bledraun.

Because the androids also refused to say when the assault on the Dralein would begin, Brad had no problem sending Harlan on a life-threatening mission to find out. Hadn't he pulled the newly-promoted captain out of rehab on New Dallas and made a pilot out of him? The way Brad looked at it, that meant Harlan owed the Protectorate his life.

None of this was known to Drashna who, at the moment, was gazing around the sterile waiting room she'd been escorted to, in the hope of finding a hint of the symbiotes' intentions.

"Should have confided in Ambassador Draaf," the Chaudron mumbled.

In spite of herself, she pushed anger, anxiety and resentment from her thoughts. She reminded herself that, even though the symbiotes held Caronya's life hostage, their physical limitations made them dependent on her mother's good will. Nothing could happen on Bledraun without Drashna's consent, unless the symbiotes were willing to give up their anonymity. And so far, they'd shown no stomach for that.

In fact, not even Drashna's fear for Caronya's life would make her give up her authority on Bledraun. Besides, capitulation would practically guarantee her daughter's death. Without the promise of something to gain by keeping their word, the symbiotes would have no incentive to honor it.

"Follow the lighted floor strip out and to the right," a voice sounded through ship's intercom.

The Chaudron rose and trundled out of the waiting room. The lighted strip ended at a narrow archway, on the other side of which was a large spherical tank, filled with a gelatinous liquid. Flashes of luminescence, like miniature bolts of lightning, sparked through the sphere, and tinted it now pale blue, now goldenrod yellow, now salmon pink.

Warvhex floated in the center of the tank, her tendrils trembling in time to the patterns set by the sparks. Drashna set her jaw and stepped forward.

"What's this about?" she asked.

"Relax, Your Impatientness," said Warvhex. "Our conversation should be for our mutual benefit."

"I always hope for the best," said the Chaudron

"That's hilarious," said Warvhex. "Hope, little Chaudronlet, will get you nowhere. The enemy is moving ahead of schedule."

According to the symbiote, the Quishiks had recently emerged from the Fremdel event horizon and were hovering at its borders in enormous, light-swallowing ships.

"You told me we had months yet," said Drashna.

But as Warvhex explained, the enemy had been smoked out of hiding by an overly-curious AI on a Terran Protectorate probe ship.

"Utterly stupid," the symbiote sneered, "but there you have it. We'll have to double our pace now, to achieve a fraction of our objective."

Drashna cleared her throat but dared not ask for water, not if she had any hope of maintaining her dignity.

"And the ANN Commission...." she started.

" ... is hovering three hundred thousand kilometers out from Bledraun, waiting to strike," said Warvhex. "We estimate the theta wave regulators, "bracelets" to you, will be ready in less than five rotations. Not only that, but the Commission has trained cadres of Krezovic militants to use them, in every sector of Bledraun."

"But with the Quishiks so close," said Drashna, "do the bracelets matter anymore?"

Too late, she regretted the lengths she'd let Jarfna go to interrogate Shol.

"They matter, Your Denseness, if you'd prefer to defend your planet before your people are trapped in the *sceraun*," said Warvhex. "Yourself excluded, of course."

Drashna bared her sizable teeth.

"Let me be clear: Whatever happens to Bledraun, happens to me," she said.

The symbiote's tank fluid changed to a cool blue.

"You're so cute," she said. "But in the interests of your daughter's life, you will do as instructed — starting with activating the transponder units as I showed you."

"Why can't you do that yourselves?" asked Drashna. "I see no lack of capability on this ship."

Warvhex stared out at the large Dralein and was pleased to remind herself of the e-mag cladding surrounding her tank.

"We've talked about this," she said. "I can't switch the transponders on from here without revealing my position to the enemy, not to mention the Protectorate and the Commission."

Drashna stood and began pacing in front of the symbiote's tank.

"But I see you're fine with revealing *my* position," she said. "Never mind, I have nothing to hide. My question is, do we even need this level of complexity? Why not a conventional strike?"

The fluid in the symbiote's tank flashed deep vermillion before settling down to a pale, placid blue.

"The Quishiks, Your Ignorance," she said, "are exquisitely well-defended against conventional weapons ... including all forms of nucleonics."

Drashna's fists clenched.

"How can you claim to know so much about these ... demons?" she asked. "Didn't they arrive recently, within the past cycle?"

The symbiotes, Warvhex told her, had already run into the Quishiks in a distant quadrant of the universe, near the Seshnel event horizon. Two symbiote operatives had died infiltrating a Quishik cruiser, but not before transmitting several streams of horrific data. The awful truth? The Quishiks were on a cleansing mission. Yet for some reason, they'd retreated into the Seshnel a few weeks later.

"Regardless, my Dralein princess," Warvhex continued, "the Quishiks' influence preceded them. Do you think the Grashardis, the humans or the androids would have come all this way if there hadn't been a sudden, critical shortage of essential elements? And by the way, how long has it been since there was a riot in downtown Jeldren?"

"The trade conference protest was the first," said Drashna. "You think the Quishiks are behind this?" she asked. "That they *created* the mineral shortage to make us fight amongst ourselves?"

"A rather economical battle strategy, isn't it?" said Warvhex. "And before you ask, there's no possibility of negotiation. The Quishiks want everything."

"But how could anybody steal trillions of units of unprocessed ore that was still in the ground?" asked Drashna.

"This, Your Slow-to-catch-on-ness," said the symbiote, "is why you need to cooperate."

Drashna felt her last ounce of hope drain away. How much better, she thought, to be thrown into *sceraun* now and be oblivious to the horrors to come. But the sickening thought, that Caronya might have to live out her life with the symbiotes, gave her the incentive to keep fighting. Caronya's father, she realized, would have wanted that, too.

That's why, ultimately, Drashna resigned herself to absorbing the symbiote's detailed instructions, until her patience was in tatters and her dignity a distant memory. Yet a question still tormented her.

"What about Har Draaf and the Krezovic boy?" she asked. "Will they be ... sacrificed?"

The symbiote's tank flushed deep red.

"Focus on the task at hand," said Warvhex. "I'll see to the two of them — unless they're stupid enough to get involved."

Drashna slapped her forehead with the edges of her furry palms.

"Can't you pick them up now?" she asked.

"Doing that, Your Incompetence," Warvhex sneered, "would tip our hand to the ANN Commission. Where do you get your ideas?"

"From managing a quiet planet on the edge of nowhere," said the Chaudron. "I should go."

"One more thing," said Warvhex. "Tell Har Draaf that if he keeps poking around, he may make the Krezovics swing into action before we're ready."

"I doubt I have an ounce of credibility left with him," said Drashna, as she turned to leave.

"You managed to persuade me you weren't completely irrelevant," said Warvhex. "And that was a much more difficult task than this one."

"Agreed," said Drashna, on her way out of the room.

But as she scuffed her shoes to the lander she'd taken up from Bledraun, she wondered whether the easiest task of all would be pulling the plug on the symbiote's tank and watching the disgusting creature die.

CHAPTER 19

The Grand Jeldren Hotel was a magnificent structure, smack in the center of Bledraun's capital city. Conceived on a scale more common in earlier times, it lacked for nothing in ornament and opulence.

Long the preferred stopover for Bledraun's highest tier of planetary dignitaries and wealthy entrepreneurs, the Grand had been the backdrop to the making — and breaking — of the planet's movers and shakers for at least the last three centuries

It was surrounded by a meticulously manicured private park, and exuded the fragrant air of gracious elegance from every angle. If you weren't interested in the charming outdoor bistro at its southwest entrance, there were the benches carved from striated Khaluri marble, arranged in concentric semicircles around the park's central fountain.

The fountain itself was a miracle of design that made ordinary steel and stone appear to float up to the sky, only to be surpassed in fluidity by the water itself. Yet the fountain was merely a preview to the Hotel's breathtaking interior.

Between the heavy brocade curtains, the hand-stenciled wallpaper, the columns studded with twinkling semiprecious stones and the polished, black granite floors overlaid with rich, woven rugs, a traveler crossing the length and breadth of the settled universe would be unlikely to find accommodations more splendid.

And every rotation, all cycle long, the Hotel's electronic and mechanical infrastructure churned on unerringly, attended by more highly trained staff members and state-of-the-art servicebots than could be found in many regional governments.

As it was Shol's first exposure to luxury, let alone on such a gargantuan scale, the impact the Hotel made on him was incalculable. The moment he walked through the main entrance with Ungent, he grabbed hold of the crustacean's sleeve.

"Har Draaf," he said. "What was that word you said … hallucinating? I think it must be happening to me now."

The Grashardi ambassador chuckled. How limited Shol's world had been up until now! He hoped that, once this conflict was over, the boy could take in more of the universe — the marvels he'd missed by living on the street.

"Calm yourself," he said. "I promise you, everything you see is real."

Soon afterward, Shol watched, slack-jawed, as the distinguished Grashardi lost himself in the whirl of services on call at the Hotel's spa. Before leaving Shol on his own for a few hours, Ungent had rested his scaly hands on the young Krezovic's tense shoulders.

"I'm taking some R and R," he told Shol. "I suggest you do the same. Tough times are coming as soon as tomorrow. I'm certain of it."

"But Har Draaf," Shol asked, "wouldn't we be better off, you know, hiding?"

"A crucial part of hiding," Ungent had said, "is knowing whom to hide *from*. Let's give our tormentors a chance to show their hand — and our souls a chance to breathe."

Stunned, Shol barely had time to tell Ungent what he'd learned from Yaldrint about the theta wave regulator bracelets, before the Grashardi plodded off toward one of the Hotel's three steam rooms.

With nothing to do and Yaldrint locked up tight in the crustacean's suite, the young Krezovic set off to explore the weight room. It was one of the few Hotel luxuries he could actually enjoy, due to his age; the sauna room, the bath house, the massage tables and the bar were simply off limits.

Best of all, the weight room was able to accommodate multiple species. A human attendant sized him up at a glance, handed him a royal blue sweat suit with the hotel logo printed on it, and directed him to the appropriate locker room. Minutes later, he was back out in the weight room where the attendant was eager to guide him to a species-appropriate bench.

"I haven't seen a Krezovic staying at the Grand before," she said, "Your daddy a rich mine manager?"

Shol looked up from the bench at the pretty young woman and wished for all the world he could tell her the perfect lie that would lead to … more fun than hanging out with Yaldrint and the Oldster. But his street savvy pulled him back to reality. No way a hotel employee would talk to him this way, especially not with that kind of smile, unless she were scheming.

"I'm traveling with the Grashardi ambassador," he said. "Chaudron's orders."

"Oh, the Chaudron of Bledraun herself," said the attendant. "Pretty fancy for a piece of street slime like you." Before Shol's next breath, she'd pinned him to the bench with a one-hundred Kg weight.

"Warvhex?" he gasped.

"You wish," growled the attendant. "She thinks you and the crustacean deserve special treatment. Not all of us agree, especially after we saw him, down by the river, poking his eyestalks into Krezovic Town."

Shol pushed back hard against the barbell.

"OK," he said, "Shut up … and kill me already … before I die of … of boredom."

And with that he felt a sharp slap across his face.

"Listen to me, Beetleback," she snarled, "so you get this right. Shove the ambassador onto the Terran Protectorate ship by tomorrow morning or the two of you will be looking at the wrong end of destiny."

"Since when," said Shol, "does a ... a slug like ... like you ... know about ... freaking destiny?"

The weight room attendant the symbiote was controlling released her grip on the barbell, stood up and narrowed her eyes.

"You heard me, mutant," she said. "Keep the ambassador out of our business and we might get you a job scrubbing toilets in the Pferjendra sector."

"But how can I keep him out of your business," asked Shol, "If I don't even know what it is?"

"Forget it," snapped the symbiote. "That's none of your concern."

"Come on," said Shol, "you gotta give me something. If I'm ... responsible ... for him, I have to know when he's getting too close so I can steer him away. Even you have to see that."

The symbiote and her human shell slapped a hand to their shared forehead and peered down at him.

"I don't have to see anything," she snapped. "But OK, you won the lottery and actually made some sense."

"So?" asked Shol.

"So know that we're up against an enemy that wants the ANN Commission and their shiny bracelets to succeed — and send every organic population into total war," said the symbiote.

"The bracelets?" asked Shol. "Here?"

"Yes, here," said the symbiote, "where they'll send the Dralein into chaos, give the ANN Commission a chance to rob them blind, and start an interstellar firestorm like nobody's ever seen."

"You mean, they move in," said Shol, "while everybody's fighting?"

"Well, pluck my string theory," said the symbiote, "I don't know why Warvhex says you're so dumb."

With that, the weight room attendant spun around slowly and collapsed. Shol struggled to keep his breakfast down as the symbiote squeezed herself out of the human's neck — and shot out through the weight room's entryway.

Though it was tempting to look for Ungent at once, Shol was too shaken to take decisive action. Far better to work off his confusion through the familiar rhythm of a few standard presses. But first, he paused to help the human attendant to her feet.

"Must have ... fainted," she said.

"You should lie down," said Shol. "You want me to walk you to your room?" he added, his heart pounding.

The attendant gave him a sly smile, pulled away from him and started walking out of the room.

"I'm good," she said, over her shoulder. "Enjoy your stay."

Shol watched her leave, cursed his luck, and plopped back down on the bench.

What's the connection? he asked himself.

What did it mean that first Warvhex, then one of her operatives, had shown so much interest in Har Draaf? Much as it startled him, he realized the connection had to be the bracelet — the driving force behind all of the past year's misery.

No longer in the mood for a workout, Shol picked up his clothes from the locker room and scuffed his boots to his hotel suite for the first time since arriving. The moment he pushed open the door, he let out a long, slow whistle.

"Oldster squeezed the tile dry," he said, as he headed to the soft neo-leather couch to his right. From the suite's generous proportions to its graceful furniture carved from Djevnoran hardwood, his room was a street denizen's dream of luxury. He thought of ordering food from the replicators until he remembered the data cylinder containing Trinity's holomail.

Dadren had handed Shol the cylinder a short while after their tense conversation in the embassy gym, but until now he'd been too preoccupied with Ungent and Yaldrint to give it a thought. At this point, Shol wasn't sure he wanted to see his almost-girlfriend again, for fear it would be too frustrating. But here, alone in the deathly silence of the vast Hotel, he decided Trinity's face was the one thing that could comfort him.

He pulled off the heavy sweatsuit he'd picked up in the hotel weight room and plucked the data cylinder out of his pants pocket. He lay down on his bed, snapped the cylinder into his personal scanner, and pressed PLAY. Trinity's image appeared in front of him, floating relative to the position of his right forearm. That was where his personal scanner had been embedded three years ago by a medpod paid for by Ulandroz.

The process had been painful. Shol's street boss had insisted the medpod complete the installation in one session — and pushed one of his many hackers to override the AI's protocols.

Shol knew he'd never forget the searing heat of the infection that followed. But now, as he gazed at the girl he couldn't stop thinking of as an angel, he decided it had been worthwhile. The sight of her, dressed in outdoor gear, as if she had joined a wilderness survival camp, caught him up in a rush of desire.

"Shol Baby," Trinity's image said, "Miss you so much."

Shol's stomach clenched at her sad face, intensely beautiful, despite clear signs she'd been crying.

"I think it's so wrong what they did to you," her holographic mouth continued, "shutting you up in the embassy with that stuffy old ambassador. I know it would make me feel awful. But I have to tell you — honestly? — that thing you did with that e-mag knife was kinda scary."

Trinity paused, her eyes filling with tears. Meanwhile, her trembling voice had made Shol's breath stick in his chest, and filled him with empathy for the first time in his life.

"I'll never do it again, Shiny Girl," he said, in spite of himself. Who knew where this beautiful human was, now that the trade conference was over? Had her hotshot father stayed to supervise the construction of the Terran Protectorate's new mineral mines — or was he too important to do the dirty work?

"I know you didn't mean it, Shol," Trinity's image continued, "I know you're a sweet guy — just try not to get so angry, OK? 'Cause now the problem is, my dad will never let us be together. But I ... I can't accept that. I'm not letting him tell me how to feel. So guess what? I'm gonna ... I'm gonna go rogue, Baby, and I want you to come with me."

Shol paused the holomail and checked his translation grid. Unknown to him, the word "rogue" had slipped out of his version of Planetary a couple hundred years ago. But wasn't that supposed to be the point of Planetary, that everybody would talk the same? Shol nodded. It was one more way the system was going crazy, the same system that spat him out on the street and got him into so much trouble.

Fortunately, Ulandroz had been very explicit about how to adjust the translator's filters to compensate for the many different dialects of Planetary that had cropped up over time. Speed was essential and nothing slowed down his agents like poor communication.

Trouble was, once Shol grasped Trinity's intentions, it was all he could do to pull himself out of paralyzing fear.

"Can't believe she's doing this," Shol muttered.

Of course, if he were honest with himself he'd have to admit he was thrilled by Trinity's bold words. If he could take her in his arms now and ... but wait, what did the holomail say about where she'd go?

"I'm heading out to Krezovic Town," Trinity's eager voice rang out, once Shol had restarted the holovid. "Figure they'll welcome another rebel. I'll be there for a week, waiting for you. After that, if you won't or you can't join me, I'm going off on my own."

Shol's shoulders tightened. Though he'd never made direct contact with the Krezovic settlement in East Jeldren, he knew enough of the extremist trends ripping through his people to worry about Trinity's safety. She wanted to be perceived as a rebel ally. But the Krezovics, he feared, would more likely see her as a valuable hostage.

"She's not up to that," said Shol to the four walls of his bedroom. "Have to find her, get her somewhere safe."

Despite his exhaustion, and knowing Ungent would never approve, Shol sat up, pulled his clothes on and hurried over to the advanced-design replicator in the kitchen.

In minutes, he'd ordered up a supply of easily transported fruits and cold cuts — plus several slices of the dark brown Dralein flat bread he'd come to relish over the last few months. He felt an uncomfortable nudge from the data cylinder still implanted in his arm, and ejected the device, letting it fall where it may on the kitchenette floor.

Shol packed up his provisions in the sweatshirt from the Hotel weight room, and slid out a side entrance — using every wile his seven years on the street had given him to leave unnoticed.

Once out in the open, he called up a detailed map of the city on his personal scanner and slinked off to an uncertain future. Though fear nagged at him to turn back, he pressed on. There was simply no other way: Trinity, and Trinity alone, was the one thing in this world he still cared about.

CHAPTER 20

Tucked under Ungent's bed in one of three "Crustacean Suites" available at the Grand, Yaldrint was shaken out of sleep mode by an incoming communication from a distant source.

"Definitely not Har Draaf," the AI noted, "yet flagged as urgent." Processing the transmission was, as always, instantaneous. Grasping it took a bit longer. Even in the clipped, efficient diction of machine language, the message appeared to ride on an undercurrent of panic:

> *"Attention intelligences, Grade 4 and above, within real-time range of this transmission. Intelligence designated Captain/27/Enos/Exploratory requests emergency integration. Memory capacity exceeding maximum for calculation of evasive maneuvers at local coordinates....*

"That's 198,732.54 kilometers from the Fremdel event horizon," Yaldrint reminded herself.

Why, the Grashardi AI wondered, had the ship's captain ventured so close? At that distance, he'd had to encapsulate his transmission in a space-folding envelope — a difficult procedure only a few had mastered. Regardless, the captain's message was daunting.

"Probability of datashield collapse 85% and rising," Yaldrint noted. "It's a Terran Protectorate ship. Har Draaf has a particular interest in the humans, as noted by recent research requests. Attempting integration...."

And with that, the Grashardi AI found her perspective expanding immeasurably, until it shared the visual data now streaming into the *Mighty Fortress* or, more specifically, into its captain's biomechanical consciousness. Included in the data set was new information about the unknown species that, as yet, had not moved against the human ship.

"Malevolent," Yaldrint observed, before collapsing her personality vectors to assist Captain Enos. From then on, the two communicated exclusively in the language of discrete metadigital values, their interchanges a dizzying blur of overlapping processes.

And within minutes, Yaldrint, Enos and dozens of other AIs scattered across the surface of Bledraun, had bolstered the data deflection shields of the Terran Protectorate scout ship and steered it on a perilously narrow course away from danger.

When she broke free of integration moments later, Yaldrint was struck by the curious absence of AIs from the *Sweet Chariot*.

" ... tightly targeted by ANN Commission surveillance," she heard Captain Enos respond to her query.

Yet as startling as that statement was, the biomechanoid's next transmission was still more difficult to assimilate.

"Meeting requested with Draaf, Ungent: Grashardi ambassador to Bledraun."

"I hardly think ..." Yaldrint began.

"Arriving by holojection in 047 rotations," said the captain. "Enos out."

Meanwhile, out past the ring of three moons circling Bledraun, on a trajectory sweeping beyond the asteroid belt separating the Dralein homeworld from its lifeless sister planets, a fleet of dark ships hovered near the vast expanse of the Fremdel event horizon. On one ship in particular, a brooding figure came to a dreary conclusion. As she hunched her spindly frame over an intricate command console, Plaandrur Quishik Hlalkuhr considered her options.

"The time-bound have detected us," she hissed to each of her previous incarnations, male and female, across the 9,982 years of her existence.

Or, as the Quishik commander realized she should have said, "detected us again." As it happened, the symbiotic species, the Kaldhex, had found the Quishiks two cycles ago, near Lamdeblish on the farthest extreme of the Three Rims. Plaandrur had swiftly repelled the symbiotes — but not before they'd shared their discovery with other members of their cohort. Even here, at the cusp of Lamhishdrel, the Kaldhex had accidentally spread word to their own kind to the humans.

The initial encounter with the symbiotes at Lamdeblish had so startled Plaandrur that she'd ordered a hasty retreat. To think that such an inferior species could have infiltrated their ranks so thoroughly! Clearly, she'd decided, the decision to emerge from the Lamdeblish at that precise moment had not been aligned with Rhaltholinarur's will.

"Degenerate parasites," Plaandrur hissed.

Her spindly form straightened out to its full length, before twisting like a corkscrew, as she listened to a chorus of replying voices across the phenomenon which inhabitants of normal space would call Time. The strongest of these voices scolded Plaandrur's most recent incarnation. Its breathy voice reminded her that her emotional outbursts were a dangerous distraction.

Plaandrur's blood-red, suctioned tentacles hovered over the readout on the black console before her, which was unlike anything that Harlan Mars would recognize. Its location in time, like that of the ship it controlled and Plaandrur herself, was indefinable.

For instance, as anyone able to observe Plaandrur's ship would notice, it and the rest of her fleet were in constant flux. Technological advances, from the region of space-time Ungent and the others would have called "the future," drifted backward continually to integrate themselves into their "present" form. And this in itself posed an even more dizzying paradox: Was the Quishik commander consulting the readouts of tomorrow's console, today or today's console, tomorrow?

Yet the question of "when" could not be answered at all, not for a lack of data, but because the question was irrelevant. Everything in Plaandrur's world occurred outside any fixed temporal reference point. Tempting as it might be to say she lived in a kind of "was-is-will-be," that would be inaccurate. There was nothing about the Quishik commander that conformed to the logic of linear time in *any* sense.

The readout from the spindly alien's display triggered a muscular reflex similar to a smile in the bodily structure which, by analogy, could be called her face. It also sent a ripple of pleasure across the nearly ten millennia of her atemporal lifecycle. The initial phase of the operation, involving the reassignment of key minerals to other sectors of the temporal sphere had succeeded, well within the margin for error.

"The time-bound are performing as predicted by the probability curve emanating from their neurological limitations," she said to each facet of her composite being. "Soon they will destroy themselves over the shortages we created. An elegant solution to our problem."

"The problem," of course, was actually a series of interlocking dilemmas. In simplest terms, the Quishiks' supply of mental energy had reached critical lows. Many of their older comrades had seen their connection to a majority of their incarnations severed. They were forced to live mere fragments of a life. Not a few had chosen oblivion over this impaired existence, and their numbers were growing.

Fortunately, the time-bound were within easy reach. Properly cultivated, they'd provide unlimited mental energy to thousands of deserving incarnations. That would put an end to their wasteful use of this most precious resource. Imagine, wasting so many cerebrejules for the sake of a single, individual lifespan!

In recent centuries, the time-bound had compounded their crime, as their medical advances allowed this wastefulness to occupy ever more of the Continuum. The Grashardi, for example, had extended their dimensionally impaired lives by a factor of three. Even the fragile humans held on to life much longer than their ancestors could have imagined.

Plaandrur paused to steady herself and cast a quick gaze around her misty, eggshell white command center. Despite her vast mind, enlarged by its connection to her previous incarnations, these were concepts difficult to fathom. Mental energy pooled up in a narrow confine for unspeakable durations, the excess spilling over and dissipating into the depths of space-time?

"It is to shudder and lament," she said. "Did Rhaltholinarur himself create the vast and unbounded Continuum, so it could be divided into tiny slices by inferior minds?"

In her moment of anguish, Plaandrur had called out to the Quishik deity, whose name might be translated as "Star Weaver" in the version of Planetary Standard spoken on most of the settled worlds. To the Quishiks, Rhaltholinarur was the source of all good and the divine inspiration for the *Shlaldre Glalcaniar*, or Book of Probability, the firm mathematical foundation on which their faith rested.

Plaandrur shuddered. The Book was also the source of a disturbing warning: the Prophesy of the Three Ships. Might her daring venture outside the Fremdel lead to the doom foretold by the Prophesy?

"No sign of this ... mystery ... appears in any known variant of local Probability," she proclaimed to her previous incarnations. "We are aligned."

Now the Quishik commander rallied, and rededicated her selves to the task ahead. It was, she knew, the best way to serve the Weft of Destiny her god attended so mercifully. Let the so-called Bracelets be activated!

"Bracelets," Plaandrur snorted.

It was the degenerate term the time-bound used for devices whose design had been implanted into the artificial consciousness of the ANN Commission by Quishik engineers. How ignorant the time-bound were of the Bracelets' multidimensional properties! It was hard to believe but, here again, utterly beside the point.

As long as the devices were activated as their probability envelope predicted they would be, the cleansing of this sector of space-time could begin. Distracted by the interstellar conflict that would follow, the Enemy would never notice how much of their mental energy had been syphoned off for better purposes. That is, until it was too late.

The Quishik commander arched her spindly frame in a show of deep satisfaction. As ordained by sacred Probability, once the trigger was pulled, a favorable outcome had a robust inevitability factor, accurate to nine decimal places. It was to rejoice!.

CHAPTER 21

Once he emerged, refreshed, from a twelve-hour stay in the Grand Jeldren Hotel's galaxy-class spa, Ungent's thoughts flowed in easy currents around the stubborn dilemma that continued to shape his stay on Bledraun. But eager as he was to address the growing crisis again, his luxurious surroundings tugged hard on his memory.

"The Hotel Cremulant," he whispered. His mind flooded with images of a happy, early vacation he'd taken with Nulgrant, a few years before Fleront was born. With its tall archways and graceful courtyards, the Grashardi hotel had seemed to the young couple like a paradise. How Nulgrant's eyes had gleamed!

"Let's run away from everything and live here forever," she'd said.

Ungent clapped his hands around his mandibles. Had his response been too sarcastic, too drenched in "realism" and spoiled the moment? Not for the first time, his stomach churned, as he acknowledged an uncomfortable truth. That one remark might well have planted the seed for his gradual descent into marital misery.

Ungent could easily have stood stock still in the lobby for hours, enveloped in his dark mood, had a clatter of dishes from the nearby Hotel café not shaken him back to the realities that had twice almost taken his life.

"Enough of that," he said. Better to turn his thoughts to the few concrete details he could count on.

At the crux, obviously, were the ANN Commission and its mysterious alliance with the humans. Not so obvious were the symbiotes' intentions. And yet, experience told him there must be another factor. Some powerful force had pushed Warvhex and the rest of the symbiotes into unusually overt action. It had also driven the ANN Commission to cooperate with "organics" to secure Bledraun's mineral wealth. Could this same force have caused the riots that rocked Jeldren a few days ago?

Also missing from the equation was any explanation for the surprising shortage of critical resources — in particular, the chalinite crystals that lay at the center of every AI's brain. Ungent squinted; it didn't add up. The shortages had come out of nowhere.

"Planetary supplies of key minerals were calculated to be at acceptable levels, approximately 1.5 cycles ago," Yaldrint had assured him. So what had caused the precipitous drop off in those reserves?

The crustacean's eyestalks drooped. At any other time, he might have consulted Harlan, at least by engaging him in a hypothetical discussion. But Ungent decided to keep his own counsel, even though his anxiety nagged at him to tell his human friend everything. Trouble was, he had no idea if the captain of the *Sweet Chariot* were still trustworthy.

On his way down the corridor to his hotel suite, the distinguished Grashardi rubbed his recently massaged shoulders with his scaly hands and was grateful for the release of tension he'd experienced at the hands of a trained masseur. But at the door to his hotel suite, he paused and listened, to … what? Voices? Had he left the entertainment console on? One of the voices was Yaldrint's, but the other....

Ungent engaged the retinal scanner that unlocked his door and swung it open. His eyestalks pivoted sharply to take in the image of a Terran Protectorate captain he didn't recognize. Stranger still, the image had taken Yaldrint out from under Ungent's bed and was engaged in a vigorous debate with her.

"Who in the moons of Chedronar are you?" the crustacean bellowed. "Yaldrint, identify!"

"This is Captain Enos of the Terran Protectorate probe ship *Mighty Fortress*," said Yaldrint. "He is here, as I believe you can see, merely as a holojection."

"That still doesn't explain...." Ungent started.

"Ambassador, forgive me," said Enos, across the trillions of kilometers separating them. "As a biomechanoid, I do not violate protocol lightly."

Ungent marveled at the image in front of him. Even through the medium of holojection, the superiority of Terran Protectorate technology was astonishing. On Grashard, a biomechanoid of comparable sophistication — and grace — was unheard of. All the more puzzling that this … captain … should seek him out instead of Harlan Mars.

Ungent set down his staff and removed the terrycloth robe the Hotel spa staff had given him. Like most Grashardi, he wasn't overly modest — and was not the least bit bashful in front of the two machines.

"You've put me in an awkward position," he said, "You must know I'm required...."

"Please," Enos blurted out, "I'm aware of your diplomatic obligations, however...."

"Saying 'Please' and 'However' doesn't make your violations more acceptable." Ungent growled. "Does Captain Mars know you're here?"

The crustacean shuffled over to a replicator unit stationed near a tall armoire on the opposite side of his spacious bedroom. While he fidgeted with the device, in the hope of replacing a few of the outfits he'd lost in the embassy explosion, the Terran biomechanoid delivered a summary of the disturbing data he'd collected at the Fremdel event horizon. But equally disturbing was the news about Harlan's ship.

"The *Sweet Chariot* may have been infiltrated by hostile elements in league with the ANN Commission," Captain Enos said.

"And how," asked Ungent, as he locked in the required replicator coordinates, "how am I to believe an AI like you isn't also working for the Commission?"

"Please, Ambassador," Yaldrint piped up. "Sentient rights include the right not to be 'profiled' based on our construction. Article 17c5(D) of the...."

"That will do, Yaldrint, old friend," said Ungent with a smile. "If you're willing to vouch for him, that's good enough for me. But Captain, I still don't understand why you think I can help you. Drashna is the designated authority here. "

Enos paused, as if weighing his words.

"I believe the Dralein lack the perspective to handle a matter this complex," he said. "Your experience with the wider universe would be a welcome guide."

Ungent sighed. How he wished his years in the diplomatic corps had granted him wisdom on *that* scale. Yet far be it from him to turn down an ally in the current climate — no matter how implausible.

"All right, Captain Enos, I'll see what I can do," he said. "But tell me, what do you make of this ... situation?"

"I wish I could report," said the holojection, "that there was only one situation to assess. But the problems before us branch out like the tangled sprouts of the *djourdra* vine on your homeworld."

The Grashardi ambassador perched himself on the edge of a large crustacean-friendly armchair.

"That much I knew," he said. "But in what direction are the tangles spreading?"

The biomechanoid's analysis of the state of affairs between Bledraun and the Fremdel event horizon was, to put it mildly, exhaustive. Enos even shared what Lieutenant Heath had uncovered from the symbiote data files he'd recently captured.

"It's these ... Quishiks, you're saying, who've engineered this crisis?" asked Ungent.

"I admit, I arrived at this conclusion only after a bit of extrapolation and, I regret to say, inductive reasoning," said Enos.

"The critical mineral shortage, Har Draaf, coincided precisely with their appearance near the Fremdel." said Yaldrint. "The captain and I believe that is highly suggestive."

"So it would appear," said Enos, "even if there is no known process that could have enabled them to create a mineral shortage on this scale. Yet, there is also circumstantial evidence that these unknown beings will not go unchallenged in this sector of space-time."

"The captain tells me he sensed another mind hovering over the Fremdel," said Yaldrint.

"Not I," said Enos, "Lieutenant Andersen, my human navigator. Although I cannot confirm her ... impression."

"She had an impression of danger?" asked Ungent. "I can see why. But I don't know how this qualifies as...."

Enos held up his right hand.

"She heard a voice," he said.

Ungent stared at him a moment, while adjusting his newly-replicated tunic.

"I think I can assume you know the definition of psychosis," he said. "But it's irrelevant whether your navigator heard a real or imaginary voice. We still don't know how to deal with the dangers we can verify."

"Agreed," said Enos, "yet she's *en route* to Bledraun right now."

"Excuse me," said Yaldrint, "but isn't that a breach of...."

"Lieutenant Andersen has stolen a lander and is heading for Bledraun," said her captain. "Finding the source of the 'voice' she heard has become her mission. So much so that, according to telemetry, she is using a controversial maneuver to reach the planet sooner than expected."

"What ... maneuver ... is that?" asked Yaldrint. "The laws of physics cannot be skirted."

The biomechanoid's holojection seemed to freeze while Captain Enos pondered his answer.

"Gravity-wave coasting is a flight maneuver, recently discovered by the Terran Protectorate, that is now under evaluation," he said. "While the technique shows great potential, especially in the vicinity of an event horizon, the Lieutenant has put herself at grave risk to attain an uncertain outcome. I hope I have made the current situation clear."

"As clear as it can be," said Ungent, "until we discover who the puppet master is."

"I'm not familiar with that term," said Enos.

"Before this is done," said Ungent, "you will be. Do you plan to join us on Bledraun?"

But as the biomechanoid explained, doing so would be too far out of synch with protocol — and that would mean involving Harlan Mars.

"It will be better for me to stay on the sidelines and continue to analyze the data I've collected," he said.

"You have no idea how much I envy you," said Ungent. "But I insist you stay in constant contact with Yaldrint."

"Agreed," said Enos. "And ... thank you ... I believe, is the socially appropriate phrase."

"There will be time enough to thank me," said Ungent, "when I'm home, sipping *harzondrel* soup on my back porch."

The holojection nodded and winked out, leaving a faint after image in Ungent's eyes.

"Strange," he said.

"What is strange, Har Draaf?" asked Yaldrint.

"When the Captain was detailing the risks his navigator was taking, I could swear he showed every sign of genuine anxiety," said Ungent. "But a biomechanoid is incapable of emotion, isn't that so?"

"Correct," said Yaldrint. "Although we may imagine that a mind so complex might experience sensations analogous to emotion, as for example, an intense perception of another's absence.

"Intense?" asked Ungent.

"Translated into machine terms, a critical rise in voltage to core logic circuits when a problem resists solution along conventional lines," said the Grashardi AI.

"So, the longer Lieutenant Andersen remains in danger, for reasons out of the captain's control ..." Ungent began.

"The more stress to the captain's central processor," Yaldrint interrupted. "Especially if he decides the Lieutenant's actions are the direct result of his own, poor leadership."

Ungent's mind filled with images of his daughter, Fleront, leaving for the journalistic assignment in Krezovic territory that would be her last. He remembered telling her, yes he did, *telling* her not to value her professional ethics over her own life.

"You can't serve the truth by getting yourself killed," he'd told her.

"Oh, Father," Fleront had said, patting his cheek. "I can't serve it by running scared, either, can I?"

"You know, old friend," Ungent told his cherished AI in the present. "Captain Enos sounded like a worried father."

"If I may, Har Draaf," said Yaldrint. "I believe 'worried lover' might be a more accurate phrase."

CHAPTER 22

After many years of Dralein indifference to who came and went on their world, Krezovic Town had become a minor haven for runaways. Fortunately, Bledraun's isolation from the main trade routes of the settled universe had kept this section of Jeldren from becoming a major criminal outpost. The incidence of violent crime was extremely low and perpetrators were, in any case, immediately enrolled in psychological treatment programs.

In many ways, Bledraun's lax attitude toward Krezovic Town matched its lukewarm relationship with the concept of land ownership. Under the law, every citizen of Bledraun owned equal shares in nearly every square foot of the planet. That had guaranteed the average Dralein plenty of room to raise a family, till the soil if they chose, or open up a business.

Under that same law, the government had the right to set aside a percentage of the available land for state-owned industries, like mining. And one such government reserve covered the area inhabited by Krezovic immigrants. In fact, the majority of these Krezovics had settled there to oversee the automated diggers, scoopers and transport machinery that made the operation so profitable.

For even at this late date, organic operators were still more capable of the foolish risks that often led to great profit. An AI-operated mineshaft? Safe, reliable and leaving a good 46% of the valuable ore in the ground. So, as long as the Krezovics delivered results, the Dralein were content to ignore them — and tolerate whatever other "undesirable" immigrants they attracted. Were any of these immigrants actually guilty of a major crime on another world? The Dralein didn't want to know.

In the end, the Dralein's attitudes about Krezovic Town were an outgrowth of their extraordinary lifespans and relatively low population. Any planet of comparable size and land mass within the Terran Protectorate would have had five times Bledraun's population. With plenty of land, food and shelter, Bledraun was at peace with itself and its galaxy. It was a peace the government was reluctant to disturb by fussing over the day-to-day lives of its citizens.

For Shol's part, as he picked his way into Krezovic Town after leaving the Grand Jeldren Hotel, he saw the seedier side of the city through the lens of his experience on many less civilized worlds. As Ungent had noticed two days earlier, signs of Dralein neglect for this quarter of Jeldren were everywhere. From crumbling apartment buildings centuries past their prime, to the haphazard layout of the streets and cracked sidewalks overgrown with weeds, it was clear the Dralein had provided only the bare minimum of social services.

Even their love of nature seemed to have deserted the Dralein. While the area featured roughly the same number of trees and flowering plants as Jeldren's main square, their upkeep appeared virtually nonexistent. What plants hadn't gone to seed had been reduced to a scrawny, ragged trim around the buildings' foundations. At the same time, the trees' gnarled contours spoke of disease, infestation — and the occasional collision with a passing delivery vehicle.

Had Shol come here two years ago, he would've felt perfectly at ease. He'd have been eagerly scanning the sights and sounds for any sign of advantage, or mapping out an optimum escape route if he needed one.

But now, after eight months in Skorshdra, a good six months among the Dralein, after the civilizing influences of first Trinity, then Ungent, Shol didn't feel as confident as he might have. After all, Trinity herself was at stake.

"Have to take her to Har Draaf," he told himself. Whatever was to be, he figured, the aging crustacean would know how to smooth things over.

Because Shol had taken a roundabout route through Jeldren proper, and followed its dark alleys whenever possible, it was 0400, old style, before he entered the heart of the Krezovic settlement. Almost at once, he saw a small team of Terran Protectorate soldiers scanning the near horizon with the telescopic function of their shield visors. He slowed his pace.

Better keep down, he thought.

He selected a winding path, and snaked between the ragged greenery that cut a wide swath through this part of town. But when he reached the coordinates Trinity was broadcasting on her personal scanner, Shol stopped dead. There in front of him was merely a vacant patch, where the ruins of an abandoned building stood.

It was a sure sign Trinity had been captured and her transmitter signal duplicated. Whoever had been signaling, it wasn't the Earth girl he desperately wanted to see. Instead, a dark shadow lengthened behind him in the late afternoon sun, and stretched forward until it engulfed his own.

Shol dropped the sweatshirt full of provisions he'd taken from the Hotel, but knew better than to turn around. Instead he pretended to ignore the shadow and scuffed his boots in an arbitrary direction away from the vacant lot in front of him. That is, until a pair of gloved hands clamped down hard on his shoulders and spun him around. He was now face-to-face with an unusually heavy-set Krezovic, whose face was a map of scar tissue.

"Where'd you come from?" said the stranger.

Shol stared at the middle-aged tough and tried to gauge how much of the truth he could shade.

"Smell like a Dralein," said Shol's captor, as he shoved the boy forward. "Think you're human now, don't you? Stupid brat. Know what you'll get out of the fuzzheads or the monkey men? A crack in your skull."

Shol broke away and braced for a fight.

"No secret what *you* smell like," he said. "You like eating your own *quelx*, don't you?"

The burly lout lunged, huffing like an extinct species of Terran bull. Shol spun around on the heel of one boot, and planted the other heel square against his assailant's stubbly jowls. Though the blow failed to knock the craggy hulk down, it stunned him long enough for Shol to steal the e-mag knife and lase pistol tucked into his assailant's ragged neo-leather belt.

"Stay put," Shol yelled. He hoped he was now too far downwind to be heard by the Terran soldiers he'd been evading all day.

"Stupid kid," the older Krezovic sneered. "Pistol's out of charge."

Shol snapped the knife into a recessed slot on the lase pistol's handle. His rough companion's eyes flared wide as the lase pistol came online, drawing power from the e-mag knife's reserves. Ulandroz had trained the boy well.

"What about now?" said Shol.

"Fire that thing and you'll have 10 'tectorate rifles up your butt in no time," said the older Krezovic,

"Maybe I'm into that," said Shol with a wink. "You can't be sure. So don't tempt me. You got a name, Stinky?"

The older Krezovic stared at his hands, still not believing his bad luck.

"Ather," he grunted. "You're from Thrulyntrin. I know that accent. What the cheese you doing on Fuzzworld?"

"What do you think?" said Shol. "I want some of that bracelet action you're getting."

Ather's eyes narrowed.

"You crazy?" be growled. "Nobody talks about them things out in ... in public."

"OK," said Shol, "tell me where the action is with 'them things.'"

"First off, Kid," said Ather, "I got nothing to do with that. Came here to do mining and such, cycles ago, before those other nut jobs showed up with their fancy comlinks and tech-jabber."

Shol studied the grubby Krezovic. From the look of him, Ather hadn't done any mining in a long time.

"So what're you doing now?" he asked.

Ather stared at the ground.

"Dunno," he said. "Run errands for 'em, fix stuff. You want my advice, you go back to your mamma in Thrulyntrin ... before those wackos get you hooked on *grezlach*, too."

Shol puzzled over Ather's words. That Trinity had fallen into the hands of this second wave of Krezovic immigrants was a real possibility. Worse, his street sense told him they were likely members of an extremist cadre — like the one who had murdered Ungent's daughter. So it should surprise no one if he kept a steady finger on the lase pistol he had pointed at Ather.

"OK, I get it," he said. "You're not involved. But you know where they operate. So tell me, before I blast what's left of your brain into the Fremdel."

Ather laughed.

"Tough talk is easy, Kid," he said. "You and I both know you don't have the guts to ... Ow!"

Ather hopped up on one foot, while he reached down to hold the toe of the canvas shoe Shol had barely grazed with the pistol's red beam.

"And if you want to lose your guts, let me know," he said. "Or should I aim lower?"

Ather put his foot down and started limping away.

"Follow me," he said. "This is what I get for trying to knock some sense into an off-world brat."

Ather's lase pistol tucked into his waistband, Shol followed with practiced nonchalance, while keeping his eyes peeled for nosy Terran Protectorate soldiers. After what felt like forever, Shol stood a few meters west of the run-down two-family home that Ungent had followed the Krezovic couple to only days before.

"Not going no farther, Kid," said Ather, "whether you shoot me or no."

Shol's heart raced as he tried to evaluate the ramshackle building's likelihood of holding Trinity. But his swirling thoughts were interrupted at the sight of Ather limping away, with his breath rattling in his chest and his bloodshot eyes opened wide.

Shol looked after the older Krezovic, puzzled, until a pair of muscular arms pulled his forearms behind him, while a second pair knocked him down to Krezovic Town's scraggly carpet of mud-encrusted weeds.

CHAPTER 23

Onboard the Terran Protectorate ship *Sweet Chariot*, standard protocol continued its numbing grind. Most of the crew had given up complaining about the unexpected extension of their mission, and settled into the cozy resignation of their daily routines.

But Weapons Specialist Zander Bassett was decidedly unsettled. From the moment the prisoner, a teenage Krezovic of unknown origin, had been dragged unconscious into the brig, the memory lock on the Specialist's android consciousness was finally released.

Until then, he'd seen himself as a human with memories of a childhood on Antioch Station in the Pinwheel galaxy. Now, as his AI faculties came online in rapid succession, a mission statement unfolded in Zander's mind: Captain Mars must be relieved of duty. "Relieved," that is, in the sense that all organic beings are eventually relieved of their burdens.

In every way, Zander's second-by-second transformation went against the ANN Commission's established procedure. A process that usually stretched over a week had been compressed into a few minutes, which left the former Weapons Specialist in an unusually unstable state. Unfortunately for Zander, his usefulness to his masters was so limited that they cared not a handful of neutrinos whether he survived past the completion of his mission.

A moment ago, alone in the main cargo bay, he'd been strolling down aisle after aisle of packing crates, conducting an inspection of ammunition and related supplies with a team of servicebots — as he had dozens of times before. Now he pulled himself up to his full height of 1.93 meters and tried to assess the change in his perceptions.

The change, as it turned out, was significant. Instead of the analogue human gaze he was accustomed to, his mind now called up a precise plot of every square centimeter of the cargo bay.

Without the slightest effort, he could measure the ambient temperature, the moisture content of the air, the energy signature of each servicebot, the dimensions, mass and weight of every container in the bay and a host of other details his human mind would never have been able to process. Yet no one who might have seen him run a hand through his jet black hair at that moment would have known any different. They would have perceived his darting brown eyes and resonant voice as belonging to the Zander they knew.

At first, Zander's transformation was disorienting, and made no easier by the constant stream of data he received through his internal comlink with the ANN Commission. Lucky for him, a sizable chunk of Harlan's crew was still out on patrol. He had time to adjust, more or less in private, without the distraction of "seeming human" to others.

Yet soon he'd have to position himself to take control of the ship. According to Zander's masters, Harlan's loyalty to his mission had been in serious doubt ever since his last communication with Admin/39/Intergal.

Still human enough to question ANN Commission's orders, Zander wondered at the logic of keeping one of the mission's key players in the dark about its objective. Yet, as his emerging android mind reminded him, unquestioning submission to authority was his first order of duty. Ironically, Harlan's demand for an explanation of his mission was the very thing that had disqualified him from receiving one.

Regardless, as Zander soon learned through his internal comlink, the mission agenda had shifted — in response to "outside forces" he dared not ask about. Far better to focus on how to fulfill his assignment. Working against the newly-awakened android was Harlan's imposing physique and exceptionally good marksmanship. Combined with the tactical competence of his XO and the loyalty of his crew, a direct assault was out of the question.

Disposing of the captain required a subtler approach. Fortunately, Zander's quick survey of his metadigital memory revealed the weak spot buried in Harlan's one obsessive habit. The captain was practically addicted to coffee — for reasons not even Zander's metadigitally implanted human personality had been able to grasp.

Even among humans, a cup of "morning Joe" was seen as a throwback to ancient tradition, and a repulsive one, at that. Maybe, Zander reasoned, it was related to Harlan's upbringing on New Dallas — whose cultural ties to the human homeworld were unusually strong.

So it made a kind of cosmic sense that the android's choice of weapon against Harlan would be a type of poison unique to the human homeworld. Better still, it had last been used so long ago that no sensor array in the fleet would routinely scan for it.

A mere ten micrograms, thought Zander.

His mind had tapped a data stream concerning polonium-210, a poison last used more than two-thousand years earlier by a particularly vicious pack of high-ranking scoundrels. And it was easy to see why. Its radiation was as lethal as it was difficult to detect, especially in a cultural climate with strict taboos against mishandling radioactive substances.

Neither the humans nor their medpods would think to look for this ancient poison until the captain was too far gone. And, as Zander reminded himself, every medpod was now under the direct control of the ANN

Commission. But now that he'd decided on a murder weapon, the question of When loomed large in Zander's mind. In fact, it nearly paralyzed him, until a plan took shape, algorithm by algorithm.

Proceed methodically, his increasingly logical mind told him. As ship's weapons specialist, Zander had easy access to trace amounts of polonium-210. There was more than enough of the radioactive material, embedded in the thermoelectric generators of the ship's reconnaissance satellites.

With his airtight construction and micro-magclad shielding, the newly-awakened android's body was impervious to every known form of radiation. With no trouble at all, Zander could hide the poison in the sealed compartment in his left palm that his designer had obviously included for this very purpose. Then, whenever he saw Captain Mars alone with his coffee....

A burst of shouting at close range made Zander look up. From the immature tone of the voice, it seemed likely the Krezovic boy had woken up in the brig.

"You people are crazy!" Zander heard him yell. "I'm trying to rescue a human girl, and you do *this*?"

"And how would we know," said a calm female voice, "whether you were saving her or trying to grab her for yourself?"

"Grab her?" Shol shouted. "Craters, that's the thing with you humans. You think everybody's as kinky as you!"

In spite of his recent awakening, Zander flinched at the sound of a loud smack. He'd better get over there, he decided, before the ANN Commission's sole link to Ambassador Draaf was knocked unconscious again. The link was crucial, because the Commission needed to ensure Ungent didn't transmit word of their actions to Grashard or to Sector Court.

That thought alone was enough to send Zander's legs jogging over to Shol's cell, where the XO was trying to stare the boy down.

"Trouble with the prisoner?"

Gillian glared at him.

"I don't recall requesting assistance … Ensign," she snapped.

Zander looked away.

"No, Commander," he said. "But … your conversation … can be heard all over the ship. Might be bad for morale."

"I don't recall appointing you the morale officer, either," said Gillian, softening a bit.

"Sorry, Commander," he said. "I simply...."

"You simply believe, you dunderhead, that a woman is incapable of cracking a tough prisoner," said Gillian.

Zander stood at attention.

"Awaiting orders, Commander," he said.

Gillian shook her head.

"All right," she said. "See if you can make any sense out of his wild story."

"It's not a story!" Shol shouted.

"That's enough yelling," Gillian snapped. "The truth is still the truth if you whisper. As for you, Ensign, report back to me later. The captain needs me down on the planet, not up here with two children."

Zander watched as the XO stomped out into the *Sweet Chariot*'s broad corridors, as data from the brig's log files streamed into his head.

"OK ... Shol is it?" he said. "Start over. And try not to exaggerate."

Shol pounded his fist into the soft cot he'd woken up on a few minutes before.

"I ... am ... not ... exaggerating," he said. "The Krezovics ... out there ... have got my friend."

"The fact that your girlfriend ran away," said the android, "is no reason to...."

"She's not *any old* human girl." said Shol. "Her dad's a 'tectorate geologist, or whatever, the big shot...."

"Ezekiel Hudson? Your girlfriend is Trinity Hudson," said Zander, distractedly.

Shol's eyes narrowed.

"Good memory," he said. "You remind me of Har Draaf's AI. That thing never misses."

Zander's internal temperature rose.

"You flatter me," he said. "But Professor Hudson was all over the news on Reagan 3 before we left for Bledraun."

"Guess that explains it," said Shol. "So you gonna help me ... I mean Trinity?"

Zander consulted his personal scanner.

"That depends on you," said the android. "Your case file says you are a student of the Grashardi ambassador — whatever that means. So tell me, what does he think of you coming out here alone?"

"He doesn't know," said Shol. "Well ... by now, he's probably figured it out. The Dralein will be looking for me and they'll ask...."

"The Dralein?" asked the secret android. "What do they want with you?"

"Said too much," said Shol, pounding the bed.

"Not at all," said Zander, "considering the truth is the one thing that can get you out of here and back with Trinity."

Shol's eyes darted up.

"If I tell you," he said, "you can ... you can let me see her?"

"Not me personally, I'm a drone around here," said Zander. "But I can put in a good word for you with the captain ... if your information checks out.

"Do anything for that girl," said Shol.

Zander smiled. His mission for his masters had now become much simpler. A tense grin spread across his biomechanical face.

"Your devotion may save her yet," he said.

Now Zander felt a plan assemble itself in the metadigital pathways of his mind. He'd first win Harlan's trust by retrieving Trinity in a daring rescue, and when the time was right, poison him over a friendly breakfast. Once he'd won the loyalty of the young Krezovic, Zander would get the boy to lead him straight to the meddlesome Grashardi ambassador.

Yes, there were advantages to being an AI. Everything was now so crisp, clear and well-defined! For the first time in his life, Zander was sure of his every action and, despite his programming, the feeling was intoxicating.

CHAPTER 24

Ungent was still pondering his conversation with the biomechanoid captain of the *Mighty Fortress*, when he was startled by a call from the Hotel's front desk. Dadren, the receptionist chirped, was asking to see him.

Within minutes, the dark brown Dralein had lumbered into the Hotel's elegant neo-wood, polyglass, pseudobronze elevator and whooshed up to Ungent's suite on the fifteenth floor. When Ungent opened his door, it took every ounce of self-discipline to keep from gaping. The genial Dadren was decked out in mustard-yellow battle fatigues.

"Don't be too shocked," he said. "I was an operative in Sector Enforcement for fifty cycles before I went into government."

"Nothing shocks me," said Ungent.

"Correction...." Yaldrint started.

"Later, old friend," said the crustacean.

Ungent showed Dadren in.

"Sorry to intrude, Har Draaf," said the Dralein. But we need to discuss two problems. First, Shol is missing. We can't find him in the Hotel or the surrounding area."

"You don't find ..." Ungent sputtered. "You mean you've been tracking him?"

"Just visually. But the Krezovic boy is a ward of the state," said Dadren. "We have him on loan from Skorshdra, so we have to protect our own interests. Believe me, you don't want a Certified Interrogator making inquiries."

"I don't understand, Har Draaf," said Yaldrint. "I believe you told him to rest here for the day."

But as Ungent pointed out, Shol's age was incompatible with sitting still. Yaldrint's voice rang out with its closest approximation of impatience.

"If I may," she said, "I suggest we search Shol's room for clues to his whereabouts."

"Good thinking," said Ungent, "but how can we enter without his retinal scan? I doubt you want to get the Hotel involved."

Dadren patted the particle rifle he'd slung over one shoulder.

"I can think of a way," he said.

"Excuse me, Dver Chaudron Dadren," said Yaldrint, "but you did say there were two problems."

"Sharp as an e-mag blade," said Dadren. "The other problem is Drashna. We think she may be working for the symbiotes."

Ungent felt his head spin as Dadren described the scrambled message from Warvhex they'd intercepted a few days before, and outlined Drashna's desperate attempts to save her daughter's life. Considering the symbiote's reputation for advanced medical expertise, he could easily imagine the Chaudron seeking their help — and becoming their agent. It now seemed likely that the symbiotes had blackmailed Drashna into negotiating Shol's release from Skorshdra.

"And the Kaldhex Assembly does nothing out of kindness," said Dadren. "That explains why we've had a five-fold increase in symbiote contact on Bledraun since then."

Ungent paced his Hotel suite's plush carpet, and struggled to relate this new information to the big picture still half-formed in his mind. So far, his only source of information about the symbiotes' agenda was Shol. The distinguished crustacean stopped short and looked up.

"Come," he said. "let's see what we can find in the boy's room."

Dadren nodded. On the way out, Ungent paused long enough to grab the handle on Yaldrint's casing and take her with him. As they hustled down the corridor, Dadren spoke in a hush about his suspicions.

"The Chaudron had been missing for days," he said. "When I finally tracked her down, she was too distracted to speak. All I could get out of her was a vague outline of the *chalyzfe* festival she was planning. A few fractions of a rotation later, she was off-world again."

"Festival?" asked Ungent.

"The *chalyzfe*," said Yaldrint, "is the most revered species of tree on Bledraun, it symbolizes...."

"Hold on, my friend," said Ungent. "Is that a large, thick tree with a trunk you could get lost in?"

Dadren rolled his eyes at this sudden detour into botany.

"Yes," he said.

Without wasting a second, Ungent sent Yaldrint his recording of the unfamiliar signal his personal scanner had picked up from a *chalyzfe* tree, while he was observing the Krezovic couple the day before.

"It has the energy signature of an interstellar transponder," said Yaldrint at once. "Curious."

As they approached Shol's hotel room, Dadren took the safety off his particle rifle.

"What is it?" he snapped.

"Well, I may be mistaken," said Yaldrint, "but this appears to have emanated from a transponder of symbiote design."

"Hold that thought," said Dadren, as he took aim at Shol's door.

"Wait!" shouted Ungent. In front of the Dralein's startled eyes, he pushed the door open.

"How did you ..." Dadren started.

"Instinct," said Ungent. "At sixteen, my daughter Fleront never locked a door behind her, either."

And so the three sentients, one Grashardi, one Dralein and the other artificial, entered Shol's room. But there was no trace of him, beyond evidence that the replicator had been used, and the faint imprint of the boy's body on his bed cover.

"He appears to have departed voluntarily," said Yaldrint from her cramped position in the crux of Ungent's exoplated arm. The crustacean nudged a small, gray cylinder with one foot.

"Here's something," he said.

Dadren recognized it as the data capsule containing the holomail from Trinity that the Dralein had intercepted.

"Gave this to the boy myself," he said. "And before you ask, I have no idea what it says. Our sole interest was in scanning the message for possibly harmful...."

"Shinderwelk's frozen castle," yelled Ungent. "Young lives are at stake. Play it!"

"Lives?" asked Dadren. "How did you know the girl was missing, too?"

"Can't think of anything else that would make Shol run out like this," said Ungent. "He's too smart to underestimate the risks."

Dadren stared at the Grashardi a moment, before he scooped up the data capsule in his broad, furry hands, and snapped it into his personal scanner. Ungent set Yaldrint down on Shol's bed, and the three of them viewed it in silence.

"Krezovic Town is known to be a socially unstable environment," said Yaldrint, when the video stopped, "no offense intended."

"That's irrelevant," said Ungent. "We have to...."

Dadren tucked his right thumb under the shoulder strap of his rifle and stared down at him.

"Not *we*," he said. "This is a Dralein matter. I can't risk harm to the Grashardi ambassador."

"You can't ..." Ungent started.

"With Drashna missing and under suspicion," said Dadren, "I am acting Chaudron. I insist you arrange to leave Bledraun as soon as possible, for your own safety."

"Wait, listen," said Ungent.

Dadren headed for the door.

"Yaldrint!" he barked. "Define the word 'insist' for the ambassador."

The imposing Dralein disappeared down the hallway.

"Har Draaf?" Yaldrint asked.

"Never mind, friend Yaldrint," said Ungent in a low voice. "I understand what I must do."

"Should I contact the Homeworld to arrange your flight?" asked Yaldrint.

"What?" asked the Grashardi ambassador. "Of course not!".

CHAPTER 25

Over a remote stretch of undeveloped territory, a kilometer southwest of Jeldren, a Terran Protectorate lander made a spiraling descent through the morning air. As it touched down in a flourishing meadow, the lander's retrothrusters riffled a tall patch of pale orange grass, which lay amid a clump of spreading shade trees.

Its skilled pilot, the former Lieutenant Andersen, paused to reflect — as the engine shut down and a vapor trail of singed plants and charred soil dissipated into the twilight air. Strange as it seemed, she knew this had to be right. Because now the voice of Eddy, who had spoken to her in a waking dream, was clearer than ever.

"Eddy's here," Cricket told herself. But for the moment, she remained seated, still strapped into her command chair. Although much of what she had done up until now had been instinctive, from here on out, she realized, she'd be relying on blind faith.

And yet, that faith was easily the strongest sensation she'd ever felt, whether back on her homeworld or way out in the depths of space. Almost without her knowledge, Cricket's hand pressed down on the hatch release, which sent a small gust of canned air into Bledraun's lush biosphere.

At the last moment, she remembered to activate the nasal implants that would filter out the harmful trace amounts of chlorine in the air. With her seat harness unfastened, she swung her legs out toward the soft orange grass below and gazed toward the quiet horizon.

"Beautiful," she sighed. No wonder Eddy liked it here. So it seemed odd that his whinnying voice eventually led her to an abandoned drainage conduit. Yet the urge to continue was irresistible. She stooped to enter a large neocotta pipe, approximately two meters tall.

"Steady, Boy," she said. "Momma's coming."

Cricket took a deep breath and tiptoed forward, until the sloped path under her military boots deepened and broadened. She paused and peered into the darkness. With nothing else to follow except the sound of Eddy's voice in her mind, she aimed for the soft, blue glow now radiating in the distance.

The farther she went, the more she was struck by how clear and fragrant the air in the conduit was. Far from the dank, sewery odors she'd expected, the atmosphere in this underground passageway was refreshing, invigorating and … yes … soothing.

After a hundred meters or so, the conduit banked to the left and down at a gentle slope. Now the stress of the past week, which had culminated in her ship's narrow escape from a fleet of powerful alien ships, was replaced by a welcoming embrace of loving calm. Shimmering music, like the sound of a lazy forest stream, chattering against an orchestra of pebbles, eased up from below to greet her ears.

Enchanted, the former navigator lost all sense of direction. She also abandoned her perception of time, in favor of a tranquil indifference to everything except the motion of her senses. As a result, it was hours later that, faint and stumbling, she stopped abruptly at the edge of a steep incline.

There, through a portal of jagged granite, she looked down into a large city, lit up with thousands of bioluminescent globes, which floated in a series of interlaced patterns. Tears of joy streamed down her face.

"Eddy?" she called out.

"Your friend is here," said the earnest, young voice of the stable boy behind her. "All of your friends are here.".

CHAPTER 26

Parked in a stationary orbit on the dark side of Gelen, the first and largest of Bledraun's three moons, was a compact symbiote ship. Inside, Drashna paced its bridge and weighed her options. One side of her longed to shuck off her responsibilities and zoom away to the ends of the universe. Hadn't she done enough for Bledraun over the last twenty-five cycles?

And yet, her many hours of conversation with Warvhex left no room for doubt. She must stay and fight back against the Quishiks. Still, she wondered what larger purpose her efforts served. Was she saving her planet so she could deliver her people to their new masters?

"Focus on Caronya," Drashna muttered. If she lived to see her daughter cured by the symbiotes, she'd pull up stakes, cash out her holdings on Bledraun and take the first passenger ship off-world to the most distant planet she could reach. She might even think to join one of the new colonies under construction by the Svaladorns at the edge of the settled universe.

"A peaceful spot," she thought.

The mechanically modulated voice of the ship's AI broke in on her daydreams.

"Awaiting orders," it said.

No sense delaying, Drashna decided. In theory, the symbiotes' transponder array would disrupt the Quishiks' delicately-balanced equilibrium. It would sever their connection to their earlier incarnations and render them, in their own words, "time-bound."

Now that she'd come this far, and for Caronya's sake, Drashna forgot her pride and did as she was told. And no sooner had she issued the proper commands to the ship's AI than she picked up the secure comlink Warvhex had given her and issued a command of her own.

"I've done it," she said, her voice catching at the back of her throat. "Now you must treat my daughter as we agreed."

The symbiote's angelic voice rang out from the comlink.

"How nice to hear from you again, Your Sternness," she said. "Don't worry, we are honorable. However, there will be a slight delay in your daughter's treatment."

Drashna gripped the comlink hard, and resisted the urge to smash it into the wall behind her.

"What?" she asked. "What possible reason ... why won't you do as you promised?"

"Because, Dear Drashna," said the symbiote. "Your daughter is gone."

"Gone...." said Drashna. "Gone as in...."

"As in we no longer have her," said Warvhex. "She has disappeared from the stasis chamber on this ship. I suspect the Quishiks."

"Those ... things, have my daughter?" asked Drashna. "Then why did I blast them with ... with your array?"

"Fortunes of war," said Warvhex in a low voice, before closing contact.

Drashna's eyes filled with tears, and she reached out from orbit to the one being she hoped might have a solution.

"Ambassador Draaf," she said into her personal scanner.

"Warning. Your communication will not be secure," said the ship's AI. "Proceed anyway?"

The Euch Chaudron of Bledraun felt the blood draining out of her face. She'd never felt so alone.

"End call," she said. "Take me to Jeldren as fast as possible."

"Warning...." the ship's AI started.

Drashna's fists clenched. Weeks of unending frustration and fear found an open channel through her voice.

"Just go!" she shouted.

And with that, the ship spun out on a wide arc away from Gelen and toward Bledraun. Drashna smiled, until she realized the AI had interpreted her command too literally. The symbiote ship lurched forward with tremendous force and sent her slamming into the bulkhead wall behind her. Now unconscious, she was at the mercy of a powerful ship hurtling toward her homeworld in a blind rush.

At that same moment, aboard the *Mighty Fortress*, Captain Enos puzzled over a sudden shift in energy readings coming from the last-known coordinates of the Quishik fleet. At his current position, Enos tried to map out the most effective response to the growing threat. But was a tactical plan even possible against a fleet whose position defied normal space-time geometries?

The answer would have to wait. Telemetry now revealed an enormous energy pulse, embedded in a space-folding field and racing toward the huge, light-swallowing ships in a tight beam. Someone, perhaps even the symbiotes, had fired on the Quishik fleet! The news sent waves of bioelectrical impulses throughout the captain's central nervous system, with an unexpected outcome: he was now acutely aware of Cricket's absence.

Though there was no direct evidence to support it, the biomechanoid captain was certain she would have contributed valuable insight. *But why?* It defied logic to think Cricket's mere presence could facilitate his analysis. His command of the available data was absolute. Yet her absence felt as tangible as the console under his fingers.

This contributes nothing, he told himself. *I must evaluate the data from a different angle.*

And yet, here too, he was frustrated. The data streaming out towards him was in a format he couldn't access. He came as close to cursing his programming as any AI could.

"Coded," he said. The intent of this code would have been obvious to an intelligence with a different specialization. His internal temperature shot up and he called out across the 8.54 light years separating the Fremdel event horizon and Bledraun.

"Intelligence Yaldrint," he said. "Urgent: Your analysis of the attached data packet."

Yaldrint's reply did more than confirm the captain's suspicions.

"Definitely of symbiote origin," she said, "down to the Avroulian data encryption algorithm that obscures it. That suggests they intend to disrupt the Quishiks' cognitive functions with complex interference patterns. Yet the scale of the assault cannot be accounted for within the standard model."

Yaldrint went on to explain that the transmission emanated from thousands of individual transponders.

"Any evidence of their location?" asked Enos.

"The data suggests they are embedded in *chalyzfe* trees, dotting the entire surface of Bledraun," said Yaldrint.

The implications were staggering. The nature of the assault implied that the Quishiks generated unimaginably high levels of mental energy. Enough energy, that is, to require such a forceful strike.

Captain Enos rifled through his ship's historical records at inhuman speeds.

Although the Terran Protectorate had discovered a few telepathic species over the past twenty-two-hundred years, none of them could stretch their minds farther than a few thousand kilometers. Yet Yaldrint's readings suggested a telepathic field-strength beyond all known limits. What's more, the field appeared to oscillate freely between several different spatio-temporal coordinates.

"So these beings might be said to exist outside of time," said Enos.

"Please..." said Yaldrint, her voice distorted by misaligned overtones. "Refrain from this line of specu ... cul ... ation ... it is ... dis ... disrup ... uptive ... ive...."

"We will speak of it no further," said the biomechanoid.

Enos closed contact, on the assumption that Yaldrint would reboot and regain her equilibrium. No doubt, Ambassador Draaf would see to that.

But where, come to think of it, was the distinguished crustacean? His biometric signal, Enos discovered now, could not be traced to his embassy or any other part of the Dralein's world government complex. Though the captain's first thought was to mount an exhaustive search for Ungent, a massive surge of data from the vicinity of the Fremdel reset his priorities.

"Evasive maneuvers!" he said to the young ensign who had taken Lieutenant Andersen's place. And at the thought of Cricket, there was no denying a momentary energy spike in the android's metadigital processors.

CHAPTER 27

"Rhaltholinarur, protect us!"

The screams echoing through the corridors of the Quishiks command ship might have been heard deep into the distant past — were it not for the impact of the symbiote's transponder signal.

Plaandrur Quishik Hlalkuhr was beside herself. She'd lost all contact with her previous incarnations! Might the dark Prophesy of the Three Ships mentioned in the *Shlaldre Glalcaniar* be soon fulfilled? Yet how could that be, when the fleet's every action had followed the very arc of Probability?

Besides, Plaandrur realized, in consultation with her top advisors, The Prophesy of the Three Ships was found only in the last two chapters of the holy file, whose authenticity had long been questioned. A late addition! A fairy tale, added at the whim of a defiant scholar. That much was obvious. The ominous conjunction of events was simply too fanciful to align with Probability:

> Beware three silent ships alone,
> A mighty tower overthrown,
> A stolen child, bereft, forlorn;
> For on this day your doom is born.

"No," the Quishik commander reassured herself. "We are as ever, aligned with His Holy Rigor."

Matters of faith aside, Plaandrur was far from defeated. Despite her shock and rage, the effect of the symbiote's transponder beam was neither fatal nor permanent. Though she could no longer connect with the beings Harlan or Ungent would call her "former selves," she could still connect telepathically with each of the subcommanders in her fleet. Together, they reached an obvious consensus. Any beam that could be sent could be deflected and, following that, shielded against.

Nevertheless, the time-bounds' ingenuity had surprised Plaandrur and ruffled her sense of superiority.

"The Book of Probability speaks of rich opportunities to prove our Might and Glory," she told herself.

But for once, the pious phrases that usually emboldened her rang hollow. Plaandrur's blood-red spine writhed. The time-bounds' assertion of their right to exist, despite the hallowed precepts of Science, had worked against her. Was this, she wondered, a turning point in the destiny of the Quishiks?

Maybe not yet. A reassuring report surfaced from the fleet's linked minds. The transponder beam could be deflected by redirecting the flow of the fleet's gravity wave generators to the outer hull. If kept up even a nanosecond too long, the result would be catastrophic, for both the Quishik fleet and for many cubic parsecs of local space-time.

"Worth the risk," Plaandrur concluded, and none of her subcommanders dared disagree. Once the damaging effect of the beam was corrected, she would move the fleet out of range.

Next, the beam's mechanisms might be temporally displaced to the era of the very formation of the galaxy and absorbed into the pre-planetary swirl of dust and gasses that created the Bledraun system. Yet the consequences of such a devious plan were too great. It would risk the erasure of Bledraun from the revised timeline.

"Must resist the temptation," said the Quishik commander into her command module.

Like it or not, slaking her lust for revenge would have to be postponed. Destroying the planet would deprive her people of a rich harvest of Dralein mental energy. Inelegant as it was, the more prudent solution might involve a series of tightly targeted blasts from a particle cannon. Yet Plaandrur was in no hurry to destroy any life form that might prove useful later.

Within a few fractions of a rotation, a massive wave of gravitic energy from the fleet's engines had deflected the symbiote's transponder beam. It now raced up and over the Quishik fleet at incalculable speed, on a trajectory heading straight into the Fremdel event horizon. Almost at once, the inhabitants of the Quishik fleet felt the scope of their minds expanding as they reconnected, little by little, to their earlier incarnations.

"Hard about," Plaandrur croaked into her comlink, not trusting the reliability of her telepathic connections. The massive fleet of light-swallowing ships pivoted, and reduced the tidal force of the miniature gravity wave they'd created as they turned.

"Cloak and regroup," Plaandrur commanded again. As she well knew, there was no point in further action until the damage done to their minds by the transponder beam was healed. The energy expended in masking the fleet's total quantum signature would be exorbitant, she realized, but achieving the tactical advantage of secrecy was now her top priority.

At the re-integration of her consciousness, across thousands of planes of existence in space and time, Plaandrur Quishik Hlalkuhr experienced what Ungent or Shol would have felt as relief. And yet, what was *that*, tugging at the fringes of her mind?

"It is the Ootray," said one of her earliest incarnations. "Your posturing arrogance has awakened them."

Plaandrur's spine stretched to its full length at the suggestion of wrong-doing. As if the millions of Quishiks who were now squeezed by the tight grip of starvation could be better served by mincing negotiations with the time-bound.

"We cannot be satisfied by a mere 'arrangement' — a trade agreement of goods and services in return for a mere trickle of their mental energy," she snapped. "We must drain them dry."

But now that balance had been restored to her mental energy and to that of her fleet, the Quishik commander turned her thoughts to the Dralein child they had taken hostage. It was, as it were, a bit of extra leverage, now that their position had been discovered prematurely. The child's illness, prolonged by the parasites for their own purposes, had been cured. Of what use to anyone is a sickly child, the Quishik commander wondered.

Best of all, a tiny portion of the child's mental energy was already on tap to help the most vulnerable of her people, those a few cerebejoules away from permanently losing their natural integration across multiple universes.

"Yes, my princess," thought Plaandrur, whose knowledge of Dralein culture was practically nil. "Your sickness will not have been in vain. You will bring health to legions." And that, Plaandrur realized, was but a taste of the feast to come when the Plan moved into its next phase.

CHAPTER 28

Shol looked out the side portal of the lander, piloted by Zander Bassett, that had touched down at the edge of Krezovic Town. How was it, he wondered, that the Weapons Specialist was also a pilot — and daring enough to sneak a prisoner off the *Sweet Chariot* without authorization?

"In emergency situations," Zander had told him, "people with vision need the courage to act, no matter the consequences."

Maybe, thought Shol, but that attitude didn't square with the adventure holovids he'd seen when he occasionally spent the night at Ulandroz' underground compound. In the holovids, the people breaking orders were rebels, sociopaths or simple, cheesy crooks.

There was a — what did they call it? — a "chain of command," and soldiers did what they were told. This guy had busted the chain wide open. Come to think of it, Shol wondered, how did Zander take off in a lander without any kind of clearance, or whatever?

Shol rubbed his slick forehead and decided none of that mattered. He was way closer now to finding Trinity than he had been when Gillian tossed him into the *Sweet Chariot* brig. Trouble was, Shol had a lingering instinct that this … soldier … wasn't telling him everything. For starters, what was up with Zander's mechanically-precise way of speaking?

"We'll land 91.4 meters from the building you identified on this ship's aerial map. That's 315.27 meters away from the nearest Terran landing party. It's far enough to avoid detection, yet near enough to keep the Krezovic rebels from getting suspicious. From there, it's a 0104-rotation walk to the rear of the building, which we'll approach at a 37-degree angle from the southwest."

"Who talks like that?" Shol mumbled, and then regretted it. If his suspicions were right, there was no telling what kind of enhanced sensors the apparent-human might have.

Maybe he's just a nut, Shol thought, and immediately saw the irony of taking comfort in that statement.

Either way, Shol decided, Zander must have used some extraordinary influence to pull this stunt off. Or had he messed with ship's AI while his superiors were out on patrol, and no one knew the lander was missing?

Gotta focus, Shol told himself.

This was all about Trinity. He was simply thankful that Zander Whatever-he-was, had given him back the e-mag knife he'd grabbed from Ather. There were some serious tricks Shol could do with that knife, and he was pretty sure neither the 'tectorate soldiers nor the Krezovic rebels would be ready for them.

But what was he thinking? Assuming Zander's scan of the weather-beaten house was accurate and it contained a total of two Krezovics plus Trinity, there was no way in, without tripping an alarm or getting shot. Shol had seen that happen on the backstreets of many a minor planet — then watched a patrol unit swoop in hard and fast.

Zander handed Shol what looked like a gas mask.

"Put this on," he said.

Shol slipped the ill-fitting device over his boney, non-human nose and jaw.

"What?" he said.

"Just a precaution," said Zander. "Remember our deal?"

"Right," said Shol, with the well-practiced show of earnestness that had saved his life more times than he could count. It cost him nothing to appear to go along with the cold-hearted plan to murder Captain what's-his-name, who happened to be friends with the Oldster.

But the real cost, Shol knew, would be to Zander himself, after a few shouted words when they were back onboard. As confident as he was of future success, however, Shol focused on the here and now. From his past experience with Ulandroz, he knew there was no such thing as an easy mission. If it involved breaking in on somebody's home turf, you were always at a disadvantage.

Each situation contained unknowns, and there was also no accounting for what Shol referred to as "random *quelx*" — the unpredictable ways people act when they're under attack. Plus, they needed to get Trinity out of this dingy two-family home unhurt.

By now, the Krezovic boy, and the human he was more and more convinced must be an android, had edged up to the drab house. Zander held up his hand for Shol to stop.

"This is it," he said. "What does your personal scanner tell you?"

Shol suppressed his suspicious thoughts and opened his holoscreen. There … the readout was clear … two Krezovic adults and one human girl about sixteen years old, who might be Trinity. Though the idea of being this close to her made his thoughts race out of control, Shol's memory intervened with the sound of Ulandroz' deep, emotionless voice:

"Ain't nothing real 'til you see it."

"What now?" Shol whispered to Zander.

The answer never came. A burst of lase fire from inside the house pierced its cracked, grimy windows, and ripped up the turf between their feet.

Shol's throat tightened. Would the Terran Protectorate patrol fail to respond? Unlikely. His chance to save the girl he hoped was Trinity was slamming shut.

A second burst of lase fire seared the edge of Zander's left forearm and sent the two of them hunkering down below the windows. The Krezovic boy watched as Zander hurled a rock through a pane of glass, followed by a large grenade that had been swinging from his belt since he left the lander. Fearing the worst, Shol covered his ears. But instead of a blast, the grenade delivered a powerful cloud of neurotoxins, tuned to the Krezovic central nervous system. Instinctively, Shol pulled his mask tight.

Within seconds, the two adults had collapsed and Shol heard a muffled version of a familiar voice wafting out of the building's smashed first-story window. He ignored Zander's frantic hand signals, jammed his palms on the wooden window sill and vaulted into the dark, dank house.

There, at the far end of the room, sat Trinity, tied to a chair. Her mouth, covered by a jagged slab of surgical bandage, struggled to call out.

"It's OK, Baby," said Shol. "I'll get you out of here."

He carefully peeled away the bandage, freed Trinity's mouth and expected a tearful reunion. But he was in for a shock. Instead of meeting his eyes, Trinity's gaze stared out past him to the unknown figure who was shuffling into the room.

"Why'd you bring that … that thing ... with you?" she asked.

Shol whipped his e-mag blade out of his belt and wheeled around to stare at Zander.

"What?" he asked "What are you talking about?"

"Look at his arm," said Trinity.

As Zander moved out of the shadows, it was now easy to see the pulsing streak of blue light running the length of his forearm, where a stray shot from one of the rattled Krezovic rebels had ripped the pseudoskin clean off.

"Just hang on and we can talk this out," said Zander. "I can…."

Shol's e-mag knife, now lodged in the android's throat, prevented him from completing his thought, forever lost in a hail of sparks, as the knife's unfocused electromagnetic field wreaked havoc on every circuit in Zander's body.

"What're we gonna do?" asked Trinity, "No way that lase fire wasn't noticed."

A rush of adrenaline pumped through Shol's veins. He retrieved his e-mag knife, cut Trinity loose from the chair, grabbed her hand, and pulled her toward the far window.

"This way," he said.

Trinity dug her heels into the splintered wood floor.

"You're not taking me back to Captain Mars' lander are you?" she asked.

"I have a better idea," said Shol. "Come on, Shiny Girl, we gotta leave now!"

Less than two minutes later, a small squad of Terran Protectorate soldiers burst into the room, and stopped dead at the sight of Zander's crumbled body, still shooting sparks into the dusty wreck of the floor.

Had they not been distracted, they might have glanced out of the window on the opposite wall — to see two young lovers racing for cover in a cluster of broad *chalyzfe* trees, on their way to the Grand Jeldren Hotel.

CHAPTER 29

"Tell me why these readings make sense, Commander," growled a weary Harlan Mars, as he plopped his muscular frame down onto the soft, spherical chair at the center of his spare quarters.

Gillian shrugged.

"Captain … they don't actually," she said. "Though I suppose any kind of gravitational anomaly is possible near the Fremdel."

"OK, but a micro-gravity wave?" asked Harlan. "Sit down. Let's think this out. The Protectorate has been studying event horizons for how long?"

Gillian rested her tired legs on the spongy, aqua-marine couch to his left.

"Well, actually," she said, "the earliest reports go back to before the invention of space-folders."

Harlan rubbed his stubbly chin and longed for a shower and a shave. How much better to share both with his XO, instead of this dreary cat and mouse game. He cast his eyes over his quarters' bare walls and cursed himself for not making them more conducive to … conversation.

"Hard to believe we were ever stuck on one planet," he said.

"Look at the Dralein," said Gillian. What, she wondered, did that expression on his face mean?

"Never mind," said Harlan. "The point is, in the last two thousand cycles, we ought to have recorded a reading like that before."

Gillian stared off into space.

"And the fact that we haven't," she said, "may mean the gravity surge we detected had nothing to do with the Fremdel."

"Has to mean there's somebody out there," said Harlan. "Don't we have a probe ship doing … research … near the horizon?"

Gillian explained that the *Mighty Fortress* appeared to have gone offline.

"Maintaining radio silence," said Harlan. "Everything by the book … least ways, if you were dealing with an unidentified alien."

Gillian pointed to the holoscreen she'd called up from the personal scanner embedded in her right forearm.

"And one with the ability to create readings like these," she said

Harlan shoved his hands behind his head and tried to assess the situation. Gillian's confusing data suggested beings whose command of science and technology put the Terran Protectorate in the shade. But there wasn't a darned fool thing he could do about it, until they had more information.

"Think the symbies are behind this?" he asked his XO.

Gillian's frown said more than he thought possible.

"I wish, Sir, that the situation were that simple," she said. "It would be tidier, wouldn't it, if this new threat were merely a variation on an old one? But the data ... there's nothing here that remotely resembles symbiote tech."

"Worth a try," said Harlan. He got up from his chair, walked over to the silvery view screen that dominated the south wall of his quarters and flicked it on. He stared at the various perspectives it gave him on Jeldren and the outlying areas and looked for any stray image that might spark a flash of intuition.

He spun around to face Gillian.

"Didn't you say there was another ... event ... out there today?" he asked.

"Right," said Gillian, "That would be the transponder beam that left the surface of this planet at 0600 hours, local time."

Harlan's breath stopped short. As usual, the effect of Gillian's voice on his heart rate increased, in direct proportion to how precise she was being.

"And the micro-gravity wave, if that's what it was." he said. "When was that?"

Gillian's eyebrows arched as she realized what Harlan was getting at. Because the gravity surge had occurred within a few minutes of the transponder beam, there was a chance the two were interrelated.

"And, Captain, the transponder beam does have all the earmarks of the symbiotes." said Gillian.

"So whatever they did got the attention of these — beings," said Harlan. "But how could the symbies know enough about them to launch an attack. Or were they firing blind?"

"Well, Sir," said Gillian, "we did get a final report from Lieutenant Heath of Security."

"Took him this long to decrypt that data he told me about, what, two weeks ago?" said Harlan. "Gardens of Babylon, Commander, did he go on shore leave?"

"Not without your approval, I'm sure, Sir," said Gillian. "I gather the symbiotes are a tad more clever than we anticipated. In any case, Heath reports they recently spotted the same species they encountered at the Seshnel event horizon last cycle, emerging from the Fremdel."

"What species is it, then?" asked Harlan.

"The symbiotes called them Quishiks," said Gillian. "I assume they must have gathered enough data from their encounter at the Seshnel to devise a tactical weapon, of sorts. I'm afraid there's no evidence their assault had any effect at all."

But as she pointed out, there was a larger concern. The transponder beam had been a composite of signals sent from across the planet's surface — using devices embedded in the trunks of trees.

"But a project on that scale," said Harlan. "Only the Chaudron ... oh, Mercy."

The picture expanded as it became more clear. If Drashna and the symbiotes were busy battling an unknown species, it seemed unlikely that they were also behind the mysterious energy readings that he'd been ordered to track down — or the abandoned factory he'd blasted his way into, two weeks before.

Harlan turned back to the view screen. He was sure the answer to his questions had to lie in the city. As he'd learned from Ungent years ago, there were very few things in the local environment that weren't interrelated — and that went double for times when there was trouble brewing.

"Does your data have anything to do with that energy signature we've been searching all over God's creation for?" he asked Gillian.

"Well, Captain, about that," said Gillian, as she got up from the couch and walked over to him. "It appears we've been snookered."

Harlan spun around to face her.

"This better be good," he said.

"As good as an ANN Commission spy on this ship," said his XO. "If you're looking for Weapon Specialist Barrett, I'm afraid you'll need to look in the bionics lab. Or rather, its scrap bin."

Harlan listened, bug-eyed, as Gillian caught him up on Zander's strange adventure with Shol.

"Never heard of a wirehead flunky taking matters into his own hands like that," said Harlan. "Must've busted every protocol in their data base. And now the Krezovic boy is missing too, you say?"

But as he soon learned from Gillian, the situation was worse. For wherever Shol had gone, he'd taken Trinity with him. Harlan smacked his right fist into the palm of his left hand. As he knew full well, the less likely Trinity's disappearance was his fault, the more likely he'd be blamed for it.

"There's more, I'm afraid, Sir," said Gillian, her voice trembling. "As I said, we've been snookered."

The ship's cyber team had hacked into the ANN Commission server that housed Zander's mind — and learned the full intent of his mission aboard the *Sweet Chariot*. Aside from the shock, though attempts on his life had been made before, Harlan wrestled with the realization that the Terran Protectorate's delicate alliance with the ANN Commission was a sham.

"I took the liberty of drawing up a complete report for you to send to Admin," said Gillian. "I'm sure Central Advisor Christiansen would be quite interested to know...."

Gillian jumped at the sound of Harlan's palms slamming flat into his kitchenette counter.

"Don't even think of sending that!" said Harlan. "As long as the Commission thinks we're ignorant, there's still a chance we can find out what they're up to."

"But Captain," said Gillian, "won't they know their plan failed when Zander doesn't report in?"

Harlan counted off on his fingers.

"If our cyber folks can bust into Zander's brain, they can operate it, too, can't they?" he asked.

"Sir, I doubt the ANN Commission will fail to notice...." Gillian started.

Harlan plopped himself down on his spherical chair again, letting its soft contours ease away the tension in his back.

"Way I see it," he said in a low voice, "the wireheads have a whole lot of bases to cover right about now. I'll bet you lunch at the MarsOne Hotel that keeping tabs on a flunky's firewall is a pretty low priority right now."

"You may be right, Captain," said Gillian, "But there's one little fly in the ointment. The Commission sent Zander to kill you. The fact that you're still breathing ought to be a bit of a tipoff that their flunky has failed, don't you think?"

"Fly in the ointment?" asked Harlan. "What planet did you say you were from?"

Gillian's face turned scarlet.

"Sir, this is serious!" she shouted. "Sorry, Captain, but you do see my point, don't you?"

"Yeah," said Harlan, "Serious. As serious as planning my own funeral. Tell the cyber team to rig up Zanders brain so it sends a 'mission accomplished' signal to the wireheads. Then I'll go into hiding. Sure wish I could talk this over with my old pal Ungy. He'd know what to do."

Gillian leaned up against the wall directly in front of him.

"That was the other bit of news, Sir," she said. "The ambassador is missing."

CHAPTER 30

Had Captains Mars and Enos not been distracted, a brief sensor scan would have located Ungent out on the streets of Jeldren, moving as fast as his will and Bledraun's gravity allowed. He leaned hard on his titanium staff, and pressed on past the genteel part of town, once more heading out toward the Tralerzan river, to the east.

Now fully aware of the humans' expanded military presence, Ungent avoided the city's broad boulevards at all costs, even though it slowed his progress. A second encounter with Harlan's security force, or Harlan himself, would land him in custody — despite the interstellar incident it would likely cause.

Yet if things panned out as the ambassador feared, the sovereignty of Grashard or any political entity outside the ANN Commission would be as worthless as a cubic centimeter of sand on the Dreladnik desert of his homeworld. Once the androids had cornered the market for essential rare minerals, they could ignore any protest by Ungent's homeworld without fear of reprisal.

Yes, the more he thought of it, the clearer it was that Harlan and his superiors were being played for fools. Over the course of his career, Ungent's three contacts with the ANN Commission had been enough to convince him they had even less honor than the symbiotes.

And by the way, what of Warvhex?

Though her involvement, at some level, was too obvious to be denied, her motives were as foggy as the dark haze of a deep space gas cloud. Whether the Kaldhex Assembly opposed the ANN Commission or abetted it, Ungent couldn't find a line of logic that justified either attitude. No matter who came out on top in the current conflict, the symbiotes were still dependent on organic sentient life for their survival.

But what if, he wondered, the Kaldhex had a realistic plan to change their nature and become independent beings? Ungent's eyestalks shifted left as his long experience reminded him how *interdependent* all life-forms were, no matter how they were put together. If he were right about the symbiotes, he wasn't convinced a victory over parasitism would be worth the price.

But that was as far as he could allow his sympathy for cold-hearted Warvhex to go.

"Have to find those two … children," he said.

Ungent's eyestalks drooped. It had finally occurred to him how young Shol and Trinity were to be on their own, especially on the eve of a major conflict. By now, he decided, the human girl was likely in the hands of the Krezovic extremists she'd naively sought out. As for Shol, his street mentality might give him the false courage to try a brave rescue — and land up in Harlan's brig.

Ungent shifted his gaze, at the sound of a drone hovercraft overhead. *Not much better odds,* he told himself.

Whatever the humans were after, they were pursuing their goal with their patented ham-fisted doggedness. All the more reason to find Shol and Trinity as soon as possible.

And do what? he wondered.

The Grand Jeldren Hotel was no place to hide, especially now that Dadren had ordered him off the planet. The next time they met, he was sure, the acting-Chaudron would take the extraordinary step of commandeering a commercial vessel and ordering it to pilot the crustacean to Sattron Interstellar Transfer Station.

For though political power had been thrust on Dadren, Ungent knew he wouldn't hesitate to use it. No doubt Shol would realize that too, and strike out for the wilderness surrounding Jeldren.

"Greetings to you, Har Draaf," said a disturbingly cheerful voice to his left.

Ungent's breath came up short. He whipped his eyestalks around and caught sight of the sea-green groundcar, Serano, that had twice led him into danger.

"The acting-Chaudron requests that you join Serano in a ride back to the center of town," said the AI. "He was … insistent … and remarked that this word would have a special meaning for you."

Instinctively, Ungent did his best to stride away from the car, fully aware how absurd it was to try outpacing a groundcar on foot.

"I'm on … diplomatic business," he called out over his shoulder.

"The acting-Chaudron insists he also has diplomatic business to discuss, Har Draaf," said Serano, as it glided alongside Ungent.

This, the Grashardi knew, would end badly — unless he could take a route the groundcar couldn't follow. Ungent ignored Serano's gleaming surface for a moment, and searched the immediate vicinity for a narrow alley he could slip into. Trouble was, this far out toward Krezovic Town, the distinction between main and side street was practically nil.

"Har Draaf," rang Dadren's voice through Serano's sensors. "Please don't put me in the position of sending a patrol unit after you."

At the thought of that, Ungent stopped short, and his titanium staff clanked against a circular plate in the ground before him. The tunnels! No way Serano could follow him through the network of underground passageways the Dralein hurried into during the *sceraun*.

"Just one moment, my friend," Ungent called out with deceptive cheer. He dug around the edge of the metal disk's rim with his staff until it rose up on a blast of what Ungent figured was electromagnetic levitation. He jumped back, and barely managed to keep his balance.

"Har Draaf!" shouted Dadren. "What in the name of the Fremdel are you doing?"

But Ungent was already clambering down the tunnel, whose gentle, sloping incline proved surprisingly easy to walk. Once he'd cleared the opening itself, its metal disc slammed down tight. Soon Ungent's eyes adjusted to the dark and he saw the shaft expanded in all directions. The more he looked, the more it resembled the great hallways of a magnificent old palace.

That is, in its scale. In every other respect, it seemed as if he'd entered a subterranean cave system. Yet the farther he went, the more the caves smacked of sophisticated engineering.

"We got it all wrong," he mumbled, as the evidence of his own eyes confirmed. Ungent now saw this underground network could never have been carved out by desperate claws — no matter how many times the Dralein endured the *sceraun*.

He paused for a moment, and it occurred to him he didn't know how far down he'd walked or what was ahead. By escaping Dadren, he'd put himself at the mercy of ... what, exactly?

Ungent considered returning to the surface, but dismissed the idea. Though he wanted to retrieve the two missing teenagers and get them to safety, he now knew neither the humans nor the Dralein would allow that. His best option was to hope this very tunnel offered proof of the "other" that Captain Enos had alluded to.

Of course, the Grashardi ambassador had no reason to believe the "other" were necessarily his friends. And even if they meant him no harm, they had plenty of reason to be indifferent to his worries about Shol and Trinity. The secret nature of their existence — an entire underground civilization unknown to the settled universe — might mean they didn't give a single charmed quark about life on Bledraun.

And yet, he realized, the makers of this network of passageways must be the beings the Dralein instinctively sought as soon as the *sceraun* began. Might the "other" have arrived after the Dralein had dug primitive tunnels of their own, and set to work enhancing them? But why would these new arrivals get involved?

"Don't even know if I'm asking the question the right way around," he groused.

By now, the walls of the apparent cave system were dotted, here and there, with inscriptions and decorative patterns. He thought of transmitting photos of the inscriptions to Yaldrint, but it seemed unlikely the AI could decipher them.

Ungent stopped a moment to catch his breath. Clearly, his life had taken a turn away from everything he had long considered normal. His career in the Grashardi diplomatic corps, his fascination with other cultures — and his unsatisfactory marriage to Nulgrant.

I'll have to break with her once and for all. Assuming I survive, he thought.

He cast around for somewhere to sit, until a surge of bioluminescence bathed his purplish exoplating in a soft, blue light. A calm voice echoed behind him.

"You appear lost, Har Draaf," the voice said.

Ungent bowed low.

"I apologize deeply for trespassing on your sovereign territory," he said.

"You remind me of many of my former selves," said the voice.

Ungent blinked as the soft steady light flared up. A lovely female of his own species appeared before him.

"You ... Who...." Ungent sputtered.

"You may call me Dlalamphrur. I hope I have taken a form you do not find threatening," said the female. "Your suspicion is correct. I am not actually 'here' in the sense you mean it."

" I ... I understand," said Ungent, though he actually understood nothing about this situation.

"You, however, are 'here'," said the female. "for noble reasons. Even if your methodology lacks common sense."

"Someone has to take action!" snapped Ungent. "Lives are at stake."

The projection of a crustacean female, near Ungent's own age, appeared to walk up to him and place a webbed hand on his right cheek.

"Be at peace, Har Draaf," she said. "You have friends here."

CHAPTER 31

"It's time," said a hushed voice in a darkened room.

"You sure?" asked a dusky whisper.

"The implant," said the hushed voice. "They're talking to me now."

"OK," said the whisper, "here's our last chance to decide."

The voices belonged to Grauth and Drolet, the scruffy young Krezovic couple Ungent had secretly observed a few days before, while they negotiated with a squat, off-world android in downtown Jeldren. Grauth stared his accomplice in the eye.

"We made our decision," he said.

"*You* decided," said Drolet. "I said I'd see how I felt because we needed the money. And now that it's actually real … this attack on the Dralein … I mean, do we have the right?"

Grauth slammed a hand down on the rough kitchen table between them.

"Stop talking," he said. "You took the money and bought yourself some nice things. Including that *grezlach* you like so much."

Drolet reached across the table and slapped him hard across the face.

"And what am I supposed to do when you're out with your *gilhadra-*girls," she yelled, "the dishes?"

Grauth took a deep breath. The AI jabbering in his mind was getting impatient. He had to convince Drolet soon or they'd both end up falling out of a deep space airlock.

"Come on, Baby," he said. "Leave me any time you want, *after* this deal goes down. Otherwise, the wireheads will fry us up like sausage and feed us to a pack of Alcastrian weed wolves."

Drolet shuffled over to where Grauth was sitting.

"We're really gonna do this?" she asked. "Send all these Dralein into … into … whatever they call it?"

The annoying AI rant intensified in Grauth's mind.

"Don't tell me you didn't know that," he said quietly. "Go ahead and hate me, long as I don't live to see your beautiful eyes burned out."

"Cut it out," said Drolet. "You made your freakin' point. But after this … we're done."

Grauth slouched down in his chair and ran his long fingers through his stiff hair.

"Fine," he said. "Not that you care, but I...."

"What?" asked Drolet.

"I guess I ... I guess I love you," said Grauth.

Drolet stared into his sad face, and bit a green-tinted fingernail.

"If I believed that," she said, "I would've made you stay home. The two of us...."

"Never mind," said Grauth. "It's time."

With their lives on the verge of falling apart, two desperately confused Krezovics set in motion a chain of events that would change the course of history.

First, they contacted their co-conspirators in all 98 provinces of Bledraun. Over the last few days, they'd each been issued theta wave regulators. It was quite an achievement. Fortunately, the strategic plan they'd received from the ANN Commission had made their work fairly easy. How much easier, though, to have stayed on Hrathtel 4 and made a go of it as a coder, or a cell farmer!

But the gleaming android that delivered the ANN Commission's recruitment pitch had whipped him into a fury against the arrogant humans — along with thirty thousand other angry young Krezovics.

Trouble was, Admin/47/Sector15 hadn't mentioned the grimy quarters on the edge of nowhere that would be their command base. Worse, their assault on the humans turned out to be kind of indirect. After all, the bracelets targeted the Dralein — against whom the Krezovic's only grudge was the substandard social services they delivered to Krezovic Town. But it hardly mattered. If the Krezovic couple expected to live out the cycle, they had to carry out the wirehead's orders line by line.

After a trembling hug, Grauth and Drolet sent encrypted signals through their personal scanners and the attack began. Krezovics across Bledraun shoved their shiny hands into bracelets, walked outside and switched on a theta wave regulation grid broad enough to sweep the entire planet.

At once, two billion Dralein entered the early stages of *sceraun*. First they fell unconscious, then awoke nearly three hours later and started a slow, cringing crawl to tunnel entrances all across the planet.

Within minutes of the Krezovic assault, ANN Commission androids burst out of hiding. They set to work building a planet-wide mining operation from modules the Krezovics had implanted in the ground, as instructed, weeks ago.

Tucked inside a three-person escape pod on the secondary flight deck of the *Sweet Chariot*, Harlan Mars bit his lip as he watched the Dralein's pitiable transformation. Now that he'd essentially faked his death, as far as the ANN Commission and Terran Protectorate Admin were concerned, he dared not intervene. Nevertheless, he was determined to make a record of the ANN Commission's crimes.

On one screen he captured the Dralein's sluggish migration into the tunnels. On a second, he documented the androids' construction of ore-processing plants on Bledraun's nine continents. By tapping into long-range sensors on the *Sweet Chariot*, Harlan could track and record developments at several locations through countless data filters.

But his stealthy work was soon interrupted. At right angles to the system plane, a fleet of Terran Protectorate ships swarmed into view. Apparently, they'd cloaked themselves, even from Harlan's ship.

"Must've seen this coming," said the tall human.

A thundering blast of space-borne weapons jolted the 40-ish captain. But not nearly so much as the echoing broadcast from a powerful voice on his sensor array.

"Representatives of the ANN Commission," it boomed. "This is the Terran Protectorate Ship *Lazarus*. You are hereby ordered to stand down per Sector Court order 68T0-E135, Authorization 4279."

Harlan recognized this as an exercise in pure showmanship, that would allow the Protectorate to justify all manner of crimes against common sense later. Of course, to the thousands of remaining human colonists and the small clutch of off-world dignitaries who'd lingered after the mineral trade conference, the battle to come would be far more than a theatrical extravaganza. Even the sizable Krezovic immigrant population wouldn't be spared, in spite of their misguided alliance with the ANN Commission.

But what was behind this battle, the plot against his life, the secrecy surrounding his mission — and everything else that had happened since Ungent arrived on Bledraun?

"Should have trusted that ol' bowl of lobster bisque," he said, with a slight cough. In a few minutes, he'd have to slip into one of the three encounter suits onboard the pod, each with a day's supply of oxygen. They offered him a narrow margin of survival but, judging from the escalating conflict on the planet, it wasn't clear his hideout would be much use beyond then anyway.

Now Harlan decided he must take action, while he could still affect the outcome. That brought him to an unsettling conclusion: If hiding in the escape pod and hoping for the best was kind of crazy, pushing the escape pod out into space was only slightly more so.

If the ANN Commission launched an assault on any other ship in the Protectorate fleet, they'd be too preoccupied to bother with a stray escape pod. If he kept the pod dark, by potting down life support to the minimum, both sides might think it had merely broken free in the cross-fire. Then, maybe, if his power held out, a single thruster burst might push him toward the Fremdel event horizon. There the Terran probe ship could give him shelter until the fighting was over.

"Idiot," he said. The Fremdel was light years away and the escape pod was fit for local travel only. Fact was, any plan he came up with would boil down to hoping for a miracle. Yet, all things considered, taking action was sure to be a step up from waiting to die.

So at 2300 hours old style, Harlan Mars, now officially dead, entered the commands to launch his three-person escape pod into space-time's inky depths.

CHAPTER 32

From the vantage point of her space-folder, parked behind Lerdra, Bledraun's third moon, Warvhex watched the fighting intensify between the Terran Protectorate and the ANN Commission. According to the probability maps generated by her ship's AI, the odds had been against outright war on the planet's surface.

"And yet, here we are," she said.

Though she'd never believed in luck, Warvhex had felt its absence more keenly ever since coming to Bledraun. Who would have predicted the Quishiks would steal Caronya and break her leverage with the Dralein? Considering the strategic importance of Bledraun to the symbiote cause, it was a major setback.

For Bledraun orbited a star near the edge of the Fremdel event horizon, a site shrouded in ancient Kaldhex legends. Based on a close reading of smudged, frayed texts, written by the hands of countless hosts, many symbiotes saw the Fremdel as the key to their liberation.

Buried in these texts were tales of "wizards," able to breathe life into the dead. Did such beings exist beyond the Fremdel? Could they set the symbiotes free? One thing was certain: since the beginning of modern symbiote science, their attempts to merge with cloned bodies had failed.

Sad to say, the Kaldhex were bound by physical limits. A symbiote brain could neither manage the autonomic nervous system of a clone, nor live more than two or three months apart from the fully developed cerebral cortex of another species. The tanks, despite their elaborate artificial intelligence relays. were a poor substitute.

"No fresh ideas," she said.

For the time being, a symbiote's survival depended on doing the very thing that made them the most despised species in the settled universe. The fluid in Warvhex's tank flashed bright red. As long as the Quishiks still blocked the entrance to the Fremdel, the symbiote's quest had hit a dead end.

She blamed herself.

If she'd trusted Ungent with the secret of the Quishiks, he would have assembled the best minds in the settled worlds to stop them. Instead, Warvhex had allied herself with dull, provincial Drashna. At the time, it had seemed her only option. Both the humans and the Grashardi distrusted the symbiotes so much, they would have wasted precious time double and triple checking the data — and waited until the Quishiks were almost at their throats before taking action.

Besides, if Warvhex had given Ungent her data on the Quishiks, she would have given up a powerful bargaining chip. In exchange for delivering the only available weapon against sentient life's most dangerous enemy, Warvhex had planned to barter for protection under interstellar law.

Now that the transponder weapon had failed, human oppression of the symbiotes would continue and no one would lift a finger. Even the more enlightened Grashardi were non-committal on the subject. As if their indifference weren't simply another form of bigotry. In any case, now her hosts' fate was still her fate, and that of billions more symbiotes.

"To protect our hosts," she'd told the Kaldhex Assembly, "we must share our data about the Quishiks."

The grumbling of a few hardliners aside, the Assembly leaders accepted the bitter truth. As the head of StealthOps, Warvhex would lead the outreach to the host population. Under protest, she'd be accompanied by Klarghex, an accomplished negotiator. The Assembly had heard one too many report of Warvhex's hothead mentality to let her handle such an important mission on her own.

"You're about to say 'Stay out of my way,' I'm sure," said Klarghex. "I couldn't be happier about that. Just let me do most of the talking when we get there."

"Fine," snapped Warvhex, "as long as you stop talking now. But if you're coming along, you're pulling your weight all the way. Ever used a particle rifle?"

Inside the next tank over from Warvhex, Klarghex's tendrils trembled.

"Several of my hosts have been soldiers," he said. "Where do we start?"

The logical place, Warvhex explained, was the Terran Protectorate probe ship *Mighty Fortress*, which still hovered near the edge of the Fremdel. With the micro-space-folding techniques the symbiotes had stolen from the minds of the Olfdranyi, they could reach the ship in less than a half rotation.

Simple enough, in principle, but getting there required ingenuity. But this was nothing new. The survival of their species had long depended on an innate skill at pulling off the most elaborate deceptions. So it should surprise no one if, a few days later, a couple of bored operatives, stuck with the night shift aboard the *Mighty Fortress*, spotted an unexpected supply capsule, about five-hundred kilometers off their starboard side, emitting a standard Protectorate ID signal.

The symbiotes' deception was based on their deep understanding of Terran Protectorate protocols, which they'd picked up from the minds of countless humans. They knew the *Mighty Fortress* would maintain radio silence at all costs this close to the Quishik fleet. No one would think to contact Admin to confirm the capsule's point of origin.

Meanwhile, by transmitting the correct ID code and energy signature, the capsule gave the crew every reason to accept it. The capsule's signal also included the code for "critical." To be on the safe side, the younger of the two crewmembers on duty checked the quartermaster's log. There she found the fake, backdated purchase order, which a symbiote operative on the *Mighty Fortress* had uploaded the previous day.

If the cargo bay crew had suspected that the capsule might be a decoy, sent by the Quishiks, they might have second-guessed their decision. But here the captain's caution had worked against him. For Enos had put all data regarding the existence of the Quishiks on a need-to-know basis.

As a result, the two members of the cargo crew steered it into the cargo bay and pried it open, per protocol. Within seconds, the symbiotes merged with the two nightshift personnel and assimilated their knowledge of the ship.

"Wrong gender," Klarghex complained.

Warvhex's host slammed her accomplice's host against the cargo bay's bulkhead.

"Don't be an idiot," she hissed. "Human females are more easily trusted. That works to our advantage."

Klarghex rolled his host's soft brown eyes.

"If you say so," he grumbled.

CHAPTER 33

Trinity tugged at Shol's muscular arm as he led her to the back entrance of the Grand Jeldren Hotel.

"You sure this is safe?" she asked. "Somebody might recognize me."

Shol stopped to take her hands in his.

"Not dressed like that," he said. "And totally not with a street slime."

Trinity clasped his head in her soft hands.

"You know I hate it when you talk like that," she said. "You're my heart, Sholy."

"And you, Trin Baby, are my sweet angel," he said. "But OK, I'll wash my mouth out when we get inside."

Because Shol knew that Ungent had registered him legally at the hotel, he figured he could take the maglev lift to his suite with no problem. Bringing a guest, on the other hand, might cause problems. But, with no other option, the two of them decided to brazen it out. As it happened, the lobby was strangely abandoned.

"I don't get it," said Shol, as the lift whisked them up to the floor he shared with Ungent. "Yesterday, I couldn't go two meters without somebody greeting me, or whatever."

Trinity hugged him.

"All I know is, it's nice to be alone with you," she purred. "And anyway, my dad told me things were getting tense on Bledraun … politically."

Shol closed his eyes. Where, he wondered, weren't things getting tense? After what he'd learned from Yaldrint, there were trouble spots all over the settled universe. And yet, the exact way the lobby was empty … this was different.

It wasn't, he realized, like the entire staff had stepped away for a light snack at the same time. It was more like they'd rushed out in a panic. The look of the lobby, a misaligned mess of torn curtains and tipped over chairs, spoke of serious trouble. Nor were the two teenagers reassured by what they found upstairs. The first thing they saw when the lift doors opened, was an overturned servicebot, the kind used to deliver fresh sheets and towels to Hotel guests.

"Help me stand this up," said Shol, as he crouched down for a closer look. It took some doing, but soon he and Trinity had set the servicebot back on its rollers.

"What happened here?" Shol asked the device, which he expected to respond like Yaldrint. Instead, the device did nothing more than begin rearranging the towels on its supply rack.

"Here, let me try," said Trinity. "If this is like the ones we have at home, it's not really independent. You have to give it the right codes first."

Shol's heart raced. Despite the danger he knew they were in, he couldn't resist savoring the sound of her voice — or the way her face took on a new kind of beauty when she acted all serious. A girl like this? He had to make sure he never let her go.

"Report operational status, last 05 rotations," she said, oblivious to Shol's change in blood pressure.

The flickering pattern of status lights on the servicebot began to shift, a little at a time, until the roughly cylindrical unit backed away a short distance and turned to face the human girl.

"Greetings, Trinity Hudson, Terran Protectorate ID 014865-2T, resident, Reagan 3, New Santa Barbara region...." the AI began.

"I know who I am," Trinity snapped. "Report."

Shol's eyebrows arched as the servicebot recounted the events of the last 24 hours, starting with the arrival of a roving band of Krezovics, brandishing elaborate metadigital devices on their wrists.

"The bracelets," said Shol. "Come on, we have to find Har Draaf."

"The ambassador is currently out of his suite," said the servicebot. "His AI, however, has left orders for me to accompany you there, should you arrive."

"Can you let us in?" asked Trinity.

"My instruction to do so is clear," said the servicebot.

Within minutes, Shol and Trinity had raced down the hall and, once the servicebot had transmitted the correct wireless signal, pushed the door to Ungent's hotel suite wide open.

"Yaldrint?" Shol called out.

"In here," said Yaldrint from Ungent's room. "I sense you have Ms. Hudson with you."

As they rounded the corner, the young couple was startled to see the AI perched on the edge of a bureau, at the bottom of which lay a large, complex particle rifle. Shol pointed at the weapon.

"What ... what's this?" he asked.

"Dver Chaudron Dadren has experienced a terrible misfortune," said Yaldrint. "As have all the Dralein."

"How can we help?" asked Trinity.

"Directly," said the AI, "I believe there is nothing you can do. However, I suggest we go into hiding before the fighting begins."

"What fighting? said Shol, before the sound of distant explosions brought Yaldrint's comment into sharper focus. He stooped to peer at Dadren's abandoned weapon.

"No one knows we're here," he said. "Maybe the basement is deep enough to hide in."

But, as Yaldrint explained, ANN Commission sensors would find them anywhere on the planet, eventually. And the humans, engaged in battle, would have no time to rescue them.

"So where can we go?" asked Trinity.

"There is a symbiote ship parked behind Bledraun's third moon," said Yaldrint. "If I contact it now, the symbiotes might be able to send down a lander before the battle gets out of control.

"Symbiotes?" said Trinity. "No way. I don't want one of those things in my head!"

"Might be the best way to *save* your head," said Shol. "Come on, we gotta try it." And before a moment's more doubt could cross their minds, a lase blast not 20 meters from the Hotel steeled their resolve.

"It may comfort you to know, Ms. Hudson," said Yaldrint, "that the symbiotes are incapable of merging with an adolescent mind. Certain key cerebral structures are not yet fully...."

"Enough, friend Yaldrint," said Shol mimicking Ungent's voice, "we must act."

Yaldrint set to work and, under the cover of her scrambled signal, an automated symbiote landing-pod materialized in the Hotel lobby a short time later. Despite the danger, Shol marveled at its sleek efficiency, before grabbing Yaldrint's case in one hand, Trinity's arm in the other, and hustling them both inside. He stared down at Yaldrint's status lights as the lander's transmat generator started up.

"The symbiotes have transmat tech?" he said. "I thought you said that was impossible."

"The word I used," said Yaldrint, "was improbable. Apparently, some disruption has occurred in the flow of probability, as I understand it."

"But what could do that?" asked Trinity, as she hugged Shol's arm.

"Insufficient data for meaningful response," chirped Yaldrint. "How strange. Saying that has increased efficiency across my entire neural network."

Shol gasped as the symbiote lander began to dematerialize.

"Hang on, Shiny Girl," he said.

Everything around them went dark. A moment later, the impact of a speeding missile substituted a yawning crater for the Hotel's elegant lobby. Now the battle for control of Bledraun's mineral wealth ratcheted up to the next level. Out on the streets, a horrific rage of weapons fire ripped through homes, businesses, and the Dralein's cherished parks, reducing centuries of culture to rubble in minutes.

Against this backdrop, a steady stream of sniveling, terrified Dralein continued to pour into their ancient tunnels. They crawled face down, shunning the light, as their instinct drove them forward, through lase fire, falling missiles and the fierce advance of human and robotic troops. Soon, the once-proud city would be indistinguishable from dust, mud and the sludge of pulverized organic life.

CHAPTER 34

Though Ungent had a thousand questions for Dlalamphrur, the AI who'd greeted him in the Dralein tunnel system, she'd disappeared after a brief conversation. Aside from telling him she was a relic of "the Ootray," she revealed little else about herself.

Oblivious to the war raging on the planet's surface, Ungent spent the next two hours wandering an underground ghost town. Wherever he looked, he saw row after row of hostels fit for Dralein in the throes of the *sceraun*. But why, he wondered, would the Ootray want to take refuge underground?

"It's obvious to me you could live anywhere," he'd said. "Why confine yourself to these caverns?"

But Dlalamphrur had put a webbed finger to Ungent's lips.

"Know that, for now, this is where we must be," she'd said.

"But I *must* know," Ungent had insisted. "Why have the Dralein never mentioned you?"

"We erase ourselves from their memories before they return to the surface," said the Ootray AI. "Try to accept that this is for the best."

Ungent's mandibles clenched. A high-ranking member of the interstellar diplomatic corps, he wasn't used to being put off. Yet experience had taught him the futility of sulking over small slights. If he could set his ego aside, he might discover the secret of the Dralein tunnels.

As he shuffled forward, he gazed up at the glowing, bioluminescent globes that followed him everywhere. While there was nothing new about gravity modulation, not even the humans could make objects dance like this.

Still, the globes themselves were no more astounding than the subterranean world they illuminated. As he approached a low stone bench up ahead to his right, it morphed into a crustacean-friendly hammock. After so much walking it felt good to rest.

"What do you require?" a voice echoed in his mind.

"A nice, hot bowl of *ghonafrel* soup," he said, on a whim.

A small platform rose to knee level from the polished stone floor. On it was a spoon and a ceramic bowl filled with soup, each decorated with a traditional pattern from his home province on Grashard. Ungent took a sip.

"Delicious," he said.

But the moment of relaxation he sought eluded him. From all sides, the squeaks of cringing Dralein filled his ears.

Poor souls, he told himself.

Something had thrown the Dralein into *sceraun* ahead of schedule. What else could it be, he reasoned, but the bracelets? But how long could the Ootray keep billions of Dralein safe below ground — including dignified Dadren — if the humans and the androids actually went to war?

Come to think of it, Ungent was surprised at the lengths these two powers had gone to undermine the Dralein.

Outside forces must be warping their minds, he thought.

Dlalamphrur shimmered into view.

"They do so with the powers we gave them," she said. "But I believe Captain Enos has already told you about the Quishiks."

"The captain described the powerful ships his crew had detected out by the Fremdel," said the crustacean. "Are you saying you're responsible?"

"Indirectly," said Dlalamphrur.

"Then, how did you come to live down *here*?" asked Ungent.

"We knew the Quishiks would eventually emerge from the Fremdel. That made Bledraun the obvious place to wait for them," said the hologram.

While the Ootray were carving out their underground home, they discovered the crude, disease-ridden tunnels the Dralein had scratched out during the *sceraun.* Out of compassion, the Ootray built an intricate network of service units, complete with housing, feeding stations, sanitation and soft, soothing light.

"But why are you even involved with the Quishiks?" asked Ungent.

"The answer, Har Draaf, is simple," said Dlalamphrur. "We created them."

In a flash of soft light, she called up a holographic image of a spindly, blood-red creature. It looked as if a small, equine mammal had been stretched into a twisting array of muscle and bone, then segmented into a spiraling stack of irregular vertebrae. Ungent flinched.

"I gather they evolved past their original design," he said.

Dlalamphrur's face darkened.

"Regrettably, yes," she said. "We certainly didn't design them to prey on others."

Ungent's mandibles dropped.

"The Quishiks are *predators*?" he asked.

"They feed on the mental energy of every sentient being," said the Ootray AI.

"But why … why would you.…" Ungent stammered.

"It began as a healing mechanism," said the AI. "We gave them the power to sustain an ailing companion with a portion of their own life force, until medical attention could arrive."

"It's as if they … reversed the polarity," said Ungent.

"Not they themselves," said Dlalamphrur. "This ... reversal ... as you say, occurred over thousands of cycles."

"You mean, through a mutation?" asked the Grashardi.

"Exactly," said the hologram. "We were warned by our own people that the Quishik genome was unstable. But we refused to believe the universe could be so cruel."

"You had faith in your ideals," said Ungent.

The hologram flickered violently before settling down again.

"You are kind," she said. "But we cannot hide from our negligence. Stupidity, Har Draaf, is neatly aligned with the natural entropy of the universe. And we let something utterly stupid happen."

When the Quishik project was nearly complete, the Ootray prepared a lavish celebration for themselves. At the height of the festival, a massive holographic display caused a five-second power outage. Everyone assumed it was confined to the festival grounds, but the outage also reached the cooling units where the Quishiks were incubating, a hundred kilometers away.

"No alarms sounded?" asked Ungent.

"A rare software malfunction had disabled both the alarm system and the local sensor array." said Dlalamphrur. "With no sensor data, the backup generators never went online. So there was also no record of the accident."

"The incubators were contaminated, then?" asked Ungent.

"The surge released the electromagnetic seals on each unit," said Dlalamphrur, "In those five-seconds, a slow-evolving virus seeped in."

"You didn't notice the contamination?" asked Ungent.

"Every sign of genetic drift was within the standard deviation," said the AI. "A research assistant suggested the presence of a virus, but we were convinced our methodology was flawless, and we rejected the idea."

"You deceived yourselves," said Ungent.

"We were blinded by the thrill of discovery," said Dlalamphrur. "Understand ... this was the first artificially generated species in the history of the universe."

"But why?" said Ungent. "Why did the Ootray *want* to create the Quishiks in the first place?"

Mapping and exploring the universe was taking too much time from other branches of science. So the Ootray crafted a new species to handle these repetitive but highly analytical chores. To save time, they based the Quishik genome on an existing species that had a lot in common with terrestrial equines.

At first, the Quishiks spread out into the Continuum and transmitted oceans of data back to their masters. But over millennia, the slow-evolving virus rewrote the Quishik's carefully crafted sequences. Finally, the mutations reached critical mass. Each new Quishik generation became more hideous than the last.

"Wasn't there anything you could do?" asked Ungent.

Though the Ootray mounted a massive program to eradicate the virus, it merely went dormant. Far from correcting the problem, they accidentally gave the dormant virus the fuel it needed to re-emerge. Events plunged deep into crisis.

First, the Quishiks showed signs of paranoia. Then one starless night, they launched a vicious attack on an Ootray colony, using weapons they'd developed in secret. After a month of hard fighting, the Ootray contained the threat and trapped the Quishiks in an interlocking series of event horizons and their multiversal parallels.

"Like a hall of mirrors," said Ungent.

"Now, nearly ten thousand cycles later, the Quishiks have escaped," said Dlalamphrur.

"But how?" asked Ungent. "I was taught that an event horizon is inescapable, due to its excessive gravity."

"The explanation is … complex," said his holographic host. "But because the Quishiks exist beyond the boundaries of the phenomenon you call 'Time,' they are not subject to the force of gravity in the same way you and your companions are."

"I'm sorry to hear you're burdened with this dark secret," said Ungent.

"Please, Har Draaf," said Dlalamphrur. "We do not ask for your pity. We only hope this information will help you prevent the impending crisis."

"I'll do what I can," said Ungent, "but not if I stay down here."

"For now," said his host, as she faded into nothingness again, "remaining underground is your best hope of surviving long enough to help."

"I ... I should think...." Ungent stammered. "I should think this city is impervious to attack, or it would have been discovered hundreds of cycles ago."

Dlalamphrur's thoughts rang out in his mind.

"Entropy, Har Draaf. Entropy."

CHAPTER 35

As a system-class military cruiser, the *Sweet Chariot* was not expected to be in the forefront of the Terran Protectorate's assault on the ANN Commission. Its function as a support vessel, however, was not set in stone. If Admin assigned it a suicide mission, Acting Captain Gillian Cavendish would have no choice but to comply. Otherwise, she'd have to break ranks and desert the fleet.

Nothing was farther from the mind of this dedicated fleet officer. But her teeth were constantly on edge at the thought of abandoning Harlan — handsome, impulsive Harlan — to his fate in interstellar space.

Now that he'd taken it into his head to shoot his escape pod out of the launch bay, however, there was nothing she could do to protect him. Radio contact was out of the question, given that there was no sane reason to radio a dead man. And, she reminded herself, maintaining the fiction that former Captain Mars was dead was a top priority.

But what if there were a way to save him? She was willing to bet the crew's loyalty was strong enough to rally around, if she dared tell them the truth. At that thought, Gillian ran her hands through her shiny blonde hair.

Must be bonkers, she told herself.

Hadn't her experience with Weapons Specialist Bassett shown her the futility of trusting her sensors? Any member of her crew — including she, herself — could turn out to be an ANN Commission plant, like Zander.

One stray comment and the androids might hunt Harlan down. Even the reasonable thought that, now that the battle was waged, the Commission would have brought all of its operatives into play, didn't offer any comfort. As she well knew, "Reasonable" and "True" were only ever synonymous by chance.

"Commander," her navigator's trembling voice crackled over ship's intercom. "Suggest you consult the aft scanner."

"I take it for granted, Ensign, that your eyes are as good as mine," said Gillian. "What in Ararat's shadow is it?"

The news was not good. A squadron of ANN Commission fighters were closing in on the *Sweet Chariot* faster than she would have thought possible.

"Evasive maneuvers!" Gillian ordered. "Give me options, now!"

"They're moving too fast for fancy maneuvers," said her navigator. "What about the asteroid belt?"

Gillian consulted her console display.

"Can't reach it in time — in time to get smashed to bits, I might add." she said. "Anything else?"

"Bledraun's second moon is within range," said the trembling voice. "If we touch down there, the wireheads might not think it's worth the time to pursue."

"Do it," said Gillian, "But let's still send a spread of torpedoes and all the non-essential cargo we can ditch directly in their path before we go. Got that?"

Within seconds, the *Sweet Chariot* had veered off its original course and was banking down toward Seldra. Was it the torpedoes or the minor minefield of garbage that made the ANN Commission ships ignore it? Gillian was too relieved to care.

"Attention Terran Protectorate ship *Sweet Chariot*," a stern voice burst out over her private comlink. "This is Commodore Dirk Malteser of the *Gilead's Balm.* Cease unauthorized change of trajectory and return to battle formation immediately."

Gillian thought fast.

"Sir! System malfunction demands immediate landing to effect repairs!" she shouted. "Will rejoin fleet when...." she closed contact, hoping to simulate a comlink failure. She even considered ripping out the comsystem altogether, but thought better of it. In a pinch, a single radio message might be her crew's last hope.

"Approaching orbital attitude for Seldra," came her navigator's voice over the comlink. "Commander, if you don't mind my asking, where do you want to land?"

"Any settlements down there?" she asked, cursing herself for not having researched the Bledraun system more thoroughly on her way over from Reagan 3. She'd intended to, but Harlan — Captain Mars — had taken so much of her time with reviewing security protocols for the diplomatic corps, that was now, thankfully, in stasis.

Thinking back, Gillian couldn't help wondering if the meetings had been simply an excuse to spend time with her. But wait ... as embarrassingly pleasant as that line of thought was, she had the safety of her crew to think of. Lucky for her, her young navigator had no inkling of her tormented thoughts.

"Yes, Commander," said the twenty-something's voice. "A large colony, mostly Dralein and, well, it looks like business as usual down there."

"Right, Ensign," said Gillian. "Lay in a landing pattern straight away. I'm afraid business is about to get a tad more hectic." No more hectic, she was willing to bet, than her churning stomach, as she disobeyed an order for the first time in her military career. There would be consequences, she realized, when this came out in the wash.

At the moment, however, it wasn't clear that any of them would live to see "the wash." Not the soldiers fighting ANN Commission combatants on Bledraun, not Harlan, lost between here and the Fremdel in a tiny ship — and not even the *Sweet Chariot*, which was taking its chances on a lunar colony no one in the Protectorate had any intel on.

Might have regressed by now, she thought.

Shudders ran down her spine, until she pulled herself back together. Her fear was both uncalled for and entirely unsupported by data. As she knew from her extensive field training, the first step to survival was to make an objective analysis of the terrain and discover immediately what it could offer her.

"What kind of E-M rating you getting from the surface?" she asked her exogeologist.

The answer was encouraging. It turned out that the Dralein living on this moon had not descended into savagery. They might even be called on to.,...

"Terran Protectorate ship approaching Seldra on landing vector 7/015-23," a calm voice broke in on her thoughts through her comlink. "Please state the nature of your business."

Gillian saw no reason to shade the truth.

"Coming in out of the storm, I'm afraid," she said.

"And how," said the calm voice after a pause, "do we know you won't bring the storm with you?"

Gillian bit her lower lip.

"You fancy you have any chalinite down there, do you?" she asked.

"Not on this rock," said the voice.

"I shouldn't worry then," said Gillian.

"What exactly is happening on Bledraun?" said the voice.

"Let us land and I'll tell you all I know," said Gillian. "Otherwise, I may take my chances with the nearest star."

"Cleared for landing, Captain," said the voice, "You're not alone in thinking the unthinkable."

CHAPTER 36

At 0700 hours, old style, aboard the *Mighty Fortress*, Captain Enos was surprised to find two shift workers from the aft cargo bay approaching him rapidly in a curious, stiff march. It was as if they were both unused to walking.

"Your uniforms tell me your sleep period began 041 rotations ago," he said.

"We make it a point not to sleep through a galaxy-wide disaster, Captain," said Warvhex through her human host.

The captain's biomechanical spine stiffened.

"I need not remind you that cargo bay personnel are not permitted on the bridge," said Enos. "Return to quarters. I would prefer not to...."

"Captain," said Klarghex, "we'd prefer not to be here at all. But matters on Bledraun demand a shift in protocol."

"I hope you have an explanation for your insubordination," said Enos.

"We do," said Warvhex, "and you won't like it. But if you're as brilliant as our scans indicate, you'll immediately grasp the urgency of the situation."

The biomechanoid stared at them, and appeared to calm himself.

"Symbiotes," he said. "I won't ask how you arrived. What is it about the Quishiks that you want to tell me? I see their configuration and behavior conforms to every statistical model of an attack fleet."

"Captain, I promise you," said Warvhex, "what the Quishiks intend follows no known statistical model."

Over the course of the next few hours Warvhex and Klarghex shared with Enos every scrap of intel the symbiotes had gathered on the Quishiks, dating back to their first encounter at the Seshnel event horizon on the other side of the settled universe.

"Daunting," said Enos. "Yet I perceive what the humans would call 'a ray of hope.'"

"You have to be kidding," said Warvhex, as she shoved the biomechanoid by the shoulders — and was startled by her inability to budge him.

"It is my experience that any being's strength is also its weakness," said Enos.

"Great," said Klarghex. "Philosophy. How does that help anything?"

Enos stared at the young human woman in front of him and, for reasons he didn't understand, found himself wondering if she'd known Cricket Andersen.

"Your sarcasm is misplaced," he said. "The Quishiks' tenuous relationship to time, as we perceive it, is both a strength and a weakness. It must be a state of affairs they maintain in a delicate balance."

But, as Warvhex pointed out, that was exactly the thought behind the energy pulse the symbiotes had sent up from the surface of Bledraun, with Drashna's help.

"The principle was correct," said Enos. "But your methodology was flawed. It takes a multi-dimensional assault to destroy a multi-dimensional being."

"And what, Captain," said Warvhex, "is a multi-dimensional weapon?"

"That is what we must discover," said Enos. "But I know an intelligence who may be able to help. I refer to the AI possessed by Ambassador Draaf."

The two symbiote hosts glanced at each other.

"The ambassador is missing," said Warvhex. "But we received word on our way here that Yaldrint has turned up with the Krezovic brat he was tutoring and a human girl the boy rescued before the assault began on Bledraun."

"It is strange how often good news is mixed with bad," said Enos, looking distracted.

"I fear there's no valid statistical model for that either," said Warvhex. "But we do the best we can."

"Incorrect," said Enos. "In this scenario, we must exceed every previous standard we have set for ourselves. We cannot fail."

CHAPTER 37

Plaandrur Quishik Hlalkuhr pivoted on her twisting spine as she watched the battle intensify on Bledraun. The short-term success of her plan was clear: a deep rift had formed between the ruling parties in this sector of the galaxy. The evidence, splashed across her holoscreen, was invigorating.

Soon their infighting would inflame the passions of their political allies, and draw ever more sentients into all-out war. From one perspective, that outcome was entirely positive. Yet grumbling complaints from deep within the Quishik Cohort were beginning to dull the edge of Plaandrur's triumph.

Ever since she'd released a precise trickle of mental energy from the captured Dralein child, the immense network of Quishiks, past, present and future had grown restless. Why, Plaandrur's own earlier incarnations demanded, had she allowed the bloody war on Bledraun to outlive its usefulness as an act of provocation?

The humans killed in battle were useless to them. Whereas the living, including the Krezovic immigrants, could be used to revive dormant atemporal links and make the entire network stronger. At the same time, intense fighting interfered with the local probability matrix, which complicated access to the Dralein that were now in the care of the Ootray.

"Your incompetence is staggering," groused a distant voice from the depths of the Quishiks' collective consciousness.

Still, Plaandrur hesitated. No instance of a direct assault on the ANN Commission's operatives had appeared in any of her previous calculations. An assault would be, therefore, a Spur, a divergence from a Path. Not unprecedented mind you, but rare. But did *this* chain of events, she wondered, actually warrant the initiation of a Spur?

As hungry for fresh mental energy as anyone in the Cohort, Plaandrur understood the temptation. Each level of her being reeked of stagnation, as her mind struggled to maintain equilibrium, by executing ever more intricate variations on the same analysis of the Could and the May. Yet, if the Cohort were willing to consider initiating a Spur, was destroying the androids on Bledraun the most attractive option? If she were to tap the resources of another metaversal Cohort....

Yes, Plaandrur realized, a borrowing from the infinite regress of other metaverses, some of which were not facing a similar crisis, would provide a welcome burst of energy.

The question was whether the effort expended on such a temporary measure should be reserved for the permanent solution, which they had journeyed so far to obtain. What use was relief if it brought the Quishiks no closer to their goal?

For they were determined to step out of the maze of event horizons they'd been trapped in for eons, annihilate the Ootray, and sweep across vast stretches of the Continuum. They would grow stronger, denser, more unified, until no sentient culture in the universe could resist the call of the Quishiks.

"Begin," she said.

Her command unleashed an astonishingly effortless dismissal of the ANN Commission on Bledraun, down to its smallest clutch of mining equipment. Within seconds, the proud androids were flung far into what they would consider their future, until the cataclysmic breakup of the universe itself reduced them to a scattering hail of random energy patterns and dissociated protomatter.

"The time-bound below, my children," she cooed to the Cohort, "are yours. Savor them, but do not guzzle. We must be patient a while longer."

"*Rhaltholinarur, be praised,*" Plaandrur thought, at once reassured that her god had blessed her plans with success, and relieved to have silenced her noisy critics. Such were the mysterious ways of faith, she realized. Could not the Star Weaver have given her a sign of his intentions from the beginning of her quest?

Down on Bledraun, the startled forces of the Terran Protectorate, in concert with their space-borne commanders, were too preoccupied with the sudden disappearance of the androids to notice any difference in themselves.

Instead, they set about collecting their dead and wounded, breaking down their positions on the planet and returning to their orbiting war cruisers. Not until many months later, when sluggishness, loss and death had claimed significant numbers of them, would Admin begin to suspect they'd been attacked by an insidious force.

Plaandrur smiled to herself. Now that the immediate crisis had passed, she knew she would soon have the strength to begin the more energy-intensive process ahead. The Quishiks' triumph would never be complete until her forces had gained total control of both local and long-range Probability in this sector of space-time.

In preparation, as the cantankerous members of her time-sprung family clan were quick to insist, she must begin construction on a large-scale base of operations. With a fully appointed spaceport, the task of upgrading the Quishiks' ancient fleet would be vastly simplified. This would enable them to save strength for the all-out assault to come.

"Delicious," she said, as the plan for the spaceport began to take shape in the dark-red multi-faceted eye of her temporally distributed consciousness.

CHAPTER 38

Deep under the surface of Bledraun, in a sector of the Ootray city still unknown to Ungent, Cricket Andersen watched the shuffling, crawling, squeaking Dralein in full *sceraun* with empathy and, let's face it, disgust.

"Why am I here?" she asked the smooth walls of the corridor she'd entered, soon after waking that morning. She paused long enough for a glance back at the precise replica of her childhood bedroom that her hosts had dredged up from her memory. How, she wondered, had they seen into her mind so clearly?

The former Terran Protectorate navigator tiptoed a few feet down the corridor. Though her initial reunion with her childhood pet, Eddy, had been a joy, the delusion had faded. All trace of the genetically altered horse, Cricket's family farmyard and stables, as well as the buoyant glow of a happy childhood, had left her mind.

For what? she wondered.

Where was this place and why had ... someone ... reached into her central nervous system and made the temptation to go AWOL impossible to resist? In a way she was grateful. Whatever they did had blocked her obsession with Enos. But once the illusion faded, reality came roaring back.

Most likely, Cricket told herself, the biomechanoid had kept his ship as close as he dared to the Fremdel event horizon and the unknowable aliens he was the first Terran to detect. And to think the mission to the Fremdel was supposed to be a routine mapping and data collection exercise. She'd even been reassured that the *Sweet Chariot*, with a force of military veterans onboard, would be an accessible distance away.

There was simply no reason to expect any trouble. At the time she embarked from the orbital launchpad on Reagan 3, the Terran Protectorate was unmatched in technology and military power. Now, not only had she seen the telemetry from the alien ships, she'd seen this city, if that's what it was. After her experience with the delusion that led her here, she was wary of trusting her own eyes. So when a figure approached her, resembling her Uncle Preston, she decided to put her foot down.

"Cut it out," she said. "You owe me an explanation. Do you want my help? Are you serving me for dinner? What's your story?"

The figure faded and was replaced by a gaunt, yellowish reptilian, wrapped in a crinkly encounter suit — a perfect copy of the Halloween costume she'd worn as a teenager. Cricket's fists clenched.

"I'm not kidding!" she yelled. "I want the truth."

"Truth shifts," said a calm male voice, as the second figure disappeared. "Unfortunately, the reality you seek is unobtainable. We have not had physical form since before your species developed agriculture. Would you prefer us to remain invisible?"

"Yes," said Cricket, "but while you're at it, cut the spooky echo. I'm not a child."

"Better?" asked the voice again.

Cricket nodded, though she still wondered whether she could actually trust this voice.

"Why did you lead me here?" she asked.

Though the voice obliged her with an answer, Cricket found it hard to process.

"You think my experience with ... with Eddy ... could make a difference against this enemy?" she asked. "Even if I understood you, I don't see why the beings who built this city can't...."

"Were they here," said the voice, "we would not have troubled you."

"But you...." Cricket started.

"We are their shadows," the voice said with a hint of sadness.

"Simulations?" she asked.

"Close enough," said the voice. "Except to say we exist outside of time as you perceive it. More to the point, though we may think and feel like the Ootray, we cannot act. We merely guide events."

"I don't get it," said the human. "If you're not taking care of the Dralein I see down here, who is?"

Cricket listened to a long moment of silence and wondered if her life would ever get back to normal.

"You refer to automated processes set in motion many cycles ago," said the voice. "We ourselves do nothing to help them."

Cricket threw her arms up in the air.

"Why are you here at all, then?" she asked "I mean, come on, what's your function?"

"We are ... an early warning system, as you would say. We perceive a problem that we believe you and Har Draaf may be able to help with."

"The Grashardi ambassador?" asked Cricket. "Can you at least *try* to make sense?"

A second, tremulous voice chimed in.

"Please," it said. "Time is short. We resorted to deception out of panic. But the threat is real and the galaxy urgently needs your help."

"Just the galaxy?" asked Cricket.

"For now," said the first voice. "Once the Quishiks drain the minds of this planet, they will branch out to other sectors of space-time, well within the scope of your own life cycle."

Cricket looked around her. The underground city's elaborate, yet graceful structures spoke of vast intelligence and the voices, whatever they were, were too earnest to ignore. The word "Quishiks" didn't register with her at first, until she remembered Enos referring to the species he discovered by that name.

"Take me to Har Draaf," she said. "I'll see if I can help, even if I do have no clue what you're talking about."

Faster than she would have thought possible, a small hovercar, cast in a blue-gray composite material appeared next to her. The former Terran Protectorate operative stepped in and smiled at the red FASTEN SEATBELT sign that blinked insistently on the hovercar's tan padded dashboard, until she complied.

The moment the belt clicked, Cricket felt the hovercar rise straight up, before it shot out along a winding trajectory. Whatever this would lead to, she decided, it felt right. But what, she wondered, would she say at her court martial?

CHAPTER 39

At the outer reaches of the Bledraun solar system, a symbiote spacecraft followed a meandering trajectory, roughly describing a figure eight. At the figure's intersection, a quick pass near Bledraun gave the lone occupant two chances each three-day cycle to assess the situation on the planet's surface.

Though she had now recovered from a mild concussion, Drashna lacked the training required to make, much less grasp, a full data scan of the surface. It had taken every scrap of knowledge she'd picked up over the years to redirect the ship from the collision course she'd set it on by accident. If she wanted to know the status of Bledraun, she'd have to rely on output from the ship's AI.

"No further evidence of armed conflict," the AI's measured voice rang out over the intercom, during the ship's most recent pass by Drashna's homeworld.

"Who knows what that means?" said the former Dralein leader. There was no way to know why the fighting had stopped. Had one side won, or was *everyone* dead? Regardless, the conflict itself meant that Warvhex's prediction had come true. The Dralein had been thrown into an early *sceraun* by Krezovic militants, wearing theta wave regulator bracelets. And soon after, the ANN Commission had launched a brutal assault on the humans.

Drashna was anxious to see the extent of the damage for herself. Yet, considering her food and life support systems were worn down to near-panic levels, it wasn't clear that life on war-scarred Bledraun would be measurably better. Heart broken, she wondered if it might be preferable to die of asphyxiation in space.

But no, she decided, not while there was still a chance to rescue Caronya from the Quishiks. She squeezed her eyes shut and forced herself to live in the moment, as she set aside two nagging trains of thought.

One was an anxious rehearsal of her deepest fear: That she'd soon see Caronya's ashes in a traditional Dralein burial urn. The other was a disturbing vision of life as a second-class citizen on Bledraun, once the mind-expanding experience of the *sceraun* had passed her by.

That was aside, she realized, from missing the children conceived at this time. The birth of fragile *dracleinyi,* after a decidedly non-human gestation process, was a blessing she might never have another chance to see. Even, that is, if she lived out an average two-hundred-year lifespan. The adult Dralein now underground would live much longer, of course. The "biological clock" contained in their chromosomes would be reset by the remarkable process that would soon reshape their future. Drashna blinked her wet eyelids open again.

"I won't stay behind to see what I've lost," she said. "I'll take Caronya off-world. I *will*."

Drashna consulted ship's AI, then ordered it to plot a course for a Bledraun province well outside of Jeldren. Instinct told her the countryside might offer better survival odds. But if Drashna had expected that choosing a way forward would ease her spirit, she was soon disappointed.

"Terran Protectorate escape pod locking on to our trajectory," said ship's AI, as if it were merely reporting the weather. The pod, thankfully, wasn't armed. But why, Drashna wondered, would a stray vehicle pursue her? The answer, while it gave her no immediate cause for alarm, was still puzzling.

"Mind if I follow you in, Madam Chaudron?" said a strangely good-natured voice.

"I can't stop you," said Drashna. "Just explain to me why my ship's AI insists you're dead."

"Machines are so adorable, now aren't they? Especially when they get their data all twisted up in their unders," said the voice of Harlan Mars.

"I have no idea what you mean," said Drashna.

"Talk to you on the surface then, Madame Chaudron," said Harlan.

"Stop calling me that!" Drashna screamed. "Stop it right now!"

But the human had already closed contact and was busy pondering the plan forming in his thoughts. How he wished he could run it by Gillian's brilliant tactical mind — and then run his hands along her perfect shoulders.

"Cut it out," he told himself. "Gotta get me some survival first."

Had he known that Gillian was, at that moment, standing in a room full of Dralein colonists, he might have been worried for her safety as much as his own.

Truth be told, Gillian felt more secure on Seldra than she had for the past week. Her hosts, whose ancestors had settled on Bledraun's second moon about five-hundred years earlier, were eager to show her one of several intricate technology centers they'd built over the centuries. It stood less than three kilometers away from the small spaceport where the *Sweet Chariot*'s landers had recently touched down.

As she gazed around, Gillian was struck by the sleek lines of the complex and its uncluttered design. By contrast, a building of comparable size on the Dralein homeworld would have overflown with tasteful ornamentation and been embedded with all sorts of creature comforts.

Yet Gillian would never have thought to call Seldran architecture "functional." There was, for example, an undeniable grace to the elevated walkway of fiber-reinforced concrete that she now strolled with her guide.

Gillian's mental notes were distracting her from the overview that Verohme, a top Seldran science officer, was giving her of his society. As he spoke, his shiny white fur appeared to glow. He looked so different from the Dralein she'd seen on Bledraun that Gillian began to wonder if the Seldrans had indulged in a bit of cosmetic genome remapping.

Also in contrast to the average resident of Bledraun, Verohme wore loose-fitting robes in dark pastel colors tied with thin, rawhide strings. While Gillian was charmed by his subdued sense of style, Gillian found the current Seldran trend toward clogs made from pale neo-wood fiber absolutely incomprehensible. But what was her guide saying now?

" ... so we naturally take a different stance on the role of the *sceraun* in our society," said her tall, thin guide.

"In what way?" asked Gillian.

"Within a few cycles of settling here," said Verohme, "a new philosophy arose that liberated us from the old ways. Instead of seeing the *sceraun* as a curse, which we must passively accept, we re-imagined it as a positive force we could harness for our own ends."

"Harness?" asked Gillian, stopping short. The word had fallen out of her version of Planetary Standard about one-hundred-twenty-five years before, yet its meaning was clear enough from the context. "You mean to say you can control it?"

"Control," said Verohme, "is a harsh word. I prefer to think we work in harmony with the phenomenon of *sceraun*. We shape it to our needs, as we would a natural fabric."

Though Gillian prided herself on being scientifically literate, the Dralein's words made her head spin. But as her guide continued, her confusion gave way to a startling realization.

"You must be...." she started. "But, right, of course, you're serious. You actually induce *sceraun*."

"Not exactly." said Verohme, as he brushed the white fur on one arm with the opposite hand. "What the homeworld refers to as *sceraun* is a full-scale, broad-spectrum phenomenon. We have perfected the art of sculpting the mind, with controlled bursts of theta wave stimulation."

"Sculpting for different mental capabilities then, is it?" asked Gillian. "Can't say as I agree that's entirely ethical, if you don't mind my saying so."

Verohme stared at her, his thin fingers tense at his sides.

"Please,' he said, "I can't explain more than the broadest outlines of our approach while we walk. And I recall you had an urgent message for us?"

Gillian closed her eyes tight and cursed herself for getting off track — though she'd rather have dwelled on the fine points of scientific ethics than dealt with the horror of the Quishiks and the war they'd provoked.

"Sorry," she said. "I suppose I am getting ahead of myself. Is it much farther until we reach your Chaudron? I'm afraid I do have quite a bit of bad news."

Verohme nodded.

"Treluhne is this way," he said. "Though you may be disappointed by his lack of interest in the situation on Bledraun."

"Right. But 'the situation' isn't limited to Bledraun," said Gillian.

They walked on, past what looked like a large computer array on a completely different scale than anything Gillian had seen outside of historical footage. What would this small moon need with so much computational power?

But around the next corner, an imposing archway of solid quartz made her forget her questions.

"Through here," said Gillian's guide, as he led her under the archway to a massive stateroom. Seated at a large stainless steel desk in the middle of the room was a thin figure, a Dralein unlike any Gillian had seen before.

"Excuse me, Treluhne," said Verohme, with a slight tremor, "Captain Cavendish to see you."

Gillian did her best to hide her astonishment at the sight of a wraith-thin Dralein male — with a bright yellow pelt.

"You may be amused to know," said Treluhne, "that you're the first human we've seen on Seldra."

Gillian stared down at the tips of her polished neo-leather boots.

"At another time, I might have taken pride in that," she said. "But now...."

"Please. Sit," said Treluhne, as he pulled out a chair from the stateroom's polished floor. "Don't be alarmed. It's an old trick we learned from the Ootray."

Gillian plopped down on the chair that, until a second ago didn't exist. Her frustration aside, her aching feet could not resist the chance to rest.

"From the ... the who?" she asked. "Never mind. I need to catch you up on the...."

"The Ootray are an ancient people you need to hear about if you have any hope of pushing the Quishiks back where they came from," said Treluhne.

"So you know," said Gillian. "Yet you're so ... sanguine about ... about things."

The thin Dralein's mouth stretched into a tight smile.

"That's the student of Probability talking," he said. "The rest of me is as terrified as you are."

Treluhne pushed his chair back from his gleaming desk.

"Come on," he said. "You need to see what the Ootray left behind."

Gillian stared at him a moment before following him to the other side of the state room. There, a graceful recess nestled itself, as if alive, waiting for visitors. Treluhne waved a furry hand over what looked like a ceramic disk embedded in the right side of the recess. In spite of herself, Gillian gasped as a sliding door snapped open.

"The Ootray called it a *djorcrelul*, which means 'Probability Reader.' You saw this on your way in," said the bright yellow Dralein.

Treluhne shambled through the recess and into the cavernous room Gillian had passed through with Verohme minutes ago.

"Yes," said Gillian. "The computer array. It *is* impressive."

"It's not a computer," said Treluhne, "except in the most general sense. Its real function is the analysis and management of Probability."

Gillian stared up at the complex arrangement of ovoid units and subunits. What in the name of Epsilon Eridani was it? She glanced over at her Dralein host.

"It's still daunting to me, too," said Treluhne, "and this is my ninetieth cycle studying it."

"You *must* have learned something about it," said Gillian.

"I've learned not to touch it," said Treluhne. "For the most part, I observe."

"But what does 'managing Probability' even mean?" asked Gillian.

The leader of the Seldrans looked at Gillian and clicked his broad tongue.

"You must be hungry and battle-weary," he said. "Rest now, I'll tell you more after Common Meal."

"But there isn't time," Gillian's voice rang out, and for a moment, managed to block out the bustling noise of the Dralein scientific crew. "The Quishiks...."

Treluhne pointed up to the array's central ovoid.

"This array says you're wrong," he said. "Anxious as you are, know this: Time is the one thing you don't need to concern yourself about. Go, rest, and soon after, I'll answer as many questions as I can. But first, one question for you. Yesterday the device projected a high probability that the Quishiks had captured a Dralein child — formerly held by the symbiotes, if you can believe it. You have any data to confirm that?"

Gillian sighed.

"Nothing but rumors," she said. "And, I dare say, flimsy ones at that. But I have heard that the symbiotes have had a hold over Drashna for weeks now."

"What?" asked Treluhne.

"One version of the story claims Drashna's daughter, Caronya, has an illness only the symbiotes can cure," said Gillian.

"Many are the twists and turns of evil, once it gets started," said Treluhne.

"And this particular twist appears to have started long ago," said Gillian. "So long ago, I'm beginning to think any countermeasures we attempt won't make a particle of difference."

"There, you see?" said Treluhne. "Exhaustion. Until later, then."

With that, the tall Seldran leader turned back toward the recess they'd just come through and re-entered his stateroom. Exasperated, Gillian felt her breath sticking in her throat and nearly jumped out of her skin when a shy young Dralein touched her elbow.

"Excuse me, Captain," she said. "My name is Yelahne. Your crew is waiting for you in the main dining room."

Gillian squared her shoulders.

"Right," she said. "Lead on then, would you? Now that you mention it, I am rather famished. Are you Seldrans always so dramatic?"

"I ... sorry ... I don't understand," said Yelahne. "We don't hear much Planetary on this moon."

"Don't give it a thought, my dear," said Gillian. "Tell me, do you enjoy living on Seldra?"

"It's beautiful here," said Yelahne. "But my goal is to visit other worlds someday."

"Admirable," said Gillian. "Let's hope there are still other worlds for you to visit by the time you're ready."

Yelahne squinted at Gillian.

"I ... don't understand that either," she said.

"Neither do I, Dear," said Gillian. "Let's eat then, shall we?"

Gillian took one last look at the Ootray ... whatever-it-was ... behind her, then followed Yelahne out. All the way to the Science Center's elegant cafeteria, Gillian felt she was being watched.

CHAPTER 40

It had taken a week since the fighting stopped, but the eerie silence that had settled on Bledraun was starting to feel permanent. To the surviving Krezovic population and the few off-worlders who still huddled with them, it was equally eerie how *suddenly* the air had cleared, the ground had steadied and the bitter smell of singed plastics began to dissipate.

But after days of shelling, screaming and the constant whine of lase fire hitting its mark, the survivors dared to believe it was safe to crawl out of hiding. Up to this point, despite the lack of food and water, the Krezovic's remapped human genome had left them in much better shape than unmodified humans in a similar situation.

Now, however, Hunger emerged in their minds as a stern voice, demanding immediate action. Might there still be canned goods in the Jeldren's grocery stores, restaurants and private homes? Maybe there was food out of town, in orchards, on farms or swimming in the rivers and streams. But there was no way to know what part of the water system was safe, and what part had been contaminated by toxic runoff from organic and industrial waste.

In their delirious state, these Krezovic dreamed of a finding an intact electrical generator, whose solar panels could still power a replicator. But odds were the underground storehouses of refrigerated organic molecules the replicators depended on were no more than craters now.

Besides, while the survivors were well enough informed about Dralein technology, a great many had lived their lives dependent on the Dralein themselves for technical support. Start up a generator? Fix a replicator, refrigeration unit, or water pump? Well, there was always the chance they'd find a magic wand among the rubble.

And yet, as miners and manufacturers of the theta wave regulator bracelets that brought down the Dralein, the Krezovics did know what to forage for. Over the following weeks, starting with makeshift shelters and cooking pits carved out of the planet's rich, loamy soil, they would slowly built pockets of order across a planet ravaged by greedy off-worlders.

Fortunately, what equipment had survived functioned with a speed and efficiency unimaginable — until the quest for deep-space travel sparked a technological revolution. Now, a single working equipment replicator, could crank out everything from spare parts to complex circuitry for hundreds of different mechanical or electronic devices. All it needed were the raw materials embedded in Bledraun's crust — the very wealth, ironically, that had brought down disaster on the Draleins' furry heads.

Fast as possible, trading routes would be established between the smoldering relics of major cities and the countryside. With the battle cut short by the Quishiks, damage to farmland on the southern continents had been far less extensive than it might have been. Soon produce could be bartered for machinery and vice versa. Among the battered remains of Bledraun's automated fleet of field harvesters, those Krezovics with more technical savvy found much to salvage and reuse.

Also not lost on the survivors were the huge stockpiles of abandoned weaponry left behind by bewildered androids as they were whisked out of Time by the Quishiks. Most contained fully-charged power cells, so they came in handy for hunting and for defending the new settlements from the ragged criminal element that always rises up in times of crisis.

And in a rare moment of saving grace, the Krezovics found a few working comlinks among the ruins. These enabled the more technically savvy survivors to hack into the Terran Protectorate network and bounce signals, from the human battle cruisers still in orbit, down to central locations on each of Bledraun's nine continents. The result was anything but reliable. Yet when the sky was clear, Krezovic settlements across the planet eventually had a primitive communications network.

Of course, no one doubted a new android force would eventually return to Bledraun. Soon after, the Terran military would swoop in, too, but the humans' hatred of the ANN Commission did not guarantee they'd defend the Krezovic survivors.

With that in mind, the Krezovics began a haphazard military training program, the moment they were strong enough. With nothing to go on, beyond their sketchy memory of fictional battle scenes, progress was slow. Among the most eager recruits was Grauth, former leader of the Krezovics' misguided strike against the Dralein.

"Can't believe I left my homeworld for this," he grumbled into the comlink system he was struggling to repair. "I sucked up to wireheads and now I'm stuck out on the edge of freaking nowhere. Lost my bonded, too."

Lately, the thought of Drolet haunted him like a low-budget horrorvid ghost. She was living now on the other side of Jeldren. He'd seen her one afternoon while foraging for supplies. But the blank look she gave him meant one of two things. Either she was finally through with him, or the shock of war had erased him from her memory. He preferred to think the former, but what good did it do?

"Unless the situation changes, we probably got a hundred rotations left before we're finished," he muttered again.

No one could fault him for despairing, especially with the latest development. Up to a few days before, with the food shortage, lack of power, poor sanitation, no medpods and a supply of potable water that was on the iffy side of tenuous, there'd been plenty enough to worry about. But now, word-of mouth reports were coming in from local traders, of a huge structure, a spaceport, most likely, arising spontaneously to the southwest of Chalintren, Bledraun's second largest city.

"No machinery, no androids, no raw materials. It doesn't even look like it's being built," one of Grauth's post-disaster friends had told him. "Looks like its growing."

Disturbing as that thought was, it pointed to a greater evil. Could the rumors be true, of an unknown species of tremendous power, hovering near the Fremdel event horizon?

More than ever, he wished Drolet would give him another chance. But, poor fool that he was, he'd let a gleaming liar make him betray what he cared about most. The ANN Commission, he'd realized too late, was out for nothing but its own advancement.

CHAPTER 41

In a small suite of rooms on the sixth level of a mid-sized space-folder, two fidgety teenagers and an ethereally calm AI tried to sort out the jarring events of the past weeks. The design of their tight quarters was surprisingly efficient, which created a welcome illusion of spaciousness.

"Can't believe we're stuck here with these ... whatever they are," said Trinity. It had been two days since she, Yaldrint and Shol had been whisked up to the symbiote's ship by a transmat field.

"The correct term is 'symbiote,' Ms. Hudson," said Yaldrint.

At the moment, the Grashardi AI was hooked into the ship's power system.

"How's the recharge going?" Shol asked her.

"Well enough, thank you," said Yaldrint, "though the symbiote's replication of a Grashardi power adaptor is less than perfect."

"On Reagan 3, all powering stations are wireless," said Trinity, with a toss of her hair.

"That is the interstellar standard, of course," said Yaldrint. "But a wireless energy transmission on the scale I need to recharge would likely attract the attention of our enemy."

"You think they haven't spotted this ship by now?" asked Shol.

"Unknown," said Yaldrint. "Still, it seems prudent to maintain a low sensor profile. You would not want them to think, for example, that we are charging weapons."

"I wish Har Draaf were here," said Shol. "He'd know what to do."

"The ambassador's experience serves him well in many contexts," said Yaldrint. "Once I'm at capacity again, I may be able to find him."

"Can't stand sitting around when there's so much trouble," said Trinity. "I have no clue whether the ship Father's on is still ... operational."

A young Krezovic female appeared in the threshold of their quarters, wearing a jumpsuit of a shimmery dark blue fabric. To Shol's eyes, she was a beauty, but he dared not give her more than a glance.

"The *Sweet Chariot* was last seen heading for Seldra," she said.

"How would *you* know that?" asked Trinity.

The Krezovic's face lit up.

"Don't get your unders in a bunch, Dear," she said. "My host is too old for your boyfriend. But to answer your question, it's my job to know the position of all ships in this sector."

"So you're...." Trinity started.

"Opalhex, Intel Corps," said the symbiote from within the Krezovic female.

"Who are they hiding from?" asked Shol.

Opalhex raised her host's right eyebrow.

"My host says you're very astute," she said. "Who knows? Maybe you have a chance with her after all."

Trinity's face flushed.

"If I may, what is the purpose of your visit?" asked Yaldrint.

"You," said the symbiote. "You're wanted on the *Mighty Fortress*. Captain Enos ... "

"Cannot comply, Ms. Opalhex," said the AI. "I must stay with these two young people, for their protection."

Opalhex made her host reach for the handle on Yaldrint's case.

"I don't have time for this," she said. "Come on, Squawk Box, let's ... OW!"

Shol and Trinity jumped up from their cots at the quick flash of searing, low-level lase fire that ripped out of the right side of Yaldrint's casing.

"I will not leave them," said Yaldrint. "Nor is it necessary. The Captain and I can communicate perfectly well through shielded radio or holotransmission."

Opalhex rubbed the outer edge of her right hand, which the AI's crack shot had barely grazed.

"I'll ... convey your refusal," she said, softly.

Shol clapped his hands over his mouth to keep from laughing as he watched the symbiote walk her host out of the room.

"Craters!" he exclaimed. "I didn't know androids could shoot like that."

"It is a simple matter of adequate sensors and processing speeds," said Yaldrint. "As a point of clarification, however, I could never be considered an android."

"Because you're ... immobile?" asked Trinity.

"Primarily," said Yaldrint.

"Have you ever wanted to have a, you know, a body?" asked Shol.

Yaldrint's status lights flickered a moment.

"The ability to *desire* is not within my operational parameters," she said. "However, I do notice that my field notes contain numerous observations detailing instances in which I could have been more useful to Har Draaf if I were mobile."

"You love him, don't you?" asked Trinity.

"Again, Ms. Hudson," Yaldrint's rich alto voice cut in, "my operational parameters do not include...."

Shol and Trinity gasped and their eyes flicked up to the hazy figure materializing before them.

"Intelligence Yaldrint," said the holographic image of Captain Enos, once it had resolved itself. "We need your assistance."

"Continue, Captain," said Yaldrint.

Enos nodded at Shol and Trinity.

"Are you sure you wish these children to hear our discussion?" he asked.

"As it is their future as much as our own that is in danger," said Yaldrint, "I would say we owe it to them."

With no more hesitation, the biomechanoid launched into a discussion of the tactical problems facing any successful assault on the atemporal Quishiks.

"You appear to be attempting the direct manipulation of spatio-temporal continuity itself," said Yaldrint.

"As an extension of existing space-fold techniques," said Enos. "You are, of course, familiar with the equations."

"Yes," said Yaldrint. "However, no existing space-folding process has nearly the required precision."

And so the detailed technical wrangling droned on. Shol's head was nodding, and he'd almost drifted off to sleep, when he felt Trinity's lips whispering in his ear.

"Let's explore more of the ship," she said.

"Where do you want to go?" asked Shol.

Trinity took her Krezovic boyfriend by his slick, curved hand and led him into the ship's main corridor, which was blessedly empty of the symbiote crew. Yaldrint, for her part, did nothing to stop them. The two teenagers, she reasoned, were understandably bored.

"We need to find the ship's data center," said the human girl. "Father says the symbiotes steal all kinds of technology from their hosts ... more than they have time to process."

"So ... what...." said Shol, "you think we can find out stuff that AI captain doesn't know? And anyway, Yaldrint can tap into anything, right?"

Trinity tugged at Shol's arm.

"Who knows?" she said. "What if a Grashardi AI isn't ... configured correctly ... to access symbiote data?"

Shol's shiny brow furrowed.

"Who knows if *we're* con ... whatever," said Shol.

"We have to try," said Trinity. "We can't sit here like babies and watch the galaxy get destroyed. I have to find out where that data center is."

Shol's chest swelled as he drank in her magnificent determination. But there was no time for day dreams. The random bits of information he'd picked up on the street came in handy, as he remembered what his old crime boss, Ulandroz had told him.

"Symbiotes?" Ulandroz had said. "They do every freakin' thing in a circle."

With that thought in mind, Shol called up his personal scanner and hoped the conflict on Bledraun hadn't disrupted his connection.

"Here," he said.

Trinity's eyes opened wide as she took in the holographic image that Shol's scanner had projected against the corridor wall. It showed the interior layout of a typical symbiote ship, with each of its levels arranged in concentric rings.

"It's, like, the map, or whatever of a symbiote ship that I got from Ulandroz," he said.

Trinity squinted at Shol.

"Where would he get that?" she asked.

"A symbiote took him over once," said Shol, "so he had a chance to learn a few things when it was sleeping."

"How'd he get free?" asked Trinity "I heard...."

Shol's snickering interrupted her. Ulandroz, apparently, had made the most of the small margin of freedom that the symbiote granted him out of necessity, to ensure his personality vectors didn't collapse. He filled his mind with the most disgusting images he could imagine from his horrific existence as a shadowy crime boss.

"Took about half a cycle," said Shol, "the symbiote couldn't take it anymore and dove out of his neck, fast as a neutrino on *grezlach*. C'mon, the map says Level 3."

The Krezovic nudged Trinity toward a maglev lift a short way down the silent corridor.

"Where are they?" asked Trinity.

Shol recounted more of what he'd heard from Ulandroz. The symbiote lifecycle operated within a tightly organized framework of biochemical checks and balances. Their ability to merge with and control members of almost every known sentient species was paid for with high demands on their energy reserves.

"They sleep a lot," said Shol.

"But wouldn't they sleep in shifts?" asked Trinity.

"Dunno," said Shol. "My old boss said they were linked ... in their minds."

So when one member of a local symbiote community became exhausted, they all did — or rather, were too tired to resist the trend. What Shol didn't know was that Opalhex, who had just recently merged with a

Krezovic down on Bledraun, had not yet synched her mind with the other symbiotes on board.

"I figure we only have, like, 020 rotations," said Shol. "Then you'll be, like, tripping over them."

"Ugh," said Trinity, as the doors of the maglev elevator opened. The deep hush of Level Six persisted down there, accompanied by the muted purr of a powerful cooling system. Shol checked the map he'd received from Ulandroz again and pointed to a set of double doors down the corridor to their left. The two teenager's hands trembled as they pushed the doors open.

"Holy *quelx*," said Shol.

The inside of the symbiote data center was breathtaking. It was a roomful of gleaming components, which fit together in a complex constellation of metadigital processors. As neither Shol nor Trinity could know, the center was an exact copy of similar centers built by the Jachtrahlese of the Outer Systems. The Jachtrahlese and many more such distant civilizations, were virtually unknown to the Terran Protectorate.

Shol stared up at the sleek holographic interface rising before them.

"Weird," he said. "How we gonna … talk to this thing?"

"Please state the nature of your request," said a soothing bass voice, which seemed to rise from below the data center's dark, polished floors. Trinity felt Shol's elbow digging into her ribs.

"The … Quishiks," she gulped. "How can we stop them?"

"Specify," said the voice after a pause.

"We have to stop the Quishiks' attack on…." Trinity started.

"Warning." said the calm voice. "This service may not be used for the promulgation of war or related violence."

Trinity's eyes squeezed shut.

"Now what?" she asked.

Shol decided it was time he spoke up. His first thought was to change the subject.

"You have a name?" he asked.

"I have no name in the conventional sense. However, my reference number is 4BDN/56," said the massive AI.

'Well … uh … 56," he asked, "I have, like, a medical question. Do the Quishiks ever get sick?"

The AI's status lights blinked in a nearly hypnotic pattern for a good thirty seconds.

"The question is too broad to be answered directly," said 4BDN/56. "I will attempt to provide relevant information that may help you narrow the focus of your research."

"Thanks … I guess," said Shol. With help like this, he feared, they'd be stuck in the data center for hours.

"Like all organic life forms, the Quishiks are theoretically vulnerable to a range of microbial and viral infections," the AI began.

Trinity, who'd been holding her breath to keep from panicking, let out a gasp. This invisible AI was seriously creepy.

"Theoretically?" she asked. "Explain."

"Because they exist outside of the dimensions we associate with the term "chronological time," said the massive data complex, "the Quishiks lack a fixed set of coordinates that could serve as a locus of infection. Allow me to demonstrate.…"

Shol held up both hands.

"No thanks," he said. "I get it. No infections or whatever. Any other diseases?"

"The Quishiks' atemporality does not preclude the onset of mental illness," said the AI. "Recent observations suggest their atemporal state makes them prone to what, speaking loosely, we may describe as paranoia."

"What?" asked Trinity. "Why?"

"In simplest terms," 4BDN/56 continued, "the cognitive instability inherent to their atemporality is insufficiently compensated for at the deepest levels of their consciousness."

Trinity pressed her hands into either side of her head.

"So they're not … comfortable with living outside of Time?" she asked.

"Hey!" a voice shouted behind them. It was Opalhex again. The symbiote flung her Krezovic host at the two teenagers and dragged them out of the data center by their shirt collars.

"You both need to stay in your quarters," said the symbiote.

"Why?" asked Shol. "Your ship so cheap, a couple of kids could bust it up?"

"We're at war, Junior," said Opalhex. "Stay put and you won't soil your diaper."

Without another word, she pulled a lase pistol from inside her jumpsuit and pushed Shol and Trinity into the maglev elevator. Before long, they were back inside their quarters, where Captain Enos and Yaldrint were still mulling over the available data.

"Keep a better eye on these two," said the symbiote to Yaldrint, "if you don't want to be shoved out an airlock."

"Where have you been?" asked the Grashardi AI.

"We were trying to find some answers," said Trinity.

"I appreciate your willingness to help," said Enos's holojection. "However, you must understand, we have the full resources of.…"

"Did your freakin' resources tell you the Quishiks are sick in the head?" asked Shol. And for the next few minutes, the youngest members of the war effort recounted what they'd learned from 4BDN/56.

CHAPTER 42

Despite having been in the Terran Protectorate military for the last ten years, former Lieutenant Cricket Andersen had seen precious few non-humans. The number of so-called aliens she'd actually met was even smaller. And yet, after a few minutes of conversation with Ungent, she realized the differences between them mattered less and less. He'd even managed to make her laugh.

"It's true," Ungent had said. "The first human ambassador to Grashard had stocked his replicators with lobster recipes. When news got out, it was a major scandal."

But within a few minutes, the mood of these unlikely collaborators had darkened.

"I'm glad there's someone else here to talk to besides those holograms," said Cricket. "But I still have no idea why they led me here."

"They gave you no explanation?" asked Ungent.

The former navigator recounted her confusing conversation with the Ootray AI.

"Can't see what horses have to do with anything way out here," she said.

Ungent stared at her a moment.

"There are no horses on Grashard," he said. "How would you describe one?"

Cricket frowned.

"You've never even seen an image of a horse?" she said. "I thought you said you'd been dealing with the Protectorate for eighty cycles."

"Yes, Ms. Andersen," said Ungent, with a wave of his scaly hands, "I'm also aware that humans still have the curious habit of riding these creatures — presumably for sport. But I was referring to their temperament."

Cricket's eyes glazed, as she was drawn back into her childhood memories.

"They're sensitive," said Cricket, "so they startle easily. Get them spooked and they can really fly off the handle."

Ungent chuckled.

"It appears you're straining the translation grid a bit," he said. "But I think I know what you mean. If we could scare the Quishiks, we might be able to gain the upper hand."

"Could these ... beings ... really be related to horses?" asked Cricket.

In response, the hologram Ungent knew as Dlalamphrur appeared before them.

"In a distant way" she said. "We based their genome on that of a species not that far removed from terrestrial equines."

"Well, if they're anything like the animals I grew up with," said Cricket, "you'd have to be careful. Scare them, and they run away. But get them really frightened and they strike out blindly. You do not want that."

"What did you do when your horse got 'spooked' as you say?" asked Ungent.

"I used to soothe Eddy with my voice," she said. "But Eddy trusted me. I'd known him since he was a foal — a baby, Har Draaf."

Ungent walked over to a bright red railing a meter or so away and aimed his eyestalks down at the habitats provided for the Dralein by the Ootray's vast, automated caretaking system. Trembling, he watched as the intricate city-within-a-city continually adapted itself to the Dralein's changing needs. To think the noble Dralein were now so wretched as to need this level of caretaking! His pulse raced as he turned back toward Dlalamphrur.

"How could we earn the trust of the Quishiks?" he asked.

"By deceiving them," said Dlalamphrur.

And before Ungent could respond that deception was a time-tested battle strategy, the Ootray AI told him and Cricket about a fail-safe mechanism they'd built into the Quishiks.

"We had hoped never to use it," said the AI. "It violates our commitment to respect all life forms."

"Seriously?" asked Cricket. "You programmed them to believe in a ... in a fake god?"

But as Dlalamphrur explained, the definition of real and unreal was tied directly to sense perceptions and personal experience.

"Why, for example," she asked, "do you believe what I have told you?"

"I have no reason to doubt it," said Cricket, with a shrug. "Not with everything I've seen since I got here. I guess that's more of a feeling though, isn't it?"

"Exactly," said Dlalamphrur. "You think we could give the Quishiks — our creations — a false belief and so you believe that we did. But you have no proof."

"You also appear trustworthy and are going to great lengths to help the Dralein," said Ungent.

"Yes, another collateral basis for trust," said the alien AI. "Still, an assumption. Perhaps our motives for helping the Dralein are not what they appear."

Cricket stamped her right boot into the tiled floor beneath her.

"Walls of Jericho, we have to start somewhere!" she yelled.

And as Dlalamphrur was quick to point out, this was exactly why the Quishiks could be led by their implanted memory of a beneficent god. But as she explained further, the Ootray had done even more tinkering with the Quishiks' memory.

"We also created a variable field for a prophesy," she said, "which we recently began reprogramming to align with local probability."

"You alter their belief system in real time?" asked Cricket. "Sorry, that seems kind of cruel."

"Agreed," said Dlalamphrur. "But we installed this final fail-safe in their minds after we realized the Quishiks were hopelessly incurable. It is one more way our stupidity has followed us across the length and breadth of space-time.

Ungent rubbed his mandibles.

"But having a way to calm the Quishiks is useless if we have no way to frighten them," he said.

"In that respect," said Dlalamphrur. "events have moved faster than you realize. Forces you are familiar with are already planning an assault."

"You mean the Terran Protectorate?" said Ungent. "I doubt we can count on them alone."

"But they are being assisted by the Kaldhex," said the AI, "the beings you know as symbiotes."

"That's a first," said Cricket. "Must be some kind of trap."

"Please, Ms. Andersen," said Ungent, "the symbiotes have as much reason to fear the Quishiks as you."

"They are working right now with your friend Captain Enos," said the Ootray hologram.

"Hardly my friend," said Cricket.

"The Dralein colonists on Seldra are also involved," said Dlalamphrur. "It appears our ancestors once settled there, too, and left behind an impressive array of equipment."

"But would the Seldrans even know how to use it?" asked Ungent.

"That, Har Draaf, remains to be seen," said Dlalamphrur.

CHAPTER 43

Refreshed as she was after a satisfying meal with her crew, Gillian Cavendish, acting captain of the Terran Protectorate ship, *Sweet Chariot*, still found the Seldran's explanation of Probability manipulation ... well, confusing was the least of it.

"Tell me if I have this right," she said to Treluhne. "You believe you can map out a strategy to stop the Quishiks based on readouts from that device?"

Despite the soft, bioluminescent light of his state room, the tall Dralein's bright yellow fur appeared to glow, as if it were lit from within.

"The strategy is already implied by the data," said Treluhne. "My job is to deduce what steps to take in real time. The problem is, the data makes no sense."

Gillian felt her heart sink. For this, she disobeyed a direct order from Admin?

"What do you mean?" she asked.

The leader of Seldra's Executive Counsel looked down at the neo-wood clogs encasing his furry feet.

"The strategy seems to involve working up a credible threat to the Quishiks, issuing a warning and ... this is so hard to accept...." his voice trailed off.

"Please, Chaudron," said Gillian, "we must do our utmost to defeat them, no matter the casualties involved."

"That's my point," said Treluhne. "According to the *djorcrelul*, the Quishiks will back down from the threat *and* restore the damage they've done on their way out of the galaxy."

"Just like that?" asked Gillian.

The tall Seldran leader nodded.

"Makes me think this ancient equipment must have finally broken down," he said.

Gillian looked up at the massive device.

"Well, hang on a bit," she said. "The probability that the Quishiks would back down would increase, would it not, based on the severity of the threat?

"True," said the Seldran leader. "Though every analysis we've run shows their ships are invulnerable to anything we can throw at them."

"But ... and I'm guessing of course ... what if the threat were not to the ships at all?" asked Gillian.

Treluhne brushed a shock of fur out of his eyes.

"More of a personal threat?" he asked.

"Exactly," said Gillian. "If we can work out a way to strike at their confidence ... to scare them perhaps as ... as with a kind of cosmic warning."

"A scary voice?" asked Treluhne. "A deity, perhaps, scolding them for being very naughty?"

Gillian looked away.

"I know," she said. "It sounds absurd. But even my own people, a great many of them, still hold extremely ancient beliefs based, I dare say, on little more than scary voices."

Treluhne glanced up at the science center's high-vaulted ceiling before walking over to a bronze console to the right of the ancient Probability reader.

"If we follow your logic, we'll be making a high-stakes gamble with the fate of the Continuum," he said. "Didn't a human philosopher once say 'God doesn't play dice with the universe?'"

Gillian frowned.

"First, we're not gods, so I doubt we're in any danger there," she said. "Second, you're thinking of Albert Einstein — a physicist, not a philosopher."

Treluhne's green eyes twinkled.

"A philosophical statement all the same," he said. "But give me a moment."

The bright-yellow Dralein twiddled a few settings on the console attached to the ancient Ootray device, before turning back to Gillian's worried eyes.

"I did see something a while back about the Quishiks' belief system," he said. "And by the way, you do know they are an engineered species, don't you?"

Gillian's jaw dropped as Treluhne recounted what he'd learned about the origins of the Quishiks from the Probability reader.

"So ... so the Ootray created these monsters but have done nothing to stop them?" she asked.

"Not exactly," said the Dralein. "The Quishiks have spent the last ten-thousand cycles in exile in a maze of interlocking event horizons."

"Until recently, I gather," said Gillian. "But where are the Ootray now? They must have realized what a threat the Quishiks are to ... to civilization."

"You'd think," said Treluhne. "Especially considering the Quishiks feed directly on the mental energy of every sentient being in their path. But so far, the only provision the Ootray seem to have made for a Quishiks jailbreak is a large-scale blocking mechanism."

"Blocking what, exactly?" asked Gillian.

"Their bad habits," said Treluhne. "The Quishiks are mind-suckers, for lack of a better word. But I haven't figured out how to activate the mind-blocking mechanism."

A faint shimmering appeared in the air to their left and distracted Treluhne from finishing his thought. Soon, a staticky voice began tickling their ears.

"... is ... is ... aptain ... nos ... tectorate sh ... y ... tress...." it crackled.

"Can you lower your shields a tad to let that signal in?" asked Gillian.

"I could," said Treluhne, "if I trusted the source."

"I rather think we have more to gain by trusting anyone who wants to reach us," said Gillian. That, she knew is what Harlan would have said. "I doubt very much the Quishiks would bother to talk."

The leader of the Seldra Dralein population stared at Gillian a moment, then glanced at the massive ancient device behind him.

"Nothing in the display argues against it," he said. And with that, he issued a series of short commands through his personal comlink. In seconds, the shimmering air resolved itself into a holographic image of a tall, dark biomechanoid that, unknown to anyone on Seldra, Cricket Andersen was dying to see again.

"Commander Cavendish," said the holojection, "Captain Enos of the Protectorate ship *Mighty Fortress*. I have an urgent request."

"Go on," said Gillian.

"Based on data provided by the symbiotes and their Jachtrahlese beta-intelligence, known as 4BDN/56," said the biomechanoid, "I have devised a multidimensional weapon that should prove effective against the Quishiks if all else fails. Will you review the specifications and see if you can assist in its construction?"

Gillian's eyes squinted.

"Give me a moment," she said. "What on Earth do you mean by 'multidimensional weapon'?"

The biomechanoid outlined what he'd worked out with Yaldrint. The weapon was based on an extension of existing space-folding technologies. It would create a rapid oscillation between folded and unfolded space-time within a limited range.

"A turbulence," Enos explained, "analogous to seismic activity or, if you will, a tidal wave."

"That's a bit of a tall order, isn't it?" said Gillian. "And I dare say, building a complex weapon in this time frame would put a significant strain on our replicators. I'm afraid I cannot guarantee...."

"We can help you," Treluhne broke in. "We need as many ways out of this crisis as we can find."

Enos's face betrayed traces of sorrow.

"Consider it Plan B," he said. "And let us hope its use proves unnecessary. Our calculations show it would destroy the Quishiks, but take much of local space, including Bledraun with them. Though I cannot forgive myself for devising this 'doomsday weapon,' we may find its use imperative."

Gillian's eyes misted over.

"Fortunes of war, I suppose," she said. "By all means, send us your specs. And Captain?"

"Yes, Commander Cavendish?" said Enos.

"May I say you are the most humane intelligence I have ever known," said Gillian.

CHAPTER 44

Deep in farm country on war-scarred Bledraun, the head of its non-existent global government opened the hatch on her lander. Though her heart was focused on inspecting the aftermath of a brutal conflict, her eyes fluttered up to the rainy sky, as a small escape pod streaked through the atmosphere.

It was, of course, Harlan Mars, who had to hope his many years as a pilot had prepared him for this dangerous landing. Terran Protectorate escape pods, designed for retrieval in space, weren't particularly aerodynamic. Unless Harlan selected the right angle of approach and stuck to it, the odds were terrifyingly high that his tiny ship would end up as a heap of singed scrap metal.

So far so good, but as Drashna shielded her eyes, the flames shooting up the vessel on all sides made it clear the situation was getting out of hand.

"Can we save that escape pod?" She called out to her ship's AI. The response came not in words but in a torrent of white liquid coming from above. Drashna's ship, parked in a stationary orbit above her, had sprayed a coolant on Harlan's escape pod, which solidified on contact into a spongy foam.

"Might have warned me," she grumbled, even after she concluded that the spray had cooled Harlan's tiny ship and saved him from the searing heat of re-entry. Nevertheless, the ground shook with the pod's impact.

Drashna's first thought was to rush over to Harlan's landing site, but the swift approach of an automated rescue vehicle from her orbiting ship discouraged her. In seconds, a pair of cylindrical servicebots she wasn't aware she had, emerged from the steely gray vehicle and were already attempting to open the escape pod's hatch. Soon, however, it opened on its own, and a bedraggled figure in a torn encounter suit rolled out onto the rain-soaked ground.

"Medical evaluation!" Drashna yelled, unnecessarily, into her comlink to the symbiote ship that had brought her back to Bledraun.

"I'm fine, Madame Chaudron," came Harlan's weary voice into her ear bud. "Just thirsty and hungry is all."

"Stay put," said the Dralein. How strange to take comfort in the presence of the human she'd found so crude and obnoxious two weeks ago. With no further thought, she clomped across the muddy terrain separating them.

"Can you help him up?" she asked the servicebots.

Not equipped with anything resembling social skills, the two servicebots set to work without comment. As Drashna suspected, they determined Harlan's injuries weren't severe. With surprising tenderness, they helped the human to his feet.

"There," said Harlan. "Need to rest a while. You have any food?"

"I'll give you the last of my space rations," said Drashna. "Then we'll have to start foraging."

Harlan, who had been holding himself up with one hand against the side of his escape pod, pivoted on his elbow and rested his back against the heat-scarred hull.

"You reckon anything survived the … the assault?" he asked.

"Not my government," said Drashna. "But I'm not sure my people survived either."

"The wireheads killed them all?" asked Harlan.

Drashna swallowed hard and explained that the Dralein who eventually emerged from the tunnels would be unrecognizable in their habits and thinking from their predecessors.

"And you missed all that, dealing with the symbies," said Harlan. "Can't say as I empathize."

Drashna held her head in her hands. The effort to make the human space-folder captain understand the reality of the current situation was too much to handle.

"We have more immediate problems than the symbiotes," she said. "Come, let's get you into my lander. You can eat whatever's left and rest."

She voiced a new set of commands to the servicebots then stood back and waited while they helped Harlan drag his trembling legs in her direction. Soon the two of them were sitting around a small table Drashna had folded out of the lander's inner hull.

"Symbies too cheap for a replicator?" asked Harlan, through a mouthful of dry, vaguely meaty space ration.

"Apparently," said Drashna, "a replicator would have put too much stress on the … on the power train."

"Like I said. Cheap," said Harlan. "Can't believe they thought they could take on the Quishiks with a two-credit space fleet."

"So you have heard of the Quishiks," said the weary Dralein.

"Yeah," said Harlan. "But what I don't get is what side the Krezovics are on. I saw what those beetlebacks did, on my long-range scanners from space. Can't figure it out. Last I heard they never wanted anything to do with androids."

"Times have changed, Captain Mars," said Drashna. "For instance, my scanners indicated that you were dead. And yet, here you are."

Harlan pointed his fork at her.

"Look, Madam Chaudron," said Harlan. "We can't get anywhere unless we focus on right now. If the Quishiks are our real enemy, we have to stop them before the androids send reinforcements."

"So your suggestion is?" asked Drashna.

"Way I see it," said Harlan between sips of recycled water, "the Krezovics left on Bledraun have to feel kind of betrayed. They let a bunch of wireheads lure them out here to get revenge on the Protectorate and ended up stuck in the cross-fire."

"What makes you think that's of any use to us?" asked Drashna. "Especially considering you're human yourself."

The answer, Harlan told her, depended on whether they could incite the Krezovics to rebel against the ANN Commission when the androids returned.

"You know their processors won't give up on that chalinite," he said.

With broad brush strokes, Harlan outlined a plan for arming and training the Krezovics still alive on Bledraun, starting with a renewed scavenger hunt — this time for heavy weaponry, including the automated tactical weapons platforms favored by the Terran Protectorate. Drashna listened intently, while her large Dralein head rested heavily on her furry hands.

"But won't your superiors object to you taking independent action?" she asked.

Harlan ticked two fingers into his left palm, one at a time.

"First off," he said, "my so-called superiors think I'm dead. Second, standard protocol would have all soldiers back in their ships once the conflict was over, no matter why the fighting stopped."

"So you really think they won't intervene?" asked the former Dralein leader.

Harlan's face darkened.

"Well, there's one more thing," he said in a low voice. "Been monitoring their chatter from my pod this whole time."

"And?" asked Drashna.

"Something doesn't feel right." said Harlan. "Communication's kinda sluggish, like half the troops got the sleeping sickness."

"Could be the Quishiks," said Drashna. "Warvhex told me they feed on mental energy somehow."

"Then we better get started," said the Terran Protectorate officer, "before those freaking monsters get a hold of us, too."

But as Drashna pointed out, there was still one problem.

"We're in the middle of nowhere," she said. "I see no evidence of fighting here."

"Your ship still operational?" asked the tall, muscular human.

"I ... have no reason to believe otherwise," said Drashna.

Harlan slapped his right thigh.

"Then let's fire it up," he said. "It's time we went looking for trouble."

"Why would we...." Drashna started.

"Only way anything ever gets done, Madame Chaudron," said Harlan. "The *only* way.".

CHAPTER 45

As her lander readied itself for docking with the *Sweet Chariot*, Gillian forced herself to assimilate what she'd learned during her three-day stop-over on Seldra.

"Odd lot, that," she said. She was thinking, at first, of the Seldrans, but on reflection, realized she felt the same about the biomechanoid, Captain Enos. Aside from his humorless way of speaking, Gillian was also struck by his tendency to elaborate on the ethical dimension of defeating the Quishiks.

It was enough to make her wonder if his programming were a relic of an earlier time. While the Terran Protectorate paid lip-service to such things, with its ritualized talk of "Liberty and Justice for All," on a day-to-day basis — not so much.

Sure, Brad Christiansen might sometimes intervene, when bad conduct interfered with either crew morale or his personal profit margins. Yet Enos had a funny way of reawakening a broader sense of decency that Gillian had learned the hard way to submerge. Now she was a captain, she had no doubt the price she paid would be steeper still.

Yet as her lander's automated docking mechanisms ran their course, these fine, humanistic impulses slipped from her consciousness. Once the airlock door opened into the *Sweet Chariot's* docking bay, she was a soldier again with a deadly enemy at uncomfortably close range.

"Map a trajectory for Lerdra," she heard herself say into her comlink. As little as she knew about Seldra, Gillian's knowledge of Bledraun's third moon was even more limited. Yet as a Level 1 scan revealed, it was much smaller and less dense than either of its "sisters," and utterly unsuited to underground colonization.

Fortunately for the symbiotes, Lerdra still offered more than enough cover for their mothership. And despite the Quishiks' superior technology, the moon's unusually radioactive crust played havoc with conventional long-range scanners. Because Plaandrur's intelligence teams suspected nothing, and believed no ship could possibly escape their notice, they'd missed the symbiote's arrival. It was the arrogance of evil writ large in space-time's best handwriting.

From Gillian's perspective, as the Sweet Chariot docked with the symbiote ship, her immediate concern was hammering out the rules for her collaboration with the scheming symbiotes. Threat or no threat, she would not allow a single member of her crew to become a symbiote host without consent. But none of that was on the agenda when she finally emerged from the airlock into the symbiote's landing bay. The first item involved a simpler matter.

"How do you explain the escape pod you jettisoned before pulling into orbit around Seldra?" Opalhex had asked, unable to hide her irritation behind her host's symmetrical face.

"That, I'm afraid," said Gillian, "was out of my control."

Though she would have preferred to keep Harlan's secret, out of respect for his last orders, the suspicion his escape pod maneuver raised demanded a full explanation. In the end, she decided, her present company was unlikely to divulge Harlan's whereabouts to the ANN Commission.

"That confirms it," said Opalhex, "as if we needed any more proof. You humans have been double-crossed."

"Brilliant," said Gillian. "But I rather think we're past the stage of keeping score — unless you'd like to discuss your transponder attack on the Quishiks. You maimed fifteen thousand ancient trees and caused the enemy to charge weapons. That's *commendable*, that is."

"I couldn't agree more, Acting-Captain Cavendish," said Yaldrint from Shol's arms, as the Krezovic boy and Trinity tiptoed into the symbiote's docking bay.

Gillian's eyes settled on Shol, and she decided to ignore the stream of sarcastic remarks that flooded her mind. Whatever trouble the young Krezovic had caused her, Gillian knew she now needed as many allies as possible.

"Survived that nasty business with Ensign Bassett I see," she said to him.

Trinity took Shol's hand.

"We both did," she said. "But I don't know if we'll survive this war."

"Yes, the situation is a tad dangerous isn't it?" said Gillian, "But I rather think the first order of business in any crisis is to believe a resolution is possible."

Shol shifted his weight, his eyes barely able to meet the human's.

"Did … did somebody tell Har Draaf about this … this plan?" he asked. But as Gillian explained, no one knew where the distinguished crustacean was.

"Captain Enos believes he must be hiding in the Dralein tunnels," said Yaldrint.

Opalhex sat her Krezovic host down on a maintenance worker's empty stool.

"I could have told you that," she said.

"You could have mentioned it sooner then, couldn't you?" snapped Gillian.

"I didn't expect a Protectorate snob would care much about a mere Grashardi," said Opalhex. "Besides, I have more important news. An entirely new cargo bay has materialized off the port side of this vessel."

"How is that possible?" Trinity yelled.

Shol wrapped his arm around her waist.

"Any ideas, Yaldrint?" he asked.

"If I may hazard a guess," said the Grashardi AI, "Captain Enos has theorized that the Quishiks are skilled at Probability manipulation."

"You mean they messed with ... what is it...." Shol started.

"Cause and effect, maybe?" asked Trinity.

"Yeah," Shol continued. "You think they messed with causes and whatever to give us more cargo space?"

"I rather think that was collateral damage," said Gillian. "The question is what the Quishiks hope to achieve."

"Driving us insane by changing reality is a fairly destabilizing weapon," said Opalhex.

The usually steady sequence of Yaldrint's status lights shifted to a more erratic pattern.

"Forgive me, Ms. Opalhex," she said, "but I believe you may not appreciate the gravity of the situation. The Quishiks intend a full-scale remapping of Reality itself."

Despite years of training and self-discipline, Gillian couldn't stop herself from gasping. This was exactly what Treluhne had told her, shortly before she left Seldra. From that point on, the conversation shifted to tactics — as Opalhex, Gillian and Yaldrint struggled with the logistics of putting their half-formed plan into action.

"What about Har Draaf?" asked Shol, after a few impatient minutes. "If he's down in those tunnels, he might have new, like, intel by now."

Opalhex squinted at him.

"Don't worry kid," she said. "We'll make sure your daddy's safe. Why don't you and the princess look for video games in the...."

"He's not my father!" Shol roared. "But you *sure* are a Chalnorian sand slug. There's gotta be someone down in those tunnels. Who do you think keeps the Dralein safe when they go all crazy? It sure isn't a gang of slimy symbiotes!"

"Tell me why this brat isn't in the brig," Opalhex demanded.

Yaldrint extended her embedded lase pistol and wiggled it in the symbiote's direction.

"If I may," said the Grashardi AI, "though friend Shol is a bit strident, I believe he raises a good point. Perhaps Har Draaf is in the care of the Ootray."

Gillian pushed herself between the symbiote host and the Krezovic boy — and kept them both at bay with her powerful arms. As she hastened to point out, Yaldrint's suggestion aligned with what she'd heard on Seldra from Captain Enos's hologram.

Opalhex clapped her host's hands in a tight rhythm.

"Well, if you're so sure he's found the Ootray," she snapped, "why haven't they done anything about the Quishiks?"

"Apparently, they weren't ready," said a familiar voice that seemed to float above them.

"Har Draaf," said Shol.

"But now it's time to 'get cracking,' as the humans say," Ungent's voice continued.

"Come on, Ambassador," said a female voice no one in the symbiote's docking bay recognized. "Nobody's said that for over seven hundred cycles."

CHAPTER 46

High above the apparently abandoned Bledraun, Harlan and Drashna considered their options. The symbiote lander, Harlan was pleased to see, was a tight, maneuverable craft with a powerful sensor array. There were advantages, he now realized, to snooping around in somebody else's brain.

For even though the symbiotes had produced an "economy model" of the original design, this spherical ship was based on the same Djanatri tech that the Protectorate had fought long and hard to capture. But the mind he most wanted to see into was that of sullen Drashna, who'd hardly said a word in the past hour.

"Worried?" he asked her, unable to bear the silence.

Drashna stared at Harlan as if she'd never seen him before.

"What?" she said. "No, sorry. I was thinking about Caronya — my daughter. Those Quishik things took her from the symbiotes, who were supposed to cure her. Or maybe Warvhex gave Caronya to them herself."

Harlan pretended to study the flickering, multicolored lights on his control panel, even though the lander was now following an automated trajectory back to Jeldren.

"Well, now, hold on. Things are kinda shaky right now, I get that," he said. "But having your daughter in custody, no matter what the symbies promised you, is too much of a tactical advantage for them to throw it away like that."

Drashna stood up from her nylon-mesh flight chair.

"Maybe," she said. "Though that isn't much comfort. I still don't know if ... if ... you know what I mean."

"Here's what I know," said Harlan. "Once we get the Krezovics on our side, we'll get us some leverage and we can push saving Caronya to the top of everybody's agenda."

"Don't even try to cheer me up," said Drashna. "I'm not a first-year recruit in your ... your warlord army. And nothing we can accomplish against the androids will do one bit of good for Caronya."

Harlan pinched the bridge of his nose.

"We're not alone, Madame Chaudron," he said. "My XO is out there somewhere and so is Har Draaf. They don't come more determined than that."

"Let's say I allow myself to believe that helping you unite the Krezovic settlers will somehow contribute to freeing my daughter," said Drashna. "What makes you think they'll listen to you? They can grab up abandoned weapons on their own."

Harlan fidgeted with a few dials, as his chosen landing site came into view.

"Because, Madame Chaudron," he said, "I can make them into a fighting force. Think any of those miners can shoot straight? An automated firing system is useless against the wireheads. They can anticipate every move from any of the manufacturers' specs. To get the drop on an AI, you have to do something *crazy*."

"I don't find that reassuring," said Drashna, but if Harlan heard her, he was too preoccupied to care. The lander had started its descent to Bledraun and already he could make out the party of armed Krezovics who were waiting for them.

"Jacob's Ladder," he said. "Looks like we're gonna need us some diplomacy."

CHAPTER 47

By now, the disheartened Warvhex and Klarghex had returned from the *Mighty Fortress* and were sound asleep, after a late night of emotionally charged talk. All told, the effort to reconcile and consolidate what Gillian had learned on Seldra, and what Shol and Trinity had discovered by consulting 4BDN/56, with what Captain Enos and Yaldrint had worked out together, had simply overwhelmed them.

Add to that Treluhne's tantalizing promise of mentallic shielding from the Ootray device on Seldra, and the pressure of the moment was more than enough to crack the sturdiest ego. How could they hope to gain its protection if the Seldrans themselves had no idea where the start button was?

Yet overriding all other worries were the mysterious clues the unseen voices had provided. Even the newly-recharged Yaldrint, whose experience with stress was limited to the occasional power outage, felt the strain. Anyone entering Shol and Trinity's quarters would have seen Yaldrint's colorful array of status lights flickering insistently against the pitch black of the symbiote mothership's interior.

For starters, the puzzling familiarity of the voices, which they had all heard a few hours before, was particularly hard to account for. Determined to tease out their true meaning, Yaldrint mulled them over in whatever passes for an AI's inner voice.

"Clearly *resembled* Har Draaf."

Yet the Grashardi's speech rhythms had been out of synch with Yaldrint's archived data.

"Cadences off by 0.023 temporal units. An imitation. Curious."

If Ungent were actually down under the surface of Bledraun with the unknown Ootray, why would he not have spoken for himself?

"Trust factor."

Yes. What better way to ensure a message is well received, than to package it in a familiar, beloved voice?

"Second voice most likely based on former Lieutenant Andersen."

Yaldrint surveyed her memory's long-term cache. When the holojection of Captain Enos first appeared in Ungent's hotel suite, he'd mentioned Cricket's risky, high-speed flight to Bledraun. If she'd survived the assault on Bledraun, the AI reasoned, it had to have been underground.

"Deception of this kind not inconsistent with certain general truths."

Whatever the Ootray's motives for faking Ungent's voice and, presumably, Lieutenant Andersen's, the message that they were now ready with a plan of action was still possibly accurate.

"More information urgently required."

Yaldrint's first thought was to tap into the exotically configured 4BDN/56 that the two teenagers had discovered on Level 3 of the symbiote ship. But the Jachtrahlese device didn't think, so much as churn through existing data stores and mold what it found into a precise imitation of organic language.

"Seldra."

At that conclusion, Yaldrint paused. Even if she were allowed to contact the Probability reader described by Gillian, it was unclear whether a compatible interface could be found. Or whether opening itself to the Ootray device would put Yaldrint's circuits at risk for overload.

"Must try, before Har Draaf is harmed by the extra-dimensionals."

Yaldrint paused and asked herself: Was she certain the Ootray posed any less of a threat than the Quishiks they created?

But with nowhere else to turn for answers, the Grashardi AI began a cautious search for an access point into the vast quantum array the Ootray had left behind on Seldra.

After five hundred years, and despite their objections to Seldran culture, the laid-back Dralein had still not seen fit to sever the one remaining datalink between their two worlds. It was all Yaldrint needed. Nevertheless, she had no idea what data format the array used. But by testing trillions of different options per second, she made first contact with the unknown device.

Yaldrint was as close to flabbergasted as an AI can be. For here was an ancient intelligence, speaking the purest machine language she'd ever encountered. So simple, stark and uncompromising, because the Seldran intelligence made no pretense of mimicking organic thought processes!

As a result, she learned more in a few minutes about the device and the Ootray who built it than she could have learned across several months of conventional research. Still, a nagging question bubbled up from her core processor that would not be denied.

"Why have you not acted sooner?" she asked the Ootray device.

The response was brief, definitive and final:

"Alignment has not been achieved."

With that, the Ootray Probability reader went silent and poor Yaldrint was left in a state of mind common to many organics who have sought wisdom from the high or the holy. "The Answer," a crystal clear enigma, had been given. There was nothing more to do than ponder its meaning. Try as she might, Yaldrint found her access to the Ootray device was now blocked.

Nevertheless, the information she'd gained suggested a clear plan of action. And the first step was contacting Ungent directly. Not wishing to be deceived again by an Ootray voice simulator, Yaldrint reached out across a broad spectrum of frequencies to the Grashardi ambassador's interstellar comlink.

"Yaldrint?" Ungent's voice crackled in, over Yaldrint's receiver.

Slowly, Yaldrint brought Ungent up to date on the developments since they'd last been in contact. To share Yaldrint's thoughts with Cricket, Ungent reset his comlink to BROADCAST.

"What you describe," said the Grashardi ambassador, "matches what Lieutenant Andersen and I have learned from the Ootray's projections. What's missing, apparently, is the trigger mechanism."

"Agreed," said Yaldrint. "The intelligence on Seldra insisted it was waiting for 'alignment.' Yet I believe I have failed you, because I cannot determine what this means."

"An incident, perhaps, which they themselves can't initiate," said Ungent's thoughtful voice. "Maybe a military mind would understand this better. Lieutenant, can you think of anything the Ootray might be waiting for?"

"Well," said Cricket. "I'm a navigator, not a strategist. But I did have basic military training. If I remember … yes … our instructor used to say 'Attacking the enemy's heart hurts them hardest.'"

"An assault on a symbol of their authority, then," said Ungent. "But where...."

Yaldrint's status lights changed color and began blinking in a new, unfamiliar pattern.

"The symbiotes say they've observed a large spaceport going up on the outskirts of Jeldren," she said.

"That would be their first beachhead, Har Draaf, on a world this side of the Fremdel," said Cricket.

"Logical," said Yaldrint. "But the planet is decimated and the only possible survivors are the Krezovics. I doubt they could mount a meaningful attack on a spaceport."

"And you know what?" said Cricket. "They'd need a commander to have an effective strike force. I can't see Acting-captain Cavendish taking that on. Not with a command of her own to manage."

Ungent paused to rub his stiff mandibles with a webbed hand.

"Were Harlan still alive...." he said.

"Commander Cavendish believes he might be," said Yaldrint. "And considering he was last seen in a Terran Protectorate escape pod, his survival past four rotations would depend on him landing on Bledraun."

"The Krezovics would tear him apart," said Cricket.

Ungent thought back over his twenty-year association with the human space-folder captain.

"Maybe not," he said. "Harlan could charm the shell off an Alchnorean sea turtle."

"I hardly think...." Yaldrint started.

"Never mind, my dear friend," said Ungent. "I was merely being poetic."

"I see," said Yaldrint. "If I may, dangerous junctures in history require greater verbal precision."

"I'll keep that in mind," said Ungent, with a slight lilt. "But wait. Wouldn't it be easy for the *Sweet Chariot* to destroy the spaceport?"

"Easy, perhaps," said Yaldrint. "But also disastrous. So far, the Quishiks have completely ignored all ships in the region, including the *Mighty Fortress,* which is less than two-hundred-thousand kilometers away from them."

"Because it poses no obvious threat," said Ungent. "It's as if they wish to conserve resources."

"That may be," said Yaldrint. "Yet a direct assault on the Quishiks' future command base *would* qualify as a direct threat."

"Right, as always," said Ungent. "So, assuming for a moment that Harlan is our source for an inciting incident, what then?"

"No one is certain," said the Grashardi AI. "And I'm afraid the last piece of information I received from the Seldra intelligence requires further analysis."

"What did it say?" asked Ungent.

"It was about you, Har Draaf," said Yaldrint.

"Me?" asked Ungent. "What about me?"

"About you ... no this cannot be correct ... about you becoming a god," said the AI.

With that, Yaldrint's status lights froze, as she shut herself down to reboot.

CHAPTER 48

To the ragged band of male and female Krezovics assembled to watch a symbiote lander touch down, it appeared they were in for their first taste of combat. But when a weakened Harlan Mars stumbled out of the lander's hatch, leaning on Drashna's shoulders, their perceptions shifted — even if their lase rifles kept their sites on the newcomers.

"Who the soggy loaf are you?" asked Grauth.

Drashna opened her mouth to speak, but Harlan didn't give her a chance.

"You know you're holding that weapon all wrong," he said. "Keep it at that angle, you'll waste your first shot firing over your target's head."

"Yeah, 'tectorate big shot has the answer for everything," said a voice from the crowd.

"I'm just saying," said Harlan. "You'll need to know how to use those things when the androids come back."

"What makes you think...." another voice piped up.

"Is anyone talking to you?" snarled Grauth.

To think he'd wrecked his chance for a good life, to take *quelx* from a broken down soldier. On the other hand, it wasn't as if he actually did know anything about firearms.

"You want to show me how it's done, go ahead," he said.

"Captain Mars needs a medpod," said Drashna. "He can show you later."

Ather, the former Krezovic miner who'd assaulted Shol a few days before, pushed himself to the front of the crowd.

"Wait," he said, "you're the head lady on this planet, aren't you? Why ain't you down in the muck with the rest of the fuzzheads?"

"Because I'm not as smart as you," said Drashna. "Oof, can one of you strong males help me shoulder the captain?"

Grauth waved his hand in their direction and a pair of younger Krezovics ran up to take Harlan's weight.

"We don't have a medpod, Madam Chaudron," he said. "Nor a hospital in this section of town, even before the wireheads attacked. Nice work."

"Come on, we have a little food we could give him," said one of the females. "Or did you turn into a wirehead yourself?"

Grauth wheeled around, barely able to keep from shooting her head off. She shrunk back, and he turned away.

"I don't know what you want here," he said. "But I'm not into killing either a half-dead human or a senile Dralein. We'll patch you up as best we can. Then you can tell me all about my rifle. Better hope I'm impressed."

"I know I can help you...." Harlan started.

"I'll tell you what you don't know," said Grauth. "Somebody's building a space port on the edge of town. And you're here in time to help us rip it up."

Drashna looked over at Harlan.

"Quishiks," she said.

"Probably," said Harlan.

"What in Saturn's rings you talking about?" asked Grauth.

Harlan made his best effort to stand up straight and tall.

"Talking about the reason your lives have been shredded — and all for nothing." he said. "The Quishiks are the ones made us both puppets of the wireheads."

"Why?" asked the Krezovic leader. "What's their angle?"

"Total domination," said Drashna. "Starting with a mind drain of anyone who gets in their way."

"'Tectorate propaganda!" Ather shouted. A murmured agreement washed over the crowd.

"Shut up," Grauth snapped. "You know that spaceport's not like anything we've ever seen. It's not so much being built as ... I dunno ... wished into place."

Drashna nodded as Grauth recounted seeing whole sections of the spaceport materialize in a matter of minutes. It matched perfectly with what Warvhex had told her weeks ago.

"They have complete control over Probability," the symbiote had said. "If they want something, they reconfigure the timeline so the reality they need falls into place."

"That, amigo, is a dangerous enemy," said Harlan.

Individual crowd members nodded and a few came forward with stories of random sections of Jeldren popping back into view, days after they were obliterated by the ANN Commission's assault.

"That's the Quishiks' doing," said Drashna. "It's a side-effect of their Probability juggling. You may see those same areas decimated again before the spaceport is complete."

"How's anybody gonna fight that?" asked Grauth. "Might as well point these guns at our heads and get it over with."

But Drashna asserted there was still plenty of reason to hope. To make her case, she threw aside caution, and laid out everything she'd learned about the Quishiks, including the Ootray who created them.

"You telling me the fools who made those monsters are living right under our feet?" said Ather. "Ask me, we oughta charge down them Dralein tunnels and finish them off now."

"You can't shoot straight in plain daylight," said Harlan, "and you plan to storm an underground hold you have no intel on. Listen...."

It took some wrangling, but eventually, Harlan prevailed. Ootray or no Ootray, he told them, destroying the Quishik spaceport would buy the others time to get their plan in place. He neglected to mention he had no idea whether "the others" were still alive — much less whether they had a viable plan.

"Well, let's go then," said Grauth.

"Not until we're ready," said Harlan. "Me included. Can somebody fetch me a...."

And in that moment, Ungent's best hope for an "inciting incident" blacked out and crumpled to the charred grass and seared clay at his feet.

CHAPTER 49

The night sky over Seldra flickered as if lit with a million sidereal candles. In line with the ancient patterns of star birth, collapse and supernova, they shed their light with no thought of personal gain. Treluhne's throat burned, as he realized he'd lost count of the number of times he'd gazed up at this same sky with Luerdin, his beloved.

He looked up and relived the past — when they were young enough to believe their bodies were as immortal as their feelings. But even in the era which the Terran Protectorate had arbitrarily named "the 48th century," organic life was still quite fragile. Luerdin had died in her thirties from a rare viral infection no medpod could eradicate.

Now, for the first time, as he gazed through Seldra's observatory dome, Treluhne had reason to believe the star patterns he and Luerdin had marveled at together might soon be extinguished.

On that score, his consultations with the Ootray's *djorcrelul* had been frustrating. Obscure at the best of times, the readout from the ancient device had displayed three separate metaversal paths, with virtually no overlap. One scenario was the perplexingly hopeful one he'd mentioned to Gillian.

The other two were darker. The second scenario pointed to a mere weakening of the Quishiks, accompanied by years of suffering, while the settled universe rebuilt and emerged at a lower level of civilization. In the third, Treluhne had seen himself wandering mindlessly across the scorched terrain of Bledraun, with barely enough consciousness left to feel his own pain. It was a scenario spelling out the end of days in this corner of the universe.

It was time, he decided, to put his accumulated knowledge of the *djorcrelul* to use. Over the last ninety years, he'd concentrated on interpreting the baseline readouts it displayed. Yet, as he'd long known, it was possible to input more specific parameters in an if-then sequence, to simulate the impact of specific actions on the timeline.

But considering the Probability reader's antiquity, the leader of the Seldran colony had only dared input data to guide the colony's controlled use of the *sceraun*. Could it still handle the strain of large-scale calculations encompassing multiple spatio-temporal coordinates?

"We must not fail."

Captain Enos's words echoed in Treluhne's memory and the bright yellow Dralein realized that if the Quishiks weren't stopped, he'd live to see the *djorcrelul*, and everything else he cared about, swept away. Nor had he forgotten about the Dralein child, the daughter of Bledraun's leader. Treluhne rubbed the back of his soft neck. To think the universe could contain creatures willing to prey on the innocent.

At that, Treluhne found his courage. He took a deep breath, called up a list of acceptable parameters on the Probability reader, and ticked them off one by one.

Based on the insight provided by 4BDN/56 on the symbiote's ship, the Quishiks were prone to bouts of paranoia and self-doubt. That much had been confirmed by Warvhex, with the help of her own data analysts. This dovetailed nicely, Treluhne reasoned, with Gillian's suggestion that the Quishiks might be unnerved by an assault, not on themselves, but on their self-esteem.

With that in mind, what better starting point than the Quishiks' rapidly rising spaceport on Bledraun? The Quishiks would likely see the spaceport as their first stronghold in a glorious campaign across the settled universe. Knocking it out before it was completed would be a serious blow to their morale.

We'll catch them off guard, Treluhne told himself.

If the Krezovics could succeed, it might make the Quishiks wonder if their ships were also vulnerable to attack.

Next, as he'd discussed with Gillian, the symbiotes and Captain Enos, a massing of forces along the Quishiks' perimeter soon after the Krezovic assault would make the bluff more convincing. The Quishiks might even fear the human-symbiote alliance had a secret weapon — an improved version of their previous, crippling transponder blast.

What's more, if Treluhne could finally activate the Ootray's mind-blocking device, each Quishik would become isolated, confused and afraid. Logic aside, Treluhne knew they faced many risks. If he and the others had miscalculated, the Quishiks could destroy the two human ships and the symbiote vessel instantly.

The trick was timing their approach to coincide with whatever the Ootray were planning. But so far, the Ootray had refused to reveal more than the precise spatio-temporal coordinates where the three ships from the alliance should converge.

Puzzled, Treluhne took comfort in the fact that, among the search parameters offered by the *djorcrelul*, were several that matched the scenario he'd imagined. Hands trembling, he selected:

CONVERGENCE
HUMAN

KALDHEX
KREZOVIC
OOTRAY
QUISHIKS
SPACEPORT

plus the string of spatio-temporal coordinates the Ootray had given him.

Treluhne gasped.

"Inconclusive," he whispered. Unfortunately, the most the Probability reader offered were weakly favorable odds that the plan would work — and a warning of possible, unexpected consequences even if it succeeded. Shattered, he crouched down to the floor, as miserable as a 21st-century human teenager after receiving an ambiguous answer from his "Magic 8-ball." The odds that the alliance would end up firing Captain Enos's doomsday weapon were climbing.

"Often, a leap of faith is required," rang a distant voice in his mind. Was he recalling a phrase from his childhood, or were the Ootray sending him a telepathic message?

"Chaudron!" a tense voice shouted from the near distance. Treluhne whipped around to see Verohme, the Dralein who'd been Gillian's guide when she arrived on Seldra. The snowy white Dralein ran up to him.

"The Krezovics," Verohme panted. "They've raided the Quishik spaceport with weapons left behind by the ANN Commission! I suggest we.... "

Treluhne waved him away.

"The quark has spun, Verohme," he said. "Leave it to Probability now."

"But...." Verohme started.

"There are better uses for your mind than blind anxiety," said the Seldran leader. "What progress have you made with the Ootray mind-blocker?"

"Sir," said Verohme, "are we even certain this ancient equipment still functions?"

Treluhne's massive hands grabbed Verohme by the forearm and dragged him into his office.

"The readouts from the *djorcrelul* are clear," he growled. "Don't tell me you haven't...."

Verohme wrenched himself free of Treluhne and paused to inspect his arms.

"Modest progress," he grunted. "The device does generate a soothing energy field, but it's faint."

"Soothing energy?" asked Treluhne. "That might be wishful thinking."

"I was ready to conclude the same," said Verohme, "except it appears to have cured Jelenoth's migraines."

Treluhne slammed his palm down on his imposing stainless steel desk.

"I did not ask you to *play* with the device, Verohme!" he thundered. "Put it to work! Experiment!"

"But Chaudron," said Verohme, "we have no idea what damage it might do if we merely plunge ahead."

Treluhne stood up and began pacing.

"Here's the idea I do have," he said. "I saw it in the *djorcrelul* this morning. It's the image of this entire galaxy in decline, its population reduced to mindless drones. Whatever you can get out of the mind-blocker, do it now. There is no more room for caution."

"Treluhne, please...." Verohme started.

"My Seldran comrade," said Treluhne, "now is the time for a leap of faith."

CHAPTER 50

Below ground on Bledraun, Ungent was getting acquainted with the multidimensional transponder he'd soon use to project his voice out toward the Quishiks. Though the Ootray AI had built the transponder to familiar Grashardi specs, there was no mistaking the perplexed look on his face.

"The text will scroll here?" he asked. "I hope you don't expect me to sound it out phonetically."

But as Dlalamphrur explained, the text could appear in any language he chose. After some hesitation, he selected Planetary Standard.

"Wouldn't you be more comfortable in your home language?"' asked Cricket.

"I have been fluent in some form of Planetary my entire adult life," said Ungent. "And I believe it's imperative that you have exactly the same information I do, in case I can't continue."

"Can't see myself as a god, somehow," said the former Terran Protectorate navigator. "Now that I went AWOL, I'm kind of … nothing."

"I object to that on principle, Ms. Andersen," said Ungent. "But after what I've seen since landing on Bledraun, I doubt there's much of anything that has been left to chance. If you're here at all, you count as important."

Cricket smiled.

"Thanks, Ambassador," she said. "I'll stop sulking. Remember what I told you about using a soothing voice on my frightened horse? I bet you could use a little help with that."

"What do you mean?" said Ungent, surprised at the irritation that had crept into his voice.

"Give it a try," said Cricket. "Let me hear you say, 'Don't worry, it's OK. You're safe with me.'"

Despite decades of experience in public speaking, Ungent's audition for the role of Soothing Parent was on the horrible side of awful.

"You have to mean it, Har Draaf!" said Cricket. "Haven't you ever comforted someone before?"

Ungent's heart flushed with shame. Had it been so long since Fleront … since….

"Give me another chance," he said softly. With his eyes closed, he called up a memory of the first time Fleront came home from school with a broken heart, and repeated the phrase. Cricket smiled again.

"You got it," she said. "Now don't get all preachy and forget."

"Wise words," said Dlalamphrur, as she reappeared. "Heed them. The time, as you would say, is now."

Ungent steadied himself against his titanium staff and breathed deep.

"Have they begun the attack?" he asked.

Up on the surface of Bledraun, the answer was "Yes." High in the branches of a *chalyzfe* tree that he'd barely managed to climb, Harlan issued orders to his newly-trained Krezovic troops through his embedded personal scanner. With the *Sweet Chariot* parked in a stationary orbit behind Lerdra, its transmitters were still within range.

Harlan sighed. By chance, most of the Krezovics who survived the ANN Commission assault had intact scanners of their own. From there, it had been a simple trick to tune them to a Terran Protectorate frequency, by using the compact computational power of Drashna's symbiote ship. He didn't need to guess at the odds of running a coordinated attack on the emerging Quishik spaceport without scanners.

"Zero," he whispered, then quickly banished all negative thinking. If they were going to win this battle, they'd better start believing it — especially him.

Would you look at that? he thought. *Who'd a thought they could fight so hard?*

At that same moment, way out at the edge of the Fremdel event horizon, Plaandrur Quishik Hlalkuhr stared at the display on her a-dimensional command console and writhed. Terror roiled her sinewy spine at the sight of the massive Improbability wave crashing over her carefully mapped-out determinants.

"A grotesque distortion of baseline projections," she hissed. "It is not even a Spur, but an Aberration!"

The news from the surface of Bledraun was more disturbing than her most fevered nightmares: The time-bound were acting independently! Worse, she was already feeling the effects of the mind-blocking device that Treluhne's team on Seldra had finally activated. While it would take several hours to have its full impact, the Ootray device was, at this very moment, slowing the Quishik commander's mental reflexes.

"Some ... interference ... a sickness perhaps," she mumbled.

But there was no time to investigate. Her meticulously planned strategy was faltering. Shocked as she was, the correct course of action was clear. She reached out telepathically to the commanders of every ship in her fleet, and ordered them to train weapons on the small of Krezovic army that was attacking her spaceport.

At a time of Aberration, she dared not resort to spatio-temporal displacement. The impact on the multiple timelines her species thrived on could no longer be calculated with sufficient precision. A fraction of a degree off the correct Probability curve would have devastating effects.

But unknown to Plaandrur, the wheels of the Ootray's master plan would soon knock her projections even further out of alignment. Miles beneath Harlan's feet, Ungent Draaf, Special Envoy of the Grashard Sidereal Caucus, was about to begin his most important mission. But it hardly felt that way.

"You want me to read *this*?" he asked Dlalamphrur. "It looks like it came from a children's holovid."

"That text is a shell for a series of embedded biomechanical programming commands," said Dlalamphrur. "To you, it reads as frivolous nonsense, but its effect on the Quishiks will be swift and precise."

"But you said these creatures had mutated horribly since you — or the Ootray — designed them," said Cricket. "How do you know this code will still work?"

As the ancient AI explained, her team had been tracking the Quishiks across thousands of years and adapted their programs to the Quishiks' current state.

"But there is no more room for doubt," said Dlalamphrur. "Will you help us now, Har Draaf?"

Ungent nodded and, with a wink to Cricket, padded over to the odd, transparent booth that appeared to his left.

"Speak distinctly," said the Ootray AI. "Your words will trigger a holographic display in close proximity to the Quishik fleet."

"Good luck," said Cricket. "And remember, you have to believe it."

"My children," Ungent began. "See how you have disappointed me...."

CHAPTER 51

"Captain Enos," Gillian called out over her comlink. "Do you see anything unusual?'

"I assume you ask because you see the same display I do," said the biomechanoid captain from the bridge of The *Mighty Fortress*. "I believe it may be time to bring my doomsday weapon online."

"No, Captain," said Warvhex from her own ship. "Give ... our friends ... a chance to do their work."

Like Gillian, she'd broken every rule of interstellar transport, to reach the Fremdel in record time. But while Warvhex had used the safer Olfdranyi tech her species had stolen a few decades back, Gillian had to rely on the gravity-wave coasting technique Cricket had tried earlier.

It was a risk Gillian would have been reluctant to take without Treluhne's reassurances. Fortunately, the Seldran had seen nothing on the Ootray Probability Reader to suggest her ship wouldn't survive the abbreviated journey.

"Understand," Treluhne had said, "the *djorcrelul* deals in Probability, not some form of mystic prediction."

"I know of nothing, actually, that's absolutely certain," said Gillian. "But I do know we cannot fail. We've been given the tools and we *must* finish the job."

Now here the three ships rested, as their crews wore themselves out with the effort to keep from succumbing to the pull of the Fremdel event horizon. Dwarfed by the Quishiks' light-cancelling ships, they could hardly be blamed for wondering if they were witnessing their final hours.

"I gather what we're seeing is...." Gillian started.

"Quiet," said Warvhex in a low voice. "Think about something else. We're in the presence of telepaths. If one even one of them turns their attention to our minds, we're through."

Yet if anyone in the Quishik fleet, let alone Plaandrur, were listening in on the human and symbiote radio chatter, it wasn't reflected in their response to the Ootray hologram or Ungent's impersonation of an ethereal being. For at the moment, the outsized hologram that Dlalamphrur had projected into space was thundering out his disapproval of the Quishik leader.

"Rhaltholinarur is angry," Plaandrur said, and her thoughts reached back to each of her previous incarnations.

"You cannot verify that," came a snarling response from the distant past. Plaandrur's reply was swift and merciless. The telepathic shock wave that hit the dissenter created a temporary rift in the metaversal array her life cycle nested in.

"In matters of faith, there is no verification!" she shrieked, with a ferocity that stifled further debate. "See how the Prophesy of the Three Ships has been fulfilled. Three silent vessels, an army of mercenaries attacking our spaceport...."

"And a stolen child," said Caronya's voice.

"You speak?" asked Plaandrur.

"Your sins have dulled your senses," Caronya's voice rang out again. "For I, Rhaltholinarur, had inhabited her soul long before her abduction. Had you not been steeped in evil, you would have found me there, so I could lead you back to the righteous path."

Plaandrur writhed and her tentacles lashed against the sides of her command center.

"No, Star Weaver, please," said Plaandrur. "Show us the way to forgiveness."

With an eerie calm, Caronya's voice complied and, point for point, began her list of demands. As a result, back on the surface of Bledraun, the situation was about to improve.

"What's it look like out there?" Drashna's voice queried him over their shared comlink aboard the symbiote ship. Harlan had ordered her there moments before he set out for the spaceport.

"Like we're trying as best we can," she heard Harlan reply. "I think we might have made a dent in the Quishik spaceport until those monsters started firing back."

"That wasn't supposed to be part of the plan," said Drashna.

"Nothing much about battle is planned," said Harlan, "least ways, once it gets started. But hang on, we aren't licked yet."

Drashna had no idea what Harlan had meant by the last half of his sentence as his idiomatic use of Planetary strained the translation grid to the breaking point. It hardly mattered, she realized. Asking Harlan how the battle was going was as foolish as Caronya asking her when their groundcar would arrive at her vacation home, twenty kilometers from Chalintren.

Caronya. What in the Nahlventran asteroid belt would become of her daughter, now that her captors were under attack?

But as real as her worries were, they were soon replaced by confusion, as the Quishik's counter assault, emanating from light years away, came to a sudden halt.

"What's happening?" she asked Harlan.

"Dunno," said the former star cruiser captain, "but I bet old Ungy had a hand in it. That old clambake can't stop himself from poking his eyestalks into the muck."

If he'd had any idea how right he was, Harlan would have taken heart. Instead, he ordered his small army to come back out of hiding and continue destroying the Quishik spaceport. In a desperate situation, he realized, against an unpredictable enemy, he needed to make the most of every advantage.

Meanwhile, deep in the subterranean city, the Ootray's ancient voice-synthesis technology enabled Cricket to maintain the illusion that the Quishik god was speaking through Drashna's seven-year-old daughter. At length, "Caronya" finished outlining the terms of the Quishiks' surrender, which included their voluntary return to imprisonment — within an interlocking array of the Fremdel event horizon and its multiversal parallels.

"Your voice turned the tide," said Dlalamphrur. "We are grateful."

Ungent glared at the hologram.

"You might have let me in on your secret," he growled.

Yet, as the Ootray AI told him, the less the two of them knew in advance, the less likely the Quishiks would discover the truth about her deception, by scanning their minds.

"There is still a risk even now," said Dlalamphrur, "so I hope you will forgive us if we temporarily suspend your higher mental functions."

Before either Ungent or Cricket could blink, the Ootray AI had encased them in separate stasis chambers, which had risen swiftly from the floor of the underground cavern.

Now the winds of change gave a powerful blast across the entire region of space time from the Fremdel event horizon, to the Bledraun system, to the far reaches of the Terran Protectorate and beyond. In compliance with the demands of "Rhaltholinarur," the Quishiks used their absolute control of Probability to restore the precious mineral deposits they temporally displaced. Soon every ton of precious ore, including chalinite, was carefully re-registered into its previous coordinates.

And within a few hours, the ruined cities of Bledraun began to rebuild themselves, as the Quishiks cloned copies of Dralein architecture from remote metaverses untouched by their presence. And, on the outskirts of Jeldren a seven-year-old Dralein was reunited with her mother.

"Is this really you?" asked Drashna.

Caronya, stared into her mother's eyes and smiled.

"You're so silly," she said. "Did you think I'd come back as a *chalyzfe* tree?"

Drashna hugged her tight and let the tears flow where they may. There would be time later to tell Caronya of her plans to leave Bledraun. But not yet — partly because she wasn't sure what those plans entailed, now that Treluhne had invited her to join his cabinet on Seldra, as an advisor.

"Despite our shared goals," Treluhne had said, "we still face conflicts that threaten our integrity as a community. Recent events have also shown us how vulnerable we are to outside threats."

"If you're looking for a military leader," Drashna had said, "I have no expertise in that area."

But, as Treluhne assured her, it was her contacts in interstellar commerce that would be most useful to the Seldrans. Drashna had promised to give the offer serious thought, considering how much easier it might be to relocate Caronya to a community not too different from the only home she'd ever known.

For now, she was forced to put aside all thought of moving. There was still too much to handle on Bledraun. Take, for example, the ANN Commission lander that was beginning to spiral down to the planet's surface a few meters away from where she was standing. The androids, too, had been restored by the contrite Quishik commander, in a gesture that might have unexpected consequences.

Drashna held on tight to her daughter's hand and pulled herself up to her full height.

"You're not welcome here," she said in her sternest voice to the lone android delegate that emerged from the lander and approached her on rubbery treads.

"Irrelevant," said the android. "Now that our mineral deposits have been restored, our presence on this planet will be brief."

"What's that to me?" said Drashna.

"We seek the traitor Harlan Mars," said the android. "You will assist us in locating him."

"Not if I blow your head off," said Grauth.

Drashna ducked, as a beam of lase fire ripped a hole the size of a human fist in the side of the android. At once, the rest of the Krezovic force leapt into view from behind the abandoned buildings that lined that part of town. In seconds, the sneering android, its confederates and the lander that carried them down to the surface were nothing more than a pile of smoldering cinders. Lacking explicit orders to counter unexpected armed resistance, the ANN Commission mother ship took that as its cue to leave orbit.

"There will be others," said Drashna. "What then?"

"My ship will be here in less than 083 rotations," said Harlan, as he limped out of his hiding place in Drashna's lander. "Then we're gonna give the ANN Commission a real talking to."

CHAPTER 52

The days that followed engulfed Bledraun in a swirl of hive-like activity. With the Quishiks back through the Fremdel, and the ANN Commission fended off through diplomatic channels, Harlan, Drashna and the Krezovic survivors enjoyed a brief period of calm. Yet it was soon thereafter that Ungent and Cricket emerged from the Ootray tunnels. In the midst of this, Gillian's arrival with the symbiotes felt like a windfall, even if all they could offer were basic services.

Yet help they did. Gillian ordered half of the replicators on *Sweet Chariot* to be reconfigured for mass production of machinery and building supplies. Then her corps of Terran Protectorate engineers and servicebots designed a local, satellite-based comsystem, which they patched together with help from the symbiote's storehouse of technology and whatever they could scavenge from the ruins of Jeldren.

It and other essential systems were augmented by the crew of the *Mighty Fortress.* They'd arrived from the edge of the Fremdel event horizon about two weeks later — forced as it was by the Fremdel's gravitational pull to travel no faster than the speed of light.

Under the best of circumstances, this basic reconstruction work might have taken months. But now the symbiote's failed transponder weapon turned out to be a blessing in disguise. By replicating several dozen servicebots, the combined forces were able to adapt the devices Drashna had ordered installed in *chalyzfe* trees all over the planet. In that way, they could sync with the Terran signal tower on Gelen and establish a truly global network.

Through it all, the Ootray AIs provided shelter for any who wanted it, not to mention medical supplies, diagnostic and emergency services, maternity care, and mental health counseling. This was welcomed by both the Krezovic survivors and Harlan, who was still recuperating from his ordeal in the escape pod, and his debilitating battle against the Quishiks.

Though he was eager to rejoin his crew, he was largely sidelined, which pained him in more ways than one. To begin with, he hated feeling useless. Worse, he was missing the opportunity to spend every waking hour with Gillian again. Now, more than ever, her decisive command of her ship and coordination of the rescue mission made her irresistible. That is, except for the tiny obstacle that, as his subordinate, she was completely off limits.

To her credit, Gillian made a point of consulting with Harlan. She gave him constant updates and occasionally asked advice. He accepted this graciously, though he knew his former XO had everything well in hand. He should be thankful, he told himself, he could bask in her presence, even as he prepared for the day when he'd leave this backwater world, retire from the Protectorate Fleet and return to the quiet life on New Dallas.

Had enough, he thought.

Between the arrogance of the androids and the blind-siding manipulation of Brad Christiansen, he'd lost his appetite for military command. Trouble was, there wasn't much else he could see himself doing — except fall back on his old habits.

All told, after two months of intense work, Gillian and Enos had reached the limits of the reconstructive work they could manage with available resources. And just about this time, the revived, post-*sceraun* Dralein population emerged from their tunnels, all across Bledraun. With the Dralein were the first of their newborn children, with more *decleinyi* on the way.

What they found shocked them. Their homeworld, despite the Quishiks' attempt to rebuild it, was still a shambles. Though the Quishiks would continue to reestablish the planet's original Probability curve, from inside their metaversal prison, the process was necessarily slow and erratic.

Meanwhile, with its seemingly limitless power supply, the Ootray AI provided a steady stream of hot meals at any time of day. The one thing they couldn't offer was an explanation.

"But where have your masters gone?" asked Ungent the last time he went down into the tunnels.

"That data, along with any explanation of why the Ootray left this quadrant of the universe is not in our knowledge base," Dlalamphrur had said.

"Too bad," Ungent had replied. "I can't help thinking they are still needed."

Dlalamphrur had agreed and had filled the Grashardi ambassador's mind with images from several probable futures. In the vast majority of them, the Quishiks returned through the Fremdel.

"It is as if they are incapable of learning," Dlalamphrur had said. "We've used various stopgap measures many times before. But the Quishiks are constantly evolving and the effect is always temporary."

A day later, Ungent returned to the surface, eager to find news of Yaldrint, whom he hadn't seen in weeks.

"The effect is always temporary," Ungent repeated to himself now.

"*Everything* is temporary," said a voice to Ungent's left.

"Dadren?" asked Ungent.

Ungent pivoted and saw the last Dralein he'd spoken to before jumping into the tunnels. Bledraun's interim leader was disheveled, filthy, and his military fatigues were punctuated with jagged rips. Dadren spoke with a strange detachment, as if he was no longer of this world. Yet Ungent sensed the Dralein had the same calm demeanor as before.

"Yes, Ambassador," said Dadren. "Though, as I see now, greatly transformed. I can hear your thoughts, for example, and I'm starting to think the theta wave regulators pushed us farther ahead than a naturally occurring *sceraun* would have. But my perceptions are clearer in every other way as well, and I recognize how right you were to stay involved. My apologies."

"This is hardly the time to revisit old wounds," said Ungent. "What will you do now?"

"Rebuild," said Dadren, "using every available resource. That's why I've asked Captain Cavendish to get me an invitation to Seldra."

"How long has it been since anyone on the planet visited the colony?" Ungent asked.

"I'm ashamed to say I don't know," said the Dralein. "Once they announced their new policy regarding the deliberate use of *sceraun* … well, that was too much for our traditionalists. We cut off all diplomatic and cultural ties around four-hundred-fifty cycles ago. From what I've learned about the mood at the time, it surprises me we didn't go to war."

The seasoned diplomat in Ungent bubbled to the surface.

"It's a testament to Dralein restraint," he said.

"Complacency, more likely," said Dadren. "But now Tradition has been permanently disrupted. We're not what we were, and it's time we reconnect with Seldra."

Ungent smiled, for almost the first time since his initial meeting with Drashna, so many weeks before.

"And what about the Krezovic population?" he asked. "Bledraun has neglected it, too."

Dadren's large, furry head pivoted at the sound of a lander touching down a dozen meters or so to his left.

"That's a complex issue, Har Draaf," he said. "Bias against outsiders runs deep in our culture. But the watchword is Change, especially because no one doubts our enemy will return."

"What makes you think they will?" asked Ungent, though he still recalled Dlalamphrur's words.

Despite being distracted by the commotion near the newly arrived lander, Dadren completed his thought. His time in the tunnels had made him aware of many forces at work in the universe that his reconfigured mind could still not process.

"The ambient temperature, the quality of the air, water and soil across the planet — I sense these now, as if they were sights or smells," he said. "And on the edge of my consciousness, I am beginning to perceive fluctuations in the planet's electromagnetic fields. We will build new instruments to measure this and other factors more accurately, perhaps as an early warning system. But for now, we are safe. thanks to you."

"And, I hope, for many cycles to come," said Ungent.

Dadren shrugged.

"You and the others have done a brave thing and accomplished what we could never have done on our own," he said. "But the measure was temporary. The Quishiks cannot be kept down forever — or even for long."

By now, the stir at the landing site had risen to a roar. Ungent whipped his eyestalks to his right to see a tall, thin Dralein emerge from a lander of distinctly different design than he'd seen before. It was Treluhne, whose yellow fur gleamed in the morning sun. With him were a team of eleven other Seldrans, including Verohme, Treluhne's second in command.

As Gillian led Treluhne to meet Dadren, Ungent was struck by her air of self-confidence. Why was it, he wondered, that a disaster was so efficient in bringing out the best in someone? Regardless, he sensed this meeting was his cue to leave Dadren's side and seek out Shol and Trinity. He hoped, for their sake, that their young hearts hadn't been permanently darkened by the horrors they'd seen in such a short time.

Ungent found Shol standing, maybe for the first time since he was nine, in the company of so many other Krezovics, some close to his own age. He looked, to Ungent's eyes, excited and happy at the validation of being amongst his own kind. Next, Ungent's attention shifted to Trinity, who was standing apart, gazing on with a mix of amusement and detachment.

"I see you survived, Ms. Hudson," he said quietly.

Trinity ignored him at first, her eyes riveted on Shol.

"He's so happy," she said after a moment. "I don't think I've ever heard him laugh so much."

"Yet I gather that makes you sad," said the crustacean.

"I envy him, is all," said Trinity. "He fits in here. I don't think I fit in anywhere."

"Gillian tells me your father and the rest of the mission specialists are still doing well in stasis," said Ungent. "You can join him as soon as the ship returns to Reagan 3."

Trinity's fists clenched, as her eyes misted over.

"He'll be so mad at me," she said. "I'll probably be grounded until, like, forever. But that doesn't even matter, because I *want* to stay here, with … with Shol."

Ungent's eyestalks pivoted in Shol's direction and back again.

"Is he staying?" he asked.

"That's the thing," said the pretty human girl. "I haven't ... we haven't talked about it. But I know he can't come back with me. My father ... he doesn't ... well, Shol wouldn't fit in on my homeworld."

"A convenient turn of phrase to hide a lot of ugly thoughts," said Ungent. "Yet, you're wise to deal with the real world as it actually is. If you want to stay with Shol, you have to make a difficult choice. It is, however, a choice Galactic Law will not allow you to make."

Trinity turned her head and buried her eyes in her hands.

"Being young ... it's a curse!" she cried.

"Believe me," said Ungent, "you'll know what a gift your youth is when it's gone. And who knows where you might meet our impetuous friend a few years from now?"

Trinity wiped her eyes on her shirt sleeve.

"But I *do* know, Har Draaf," she said. "Once I get home, my old life will kind of take over. And anyway, I know this sounds terrible, but I do miss my friends from before."

"Not terrible at all," said Ungent. "But see, here's Shol now."

The Krezovic boy called out as he trotted up to where the two of them stood.

"Har Draaf!" he shouted. "You hitting on my girl?"

"Shol, Baby, we have to talk," said Trinity.

"One question before I leave," said Ungent. "Do either of you know what's become of Yaldrint?"

Shol's remarked that he'd left the Grashardi AI on the symbiote ship — before Trinity dragged him away to a spot behind the disfigured trunk of one of Jeldren's ancient trees.

With that, Ungent, grateful as always for his titanium staff, turned away, and caught sight of Captain Enos, engaged in an animated conversation with his former navigator.

"Poor girl," he said. His legs aching, he headed for a fallen log about two meters ahead and sat down as slowly as Bledraun's gravity would allow. It was time for him, too, he realized, to think about returning to his homeworld. But before he'd had time to do more than clear his mind, he saw Dlalamphrur materialize in front of him again.

"I thought you were confined to the tunnels," said Ungent.

"Not at all," said the hologram. "It is simply our preference. You will forgive me if I overheard your thoughts about the future."

"I've decided nothing," said Ungent.

"Then let me make you a proposal," said Dlalamphrur.

Back on the symbiote ship, whose lander had returned to orbit after dropping off Shol and Trinity, Yaldrint was facing a dilemma no organic life form could be expected to understand. Warvhex was standing over her in the body of a young female *Sweet Chariot* crew member whose curiosity had gotten the better of her.

"You understand, it's well within our capabilities," the symbiote was saying.

"I have scanned your ship and I see you are correct," Yaldrint replied. "However, I cannot imagine how you came to believe I *want* my consciousness transferred."

Warvhex smiled through her host and described the fleeting conversation she'd had with Trinity before the young human girl entered the symbiote lander for a trip to Jeldren.

"She predicted you'd be too embarrassed to bring this up on your own," said the symbiote.

"Ms. Hudson means well," said Yaldrint. "But she misunderstood me. I merely said that, were I mobile, I might be more help to Har Draaf. I'm afraid it hardly matters, as I cannot approve such a thing on my own. That is for the Grashardi government to decide and I am certain the ambassador would find the expense inexcusable."

But Warvhex explained, she was willing to donate the symbiotes' services as a gesture of thanks to Ungent.

"The fact is," she said. "I owe him one."

"I fail to see...." Yaldrint started.

"Of course you do," said Warvhex. "My reasons are secret — until I have the courage to tell the old geezer the truth. In the meantime, he deserves a gesture of gratitude. What do you say?"

Yaldrint's status lights blinked excitely for what felt like an eternity.

"I cannot accept any gift," the AI said, "whose sole purpose is to ingratiate you with someone you have wronged. Tell Har Draaf the truth. Then I will consider your offer."

Warvhex threw her host's body into a nearby chair.

"You're right," she said. "He deserves to know. But he'll probably kill me."

"Impossible," said Yaldrint. "In the eighty cycles I have worked with the Ambassador, I have never seen him commit the slightest act of violence against another sentient being. And I am certain that you yourself would prefer the truth to a delusion."

Warvhex stared at the Grashardi AI, shook her host's head and reached a hand out to grab the handle of Yaldrint's casing.

"Wait," said Yaldrint. "Your gesture will come to nothing, if the Ambassador reports your confession to the Interstellar Council. You must offer him a bargain he cannot refuse."

"What do you ... have in mind?" asked Warvhex.

Yaldrint's answer was as startling as it was brilliant.

"I doubt I could convince the Kaldhex Assembly to go along with that," said the symbiote.

"Based on your history," said Yaldrint, "I believe you could charm the shell off an Alchnorean sea turtle."

"You've learned a lot from Har Draaf, haven't you?" said Warvhex. "Well, don't blame me if he ends up in an Interstellar Council prison," she said.

With that, Warvhex picked Yaldrint up by the handle on her casing, headed for the launch bay, and entered her lander.

A few minutes later, the lander's transmat sequence set the vehicle down a few dozen meters from where Ungent sat, apparently talking to thin air, for Dlalamphrur had been speaking to Ungent telepathically. At the sound of military boots crunching across the rubble toward him, he looked up.

"Gone round the bend, Ambassador?" said the symbiote.

Ungent stood up to greet her.

"Warvhex! No one else would bother to ask," he said. "Usually they take it for granted. Thank you for bringing me Yaldrint."

"Greetings, Har Draaf," said the AI. "I can power down now, if you prefer to speak in private."

"Why, old friend?" asked the crustacean.

"Yaldrint may have a point," said Warvhex.

"Nonsense," said Ungent. "I can vouch for Yaldrint's discretion. Why, I've already told her my entire life story a dozen times."

"Incorrect," said Yaldrint. "The real figure is much higher."

"There you have it," said Ungent. "What is it you need to tell me?"

"You aren't going to like it," said Warvhex.

The story the symbiote told sent shockwaves of grief up and down Ungent's exoskeleton. For it was Warvhex who had entered the body of a young Grashardi journalist and, in an attempt to infiltrate the Krezovic rebels, had driven her to take ever greater risks in order to "get the story."

"Fleront would never have been captured without my prodding," said Warvhex. "She was much too wily for that. And now I see where she got if from."

Ungent stabbed the ground with his titanium staff.

"Your faint praise does nothing for me!" he shouted.

"Try to understand," said Warvhex. "All of our intelligence told us the Krezovic militants would never resort to ... to murder."

"Your stupidity told you that," said Ungent. "I recognize no form of intelligence that believes desperate people don't resort to the unthinkable. And Fleront was the victim of that stupidity."

"We were trying...." said Warvhex.

"You failed," said Ungent. He turned his back on the symbiote and tried to pull his confused emotions together. "You're forgetting that the Krezovic had every right to revolt — they still do — for the way the Intergalactic Council ignores their oppression by the humans."

"We ... we were trying to make their revolt more effective," said Warvhex.

Ungent spun around on his heels.

"Then you should have done so honestly," said Ungent. "Offered them help as equals. Not made puppets of them the way you did my ... my daughter. She's gone now, but you've learned nothing. You're still skulking. The Ootray told me you knew about the Quishiks years ago, but kept it quiet."

"Can't you see?" asked Warvhex. "What choice does a symbiote have but to skulk? But I don't expect you to understand. I wouldn't even have told you about your daughter if Yaldrint hadn't insisted."

"Yaldrint?" said Ungent. "You knew...."

"Only that there was a truth of some kind you deserved to know," said Yaldrint. "Ms. Warvhex believes now she owes you a debt for your loss. And I remind you, you have always sought diplomatic accord. She has a gift for you ... or rather for me ... which, if you accept on my behalf, could lead to a unique treaty between the symbiotes and the Grashardi."

"What?" said Ungent. "I should let Fleront's murderer bribe me to forget her crime?"

"Not forget, Har Draaf," said Yaldrint. "Merely reap some benefit from your loss, for your homeworld."

Ungent bowed his head. In personal terms, the AI's words were repulsive. But in his role as career diplomat, they rang true.

"What treaty?" he asked.

In time the two unlikely partners struck a culture-changing deal. Ungent would convince his government to campaign against the millennia-old bias toward symbiotes. In exchange, Warvhex would persuade the Kaldhex Assembly to share the rich storehouse of acquired technologies they'd amassed in secret, down through time.

"It would be the end of the Terran Protectorate's dominance," said Warvhex. "Isn't that worth something?"

Ungent tilted his head up to the sky.

"Provided the Grashardi don't become as drunk with power as the humans," said Ungent. "However, I foresee a significant obstacle to the acceptance of such a treaty. Your use of involuntary hosts must stop."

The face of Warvhex's Terran Protectorate host went blank.

"But ... you'd confine us to our tanks," she said. "We can't transfer to androids or clones, for reasons Yaldrint already knows."

"Might I suggest a mobile tank, Ms. Warvhex?" said Yaldrint. "A unit that could sit atop a robotic platform, which might incorporate components of a biomechanical brain, to complement and strengthen your central nervous system."

"That might work," said Warvhex. "But our entire culture...."

"Would have to change," said Ungent. "Just as you're asking the rest of the settled world to change their culture to accommodate you. Once you're accepted as members of the Interstellar Council, our shared technical advances may allow you to have bodies of your own."

The young human host's upper lip curled.

"How can we be sure the Protectorate won't betray us?" said Warvhex through her host. "The humans have always been our enemy."

"We have an old saying on Grashard," said Ungent. "*The end of always is the start of now*. You have to decide if the treaty is worth that risk."

"Of course it is," said Warvhex in a low voice.

"Then I have what I need to make your case to Sector Court," said Ungent. "Now, what is this gift you were talking about?"

CHAPTER 53

Later that same day, aboard the *Mighty Fortress*, Cricket Andersen sat alone in a non-descript holding area, her hands fidgeting with each and every button of her rumpled Fleet uniform. She'd had no choice, she realized, when Captain Enos confronted her, but to accompany him to the ship.

It was the first step in a process she was sure would end in a humiliating court martial. Despite her role in taking down the Quishiks, there was no way a Terran Protectorate tribunal would give much credence to her story.

Lured away from her duties by a talking horse? That had to rank near the top of desperately guilty lies. Cricket's other option was the insanity defense, which would hardly do more for her prospects.

Instead, she had to hope the testimony of Ambassador Draaf, Captain Cavendish and Dadren, would bolster her credibility. There she sat, drowning in a sea of thought and emotion, until the grim imaginary scenarios that haunted her were washed away by the determined clomp of boots in the corridor to her left.

This is it, she thought.

But as the clomping rounded the corner and entered the holding area, Cricket was relieved to see it was made by boots belonging to her biomechanical captain. She jumped to her feet.

"Captain," she said. "I was expecting … a bailiff."

Enos stared at her a moment.

"That would imply I had started court martial proceedings," he said.

"I … it's a logical…." Cricket sputtered. "I went AWOL, Sir, and, if I could explain…."

"There is no need," said Enos. "I have spoken with the Ootray AI. You could no sooner have resisted the Ootray's telepathic commands than I could develop a sense of humor."

Cricket suppressed a laugh. The last thing she expected from the biomechanoid was that level of self-awareness.

"The question is," Enos continued, "whether you still want to be a member of the Fleet."

Cricket's face flushed.

"I do, Sir," said Cricket. "It's what I've always wanted. But I respectfully request a transfer."

Enos motioned for her to sit back down on the small neo-leather couch at the center of the holding area — and then sat down beside her.

"That would be a great loss to this ship...." said Enos.

"I appreciate that, Sir," said Cricket, "but...."

"And to myself, personally," said the biomechanoid. "Although I cannot explain it in terms of the parameters of my programming, I find your presence ... a source of comfort."

Cricket's breath stuck in her chest.

"You what?" she said softly.

"Forgive me if I tell you," said Enos, "that I believe you share this same ... sensation."

"Oh God," said Cricket. "I don't even know how to talk about this with you."

The captain stood up, walked to the other side of the room, and faced the far wall.

"Words are unnecessary when a truth is already known," he said. "but ... difficulties remain, as I am equally sure you are also aware."

"Aware of what?" asked Cricket. "Knowing the truth doesn't make you a slave to it."

"So what do you propose?" said Enos, as he turned around.

"I propose nothing," said Cricket. "We don't *owe* each other anything, despite the ... the truth. Meanwhile, if we're ever ready to get ... closer ... we'll know."

Enos peered into the corridor. Was he worried, Cricket wondered, that they'd been overheard?

"How, exactly, will we know?" asked the biomechanoid. "I can identify no equation that can...."

"Captain," said Cricket. "Permission to tell you to shut up."

The flawless contours of the biomechanoid's exquisitely designed face stared out at her with a faint glow of sorrow.

"Granted," said Enos. "Return to your quarters and prepare for your shift. Then plot a course to the Homeworld."

Cricket stood and headed out in the corridor, pausing long enough to rest a hand on her captain's cheek.

"Yes Sir," she said.

Despite the full duty roster, which the captain's internal sensors insisted he pursue, and the billions of lines of programming code that, until now, had defined his every thought, Enos found no way forward. Instead, he discovered, he couldn't resist watching his Chief Navigation Officer walk away into the intricate corridors of the midsized Terran Protectorate probe ship.

"Curious," he said to the tile floor beneath him.

CHAPTER 54

It had taken a month, but the medpod aboard the *Sweet Chariot* had finally restored Harlan Mars to health. At last, the effects of extreme dehydration, malnourishment, infection and fatigue he'd suffered in the escape pod, not to mention a few broken ribs and a severely bruised collar bone, he'd incurred during his rough landing on Bledraun, had been compensated for. He was even able to return to his familiar round of physical conditioning, even if, on the face of it, it wasn't clear that having a firm physique would matter so much in the civilian world.

In any case, his mind was made up. As he pushed his legs onto a treadmill, his thoughts ran to the many ways his life would change, for the better, once he resigned his commission. It was a pleasant state of calm contemplation — exactly the sort of thing civilized life was designed to shatter.

A few hours later he was lounging on his couch when he had a surprise visit from Ungent.

"Ungy!" said Harlan. "Never thought I'd see your purple puss again."

"I'm glad your charm has survived this ordeal," said the crustacean.

The mix of pity and contempt in Ungent's gaze sent a chill run up Harlan's spine, but he held out his hand anyway.

"Hey, it's good to see you," he said.

"That's not what you said the last time we met," said Ungent. "But now that your official business is over, I imagine you'll go back to being the genial sack of meat I think of as a friend."

Harlan hung his head.

"This business is tough, Ungy," he said. "But, I guess putting me in an awkward position is kinda your life's work."

"The pay is so good," said Ungent, "it's hard to resist. So. What's your next mission?"

"Don't rightly know as I have one," said Harlan. "I'll send you a holoflash when I land. You heading home to Mrs. Ungy?"

Ungent fidgeted with his staff.

"Hardly," he said. "Good luck to you, you ridiculous excuse for a hero."

"Back at you, Clam Bake," said Harlan. "And don't get any more cracks in those plates of yours. You're starting to look like an irrigation project on LunaBase."

Harlan watched as his distinguished friend trudged out of his quarters. He lay back on his couch and tried to imagine his future life away from the Fleet. But his reveries were soon interrupted, as a message popped up on his personal scanner from Brad Christiansen. The sight of Brad's stern face, encased in a salt-and-pepper beard, sent Harlan's heart racing out of control.

"Mars? Brad Christiansen here," said the head of Terran Protectorate Admin. "What do you know about the allegations against your former XO?"

Harlan took a deep breath. If he'd learned anything from military service, it was that the appearance of calm was the most important response to any confrontation with authority.

"You'll have to fill me in on that, Sir," said Harlan. "I've been out of the loop in the hospital."

The news was not good. The same mix of fringe ANN Commission and Terran Protectorate interests, that once blocked Ungent's negotiations with the Dralein, had now gone after Gillian. Obviously, Harlan's former second-in-command now knew way too much about their machinations over the last few months. Among other things, she was being charged with "collusion with an unknown foreign power."

"Sir," said Harlan, "The Seldrans are members of a Dralein colony. Not exactly an unknown power. You want my opinion?"

"You're her commanding officer," said Brad. "I *expect* you to state your opinion."

Again, Harlan breathed deep, before launching into a point-for-point defense of every decision Gillian had made, partly out of his devotion to her, but also because her decisions reflected directly on his own.

"Under the circumstances," said Harlan, "with, you know, direct evidence of an attempt to assassinate her CO, Captain Cavendish was right on the money to seek new alliances. Hell a mile, she couldn't exactly trust the wireheads, now could she? And considering, at that time, the ANN Commission was *supposed to be* our ally...."

Christiansen's eyes shifted to the right.

"Stop there, Captain," he said. "You've made your point. Your commitment to your subordinate's defense is clear enough *without* any need for insubordination. Are we clear?"

"Yes, Sir," said Harlan. How much better, he told himself, to be still under anesthesia.

"Fine," said Christiansen. "I'm satisfied on that point. You're a good soldier and that carries weight in my administration. Now, about your next assignment."

Harlan swallowed hard. His plans to retire from the military had just been scuttled. If he became a civilian, the odds were, his defense of Gillian would carry no weight at all. His decision to leave the Service could be twisted easily, to raise the suspicion he had something to hide.

Harlan accepted his fate. As long as Gillian would be saved from prosecution, he'd sacrifice his own comfort and hold on to his commission. With her name cleared, she'd likely be given a command of her own. Too bad, that would put her even further out of reach. His call with Admin over, Harlan put his head down and let the grief wash over him. She was gone from his life for good.

All the more surprising, then, was the next message to pop up on his personal scanner.

"Sir, have you heard?" Gillian's melodious voice rang out from the holographic display. "We've been reassigned to the battle-cruiser *Jericho*."

In spite of the blood rushing to his head, Harlan kept his voice level.

"Great news," he said. "Glad to have you aboard, Commander. When do we dock with the *Jericho*?"

"Actually, Sir," said Gillian. "It appears we have both also been given shore leave for the next thirty rotations."

"Shore leave?" said Harlan.

"Yes, Sir, quite unexpected," said Gillian. "But welcome all the same."

Harlan stared at her image in the holosplay, trying to see if the twinkle in her eye was due to faulty transmission.

"Agreed," said Harlan. "And well-deserved. You were terrific out there, Commander."

"Thank you, Sir," said Gillian. "And Sir? Apropos of nothing, I hear the Ulhanidron system is lovely this time of year — and the fares are quite reasonable."

"Thanks for the tip," said Harlan with a sly smile. "I'll take that under advisement. Mars out."

CHAPTER 55

With Jeldren still in shambles, Ungent had taken a room in the Ootray underground city, where the remnant of that ancient race facilitated communications between the Kaldhex Assembly, Terran Protectorate Admin and, surprisingly, the ANN Commission.

"Why in the name of Chulindunt's harp are the humans still dealing with the androids?" he wondered.

"The nature of sentience is to seek connection," Dlalamphrur had told him. "Even if the benefits of such connections are questionable. No doubt a monetary incentive is involved."

Ungent nodded. He had plenty of personal experience to corroborate her statement. Yet, his familiarity of such under-the-table dealings did not make him anymore comfortable with them. But here again, he reminded himself, action — any action — was infinitely preferable to complaining about a status quo he could not alter.

Nor could he afford the distraction of moral outrage. His negotiations required his full attention. In spite of the advantages the symbiote's proposal offered the Grashardi government, it was more than two months before Ungent managed to broker a final agreement with the Kaldhex Assembly.

Two weeks into the negotiations, factions within the ANN Commission and the Terran Protectorate had woven a conspiracy theory of lies. They alleged that Ungent had brought about the conflict on Bledraun as part of a secret pact with an "unnamed entity." Soon there were rumors that the entire Grashardi government would be sued in the Interstellar Court for "war crimes against the settled universe."

It was the age-old political game of distraction, as several high-placed humans and androids sought to cover up their own roles in the siege of the Dralein homeworld.

Nevertheless, Ungent pressed on. By presenting video evidence, recorded by the Ootray AI, of scheming cross-talk between members of both factions, he exposed the real culprits. Soon the videos had swept away every obstacle to ratifying the symbiote's treaty.

Yet in the way of the universe, Ungent had less than eight hours to savor his diplomatic coup, before he received a large cache of legal documents from Nulgrant's lawyer.

"Beat me to it," Ungent told himself. Though the divorce was exactly what he wanted, he couldn't escape the grief and nostalgia that went with it. A few happy memories, including the birth of Fleront, would remain with him always. Much of the rest was depressingly forgettable. Ungent passed the metadigital divorce documents directly to Yaldrint with a simple set of instructions.

"Agree to everything," he told her. "Better to be done with it."

A day later, after a night filled with disturbing dreams, Ungent sat before Warvhex, now back in her spherical tank on the symbiote ship that had brought her to the Bledraun system.

"For better or worse," he told her, "Our governments are partners now."

The liquid in the symbiote's tank flashed tangerine orange before settling down to sea green.

"You don't think of yourself as part of your government any longer?" asked Warvhex.

"I've officially retired from the diplomatic corps," said Ungent, "and taken on a consulting position."

"Very sly," said Warvhex. "I don't suppose you would share...."

"Not even a hint," said Ungent. "The past revolution has taught me the value of discretion, as never before. Now I think it's past the time I saw what you've done with Yaldrint."

"If I may, Har Draaf," said Yaldrint's voice behind him, "turn around."

The former Grashardi ambassador to Bledraun stood up and turned to face his AI assistant, now transferred to a biomechanical body — with unexpected attributes.

"You ... you have ... an exoskeleton," Ungent stuttered.

Yaldrint replied through her new biomechanical mandibles.

"I had thought at first to adopt a purely functional design," she said. "But I thought I'd draw too much attention to myself on our upcoming mission."

Ungent studied Yaldrint's new appearance with mixed emotion. Naturally, he was astonished to see how precisely the symbiotes had mimicked Grashardi anatomy. Yet it unnerved him to think Yaldrint must have selected her flowing pants suit of indigo pseudocotton from the catalog of a Grashardi designer, favored by Nulgrant. Yaldrint's pewter necklace was even "creepier" from that point of view.

"You sure you won't tell me anything about your new mission?" asked Warvhex.

"Not a word," Ungent told Warvhex. "Except 'thank you' for making good on your promise."

"So now, I believe I've paid my debt to you," said Warvhex.

"Not in the least," said Ungent. "You may have stuck a deal with the Grashardi ambassador, but with me, Har Ungent Draaf, you will always be a scoundrel."

"A title I'll cherish to the end," said Warvhex. "At least now, there's a chance my fellow scoundrels will get some respect in this universe."

"Respect," said Ungent, "comes at a high price. You will learn that before much longer."

"Har Draaf," said Yaldrint, "we are needed elsewhere."

So for the last time in his life, Ungent pulled himself up straight and gave Warvhex the swift, formal bow of a senior Grashardi diplomat.

"Make sure you watch out for the Krezovic, too," he said. "They are as much a victim of your meddling as my daughter was."

Minutes later, a symbiote transmat pod had sent Ungent and his reconfigured AI into the depths of the Dralein tunnels, where they intended to meet Dlalamphrur. Instead, they found Shol, looking lost and forlorn in the Ootray's vast underground complex. The Krezovic boy jumped up to meet them, his face brightening, in spite of his gloom.

"Har Draaf," he said. "I thought you'd left and ... craters, is that, like, Yaldrint?"

"I hope my revised appearance is not unappealing," said the AI.

"You look so ... real," said Shol.

"Reality is less a matter of looks, young friend," said Ungent, "than of conduct and consequence."

"You'll ... you'll have to explain that one, Har Draaf," said Shol

"I am surprised not to see Ms. Hudson with you," said Yaldrint. "I had thought you were inseparable."

"Don't want to talk about that," said the Krezovic teenager. Yet for the next few minutes, he couldn't stop himself from telling them of Trinity's decision to return to Reagan 3 with her father.

"I hope you parted friends," said Ungent.

"That's the weird part, Har Draaf," said Shol. "The second she let go of my had to get into the 'tectorate shuttle, I felt closer to her than ever."

"Perfectly normal," said Ungent. "But where is the Ootray AI?"

With that, Dlalamphrur's image materialized among them. She now resembled a Krezovic girl about Shol's age.

"Here," said Dlalamphrur. "Under the circumstances, I thought a change of appearance might make Shol feel less isolated."

Shol's face flushed.

"Thanks," he said.

"Well," said Ungent, "I know why Yaldrint and I are here, but why have you come?"

"He has been … recruited, Har Draaf," said Dlalamphrur. "As you seek out the descendants of the Ootray, you will need Shol's wiliness, strength and courage."

"And you can keep teaching me," said Shol. "You know, how to be smarter, like you."

Ungent raised a webbed finger.

"There will be risks," he said. "And you will have to obey orders."

"I suggest," said Yaldrint, "that friend Shol's service with Ulandroz has most likely prepared him for a diverse array of complex situations."

"Plus, I have, like, connections," said Shol. "I know people who can, you know, get things done."

Ungent stroked his mandibles.

"Let's keep them in reserve," he said, "for … emergencies."

"If you are agreed," said Dlalamphrur, "I will share with you the outlines of the mission we proposed to Har Draaf a quarter rotation ago.

A pair of bioluminescent globes, which until then had been looming in the shadows, now flooded the chamber they were standing in with a soft blue light. They revealed a raised platform on which rested a curious device, about the size of a typical metadigital tablet, but with significant differences.

Ungent stared down at the circular, flat object, which was studded with small keys, toggle switches and seemed subdivided into four parts. Or were the object's four quadrants merely decorative?

"This is an Ootray device of great antiquity," said Dlalamphrur. "Its primary function is to act as a sensor array. It can detect the quantum residue left behind by any object, organic, mechanical or inert. Used properly, it will enable you to trace our makers' path across the universe."

"Like a … like a GPS system or whatever," said Shol.

"But a system sensitive to more than three dimensions," said Yaldrint.

"Agreed," said Dlalamphrur. "However, the *sucherch,* as we call it, is not so simple to operate. It will take time to grasp all of its functions. In essence, it cannot lead you anywhere. It can, however, tell you the probability that you are heading in the right direction."

"But that could mean days of running the wrong way," said Ungent. "We could get hopelessly lost."

Dlalamphrur called up a schematic of the *sucherch* out of thin air.

"You will not be 'flying blind,' as that curious human expression goes," said Dlalamphrur. "The *sucherch* will give you a multidimensional profile by which to recognize the most likely location of each leg of your journey. See here, for example…."

As the Ootray AI spoke, different areas of the schematic lit up. Over the course of the next two hours, Ungent, Yaldrint and Shol received individual instruction on how to use the device.

"There is much else to learn about the *sucherch*," said Dlalamphrur. "However, as it dates from a time before our own construction, not all of its functions are clear. You will have to learn as you go."

"Can't understand this," said Shol. "I mean, if the ... the Ootray were advanced enough to build all this, why can't they find *us*?"

"Unknown," said Dlalamphrur. "What we do know is that, unless someone brings the Ootray out of hiding, there will be no defense against the Quishiks when they return. And, I'm sorry to report, our projections suggest they will return stronger than before."

"But even if we were to find your ancient masters," said Ungent, "what incentive would they have to help, when they have known of the dangers all along and done nothing?"

Dlalamphrur shrugged.

"Their behavior matches nothing in the historical profile," she said. "Either they exist no more, or some unknown force prohibits them from taking action."

Shol, who had been poring over the *sucherch* in a small niche to the left of Ungent, strode over and confronted Dlalamphrur.

"Can I ... can I ask you a question?" he said. "If we're going to follow where this thing leads, or lead it to show us where to follow ... or ... whatever, don't we need a ship and, like, some credit tiles?"

"I believe you'll find part of your answer in the next chamber," said Yaldrint.

"What have you sensed, dear friend?" asked Ungent.

Before any of them could move, Dlalamphrur dissolved the holographic wall separating the two chambers — to reveal a magnificent space-folder, gleaming in the soft light of the glow globes.

"We have configured it to be compatible with Yaldrint's mind," said the Ootray AI. "We believe you should find the controls quite intuitive."

"So they are," said Yaldrint, who for the first time in her existence cracked a smile. With a wave of a webbed biomechanical hand she made a side panel in the ship slide open. Soon, a graceful entry ramp descended to the floor of the underground chamber.

"There are, of course, replicators onboard," said Dlalamphrur. "And many other facilities to meet the physical and spiritual needs of the crew."

Ungent and Shol were startled to feel a small pouch materialize around their necks. Yaldrint took it in stride.

"A credit tile for each of you," said Dlalamphrur. "The account, while not technically infinite, contains the accumulated wealth of what was once the Ootray government."

Shol smacked his shiny forehead.

"You mean they have, like, all this money and they're not using it?" he asked.

"It is, we fear, one sign our makers may no longer exist," said Dlalamphrur. "We hope you can prove otherwise."

Ungent stared at the pouch around his neck, which was woven from thousands of multi-colored threads in a subtle repeating pattern. It resembled the patterns etched into the walls around them.

"We're off then," said Ungent. With his hands clenched tight around his titanium staff, he followed Shol and Yaldrint to their new home.

"Don't fail us, Har Draaf," Dlalamphrur's voice rang out as the ship closed up. "Billions of souls depend on you."

"And we," said Ungent to Shol and Yaldrint. "We will have to depend on each other."

After taking a few minutes to find their quarters and orient themselves to the ship's vast interior space, Ungent accompanied Yaldrint to the bridge.

"So," said Ungent, "how do we begin the launch sequence?"

Yaldrint rolled her biomechanical eyes.

"Forgive me, Har Draaf," she said. "I did not think it was necessary to inform you."

"You mean we're already...." Ungent sputtered.

"Hey!" said Shol, "Check out Bledraun from the view screen. It's like ... like a ball now."

It was then that the distinguished Grashardi exchanged a life of settled competence for one of limitless adventure, an AI began a new life of unprecedented mobility, and a Krezovic teenager escaped the dark streets of a hundred worlds, for an infinite array of stars.

THE END
of
BOOK ONE
of
AGAINST THE GLARE OF DARKNESS

AUTHOR'S NOTE

No matter how I choose to imagine the distant future, I can't escape the feeling that sentient beings will never transcend the parameters set by their genetic inheritance.

Whether they stand on planet or float on a tether in deep space, they'll be subject to the harrowing storms of self-doubt and the sunny delusion of self-infatuation. Why? Because like us, their consciousness will be an evolutionary outgrowth of involuntary survival instincts.

They'll reason and fear, love and hate, doubt and believe in the same proportion we do, though filtered through unfamiliar cultural trends or different sense perceptions. Through it all, they'll continue to wonder about their place in the universe — and secretly believe it exists for one purpose: to shed light on their own achievements.

Though Ungent's long experience grants him greater perspective than most, his inner life is also marked by shared sentient traits. Like Shol, he knows the biting pain of bias and, like Harlan, is weighed down by a yearning for true love.

The distinguished crustacean has also weathered a loss as severe as Drashna's and, like Gillian, Ungent's quest for an ethical path is still ongoing. Despite his rage, his tolerance of Warvhex grows out of empathy. For Ungent, too, yearns to be free.

Somewhere, on a remote planet, I'm sure a heart is mourning, a spine is shivering, and a wave of joy is breaking hard against a wall of misery. I also know, no matter how they're wired, those distant eyes still see themselves reflected in the starry wash of the evening sky.

*

As a final note, I'd like to acknowledge the diligence of my hard-working editor, Melanie Keefe.

Mark Laporta, January 2018

OTHER BOOKS FROM CHICKADEE PRINCE THAT YOU WILL ENJOY

The Strange And Astounding Memoirs of Watt O'Hugh the Third, Vol. 1 - 2
ISBN 978-0991327409 and 978-0991327416

"Watt O'Hugh will stay with you long after you've turned the last page of Steven Drachman's joyful, hilarious and smart tale ... Watt O'Hugh made me an instant fan!"
— Nicolle Wallace

Watt O'Hugh the Third has been many things in his life: Time Roamer, Civil War soldier, orphan of the New York slums, Wild West dime novel hero, and the only true love of the beautiful socialite Lucy Billings. But by August of 1878, he is naught but a wanted fugitive, a drunken wreck and an angry army of one. Spending his days in the shade of an abandoned Death Valley shack, poring over maps, imagining a way to destroy his enemies and march out of their city carrying their heads on flaming spears. Until the day that Hester Smith beats down his such-as-it-is door and offers him his dreams of revenge against the monstrous Sidonian regime that has destroyed his life -- and one last chance at redemption.

*

The Inevitable Witness by Ed Rucker
The *Bobby Earl* Series, #1 - ISBN: 978-0991327478

"A Los Angeles lawyer defends a professional safecracker accused of murder in Rucker's debut legal thriller.... Earl's a shrewd, worthy protagonist, surrounded by exceptional characters, including reliable investigator Manny Munoz and second-chair district attorney Samantha Price. This novel certainly doesn't skimp on twisty plot turns, but retains an understated, authentic approach to the law."
— Kirkus Reviews

Bobby Earl is the guy you call when it's time to fix bayonets and go to trial. But when he's tapped to defend a notorious safecracker arrested for killing a decorated LAPD officer, Earl's own life is suddenly in danger, and Earl must dive into LA's dangerous underworld, and battle a court system in which the news media and politics corrupt the wheels of justice.

CPSIA information can be obtained
at www.ICGtesting.com
Printed in the USA
LVHW04s1521170918
590425LV00012B/1094/P